Miles Apart

TANVIER PEART

frenchy
PRESS

The Frenchy Press

5325 Sheridan Drive, Suite 1196

Buffalo, New York 14221-9998

thefrenchypress.com

ISBNs: 979-8-9875061-3-4 (trade pbk.)

Library of Congress Control Number: 2024909650

First Edition: October 2024

Printed in the United States of America

1st Printing

Also by Tanvier Peart

Chance at Love Series

The Seven Month Itch (available as an audiobook)
Miles Apart
Tender Offer

Standalone

Ella Gets the D
Untitled Mafia Rom-Com (coming 2026)

Buffalo Steel Rugby Series

One Knight's Stand
Buffalo Rugby Romance Book 2 (coming 2026)

Author Note

Miles Apart is a romance novel with enough spice to make your mama blush (mine likely will). It uses strong language and has *spicy* scenes with vivid descriptions of sex. Parts of the book overlap with *The Seven Month Itch*, which includes mention of early pregnancy loss (off-page) and forcible touching (off-page, over the clothes, and not between any of the couples) during a '90s party. Miles experiences an oral transaction with a woman who isn't Emma. This happens before they get together very early in the story, so don't come for my head. (He didn't cheat.) There is mention of a secondary character losing his wife to breast cancer, and a date following Emma home (both off-page). Emma contends with a mother who appears in parts of the book and displays elements of emotional abuse.

This story takes place over the course of months and travels to different locations that prove you can't escape love.

Buckle up, secure all lace fronts, and enjoy the ride.

(And take care of yourself)

You are worthy of a love beyond this lifetime.

THE PLAYLIST—PART I

#1– "Wild Side"—Normani (ft. Cardi B)

#2 – "Permission"—Ro James

#3 – "Freek'n You"—Jodeci

#4 – "Touchin'"—Honey Bxby

#5 – "Red Lights"—RINI (ft. Wale)

#6 – "Do Not Disturb"—Teyana Taylor (ft. Chris Brown)

#7 – "21 Questions"—50 Cent (ft. Nate Dogg)

#8 – "Unravel Me"—Sabrina Claudio

#9 – "Pheenin"—Eric Bellinger x BJRNCK

THE PLAYLIST—PART II

#10 – "Situationship"—Snoh Aalegra

#11 – "Living Room Flow"—Jhené Aiko

#12 – "You"—Raheem DeVaughn

#13 – "I Like"—ROE

#14 – "Sweetness"—Elmiene (ft. Leon Thomas)

#15 – "Where Do We Go"—Andra Day

#16 – "Lately"—Tyrese

#17 – "By Your Side"—Sade

#18 – "Fortunate"—Maxwell

Chapter 1

Emma

"**D**o you have to go?"

I glance up at doe eyes in the mirror and bite back a smile. West waits for me to change my mind, and for a brief moment I allow myself to entertain the thought that he wants me to stay for more than my body.

He's cute—adorable, even—but he has much to learn.

My attention falls back to the concealer in my hand. It will be a miracle if I don't walk out looking like a yellow highlighter. This lighting is awful, even for a standard hotel room decorated in three shades of beige. I drop makeup into my overnight bag and adjust the strapless sweater dangling off my shoulder. "I had a good time last night," I say.

Gracious tongue.

Steady strokes.

Four out of five stars.

West sits up in bed with a grin too big for a woman about to leave him. The tartan duvet pools at his waist, showcasing an array of lean muscles engraved into tanned ivory skin.

"So let's do it again," he begs, his lower lip dipping into a pout. There's a lightness in his tone, one mixed with confidence and the hope that his ability to please is enough to keep me here. Firm hands tatted at the forearms push the rest of the decorative pillows to the floor. West leans against the wooden headboard and spreads his legs to stroke his length over the sheets.

Tempting.

Men in their twenties are wild cards. Most fuck with the intensity of a jackrabbit, which is why I keep them at bay. Not this one. West was a pleasant surprise who didn't let direction hurt his ego. Guys my age could learn from him. Even at twenty-nine, five years younger than me, he took the time to discover what pleased me instead of what got him off.

West and I met at the kickoff mixer for the weeklong singles' retreat. I'm not here for the hope of a happily ever after. I'm here for dick and to pull my best friend out of the fortress of her home back in Austin. She's on her way to divorce, but that doesn't mean life is over.

Justice's night ended exactly as expected. She took one look at people on the prowl for love and lust before she headed up to our suite and spent the night with room service.

I had other plans.

West caught my eye behind the bar across the crowded room. It didn't take long for our stares to linger before I sat on the stool in front of him. We exchanged names while he made my martini. His forearms flexed under the rolled sleeves of his white button-down. The lust in his eyes reflected in mine as our fingers touched on the stem of my glass. We went up to his room after midnight with the promise of orgasms.

A delicious welcome to Vail, Colorado, after a full day of traveling.

Hooded blue eyes pierce mine in a silent plea for me to stay. One night is all I'll give.

There are the Joan Claytons of the world—women like Justice who color-code their linens and believe in soulmates. I never felt an itch to attach forever to a partner. I'm with the Toni Childs of the world—those who try you on for size before swapping you out with their outfits. Relationships slow you down and expose you to wounds. She tried the "I do," and look what happened. I've seen a loveless marriage up close. Now, I'm witnessing the aftermath of a broken love story with my best friend.

I'll pass.

The hiss of the zipper on my thigh-high boot breaks our stare. West moves to pull me down when I saunter over to the bed, but he isn't quick enough. I meant what I said. Last night was enjoyable, but this eagerness for me to stay is why I don't make a habit of sleeping over.

I saw.

I conquered.

I came—more than once.

"Now, West." I straddle him for no other reason than to be a tease. "You were good." My lips press to the shell of his ear. "Let's see what this week holds. I know where to find you." I ruffle the dirty blonde waves I gripped when he explored the depths between my thighs, grab my overnight bag, and make my exit without a last glance.

West is a fuck boy in its purest form. He reeks of it, much like his Old Spice deodorant. His boy-next-door good looks and pickup lines might leave others pressed, but not me. I'm not a woman to look for more out of a one-night stand. We take what we need and move on. No idling. No waiting by the phone. No pouting of any kind—a lesson for West to learn fast.

The best way to teach is by example, right?

The front door closes behind me with a soft click. I didn't expect to sleep with someone this early into the retreat, but what can I say? West is good with his hands, behind the bar and in bed. He had the stamina to match my pace, but when I'm done, I'm done.

I like sex—love it, crave it—and enjoy the act with whatever flavor I want to taste for the night. Sleepovers are usually off the table unless I want seconds. I did with West, but now we can move on.

My phone pings with a text that pulls a smile at the *Sister, Sister* melody. No matter the years that pass—twenty, in our case—my best friend always checks in to make sure I'm okay. I don't tolerate many people in my life, but Justice will never not be my person.

Justice

> Hey, about to order room service for break-fast. Want anything?

A room service attendant smiles at my nod and stops in front of a door across the hall. The scent of eggs and French toast wafts from plates on the cart. Breakfast does sound good.

I shift my overnight bag on my shoulder to type out a message to Justice I'll be up to our suite soon. Unlike the standard rooms, ours has two bedrooms, one on each side of the wide living space. There's a fireplace and jacuzzi on the balcony with views of the surrounding valley. It's rich in luxury and knotted wood flooring.

Hey, hon.

Another message appears once I hit send, stuttering my silent walk over plush carpeting to the elevator. My jaw tightens at the name on the screen, one that paints my cheeks the same color as my manicure.

Carter Davis.

Carter

You can't ignore me forever.

The hell I can't.

Doesn't he have more important matters? A press conference? The rider that guarantees my father's favorite almond brand will be at his next event? Annoying Senator Douglass's daughter is not on his congressional to-do list, I'm sure.

I flip back to the text with Justice in a huff. The problem with a twenty-year friendship is that will see right through any attempt to act normal, and she will push for answers. It's in her nature to care, the same way it is to hug for no damn reason. I'll handle Carter myself. This week is about Justice, not me. She went through too much for me to pile on my mess.

In less than twenty-four hours, we discovered the estranged husband she left seven months ago is at this retreat, which I picked for our annual girls' trip. She needed time away from drowning herself in work as a distraction from her separation, to meet new people and decide if divorce is what she really wants. Clearly, her ex is wasting no time getting back in the game.

Our trip comes with a week's worth of activities I'd choose a colonoscopy over doing, but if snowmobiling and horseback riding put a smile on Jay's face, I'll grit my teeth. I slipped in a spa day and a whiskey tasting to lower her guard. Speed dating and the private date that comes with it will be a tough sell, but Justice will survive.

Carter

Call me. You have ten minutes.

This asshole.

I close my eyes and draw a deep breath. *Why do you fight us?* Carter's words in my father's study last Thanksgiving play on a loop. The way he whispered them while my mother argued with the kitchen staff about cranberry sauce in the hall still makes me shiver. How his hand crept up my arm to trace his thumb against my throat. He's always been an arrogant prick, but he never touched me. Not like that.

I don't mind a man who takes charge, but I prefer him not to have an affiliation with my family. My mother's constant reminders that I'm not living up to our family legacy and am wasting away my "childbearing years" are bad enough. They're the reason I keep myself on the opposite side of the country, with good weather, a lucrative fashion career, and access to all the dick I want without shame or judgment.

Juliette Douglass would pick out my wedding china tomorrow if Carter was serious about pursuing a relationship. He comes from money, is a loyal lapdog to my father, and is the only one in her eyes who could tame me out of my "wild ways."

My defiance is a declaration of the love I have for myself and the life I create for me. I adore my body, feel empowered by the autonomy to share it, and have no desire to be a mother. It doesn't make me less than or undesirable.

The elevator doors open to an empty car of mirrored walls. My fingers hover above the button to my floor. I can't see Justice right now. She's no stranger to Carter or my family drama, but, given her Terrence sighting, she needs her own space to process without distractions.

Worked up an appetite last night the menu won't satisfy. See you at lunch.

Let Justice think I'm still in someone's bed.

Now to deal with Carter.

ell

"Emma." My name is a taunt on his lips.

"What do you want, Carter?" My sigh travels between time zones and the thin fibers of my patience. This is fucking up my post-coital high.

"Did you lose your manners in the mountains?"

My eyes roll at his chuckle. I don't need to close them to picture Carter seated in his leather office chair and bespoke suit. His ego matches his six-foot stature. It's big enough to fill Congress and this restaurant.

I signal to the bartender for another Bellini. I'm at the end of the bar tucked between foliage and a wall of mirrors, the perfect spot to people watch and eat breakfast. If only I hadn't lost my appetite because of this call and the person on the other end.

Carter is attractive, but I can't stand him. My regard for him shifted over the years he's worked for my father. No amount of fine can fix that awful of a heart.

"Does my father need something?" I push out the question to rush Carter off the phone.

"I need you," he says, his husky tone licking my ear. "John has a fundraiser this weekend in Denver. His only daughter should make an appearance."

"Is Blair not available to play poster child?" My cousin is everything the good senator wants in a daughter: obedient, vanilla. Throw in a ride on the private jet, and she'll do a special cheer.

There's a pause before Carter lowers his deep voice. "She's not you."

Silence dances between us with the intensity of a livewire, one I've reinforced since I met Carter when he interned for my father during his sophomore year of college. He ignored my high school crush until I graduated from Bodie University. I was no longer the same girl who made every excuse to stop by my father's office, knowing one of Virginia's senators was too busy to see his daughter. I became a woman who grew into her own, wanting more and no longer willing to chase after anyone in order to be seen.

It pissed off my family that I chose a lesser-known institution in California over my father's Ivy League alma mater. They couldn't control my desire to attend the same school as Justice, nor my decision to put the middle of the country between us. No matter their efforts, the money they threw at me to come back home to the DMV, nor the threats to take away the trust fund I never used, I held my own—unbought or sold.

Carter took notice of my rebellion, and so began the decade-plus game of cat and mouse. I became the unattainable trophy to acquire, driven by lust and his desire to please my father. Carter evolved into another desperate-for-power suit on Capitol Hill. He's remained on my Do Not Fuck list, which is a testament to my willpower.

Low-cut fade.

Caramel skin.

Blue-green eyes.

Carter is Jesse Williams, a self-absorbed version doused in fine.

I love dick, but not everyone gets admission into this pussy.

"You are John's daughter," Carter declares as if I'm the one who needs the reminder. "You can afford a few hours to support the campaign."

"I'm here to enjoy a trip with my best friend, not bend over backward for donors to make my father look good."

"Saturday night. We'll charter a plane to pick you up and take you back. As for how far you can bend"—Carter's voice drops—"we'll test your limits later."

"I told you, I have plans." I clear my throat after a long swallow. My boots rub to keep my knees from parting. The change in altitude is messing with my head because my Do Not Fuck list might make a liar out of me if he keeps this up. I'm strong, but shit, I'm human too.

"Cancel them."

"Not happening."

Growing up, Justice and her family welcomed me with open arms. I was the kid of an influential politician with access to privilege but without the one thing money can't buy. Some fancy jet and a twenty-thousand-a-plate fundraiser aren't enough to ditch my friend. Nothing is.

"Is that an invitation to come get you?"

I hang up without a second thought. It's too early for all that. The devil is a lie, as Justice's mother says.

"Someone's testy," a familiar voice says from behind, raising every hair on my neck.

Miles steps next to me, and I ask God what I did to deserve not one but two men tempting me to pose for a mugshot. "How in the hell are you here?"

"You want my flight number?" Miles rolls his thick lips between his teeth. I follow the wet path of his tongue and scoff at the grin forming.

My now-room-temperature parfait streaks my bowl as I take in the ripped figure in my private corner, the one with a smirk on his goatee-framed mouth and a gaze up to no good.

Of course, he came.

Miles is a threat in ways Carter will never be. I'll dodge the latter without issue if I limit my trips home to Alexandria, Virginia, which I do. Miles is a different story. If Justice and I are a package deal, so are Terrence and Miles. They've been friends since they were damn near babies, and that pushes us together for obvious reasons. Our paths don't always cross, but when they do, it's this mix of sexual tension and contempt.

I've sidestepped Miles, those thick arms, and rich chocolate skin, for over a decade. We've been doing this dance since college, when Justice and Terrence started dating. He tosses a dig my way, and I toss it right back. The problem is, we both love sex, which isn't an issue until you almost do it during a trip to your respective best friends' house. We shouldn't have come that close, which is why I've kept my distance and double-check before visiting to make sure he's not there.

Test-driving the best friend of my best friend's husband is out of the question. Miles hits too close to home, even if a juicy ass and solid chest deserve a look under the hood.

Miles assesses me from the corner of his eye before turning his full gaze on me. The soft arch in his brow lifts, and a smile ghosts his lips to show white teeth. He folds his arms crowded in thick muscles over his chest, pulling the black tee and outlining every muscle in his torso.

I tear my eyes away to look at anything other than the amusement flickering in his, and my gaze lands on the gray beanie covering the fade he keeps fresh.

Fuck him.

We cannot.

"It's nice to see you, Em."

"Wish I could say the same."

"Is that how you feel after the last time we were together? What was it, two years ago?" His expression darkens, daring me to pretend the night in question didn't sear itself into my mind.

Memories filter back to the long walk to my guest room, fresh from a cold shower to keep my vagina in check. I passed Miles's room as he came out in sweats, headed to the bathroom that I left to soap down every hard muscle on his body and what lies between his legs, which left an imprint against the gray cotton.

We stood inches apart, no best friends around to force us to retreat to our corners. We argued as we always do. The source of our ire that evening? Movie trivia. But at that moment, I couldn't stop my eyes from raking over the shirtless torso before me. It was at the perfect height with our size difference.

"Ready for a taste?" Miles teased. His words were playful but his tone was sharp. Hungry. The man matches energy, and his stare told me to run.

I locked my bedroom door behind me to keep from sleepwalking and sucking the skin off his dick. By morning, Miles left. Something about a work trip. I stopped visiting Austin at the same time he did since that night. The energy between us threatened to crush my lungs, and a bitch enjoys breathing.

Carter is a lot to handle at times, but Miles is a different force.

I unclench my hands and steady my glower. "Do us both a favor. Keep yourself and Terrence far away from me and Justice, or there will be hell to pay."

If a single look could kill, Justice would choose my tombstone instead of an omelet from a room service menu.

Miles's stare coasts down my neck to where my heart is drumming inside my chest. He considers me, the light from the bistro chandelier catching in his diamond stud. The cloud lifts from his eyes, and he winks. "Put your claws away, kitten. Junior must not have satisfied you if you're still this wound up. Is he up yet for round two?"

"I am not wound up," I say too quickly. "And stop watching me, stalker."

Miles must've been at last night's kickoff mixer. I saw Terrence, who made a beeline for Justice after a man in an Al Bundy outfit hit on her. Miles was nowhere to be found. But he clearly saw me. He always does.

His shoulder lifts to shrug off the accusation. "You're hard to miss." He nods to my phone on the counter. "When you're ready for a grown man to take care of you, come find me." Miles leaves with a casual strut, too unbothered to rush, and an ass that would make Calvin Klein billions.

The bartender returns with a folded paper bag he places next to my bowl. "Would you like another to-go box?" He motions to the untouched berries and granola sliding through low-fat Greek yogurt.

"Yes, thanks." I frown at the bag. "Is this for someone else?"

"The gentleman settled your bill and asked us to rush an order." He checks the taped receipt. "Pancake and eggs from our children's menu. For Junior?"

A smile breaks.

Let the games begin.

Chapter 2

Emma

The valley shines from the windows next to the fireplace. It's tranquil, unlike the stillness pressing into our living area with all its might. Justice and I sit on the sectional in our suite with a bottle of wine between us.

"Did you know she was here?" her voice shakes as her fingers wrap around her glass.

I look down at my wine and take a sip. "There was someone last night who looked like her." Merlot and guilt coat my tongue in a bitter mix. "I'm sorry, Justice. I wasn't sure, and the last thing I wanted was to put you on high alert with Terrence here." *Like you are now.* "I know how much you questioned your marriage because of her, and I didn't want history to repeat itself."

The ploy to boost my best friend's spirit backfired. In a sick turn of events, the woman pining after Terrence for the last fifteen years is here. A long time to be sprung on dick if you ask me. Married dick at that.

It was a miracle Justice and I kept our lunch down when Madison came by our table to broadcast that she and Terrence spent time together after the mixer last night. I'm proud of her for sticking up for herself, but I know my friend. I would be a mess too if I came face-to-face with my ex for the first time in almost a year, and *I* don't do love. If that wasn't a slap in the face, doofus—Terrence—showed up at our suite this morning looking for Madison. It wouldn't surprise me if Justice made a run for it back to Austin and left a full-size cutout of her silhouette in the wall as a parting gift.

Justice hangs her head, her natural black curls unable to shield her trembling chin. "I need to get used to him dating...even her."

Madison and Terrence dated for a couple of months at Bodie before she ended their relationship to go to Paris for a study abroad trip. Justice and I took as many classes together as possible since high school. The one time we didn't, she met Terrence, who couldn't take his eyes off her. The shy freshman with the junior football player who shed his playboy persona faster than he could chase after Jay. Madison came back, heard the ex she wanted again was smitten with my friend, and hasn't let her quest go ever since. She uses every chance she gets to toy with Jay since she and Terrence run into each other on occasion for work.

I don't care if Terrence has a diamond tip between his legs. It costs nothing to display human decency. A decent person wouldn't go after someone in a committed relationship, but here she is in Vail.

This is our first girls' trip since Justice and Terrence split. I wanted it to be memorable, a fresh start with toasty drinks and hot men to keep us warm in a mountain setting that reminds Jay of those cheesy movies she loves. That was the plan, at least. One that took a considerable amount of planning, secrecy, and gentle kidnapping when I showed up at her house yesterday and told her to get on a plane without details or explanation.

Justice struggled through her first Christmas alone, prompting me to speed up our annual getaway by a month. Because that's what we do; pick each other up when we're down. God knows she's dusted me off more than once.

"Do you still love him? I know we swept this conversation under the rug, but now might be a good time to revisit it, given the circumstances."

Brown eyes weighed in sadness flick to mine. The smile Justice struggles to hold falls. "I'm so mad at him," she says between sobs.

A tightness seizes my throat. Watching my best friend cope with early pregnancy losses and the end of her marriage was agony. It still is. She deserves the world, and it breaks my heart that the wounds she's fighting to heal reopened.

I wrap her in a hug, my bracelets chiming against her oversized charcoal sweater. No man will have this much power over me. "Whatever you decide, I'm here for you. And if we need to get Madison out of the way, I'll push her off the mountain myself."

Justice snorts through a ragged sigh. "Love you."

"Love you back."

"Sure you don't want to stay in?"

"Not since the last time you asked five minutes ago!"

"Smartass!" I chuckle and reach for my mascara.

"I am smart and happen to have a great ass!" Justice's voice carries through the living area separating our bedrooms, a world of knotted wood flooring and earth tones between us. The valley is now at rest, darkness covering the small town encased in mountains. Lights from nearby businesses and homes twinkle in the moonlight. It's freezing but gorgeous here.

After the surprise cameos, I assumed Justice would want to hole up with room service and *Girlfriends* reruns. Given the circumstances, her elder tendencies are fair game, but she surprised me by getting ready for the first of many events happening at the retreat this week.

She's not ready to date again. A relationship isn't on the table or the purpose of this trip. Sex is a different story—if Jay wants someone to blow seven months' worth of cobwebs off her vagina. Doubtful, but we'll see.

Who wouldn't feel appreciated with a week's worth of doting from admirers you'll never see again? They would treasure her like the queen she is and be a reminder life isn't over if your marriage is.

Tonight's event is a '90s pajama party, one about to get my lack of rhythm and her blues.

My phone buzzes next to my makeup bag I'm sifting through for red lipstick.

Declined.

Carter can go find someone else's ass to crawl up and suffocate. Between his nonstop messages and Terrence here to mix and mingle, we need to turn this trip from a future funeral to a celebration fast. If that means dancing off-beat, so be it. Tonight, we're wiping the slate clean, from Madison and Terrence.

Miles?

This little Bodie reunion is a rash on my ass. I can handle Terrence, and I *will* handle Madison if she tries anything else. Miles requires me to be at the top of my game. He'll show his whole ass otherwise.

What an ass it is.

Hush.

"Ready." Justice breaks through the memory of Miles pinning me to the wall with his stare at my body wrapped in a towel. Two years clearly wasn't long enough to stay away. She pops through the oak-framed door, looking like an extra from a TLC music video, down to her oversized tee and slouch socks. Lips once bowed from frowns now curl at the corners. "Don't."

"Sistah, sistahhh!" I belt into my lipstick with 702 intentions that misses the mark. Tia and Tamera have a long-lost sibling.

She cackles. "You're one to talk, Ms. Andra Day. Now rise up from that ottoman so we can get this party started."

I stare at her reflection. "You sure, Jay? We can stay in."

"Kid gloves don't go with red lingerie, Em." A half smile crosses her face at my matching silk robe teasing at my knees. It's a far cry from her baggy ensemble, but we do what makes us comfortable. The only difference is a man will be on my menu tonight. "I'm good. Come on," she grabs my hand, "your Victoria's Secret runway awaits."

Chapter 3

Emma

A '90s dance party should be just that: butterflying to throw-backs that remind us our membership to the forty and over club is only a few years from hitting our mailbox. Justice Tootsie Rolled her heart out in a circle of women who matched her energy. They dipped and turned for hours among attendees reenacting *House Party 2* in their pajamas. Jay's stamina runs laps around mine on the dance floor for the simple fact that I don't dance.

I had no shame leaving her but felt it charge up my throat like bile pushing through a crowd to get to her. It was too late to notice the group she was dancing with left, leaving my best friend to fend off the man towering over her. No one thought anything of him caging her to his chest. No one except Miles, who wasted no time knocking the guy unconscious.

How he got through the crowd and to Justice so fast defies physics. By the time security came, Miles had her behind his oiled frame, ready to strike again if the six-foot-plus creep with disheveled hair tried to resurrect himself from the ground.

I'm not a crier. But I couldn't stop the tears once I reached Justice and threw my arms around her. I was too busy eye-fucking Miles like a full-time job with benefits to notice some asshole groping her on the dance floor.

Justice's hand covers mine underneath the table at our booth with a squeeze. She waves the other at Miles, who joins us for a drink at her request. Jay is pretending she's okay, but Miles and I know what happened still rattles her. She forces a smile, telegraphing a happiness that doesn't lift her cheeks or brighten her brown eyes. She won't bring up the incident anymore, and I won't press her.

"So, what's new?" she asks Miles, who's at the other end of the booth absorbing every inch of space. Terrence wasn't with him, and there's no way he'd let anyone violate Justice's personal space if he were.

Miles grazes my knee with the shift of his weight. The touch is innocent but ignites a rush of heat through my skin, which he notices when I move away. "You know me," he says. "Work. Travel." His eyes trace the outline of my breasts in my nightgown. They take their time to admire the silhouette of my nipples, moving up the column of my neck and licking my jawline. He holds my stare when he says, "Women."

I look awful, but Miles takes in my puffy eyes and a red nose from crying like I won first place in a beauty pageant.

"What's good, Em?" Thick lips spread into a grin.

"Not on your best day." I avert my eyes from his bare chest, slicked in baby oil, daring me to lie again. The bar's lighting creates a halo around the hard edges of Miles's upper body. He put it on full display for the '90s party. Every muscle threads to create the masterpiece before me in nothing but silk boxers and slides. It takes several reminders that the man threatening drool is still Miles. He is not an option to play Slip 'N Slide with in bed.

"Ouch." Miles's hand grips his heart. "Why do you deny the inevitable?" His grin widens. "It's only a matter of time, kitten."

He can go straight to hell.

Justice's eyes bounce between me and Miles. Curiosity lifts her brow at the nickname, but now is not the time for show-and-tell. Jay doesn't know that Miles and I ran into each other earlier today. She also missed our silent game of I Spy on the dance floor.

I spent most of the night dodging Miles's stink eye across the room, which turned into daggers when he saw West behind the bar. My smirk was ready for the Jumbotron. I have no interest in West, but I shook my ass next to other men as best I could without simulating the need for medical attention to raise Miles's blood pressure. His gaze turned possessive, like he had a claim to me.

The strobe lights and slow jams felt like a bad '90s romance. I kept my distance from the man with thick thighs in boxers and that damn baby oil glow. Those stupid pink cupids printed across the fabric did nothing but piss me off and turn me on.

It's a crime for Miles to roam the Earth in next to nothing—least of all at a singles' retreat. Don't believe me? Try to keep it together if Trevante Rhodes strolls by wearing silk underwear.

I don't think straight around him. Tonight proved that being half-naked in the same room is dangerous, like two years ago. Our slow dance from the sidelines of the dance floor was quiet, a series of lingering glances and glares. Then, maple eyes flashed black before

Miles sprang into action to protect Justice. The two bicker like brother and sister, but he'll always make sure she's okay.

His focus is now on me. Locked, eager, and ready to cross the line.

My heart beats like a war drum, daring me to accept the challenge. Miles waits for what feels like an eternity for my response. His expression is impassive as he leans against the back of the booth, completely relaxed. I never back down from a challenge, but I heed the voice warning me to stay away.

Men are for a moment, and this one is too close.

"I don't have time for your little antics," I say over the rim of my French 75 and take a sip.

Something flares in Miles's eyes, now hooded under thick lashes. His tone lowers for only me to hear. "Baby, there's nothing little about me." Miles changes the subject, and it takes a superhuman effort not to imagine how big "nothing little" is.

This damn man has me by the throat from across the booth with his words and knows it. Victory flickers in the corner of his mouth he curls while speaking to Justice. It's subtle to anyone else but is a billboard that says "Got you" in living color. Jay catches pieces of the silent tango but brushes off the energy. I can't. Miles Walker is a temptation I want to sample. I don't shit where I eat and remind myself to put a force field around my pussy.

He ends our connection by chasing after a woman in red, leaving Justice to polish off two glasses of whiskey and me hot and bothered. "Get some for the both of us," are her parting words before she goes upstairs for the night. I migrate to the bar across from our booth and fail miserably to ignore an emotion that is testing my willpower.

Why do you deny the inevitable?

It's only a matter of time, kitten.

"Want to talk about it?" The bartender's toffee gaze rakes over my face. He's handsome, with classic features in Viking-height packaging. Fuckable, but not the one to whet my appetite.

"No thanks." I take another French 75 with a half-smile. Miles will pay for the stunt he pulled at breakfast and for making me this undone. I need him out of my system.

A keycard slides across the onyx marble counter. "This might cheer you up," the bartender says.

My fingers skim over shiny black plastic and gold letters spelling out "Ravenous." "What's this?"

He stands taller, his tawny-gold hair tapered behind his ear. "A test run. There's a pop-up club traveling around our resort locations. To enjoy after dark. Take the elevator to the third floor. Once you show the key, an attendant will greet you in the ballroom. Don't share it with anyone else, and don't speak about Ravenous."

The distraction I need.

I'm flustered, horny, and need Miles Walker out of my mind before I lose it. This will work.

"What happens at Ravenous stays at Ravenous."

"Something like that."

Black satin drapes from the ceiling, creating a pathway of partitions between crystal chandeliers. Dancers roll their bodies to music that funnels through hidden speakers. Some hang from aerial silks, while others command attention from gilded cages that match diamond-crusted masks and heels. They're completely naked, a showcase of soft curves in nudes and mahogany.

Entrance to Ravenous means a signed NDA and a consent form. After that, you get a masquerade mask and black cloak. No cell phones. No alcohol. No intercourse. Here, femmes call the shots, granting access to look. One can only touch after expressed consent.

The makeshift hall opens to circular sofas scattered around a parquet dance floor. Cloaked guests hold whispered conversations as performers weave through voyeurs without missing a beat.

"Would you like to have a blind date?" Dark eyes under long lashes flutter over rose cheeks. Her almond skin with bronze undertones glows as her tongue dips between thick lips. "You watch me dance in a private room, next to a partner of my choosing."

My heart beats in time to the music. I've enjoyed dances in countless clubs, but a dungeon is new. So is a private session with a stranger. But Justice did say to get some for the both of us.

She would never step foot in here. Me, on the other hand?

"What do I call you?" Behind a string of pearls that cascades to her belly button, rosebud peaks harden under my appraisal.

"Aeris," she says, her voice low and full of lust.

"After you, Aeris."

She leads us beyond the dance floor, past a small crowd watching an aerialist pleasure herself with a vibrator midair. We reach double doors covered in the same black fabric as the entrance to a carpeted hall with hotel rooms appears.

Two men wearing yellow "Monitor" armbands roam quietly outside the open doors. Aeris stops at a room on the left. A pole stands in the center of the space across from a sofa where a large figure sits. Aeris extends an arm and waits for me to enter. Her platform heels put us around the same height, tempting our chests to graze as I pass through the door.

I move to a corner wall and peek back at the sofa, doing a double take at the parted thighs and slides I missed coming in. The black cloak spreads to silk boxers with tiny cupids wrapped around muscular legs.

Miles.

Strobe lights shower the walls in colorful patterns at the chime of Jodeci's "Freek'n You." The intricately patterned black mask that covers part of my face dips to my cheeks. Can he tell it's me behind the lace?

Aeris struts to the pole in relaxed steps and swivels her hips, whipping the strings of pearls with each body roll. Loose black waves tumble down her back as she bends to flip her legs around the erect metal, locking her heels in place. She inches down before opening her legs into a split with hypnotic fluidity.

She climbs the pole again and tips upside down, making her body into an "X" position. I'd drop twenties if the teddy I'm wearing had pockets. Aeris rights herself, unclasps the pearls from her body, and stands in nothing but a thong and heels.

"Come here." She curls her finger, beckoning for me to join her, but this will end in a solo act if she expects me to defy gravity or pretend I'm an extra in *The Player's Club.*

Petite breasts stare back at me as she circles her hand in wait. I chance a glance at Miles and find him watching me. His black mask conceals most of his face, but not the muscle tensing in his jaw or the sharp eyes assessing if I'll obey.

Aeris pulls an upholstered dining room chair in front of the pole and pats the top. Her fingers glide over my satin-covered shoulders when I sit. Directly in front of Miles.

"Can I touch you?" She hovers over me at my yes, blocking my view of the last man I want to see. "You're gorgeous, red." She twirls a loose strand of my mahogany hair.

I appreciate the beauty of femme forms, like the diamond tips that are dangerously close to my mouth. But I've never been with a woman. Curious? Yes, but there is no urge to seek or taste. But as my eyes peer around Aeris's shoulder at the man whose gaze is trained on my face, the prospect of fucking with Miles without touching him excites me more than it should.

Time for that payback.

"Let's give you a show, hmm?" Aeris stands.

Miles's focus shifts from me to Aeris, who's now between his legs. She asks permission to touch him, straddles his lap at his verbal consent, and moves in slow circles. He doesn't touch her, just shifts his weight to lie back on the button-tufted sofa. Miles is a king at ease, his wide arms stretching across the couch.

Aeris changes pace and lifts her hair. My nails dig into the chair on a hard swallow. I tell myself I want to be Miles, spread out to welcome Aeris's heat with open arms, but it's a lie. I want to be *her*, gripping his entire length until his eyes roll to the back of his head.

I recross my legs to stop my clit from pulsating and remind myself I'm free to have any single man except Miles Walker, who I tolerate because of my best friend and her future ex-husband. It's rare for him to be this quiet, which should explain the confusion in my urge to taste him inch by inch.

Aeris stills in his lap and follows his focus toward me. "Interesting," she says in a sultry tone. My brows furrow at her graceful dismount, and soon she's behind me. "He doesn't want me, love. But does he want you?" Her knuckles brush the side of my neck.

Miles straightens, desire pooling in his eyes behind the mask. I can't look away as I give Aeris consent. Blood pounds in my ears as she parts the black cloak, revealing my red lingerie behind it. It's nothing he hasn't seen already. He was tracking me from across the dance floor like a bloodhound.

A beautiful woman stands behind me, damn near naked from head to toe, but Miles is committing the outline of my curves to memory.

"Tell me to stop if you get uncomfortable," Aeris says in a hushed command. Little does she know, I'm neither shy nor worried.

I'd strut my ass out of here in only these red heels if I wouldn't catch a case.

My body is a gift I don't give freely to just anyone. But tonight, I want to poke the beast behind the dark brown eyes, simply because I can.

Cool air puckers my nipples when Aeris pushes the straps of my nightgown off my shoulders. A smirk builds at the erratic rise of Miles's chest and the impressive tent forming between his legs. She cups my exposed flesh and massages the buds between her fingertips. Her breasts press into my back. "He looks ready to explode," she says.

I spread my legs and drag a hand up my thigh. "Not yet." Miles follows my finger inching closer to my sex until I dip two inside and rub my clit with my thumb. He's frothing at the mouth when I come on a moan, rocking against my hand as the last waves spread through my body.

Aeris releases me, and I stand and make my way over to the man who's panting in front of me. Our gazes lock, and a tremor heats my core at the turbulence of passion swirling between us. It's always there, dormant, until a magnetic force unites us.

"Mind if I join you?" A grunt is all he gives in return.

Miles's hands flex into fists, threatening to crack his skin, until I straddle him and push him against the sofa. My hand travels between us to massage my pussy and grazes steel. He jerks at the touch and leans his head back, unable to keep his focus on my face or my breasts less than an inch from his lips.

I rock into him, pulling a mutual groan, and grip his chin, with my hand glistening from my juices. "This is the closest you'll ever get to tasting me," I say, returning the words he arrogantly uttered years ago. Miles is cocky in every sense of the word, I'll give him that. "Open." I dip my thumb into his mouth, and he happily takes it. With his eyes locked on mine, he twirls his tongue around and sucks another finger, forcing me to suppress a shudder. I hop off, adjust my straps, and retrieve my cloak. "He's all yours."

Toying with Miles might be playing with fire, but damn it if I don't enjoy the flame. I leave the room with a smile on my face—and the promise of another orgasm once I reach my suite.

That will teach him.

Chapter 4

Miles

The steady thrum of pattering water muffles the sounds of the woman on her knees in front of me going to work on my dick. They say spas are peaceful, but damn. Getting topped off butt-ass naked inside of a room with water falling from the ceiling wasn't on the agenda for today, but I'd be a dumbass to say no. It's dark enough. No one will see shit anyway.

The woman beneath me moans as she takes me to the back of her throat. I try to trick myself, but her voice doesn't match the one from last night. Her hair isn't the mahogany shade I imagined splayed across my pillows.

Emma Douglass is a witch who summoned the dark arts to cast me under her spell after one taste of her pussy. After I got back to my room, I came so hard in the shower I searched online to see if buckled knees and enough nut to finger paint tiled walls weren't signs of a stroke.

Yeah, she had me by the dick last night, but only one of us repeated words from years ago. The tension between us was thick enough to suck the oxygen from the hallway. Em wasn't in my lap, grinding her pussy into my erection back then, but she still tempted me to risk it all. I saw it, the desire lit in her eyes. Shit, I *felt* it. Had we not been in T and Justice's house, I wouldn't have thought twice about driving my tongue into her before consuming her with deep strokes.

My hands anchor to the wall as I roll my hips into Melissa's (?) warm mouth with gentle thrusts. Melanie (?) groans, reaching down to thrum her clit.

Fuck, why can't I remember her name? There's an M in it.

She chokes but quickly recovers and flattens her tongue.

"Breathe through your nose. Good girl." I pat her hair, cautious not to fist it and fuck her mouth the way I want to.

Marisa and I met at the lodge this morning. Terrence was on the slopes, heard Justice's Tia and Tamera cackle, and skied his scared ass away to put distance between them. The man is still gone for his wife—not that I expected any different. He and I went our separate ways after that. I gave him space and met up with the brunette who was clocking me from earlier. One thing led to another, and here we are alone in a spa room.

Getting pussy is neither rare nor a challenge. If that makes me a dick, so be it, but that's exactly what you get—dick. I pride myself on pleasing the women I'm with. It's rare for me to put my mouth on anyone, but my stroke game will have you speaking in tongues.

Once we're done, it's over. Out of sight, and the furthest thing from my mind.

I focus on a crack in the wall to block out the moss-green eyes behind a lace mask. Full lips parted into ecstasy at her self-play.

"Fuck," I groan.

I've always been attracted to Emma, but last night almost had me begging. I was ready to hand over whatever she wanted—my car keys, house, routing numbers—to relive her fingers dancing across her glistening lips while Aeris stroked her nipples. She exceeds every fantasy, and she's as beautiful now as she was fifteen years ago when we first met. We've always circled each other. Twin flames with an instinct to fuck and an inclination to argue.

Emma is Justice's friend, not mine. I don't dislike her, but she grates on my nerves in a way no one else does.

This is the closest you'll ever get to tasting me.

We'll see about that.

She is the source of my frustrations and desires who thinks she bested me last night but showed her hand. I'm sure I'm not the only one who still thinks about the time we nearly had sex, but I need to correct that shit fast. Em's nectar between her legs seared itself into my taste buds, but I'm not about to be sprung.

I quicken my pace as my balls tighten. What's this woman's name? I need to figure it out before she swallows.

A faint giggle registers over my shoulder. No one should be in the rain room except for me and Mary.

Madeline.

Molly.

Fuck.

I cock my head to the side at whoever's interested in my bare ass, squinting to make out the figure behind me. "What the fu—*Justice*? Is that you?"

I always knew she had kinks buried underneath the Target clothes and church girl personality. Terrence had a reputation for his sex drive, but my guess is she gives him a run for his money.

Justice trips over the lounger behind her as she scurries for the door, showing her whole ass underneath her robe. Laughter rips through me at her audacity to act surprised. She's the one who interrupted me and Mackenzie. I advert my eyes to give her the privacy to readjust herself before I go to help her off the stone floor.

"Wait here," I tell Maleficent. She looks between me and Justice and retreats to a dark corner. "What are you doing here, kid?" My attention shifts to Justice whose eyebrows are as high as I'd like to be.

She moves toward me but thinks twice and covers her eyes. "Can you put some clothes on, *please*?"

We can't see shit in here with the fake candles on recessed shelves around the room, but there's no mistaking her *Preacher's Wife* performance. It's like she hasn't been around a dick or people fucking outside a bedroom. Maybe not the second, knowing her.

"You're such a kid," I say and lift her to me after I cover myself.

Justice is a pain in my ass even when she's not being stubborn—which is never. She tries to wiggle free from my arm wrapped around her waist, and I laugh my ass off as her hands cover her face, shielding another glimpse at my shaft.

"Relax, I have a towel on. I won't smack you in the face with my dick." Light from the hallway reaches into the room when I open the door.

Jay spins on me when I put her down. "What the hell are you doing, Miles?" With our height difference, she's yelling at my chest. Her breath comes out in an angry huff and blows a curl falling from a lazy bun out of her face.

I shrug. "Thought it was obvious. I would say it's been a pleasure bumping into you again, but you interrupted my happy ending." With Margaret. "Now be a good little girl and go back to your suite." I motion to the locker room and nudge her to take the hint.

She stares at me with the same look she had when she Lysoled me during my last visit to her and Terrence's house. "You're disgusting."

"Coming from you, Mother Teresa, I take that as a compliment," I say and head back into the room.

The hum of water showers the space with white noise as an outline of petite curves comes into view. Water trickles down her breasts, and my dick springs back to life.

She fists me under my towel and licks her lips. "Where were we?"

Trying to forget Emma and remember your name.

A replay of last night, her hand sliding down the swell of her amber breasts, drifts back to memory. Head in the spa isn't enough of a distraction to erase the image of Emma's fingers dancing over her inner thighs. I push the thought from my mind to focus on... "Mya, I have to go soon."

She pouts but doesn't correct me about her name. A win is a win.

I had no plans to fuck her, but I am a giver. The pad of my thumb grazes her nipple. *That's right, focus on her.* Her back arches, and I lift her to a nearby table, where I lay her down, spread her legs, and bring her to orgasm with my fingers.

"Would you stop looking over your shoulder?" You'd think Terrence has a warrant out for his arrest the way he keeps scanning the room and eyeing the exits.

He peeks over his menu to give me the finger, a salute I'll take as a good sign. Bro is in a dark place. My rundown on what happened to Justice at the '90s party last night, and her thinking he started fucking on Madison, got to him. He's been ducking not one but two exes at this retreat. It doesn't make me envious, nor does it spark a desire for relationships beyond casual sex.

Justice stomped the shit out of his heart when she packed up and left him while he was out of the country on business. They hit more than a rough patch a couple years back and haven't been able to fix it. T is my bro, but I'll admit that throwing himself into his job caused more problems than good. That doesn't warrant radio silence and moving out in my book, but what the hell do I know about marriage?

I doubt Terrence anticipated that his other ex would be here also, but I'm sure he mentioned it to Madison in passing, given they run in similar circles. He's a strength and conditioning specialist to celebs, and she's a personal stylist.

He should be sweating that he pretended to lose our bet just to drag us here so he could see his wife. I'm many things, but Boo Boo the Fool ain't one. My IQ is too high for that. With all the traveling we do, he randomly chooses a made-for-TV location in the dead of winter?

I don't have proof, but I don't need it.

I flip through the menu and resist the urge to call him on his bullshit. If he wants to fight for his wife and prevent a divorce on the sly, fine. But do it somewhere warm, where I'm not freezing my nuts off.

"You know what you want?" Terrence scrubs a hand over his goatee, his eyes focused, and his brows drawn at the mini binder of lunch options before him.

She's not on the menu.

After I walked Mya out, I signed up for a deep tissue massage and ran into Emma. After all that shit-talking I did, I ate every word as I took in the wet ringlets swaying at the nape of her high bun. Her cheeks heated under my gaze, like she'd just come from the sauna. I've never been a jealous man, but my nostrils flared at the cotton fabric nestled between her breasts, the same way they did two years ago in the hallway. She hiked a brow, silently asking why I was staring her down. So I did us both a favor and left.

"Bro, you good?"

Shit, am I? "Can't decide between steak or fish."

Terrence stares at me for a beat before he goes back to his menu. I'm full of it. He knows it, but he won't press me, just like I won't press him about how he really feels about his wife. There's no need to. Not when his actions speak louder than words in Aretha Franklin syllables. When we're not out, he's in his room. I dared him to sleep with Madison, or any other woman here. Seven months is a long time to jerk your dick. If it's Justice he wants, go get her. If not, move on.

Regardless, I got his back. Terrence is my brother, my friend since we were small kids getting into all types of shit in Newark. I might give him hell for being whipped—what kind of friend would I be if I didn't?—but I love him and Justice together, even if I want to fling her ass away from time to time.

Time passes amid chatter and forks scraping plates. Terrence is rehearsing the apology tour he's contemplating once he gets the courage to actually *talk* to Justice. I'm running programming simulations in my head, trying not to think about his wife's friend who's living rent fucking free in my mind.

"You, uh...want to talk about anything?"

I'm a few years older that Terrence, and I have always shielded him from the bad shit I didn't want to touch his life. But his anguish at being separated from Jay is beyond my control. Feelings are foreign to me. I have them, but I don't sit around trying to process them. He does, and that's probably why his constipated stare is stuck on confused. We don't talk about shit like emotions.

He runs a hand through the black curls ruffling on top of his head. "I'm"—he frowns but recovers with a smile that's more forced than natural—"good."

"Cool."

"Yup."

"Okay then."

We mirror each other in dark jeans and Henleys, his gray and mine black. We're also dumbasses, unable to fess up about the important shit. Terrence and Justice will reconcile. It's in the cards for them.

Me and Emma? We're about to get into some shit.

Chapter 5

Emma

Only Justice would catch Miles with a woman on her knees at the spa. The Ravine is a white colonial revival mountain resort, the largest in the valley. The square footage alone should afford us the privacy to not run into her ex or his best friend. But fate works in mysterious ways, and apparently it wants to be a vindictive bitch on this trip. Miles's exhibition is the running joke of our lunch. Justice is bewildered that public sex is a thing, and I'm pretending that his being in another woman's mouth doesn't bother me. Because it doesn't.

I left him in Ravenous last night drooling and ready to burst. He didn't know what to do once my fingers touched his lips with my essence. I slept with a smile and the satisfaction of knowing I had the upper hand in this game we've played for a decade strong. But Miles one-upped me, and I hate it. I don't give up power, and his ability to make me feel is new territory I don't want to visit.

My guess is he's with the woman who was hovering over him at the lodge. Justice and I spent the morning on a snowmobile, which put us with other singles who were hitting the slopes. Terrence was there. Justice didn't see him—thank God—but I did. I also saw his friend, stretching a snowsuit over his burly frame and good looks.

No one would judge me for doing a double take at the man with the beanie and trimmed goatee. I did, and I wasn't alone.

The woman in question locked eyes with him from across the pine-walled registration room. She was pretty, with wavy dark brown hair, rosy cheeks, and heart-shaped lips—not that I paid attention. I grabbed Justice and my gear, put on my helmet before Miles caught me staring, and took off for the winter cold.

Justice and I cruised through tall pines on a trail coated in snow against a backdrop of mountains. I'm not what you'd call an outdoor person by any stretch of the imagination, unless it involves a beach or the Mediterranean coast. I live in Malibu for a reason. It's a miracle I don't have a concussion the way Justice flew over snow mounds like they were speed bumps and not knee-high tickets to the ER. This face is too cute to ruin, and I focused on the crisp air and sunshine to ignore my life flashing in front of my visor. But I stuck it out and have the keychain to prove it.

We wrapped hours ago and have been inside this bistro ever since.

"This is nice." Justice leans into her rattan chair with a content sigh.

"Good food and cocktails will do that for you."

She rubs her stomach over her sweater and reaches for the mug cake she has no chance of finishing.

"Does your ass feel better?" I ask.

Only my friend would twerk and get a cramp after driving us on a two-seater snowmobile. She couldn't help herself once she got the hang of it after our safety course. Justice gets a gold star for not crashing us into a ditch, but that's our friendship: riding until the wheels fall off.

"Yeah." Justice squirms but nods. "It would feel a lot nicer if I didn't have a thong wedged in my crack."

My grin widens at her glare. "You'll thank me later."

This singles' retreat is full of surprises for Justice, starting with her cluelessness about our destination and me packing her bag—which includes nothing but thongs. We've managed to keep our weeklong vacation tradition since college, which is a small miracle. Jay is busy being VP of marketing for her firm, and I'm the senior creative director of a luxury lingerie company.

What better way to decompress than at a resort in a winter? If Justice could jump into a Hallmark movie with a small town, tree farms, and mistletoe kisses, she'd disappear and send me a postcard. She grew up in Alexandria like I did, but she eats up those cookie-cutter stories in rustic locations with guaranteed happily ever afters. That's my friend: a believer of love and cheer. Me? I'll take the lumberjack in plaid whose ass looks good in jeans. Keep your sleigh rides.

Vail was supposed to be a place where Justice could clear her head, sleep in, and recharge. Who am I to judge if she gets over Terrence by getting under a new man? I love him like a brother, but I support my girl first and always.

Cobwebs, remember?

My worrisome friend gets nervous easily. While I anticipated Justice using true crime scenarios as an excuse not to socialize, Terrence's presence is a trigger I never saw coming—same with Madison's thirsty ass lurking in dark corners to chase after him. She already tried goading Justice at lunch yesterday, and it won't happen again. Not on my watch.

This is only day two of the retreat, and it has to turn around.

"I need a nap and someone to roll me out of here." Justice eyes her Nutella martini.

"Your sweet tooth always gets you in trouble," I snicker. "Remember our junior year of high school, when you had the bright idea to melt all of your chocolate bars into a drink *before* stuffing your face with ice cream?"

She groans. "Mom turned it into a hot chocolate recipe. She still uses it today."

Angela Garvey isn't my mother by blood, but she took me under her wing and hasn't stopped loving me since Justice and I met in homeroom during our first year of high school. She doesn't want to replace my mother, nor step on her toes, but she has been a constant maternal figure in my life. Justice's parents showed up to school events when mine were too busy, and they made space for me in their home.

I sat at the Garvey dinner table almost every school night. I learned how to drive with Justice and her dad and spent weekends—and some weekdays—sleeping over.

State dinners and congressional connections were far more important to my parents than the memories I created with Justice's family. That's why she calls Ms. Angela "Mom" and not "my mom." I'm her second daughter, someone she made room for in her big heart.

We end our lunch stuffed and talking about nothing important.

—— ele ——

"Holy shit, Jay!"

"Do you think it's too much?" Justice smooths the sides of her black silk dress. She is out to make a statement tonight in peep-toe booties, her natural curls in full bloom.

"Honey, if I didn't love dick so much, I would take you home with me tonight. You look *amazing*!"

After three hours in the bistro, we're back in our suite, laughing and catching up. Justice and I are close, but texts and phone calls don't cut it. I miss her, and I wish we lived closer. My introverted best friend is off to a whiskey-tasting tonight, and she's going solo. The fact that she hasn't run back to Austin yet is a testament to the strength she doesn't realize she has.

I wish I could take away her pain of loving someone until it hurt too much to stay, but I've never known that type of adoration, and I struggle with how to show up for her—even if she tells me I'm enough.

"Where are you off to tonight?" Justice puts the finishing touch on her red lipstick and glances at me in the mirror.

"You know, a little bit of this and a little bit of that," I force out. "There's a poker game on one of the upper levels I want to check out."

If I could kick my own ass, I would. Miles is still on my mind, and I'll be damned if a man has me this ruffled. He's loud, obnoxious, unfiltered, and enraging. He's also a clit tingler and a panty soaker, with that hypnotic grin and the way he sinks those white teeth into his thick lower lip. I haven't seen so much as a dick hair, and I still have his tip on my mind, wondering if Miles feels as good as he smells.

Lunch wasn't a distraction. Neither was snowmobiling. Miles is everywhere—in my thoughts and wherever I turn. But I won't fuck him, so *fuck him*.

I'm not on my way to poker, but I would clean house and take the deed if I were. I learned how to school my features at a young age, and that comes in handy with people who underestimate me. What little time I spent with my father growing up included his beloved card deck and his Congress buddies placing bets. I enjoy poker, but that's not the game I want to play tonight.

My lie is believable enough for Justice not to look at me sideways. She doesn't question my whereabouts. Another trip to Ravenous is how I'll end my night.

It's time I take my own advice.

The best way to get over a man is to get under a new one, right?

"This might be the best idea you've had in a long time," I say to Justice through the hotel phone. Rising steam from the bubble bath creates a thin cloud of lavender from the tub.

Tonight was a complete bust that requires pampering.

I made it to Ravenous, fully prepared to enjoy all of its pleasures. The crowd was smaller than last night's, but sex and kink reigned thick in the air, and I was ready for my high.

I looked flawless.

I felt amazing.

Even cloaked in layers of satin, eyes gravitated to me, hungry for the chance to see what was underneath my black robe and lace mask.

I didn't need their lust to reaffirm what I already know: I'm fine as hell, and I could have any man I want on his knees at the tips of my open-toe heels.

If only they were the one whose desire mixed with pain at not touching me when I teased him within an inch of his life.

Every dark figure became an apparition of the man haunting me, the one I can't escape. I saw Miles in the shadows at Ravenous, in the hooded gaze of masked figures who matched his build but lacked the fire in their eyes to incinerate me with a single look. Miles was everywhere and nowhere, with a hold on me as vivid as the memory of us in Justice and Terrence's hallway that keeps seeping back into my mind.

"How's your chocolate cake?" Justice asks.

"It would taste better if it could erase the memories of a certain dick," I confess.

"A person or an organ?"

"Both."

After Ravenous, I rushed back to my suite with my tail between my legs, unsure how to extract myself from the nightmare of the man I can't stop thinking about. I opened Pandora's Box, and wish I could close it again.

"I'm surprised I didn't find you with your suitcases ready to go when I came back."

Looks like I'm not the only one whose night went to shit. Justice freaked out after seeing Terrence with Madison at tonight's whiskey tasting event. The details are blurry, like why he walked in with her *and* Miles, but Jay acted out of character. She saw West and pretended to flirt to guard her heart, which blew up in her face once Terrence followed them into a back room. The only thing he walked in on was Justice keeping West company while he retrieved wine bottles. But that didn't stop an argument with years' worth of heartbreak thrown at their feet.

"You should've seen how much I hurt him tonight," Justice murmurs under a long breath. "Terrence was as mad as the night I left him."

I was on a plane out to Austin the same night Justice called me to say her marriage was over. The swell of her pain was beyond tears when I finally reached her. She was numb, a fragment of her cheerful self, who was slipping away. I wanted to do something—*feel* something—for her to transfer the agony. Hurt lay naked in her eyes seven months ago, the same way they did tonight when she finally came back to the room.

We're on the phone with each other from our bathrooms now, soaking in our freestanding tubs with dessert trays to comfort us. If only they worked.

"You two spent close to a year not talking," I tell her. "It was only a matter of time before things erupted. You're hurt. He's hurt. You both lost so much, and you haven't properly healed." I don't pray, but in this moment I do in hopes it will soothe her. I can't erase the fight Justice had with Terrence, but I can be here for her however she needs.

"You know, you have some pretty good instincts for someone who hates relationships." The first glimpse of humor cracks through her voice.

"I'm not sure I'd know how to be in a relationship if I tried." My words stun me to silence. I don't know what possessed the admission. It's nothing new, nor a secret. Casual sex guards your heart, to keep you from giving it away to the wrong person.

How's that going?

"Em, you okay?"

"Never better," I blurt. "Are you ready to get out? I'm a prune, and it's not a good look."

We're in the living area fifteen minutes later with our robes and hot chocolate. I try to nudge Justice to skip speed dating and put some distance between her and Terrence. And me and his sexy ass best friend.

She doesn't bite, but come tomorrow, maybe I will.

Chapter 6

Emma

I tell myself to focus on the men playing musical chairs in front of me and not the one whose cologne has me in a chokehold from several seats away. The stubborn, conceited face I've wanted to smack and ride, who's now in front of my best friend at this damn speed dating event.

Dancing through my mind and on my last nerve.

"Mind if I join you?"

My gaze shifts from the sharp edges of Miles's profile, his generous mouth, to a man in all black with a matching crop of thick hair. He's tall and slender, a contrast to the gladiator frame tempting glances at the fitted turtleneck stretched over his chest.

Dark eyes look down at me in wait. They're missing the warm flecks of brown I'm trying desperately to scrub from my thoughts, but they are still handsome.

Heat creeps up the side of my face at Miles's stare. It's overpowering, ready to call me on my bullshit for pretending to have more interest in the man across from me than I do. I press a hand to my chest and smile, present onlookers be damned. "Of course," I say, my face splitting into a wide grin for no other reason than to give Miles the finger from feet away.

Black Suit unbuttons his blazer to slide into the seat, his eyes careful not to linger too long on my little black dress or the mesh panel that exposes my skin from my right breast to my sternum.

"I'm Spiro."

"Emma."

We shake over rose petals and scattered tea lights on the white linen tablecloth between us. I want to gag at the first date clichés, but I won't complain about the floor-to-ceiling view of the snow-covered valley.

"What do you do, Emma?"

Strike one.

I pull a sip of champagne to keep my eye roll at bay. Did this event come with notecards of basic questions? I'm sure Spiro is nice, but *What do you do?* and *Where are you from?* don't get my panties moist.

"I'm a creative director." I leave out the lingerie part. Too many salivate the moment I say it, like it strengthens their chances of seeing what color bra and thong set I'm wearing.

A brow quirks. "Impressive. I work on Wall Street."

"Mmm."

Strike two.

"Where are you from?"

Check, please!

If only I'd pushed Justice to skip tonight's organized matchmaking for room service and reruns. Jay isn't ready to face her estranged husband, who's currently showing every damn tooth in his mouth to Madison. She wouldn't be seeing his charm on display, and I wouldn't be smiling my ass off at a man who does nothing to my mind or pussy because I'm dodging the one who does.

Miles has served Trevante Rhodes for the fifteen years we hopped in and out of each other's lives. He's a full meal with a side of 50 Cent audacity. His quips and level of fine are a deadly combination. Forbidden fruit luring my lips to taste.

I brush my chin over my shoulder to peek at Miles, whose eyes are still on me. Justice is talking a mile a minute, but his fixed stare teases goosebumps over my skin.

How am *I* dickmatized over someone whose dick I haven't even seen? I poke fun at Justice about Terrence, but this is worse. Miles and I never dated. Hell, we're not even friends. There's at least twenty people in the room, and it's a miracle no one has choked under the pressure of our energy stretching across the restaurant.

You are not this sprung.

"Emma?"

"Sorry. What did you say?" Spiro is classically handsome—square face, thick brows, aquiline nose—but he's no match for Miles.

A shiver massages its way down my back. What the hell is wrong with me?

Focus.

Spiro's smile widens, his white teeth in contrast to his olive tone. "Where are you from?"

"Alexandria, Virginia. You?"

"Greece. My family moved to Long Island when I was little. Interested in a nightcap? Our time is almost up." His fingers stroke over my hand. The touch is smooth, but it doesn't spark the urge to go back to his room.

"It's still early. Let's see what happens," I say.

The hostess calls time, signaling for Spiro to move to the next woman who might show more enthusiasm for gelled hair and a gold Rolex. Have I fucked bankers before? Sure, but I'm not adding this one to the roster.

Faces blend into each other as the speed dating event winds down to the last two chances to make a connection and go on a private date. I want it to end so I can get out of here—to the opposite side of the resort, where I won't see Miles or those damn muscles wearing the hell out of that turtleneck. I need to take the edge off, preferably by edging myself to an orgasm so intense, it puts me to sleep for the rest of this trip. These hot flashes are ridiculous.

Terrence all but power walks over to Justice. They can't take their eyes off each other, caught between silent longing. My friend did not come to play in her black blazer and curve-hugging ankle pants. The black shapewear underneath looks like a bra, a far cry from Justice's usual look.

I try to ignore the strange ache at their reunion. There's desire and then there's devotion. What they found in each other is rare, the kind of love to pull at your heart with the promise of eternity.

Marriage is not in my vocabulary after growing up in a home where status trumped love and intimacy. My parents were tolerable as individuals, but as husband and wife, they were far from #CouplesGoals.

"They look good together," Miles says, taking in the same view.

"They do."

We put our differences aside to watch our best friends finally have a discussion and not an argument. The hurt of their early pregnancy losses and Terrence's international work schedule made it hard to hear each other. Hard to heal. We stood by them eleven years ago when they exchanged vows, and we watched their love grow during the better times until the worst became too much to bear.

Miles takes a seat. He sighs and clasps his hands together before facing me. A smirk curls his mouth, and the weight of our tension settles back over us.

"You owe me."

The statement hangs in the air, held up by his nerve and my curiosity.

My brow dips. I'll bite—figuratively and literally, depending on his response. "Owe you?"

His jaw tightens, his eyes firm. "You think you can play with me without consequence?"

The silken thread of the warning tightens my nipples. Miles is playful, heavy on sarcasm, and I never take him seriously. But the edge in his tone knocks the breath out of my lungs.

It's a good thing we're in public. I wouldn't trust myself not to climb over this table and maul him otherwise.

No.

Miles might pique my interest—more than any man, Carter included—but no one will have a hold on me. "You must have me confused with someone who gives a damn," I throw back.

"You like games, Em. Let's play—tonight."

Don't do it.

"What do you have in mind?" I do like games, especially the ones that tie you up.

His eyes drop from my lips to my cleavage and drag up the base of my neck. "Meet me at Ravenous in two hours. No one else. Just me and you." He tips his head to the side. "Can you handle that...kitten?"

"Handle what?" Temptation reaches for my throat and squeezes.

The muscles in Miles's shoulders contract as he leans forward. Large hands fold together, stimulating the veins in his smooth forearms. "Us."

The host signals the end of speed dating. We stand, neither giving the other an inch. A challenge lies before me. The safer option would be to find someone else for the night.

My eyes leave the man whose gaze is licking my pleasure points and find Justice at the bar talking to another woman, who rubs her arm and laughs with a force that crinkles her eyes.

I drop my voice and pin Miles with a glare. "One night."

"I couldn't stand you longer."

"Jay and Terrence can never know."

"Obviously," Miles scoffs.

"No sex." My mouth lifts at his eye twitch. "You don't deserve this pussy."

"You flatter yourself," Miles says. "You'll beg for this dick before I'd ever fuck you."

"Let's get one thing straight." I shift closer, inches away from broad lips pressed into a hard line and a goatee trimmed to perfection. "You want to play with *me* tonight. Consider it a gift. My vagina is perfection." I lean back and look at the obvious tent in Miles's pants. "Don't challenge me. You'll lose every time."

I leave him pissed and with a painful erection, my head lifted and my panties drenched. I want to rid myself of our sexual tension, but I am no fool. If Miles puts it down how I think he does, I might follow him home. Ravenous's no sex rule is a safeguard.

Time to get ready.

Chapter 7
Miles

I said I would leave Emma alone, but my intentions went right out the window the moment she stepped into the restaurant for speed dating. Em put everyone to shame in the black getup she called a dress. Mesh from her breast to the top of her belly gave a peek at the soft skin underneath, and she quickly became the fantasy of everyone in the room. Except for Terrence, who clocked Justice coming in and walked off adjusting himself.

My dick bricked to the point of pain at Emma. Watching her. *Wanting* her.

She is perfection. Thick lips. High cheekbones. Ample breasts. Hips for days. Physically, Emma is in a league of her own, but she's more than just her looks. Her thick mahogany hair swayed across her back as she scanned the room, sizing up the men who'd sit before her. Men worthy of her time might think they're in control, but Emma already made the decision to let them pursue her. She's calculated. Intentional. Precise.

None of that matters. No one can satisfy her the way I can—and will. Emma never found someone who can keep up with her, and I'm up for the challenge. The draw to her is too strong to not taste her again after years of staying away.

Tonight I decided to go against logic and the sirens warning me that whatever happens will change the trajectory of whatever it is we are. If T and Jay actually go through with their divorce, there won't be a reason for Emma and I to see each other. We can have tonight if we keep our distance after.

"Bro, are you pouting?"

"Shut up." Terrence sucks his teeth and swivels back to the mini bar in the dining area of his room. He ditched his button-down and jeans from speed dating for a white tee and joggers. I'm still in my slacks and loafers but swapped my turtleneck for a black shirt. I meet Em in less than an hour, but I had to hit him up to make sure he's good. He's been nursing the same manhattan since I got here over an hour ago.

Bro hasn't been right since yesterday's whiskey tasting, where he saw Justice flirting with that bartender Emma was with. Jay only acted out of pocket because she thinks T is with Madison. In his defense, he and I hit up the tasting together. It wasn't a good look that Madison happened to find us, and the optics weren't in his favor. That led to an argument, and now Justice is back to pushing for a divorce.

A damn mess.

Terrence traces the rim of his glass and exhales slowly. Bro is going through it. "It's over. For good this time," he says after a hard swallow.

What the hell do I say? "Pray on it or something."

"Pray on it?" His brows bunch.

I shrug. "I know you do, and the shit works for my mama." Deborah Walker keeps the oil in her pantry stocked for prayer and the best consecrated chicken you'll taste.

"I fucked up." Terrence nods to himself, his eyes fixed on the marble countertop. "I let work get in the way of being there for her. Through…" His hand drags over the back of his neck. "It doesn't matter anymore."

"Yo, be easy on yourself, bro. You're a good man who's not with the bullshit. Just give it time."

Terrence acts like he was slinging dick across the seven seas. I've never seen him love someone and dedicate himself the way he does with Jay. I don't know the first thing about marriage and won't pretend I do. Terrence is a better man than me—the best I know, aside from my mentor. He set the bar high on loving the one you're with. Not that I'd attempt to reach it.

Commitment isn't for me, end of story. I don't have any desire to attach myself to anyone, and I'm not sure I'm capable of giving the love required to do it.

"You're alright with pep talks when you're not being an ass," he teases.

Pfft. "I got range." We laugh. "Jokes aside, keep your head up."

Terrence nods. "Thanks."

I slap my knees and stand. T and I are brothers, but we can only share so many feelings. Guys where we come from weren't setting examples to follow, so we didn't.

"I'll get at you tomorrow."

"Where you off to?" Terrence lifts off the barstool to dap up.

"To do what I do best." I smile. "Me."

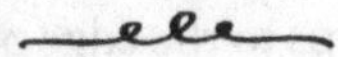

I check in with the host once I arrive at Ravenous, recommit to the consent policy, and take a cloak to cover my black slacks and tee. Tonight's guests crowd around the main stage, where an education on ropes takes place next to performers cascading down poles stationed between silk panels. I follow signs for the meeting rooms and stop in front of a room illuminated in red with matching fabric on the wall. The play space is empty except for wooden crosses on either side of a table where open briefcases filled with leather whips and other accessories lie. My eyes land on a leather chair with stirrups similar to an examination table but with—are those restraints?

What kind of freaky shit goes on in here?

Play parties aren't a personal kink of mine, but if it's your ministry, it's your ministry. I keep sex to the privacy of my meeting place of choice. No one is in here, so it will do. Maybe Em will test drive this chair since she's on her bullshit.

"You're late," I say once she shows. Twenty minutes late.

"You waited." Emma stands taller in heels that put her below my chin. She drops her purse with a green tag next to the chair. "Come play." Yeah, she's on that bullshit, alright.

I drag my tongue over my bottom lip before I pull it between my teeth. Then I close the distance between us until my black loafers touch the tips of her pumps. Her moss-green eyes light with a glow.

She knows she'll pay for her lateness. I let my gaze drag down her cloak. "Careful, kitten."

My mellow baritone seeps to the edge of my control, and the lines of my face harden as I stare down at Emma. I'm all but breathing fire after warning her not to play in my face. She better think twice about pissing me off.

"What's in the bag?" I nod to her purse without breaking eye contact.

She widens her stance and crosses her arms to extinguish the heat rising between us. We're not wearing masks anymore, which gives me a full view of her smooth amber skin over a kissable jaw. "Toys."

"Get in the chair," I growl. I got a game her ass can play since she wants to so bad.

Emma settles into the leather pressing firmly at her back and parts her knees to rest against the stirrups. Her fingers curl around the edges of the black satin ties that hold her cloak together and tug. Emma's eyes darken under the scarlet shimmer of the playroom as I take in the lingerie she wore for the evening. Black lace weaves with satin in a makeshift collar from her neck to her sternum, arching over the thin fabric that covers each breast. A barely visible lace garter belt clips to French thigh-high stockings in black.

Fuck.

Her legs open, dragging the cloak with it. My inhale is sharp, unable to control the yearning to devour every inch. I step forward to touch her but hesitate.

"You okay with my hands on you?" My swallow is audible over the seductive music piping through the ceiling.

Please say yes.

Minutes ago, I was ready to test the limits of Emma's submission for her being late. Yet one look under this fabric, and I'm singing a different tune.

Emma's arms reach back for the headrest. She swings her knees open. "Of course," she says with an evil smile.

"You're okay with me using toys?"

She closes her eyes and tips up her chin. "Yes." Emma frowns when I step away.

"Keep your eyes closed," I command from a distance. I'm back in front of her seconds later, rubbing a thumb over the top of her thigh. My voice drops to a whisper. "Tell me if it's too much. What's your safe word?"

The edges of Emma's mouth lift at my underestimation of her pussy's stamina. "Vanilla, but I won't need it. There's nothing in that bag I haven't—" The words die on her lips when I set said pussy on fire. Em's eyes grow two sizes at the riding crop in my hand and the devilish grin on my face.

I tap the leather tongue over her mound. "You were saying?"

"Why don't you let me smack you in the balls with it and see how you feel?"

"I wasn't the one who was late," I chuckle with a shrug. Emma jolts as the tongue slides up and down her seam under lace now soaked and scenting the air. I want to get lost in her, but she needs to learn about me, and quick. "You're fine, Emma, but that doesn't mean you can play with me. Be here when I tell you."

If she's panting this much from a pussy slap, it won't be a long night. I'm ready to bust in my pants, and she's breathing like she sprinted up a flight of stairs.

Emma brushes strands of hair out of her face with a frustrated sigh, one she sucks back in when I lean over her and press my weight—and this bulge—into the chair. She shudders at my lips gliding up the length of her neck. My mint breath licks her skin. "I'm in charge tonight, kitten." I cup her chin. "Do you trust me?"

I've had many partners before, but never any I wanted this much. She bites her lip and nods.

"Words, kitten. Use them. Do you trust me?"

It surprises us both how quickly her "Yes" comes. Her voice is a husky purr. I don't know what they put in the drinks at speed dating. I'm still thirsting over the woman who's been off-limits for fifteen years.

I secure a restraint around her ankle, kiss the skin above it, and secure the other foot. "Can I trust you to keep your hands to yourself? No?" I laugh at her glare and add restraints to Emma's wrists.

My kitten is spread wide, unable to put hands on me or herself. *My kitten.*

Pleasure pools straight to my dick when I skate two fingers up her thighs. "Think you can handle what I'm about to give you?"

"Please." Emma rolls her eyes and leans back into the headrest. "You're all talk so far. Don't bore me."

A chuckle rumbles in my chest and bends the edges of my face into a wide grin. "Says the one about to nut." She gasps when my hand cups her pussy, and she fights the impulse to rock into the touch. My thumb massages her throbbing clit. "Your body betrays you."

Emma's nipples harden beneath the thin fabric as my other hand kneads her breast. The sting of my pinch heaves her chest as I tend to the other breast.

"Shit, kitten. You're soaking my hand, and I'm not inside you yet." I tug the fabric between her pussy, generating friction against the sensitive flesh. Emma bucks forward to rock into the hand that's palming her and cries out.

Fuck, she's gorgeous.

She's damn near convulsing when I slip my fingers inside her panties and taste her nectar.

"Delicious." I squat to sift through her purse. *What the fuck?* "Jesus, woman. Leave anything behind at Lowe's?" I chuckle. She's got enough bullets and vibrators for ten people.

I pick up the rose but think twice. "I'm not causing no shock therapy," I mumble. All sorts of shit is in here. Suction devices. Squiggly things. Dildos with spinning accessories. I stall at the hot pink anal beads and look up from her bag. "Remind me why we never got together?"

"*Tonight*, Miles."

"How'd you get all this shit through airport security?"

"Miles!"

"Calm them titties," I say and stand with a purple and white vibrator that buzzes to life. "You must not get fucked right if you're packing this much inventory."

Emma bites the inside of her cheek and looks away. *Thought so.* Her breath hitches as the vibrator circles her nipples through her bra. It's on the lowest setting, but it's turning those pink buds into diamonds as a flush creeps up her neck.

"Can I kiss you?" My voice is a murmur that lacks its usual confidence. The draw to her is unlike anything I've ever felt. I don't put my mouth on anyone I'm with, but I want to with Em.

I run the vibrator down Emma's stomach and pull out another moan with the toy humming up her breasts. Her hands fist at the heat of her flesh on fire. Desire blazes in her eyes.

"Just one," she says, out of breath. I waste no time moving her panties to the side and slipping the vibrator into her heat. The steady rhythm rubs over her G-spot with expert precision.

Emma gulps at the tide surging between her legs. It becomes a shockwave when I press my mouth to hers. I grab her by the neck to deepen our kiss, a drugging mix of tongues probing and sucking. It's a gentle contrast to how I'm fucking her with the vibrator in deep strokes.

Her knees shake, and she shudders under another orgasm I swallow. I pump slow into her pussy, slurping the toy with her juices. Our lips part, and I steady my breathing to take in the woman who has me looking like I swam across the ocean for the hell of it.

"Touch me, Miles," she pants, spreading her legs as wide as the chair allows. With my eyes on her, I toss the vibrator, glide two fingers inside, and curl to reanimate her G-spot. "*Yes,*" she moans through a kiss, rolling her hips into the pressure building between her legs. "Right there."

My tongue drags up the center of Emma's throat as her head falls back. "There's nothing wrong with toys, kitten, but when you have the right partner, you won't rely on them so much." I lick my way back into her mouth. "Come for me again."

Emma's muscles tense, parting her lips to set free a moan. My eyes roam over her face with pride. It takes several breaths for her to come down from the high. When she does, she looks behind me. I follow her eyes to find multiple faces in the distance. We're not alone.

My body is wide enough to cover her from voyeurs, but I make quick work of the restraints and lower her cloak. Once she's covered, I secure her mask and help her out of the chair, grabbing wipes nearby to clean off the leather surface and the toys we used.

A couple holding hands approaches. "You are exquisite," the blonde says to us. "Any interest in joining us back in our room?" She nods to the man next to her, who's eye-fucking me. "He likes to watch."

"Thank you, but we have to go." I take Emma's hand, and soon I'm moving so fast, I have to slow down for her to keep up.

"What's the rush?" She's speed walking to keep up.

"Em, I'm all for adventure, but I have limits. Fucking around with them extras from *The People Under the Stairs* is a good way to never to be seen again." I smile at her snort. "Plus"—I steal a glance—"I'm not done with you," I say with a wink.

Chapter 8

Emma

"Remind me to kill you later for only packing thongs!"

I smile and shout right back at Justice from my room, "Thank me after a man helps you take them off!" She'll survive ninety minutes in jeans on a horse. I'm no better in leggings I had to buy in the gift shop. Trotting in leather pants is stylish but foolish. In my rush to get this trip ready, I did not pack accordingly. I don't own a pair of jeans or leggings, and usually my closet is just fine for it.

Jay clowns me all the time for my wardrobe, but I am who I am. The same way she could be the face of Target, I love high fashion but draw the line. Yes, overpriced jeans are a thing, but I'll be damned.

I pull my hair into a low ponytail and button the rest of my blouse to meet Justice in the living room. We head down to the back of the resort for our excursion.

Jay has been in pretty good spirits since speed dating last night. She and Terrence wished each other the best in an attempt to move on, one I doubt either will uphold. Some people are perfect matches, and these two are it.

What about your match?

I hold back a groan at my vagina pulsing from the reminder of last night and pop on my sunglasses.

"You okay?" Justice peeks at my profile on the way to our small group near the stables.

"Mm-hmm!" My answer is too bouncy for my personality. Jay is the chipper one, not me.

I called Miles full of shit when he told me he'd put me to bed. I wanted to even the score after our time in the red room. I've never came so fast from a hand job. It's usually impossible for me, like licking your own elbow. The way Miles read me and commanded my body without breaking a sweat is shameful.

In the heat of passion and frustration, I challenged him to another go, away from curious eyes and the possibility of running into one of our best friends.

We put every toy in my bag to use.

Never once did Miles make me feel guilty for my "arsenal of power tools," as he called them. He took digs at the men who've failed to bring me pleasure but never felt threatened putting my toys to work. I wouldn't give a damn if he did have something to say. A healthy sex life doesn't guarantee that the person I'm with will get the job done. Half the time, I'm directing men to my G-spot like I'm landing a damn 747.

Not Miles.

We spent the better part of three hours with my toys, taking breaks in between for drinks and snacks. Miles promised not to use his mouth or fingers, which I assumed would give me the advantage, but he made a liar out of me once again. A screamer and a squirter too.

By two a.m., Miles was ready to tap out, but then he switched up and used my rose. I creamed all over the damn thing, rode out the aftershock for twenty minutes, and fell asleep in a pool of my own sweat.

I had every chance to end our game and go upstairs to my suite, but I didn't, and I don't know what that says about Miles and how I feel when I'm with him.

Men like West are easy: flirt, fuck, and leave. There are no attachments, no second thoughts, and no feelings. Last night was different. I *felt* like staying, not because of the potential for more orgasms, but because I was comfortable.

I woke up alone. The other side of the bed remained untouched, like Miles didn't sleep. Maybe he did, but not with me. I was back in my suite in time to grab lunch with Justice and push away all thoughts of him. It shouldn't bother me that he left, but it does. More than I'd like to admit.

What happened is over. We got each other out of our systems, and now we can move on.

I focus on the valley and the snow glittering on tree branches through streams of sunlight. Justice and I receive our instructions and set off on a trail with our assigned horse. Mine is Meadow, a spotted Appaloosa with a fabulous mane, who guides us deeper into the valley under blue skies. It's not uncommon for me to complain about recreational outdoor activities that don't include a penis, but this is nice.

My annual girls' trip with Justice is the extent of my vacations. I travel often for work, shuffling between fashion events, but I don't take time for myself like I should.

A man in a red cap trots up to me. He's handsome in a rugged Chris Evans way, which is funny considering I told Justice when we arrived that I would find a mountain man.

How things change.

"Hi."

"Hi," I smile. I have no reason to be rude. Sunlight catches on his beard and the camel-colored hair peeking out of his cap. His blue eyes are the color of the sky, and he's got a juicy lower lip and a crisp jawline.

Justice is farther back on the trail, grinning at me from ear to ear. Always the hopeless romantic.

"I'm Brian."

"I'm—"

Not interested.

The thought summons a side-eye from Meadow, who's wondering what the hell is wrong with me.

Wish I knew.

I entertain a friendly conversation before letting Brian down easy. There's no denying what I want, and it's not him.

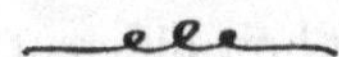

"You're not going out?" Justice adjusts her shirt dress in the floor-length mirror in the living area. Her Tinker Bell shape is perfect and will look even better with my thigh-high boots she's borrowing for a date.

A date.

My girl is going out with the instructor from horseback riding. Preston's name sure as hell didn't match his face or his body. He's fine. Tall. Dark hair. Olive skin. Muscular frame. He doesn't look like he works at the resort, certainly not outside.

I can't place where I've seen him before. But I know I never fucked him, so that's a plus.

"I'm staying in for once," I say, propped against the pillows I piled together on the chaise lounge.

Justice's hand stalls. She sets down her blush and faces me. "Are you sure everything is okay? You seem...different."

"How so?" I rub the same spot on my throat where Miles held as he fucked me silly with one of my vibrators.

She shrugs. "I don't know, like you have a lot on your mind. If you want me to stay in, I can—"

"No. I'm alright, Jay." Our stare reflects decades worth of friendship. We tell each other everything, which has made these last few days difficult. How do I share what I feel when it confuses me?

"It must be serious if it's got you tongue-tied." Justice takes a seat on the chaise next to me. She curls her legs under her, rests her chin on her palm, and waits.

I can't help but laugh at how different we are. Justice thrives on *Full House* moments that end in a hug. She feels better, and I break out in hives. It took time for me to open up to her. I don't exactly come from a household with loving parents who emulated a support system that made me feel safe. I have that with Jay, whose knowing grin says she understands.

"Fine." I throw up my hands and surrender to a conversation I'm not ready to have, with myself or her. My lower lip sinks between my teeth as I wonder how much to share. Miles and I have only had two interactions at this retreat. Two. The first was a coincidence. The second...the second has my mind scrambling to make sense of why this man is still in it. Intercourse wasn't involved, and he already has me undone.

"Should we order wine?"

"There is someone who has me...unsettled." I frown at the stars in her eyes and roll mine. "Keep whatever you're about to say to yourself if it's—"

"What if you find your soulmate here?"

"Cheesy," I finish. I'm revoking her Hallmark subscription.

I stop Justice from jumping up and down and ranting about divine intervention and love written in the stars. "Why don't we talk about your date, Lady Soulmate."

Her face drops, releasing the smile once plastered across her cheeks. I open my mouth to apologize, but she cuts me off. "It's okay, Em. I'm"—she takes a deep breath—"fine, or will be. Maybe you were right about marriage being a sham."

"Jay." She waves me off when I reach for her. "You don't believe that."

"I don't know what I believe anymore, but I'm tired of being sad," she whispers.

My heart doesn't break easily, but watching my best friend stumble to pick herself up will do it. Justice's marriage, while imperfect and full of its shortcomings, was one of the good ones—a hell of a lot better than the one my parents have. She and Terrence didn't treat their love like a business transaction, only showing affection when the media is watching. I never understood how anyone could stay comfortably miserable. There isn't enough money or power for me to sacrifice my happiness.

I take a page from Justice and pull her into a hug. One date is harmless, unless Preston the Mysterious turns out to be Preston the Jerk. I'll dissolve his body in acid if he disrespects her.

"Who's the *Sister, Sister* now?" Justice sniffles and squeezes tighter.

"Hush," I laugh. "Enjoy your date, but don't do anything you're not ready for, okay?"

"Okay. Em?"

"Yeah?"

"Don't hide yourself if you like someone here. Staying in our suite with room service doesn't work. Trust me, I've tried."

We snicker.

"Be safe tonight and have fun," I say.

"Love you."

"Love you back."

Chapter 9

Miles

"**B**ro, I fucked up."

"Sounds like it."

The BET-level of drama at this retreat deserves an Emmy. T had a front-row seat to Justice on a date with a guy last night. I almost caught a fist for laughing at the irony that *Fifty Shades of Grey* was the pick for the movie event. Jay is many things, but a clit flick enthusiast? Nah.

She spent the whole movie sharing snacks with some model-looking prick, while Terrence sat rows behind her, seconds from shitting himself. That was until he started tonguing down Madison, who happened to be there too. His lip-sucking caught Jay's attention, and off Sonic the Good Girl went to get away.

I wasn't a hundred percent serious when I said he should fuck around with Madison to get over the ex who's ready to serve him divorce papers. The only person he did fuck was himself last night. I'm not about to rub salt in his wound, but it's too early for this "Cry for You" Jodeci performance.

Terrence stops pacing. He runs a hand through his hair with a sigh like he's about to hyperventilate. "Go sit somewhere," I say. I love him, but I'm not about to do mouth-to-mouth if he passes out.

I spent the last fifteen minutes trying to calm him down and assure him there's still time to win Justice back. Love makes you do crazy shit—like hack into the hotel's computer system to figure out who the hell she was with last night.

"Did you find anything else?" Here he goes pacing again.

"Give me a minute to work my magic, man." Damn. I don't need him breathing down my neck every two seconds.

Somehow, T got the guy's name. Preston is both a prick and a ghost. He's not showing up in any records. "No registration. No room number under his name," I say. "There's not even a restaurant bill for him."

I spend another twenty minutes running through the resort's database. Terrence finally stays in one place to lean over my shoulder for a closer look at one of my four screens. "Bro, how in the hell do you know how to do all of this?" His face scrunches like he didn't barge in here and beg me to commit a felony.

I shrug. "The less you know, the better."

On paper, I'm a data security specialist who helps groups protect their data assets and mitigate risks. Hacking isn't on my résumé, but it comes into play for the right person and the right price. Vulnerability assessment, incident response, and encryptions are some of the services I provide. It sounds like a mouthful of *What the fuck?* so I usually tell people I work with computers and leave it at that. My clientele is by referral only, and I don't advertise.

Terrence has been asking nothing but questions ever since he peeped my setup. Four monitors, two laptops, and a couple of towers might seem like a lot to him, but this is an ordinary day for me. A special courier transports my tech when I need them to.

Everything else is need-to-know, and right now, he needs to sit his ass down somewhere.

A video pops up of Justice storming out of the movie with Preston on her heels. They walk through the ballroom to the balcony outside, where Justice lunges at him lips first.

"No shit." Guess Tia and Tamera's missing sister ain't afraid to get down in public.

"Turn it off now!" Terrence snaps, seconds from ripping out his hair.

I cut it off and stand to pat him on the shoulder, unsure what to say. *Didn't think she had it in her* will have him ready to box my mouth.

I'm shit at pep talks, but I think back to one of those stupid love movies Justice forced me to watch last time I came to Austin to visit. "Everything will work itself out. You two have been through hell and back. You'll get your wife, bro."

"I'm not so sure anymore. I think I pushed her too far."

"Oh, please. It's clear as day you two still love each other. You burned her with Madison, and she burned you with that guy. You're even. So go heal together, or whatever the hell it is you married people do. I've never seen you give up when you want something, and we both know Justice is worth the fight."

She'll likely cause many of the fights, but that's semantics.

It takes a few more searches to pull up Preston's personal information, which has us saying, "No shit" in perfect harmony. Terrence better thank Jesus that Justice is so low-maintenance. His wallet would have a stroke trying to compete with a damn billionaire.

Preston Donnelley is the heir to a global hotel and resort brand. He spends most of his time in London, which doesn't explain why he's here in Colorado. The Ravine is one of hundreds of properties he owns. Why here?

It's one in the afternoon by the time Terrence is ready to leave. Two hours of digging finally revealed the mystery of who he's up against—not that he needs to worry about competition. He'll get it right with Jay one day.

We dap each other up one last time before he heads to the door.

"Thanks again for your help." Terrence stuffs his hands in his jeans. "You and Em got my head right."

I tense at her name. "You saw her today?"

"Yeah." A crease forms between his brows. "I texted her this morning, to run a few things by her about Jay."

"How's she doing?"

"Breathing and walking the earth, so fine I guess. Since when do you care about Emma?"

Since I played with her pussy and she snuck out my room.

Cut that shit out.

I clear my throat with a dismissive shrug. "I don't." The words rush out with too much force. "Surprised Thelma and Louise haven't been kicked out for being a nuisance."

He huffs a laugh and reaches for the door. "That's my wife and her friend you're talking about. Em said they signed up for salsa lessons at three. I'mma head over there later." He frowns. "You sure you're cool? You can come with me."

"Nah, I'm good. Get your wife back."

Terrence dips, and I go back to a data-masking project I worked on last night. I couldn't concentrate, thanks to a certain mahogany-haired knockout with a pussy that would win first place in an Ironman competition the way she took her toys. I don't pine over women, but Emma has me in a weird headspace.

It's a miracle no one called the front desk about her hollering the commands she hurled at me.

Harder, Miles!

Faster.

Deeper.

My hands cramped like I was playing *Call of Duty* with T. There's no cheat code for Emma, but I was determined to unlock every moan.

She fell asleep in the adjoining room I intended to use for guests. No one has been in it but her, but I like my personal space without looking like a dick after giving it. I don't sleep with anyone. People get too comfortable. They fuck around and catch feelings.

Neither of us anticipated a sleepover, but I covered her with a comforter the moment her long lashes fell closed. She let out a relaxed sigh at the warmth over the lingerie I wanted to pull apart with my teeth. The memory of our time at Ravenous had my ass back in the other room with a head shake and a hard dick.

There are certain lines I don't cross, and fucking around for real with Emma is up there with messing with wives. She hits too close to home and will force you to break every rule. That makes her dangerous.

I got my own nut in the shower, jerking my damn dick like a Shake Weight while thinking about her. Then I threw on a pair of sweats and sat in front of my computer to work. Every so often, I'd hear soft snores pulling me back to her room.

Emma slept face-down under a halo of curls, her arms outstretched and a smile edging the corners of her bow-shaped lips. Justice would kick my ass if she found out Emma spent the night in my hotel room.

She was gone when I woke up the next morning, and there hasn't been a sighting or a run-in since. Women who don't spend the night don't overstay their welcome, but how long did she wait to sprint her ass out my room like there was a plague in the sheets with her?

There's a knock at the door before a gold envelope appears underneath. What is this?

Chapter 10

Emma

"Are you keeping warm? I can send thick socks."

"I'm warm, Ms. Ang," I chuckle. "We only have a few days left here."

"Okay, sweetie! You know I worry about my girls."

Like mother, like daughter.

Angela Garvey will ship heaters and a wardrobe full of flannel if I sneeze wrong. She hasn't stopped loving me since Justice invited me into their home twenty years ago. She taught me about curl patterns. She showed me how to care for my thick hair without using the flat iron my mother pushed to "tame" it.

I learned about unconditional love from her. I still smile, years later, when she asks if I'm drinking enough water or getting enough sleep.

No judgment.

No snide comments.

Only acceptance.

"When will I see you?" Pots clamor on the other end of the phone. Ms. Ang loves cooking, even on a Friday night.

"Not sure," I say. "You know how work goes." I always try to swing by Alexandria to see the Garveys. Their place still feels like home twenty years later.

"Always on the go." Pride shines in her voice. Justice is a carbon copy of her mother, from her face to her heart. "Make sure you take time for yourself. Are you drinking water?"

"Yes, ma'am," I smile.

"How's the retreat? Any prospects?"

Come for me again.

I swallow hard. "I'm keeping my options open," I say.

"Good for you, sweetie. Whether you decide to take a life partner or not, never settle. You'll know once you're with the right person."

"How will I? Just curious."

"When the love feels safe for you to be your full self," Ms. Ang says with the warmth of a woman in a healthy relationship. "Is Justice around? I haven't heard from her since you two first arrived."

"She's...busy."

Getting her guts rearranged in her room.

Justice and Terrence are making up for lost time. They are trying every sexual position possible in a hotel room. There are a lot, for the record.

Terrence showed up at the salsa lesson this afternoon. Jay doesn't know that he all but begged to meet me earlier this morning. He wants his wife back and the past behind them. One thing is clear: Terrence never pursued Madison. Their run-ins at the retreat have been coincidental, though I don't put it past her to have put a tracking device on him.

Justice and Terrence finding their way back to each other tugged at a desire buried deep. I've never pictured myself with anyone, and now I'm telling myself that whatever I feel is a fluke—a moment of weakness—because of *him*.

Every time I close my eyes, I see his lusty, maple eyes. I recall his joggers, outlining the dick I felt but have never seen. Miles took care of me the night we played in Ravenous. He put my needs above his, with a kiss to my curls frizzed from the room we set on fire. What started as a battle of will became a comfort I always avoid.

He threw me off my game so hard that I might need training wheels the next time I ride a man.

"Emma, you there, sweetie?"

"Yes—sorry." I push out a breath. *Get your shit together.* "You were saying?"

"I'm holding you up. Go enjoy your night. Have a ball. Please tell Justice I called and to talk to Terrence when she's ready." She chuckles. "What are the chances they'd both end up at the same retreat? Love always finds a way. Love you, sweetie!"

"Love you too, Ms. Ang. Thanks for calling."

Her laughter is warm, like the chocolate chip cookies she bakes on Saturdays. No one gets close enough to attach their heart to mine. Except for Justice and her family, who pulled me in and never let me go.

"What did I tell you about that thank-you?"

I smile. "Not necessary."

"Exactly. Go enjoy that singles' retreat to the fullest."

Plan to.

I'm downstairs in the main restaurant for a nightcap with the person I matched from speed dating. The invite in a gold foil envelope was vague, but I need a reset fast.

No name.

No photo.

Instructions to be here at nine.

I lift a smile at the brunette in a black button-down and slacks and give my name before following her to my match, who's waiting at our reserved table. A match with a fighter's body outfitted in a form-fitting V-neck sweater with almond-shaped eyes, a thick nose, and heavy lips.

My glitter heels startle on the stone tile that leads to the cognac leather booth where Miles waits with a glass of brown liquor. It's a sin how good the color lavender looks on him.

"Oh, hell no." I shake my head in the spirit of Maya Wilkes, wishing one of those *Girlfriends* was here now. I played around with Miles to get off, but this can't happen.

"There's a mistake." I shift to the hostess with furrowed brows. "I'm here to meet—"

"Your match," she says with a smile. "He's your match." The clueless woman extends a hand to the man I've despised..

The resort determined our matches based off of our scorecards. Someone didn't carry the two, because I didn't mark Miles. At least, I don't think I did.

"I got it. Come here, Emma." My pulse skitters at the command and outstretched hand.

I glance at the hostess, who's waiting for me to get my head out of my ass. She takes one look at Miles and walks off with heart eyes. Let her take this date if she's that sprung.

My hand slips into his, and I sink into the memory of the last time our fingers touched. A bolt of heat scorches my body. Miles's fingers cover mine, and I let him guide us to the booth in a haze of musk. I settle opposite him and shift my legs behind me so as not to rub knees as he spreads his wide thighs.

"We need to talk." Hooded eyes roam down my olive-green dress and trace the contours of my body through the material.

There's no disguising my reaction to Miles. Not the way my chest expands to accommodate the low, steady breaths through my parted lips, nor how his focus darts to my tongue instinctively swiping the edge of my mouth.

"There's nothing to discuss," I say. "We played. You left."

My body might want him, but my mouth is ready to cuss him out. Everything I told Justice was true. I'm unsettled. I'm also confused and frustrated. Confused at my reaction to the man sizing me up from across the booth. Frustrated with myself for allowing a man to unsettle me in the first place. Every moment alone with Miles takes a piece of my guard with it. I can't do *this* kind of naked.

"Left?" Miles takes in my frustration. He rubs his index and pointer fingers over his bitable lip. "Is that how you have it?"

"It's what I know."

"Which is shit."

"Excuse me?" I fold my arms over my dress. Diners pass our silent showdown. I should leave, but part of me wants to hear his explanation. The other part wishes I didn't care. No emotions is safe. It's what I know, what I'm good at.

Miles's voice is soft with a tenderness I'm not used to from him. "I was working in the other room, Em. I sleep alone and didn't want to disturb you. When I woke up, *you* were gone." He gauges my reaction, which is stuck somewhere in denial. What is happening?

"Come back to my room." The request surprises us both, but Miles holds steady. "We're not done."

"No." My tone is firm, the final nail in a coffin I refuse to exhume. No penis will leave me this rattled again. Distance worked for us before and will have to now.

"Here you go, treating me like a stranger," he says with a playful chuckle and the smile he wields to sear the panties off of women who fall under the spell of his charm and big dick energy.

I'm not wearing panties tonight, but I still clench my thighs.

"What are you afraid of, kitten?"

Everything.

I can compartmentalize the act of sex from any attachments that come with it. That was true until Miles, and I won't risk getting caught up more than I already am.

"What happened was a mistake, one we won't make again." It's a lie, and a shitty one at that.

"A mistake." Miles tilts his head and weighs the word. "Bullshit, Emma. You can't hide from me, kitten."

My eyes threaten to roll into the back of my head at his smirk. Under normal circumstances, I'd stop our flirting before things got out of hand. Distance and willpower made me immune to Miles's wiles, but I'm damn near feral. A lack of action will have you doing wild things. Like entertaining whatever is about to come out of his mouth.

The word "risk" waves in front of my face, daring me to be stupid. The problem is, I'm curious if his stamina matches the precision of his fingers.

"How does this play out for you?"

Miles flashes a grin. "Simple. We fuck until it's time to leave. There are only a few more days left, and last I checked, our best friends are too busy getting busy to care. Once Monday hits, we go back to not speaking to each other."

"Just like that?"

"Just like that."

Using a man to tide me over on vacation is nothing new. I love sex and consider it weekly cardio. I never miss a partner once it's time to pack up and go our separate ways.

But this is different—it *feels* different. There's an energy between me and Miles calling us together, and that alone makes this proposal a problem.

"We don't have to tell them," he says about Justice and Terrence, reading my mind. "I guarantee they're still in your suite and will be for the rest of the night—if not the weekend. Come with me to mine."

The fact that I haven't told Miles to find another woman to keep the sheets I slept on warm is another warning that the wall I erected between us is on the brink of collapse. I'm ready to list all the reasons we need to find other partners, but I stall. Behind the desire swirling in his eyes are embers of hope. His entire demeanor shifted, and he's ready to cling to every word I've yet to utter—not because I don't want to say the words, but because of the man making his way to our table.

One who shouldn't be anywhere near this resort but threatened to come and get me if I didn't get on a plane to see my father. The event is tomorrow, but Carter is here today.

His stride is a tailored trajectory of arrogance and disruption. I haven't seen him since I visited my parents for Thanksgiving, which turned out to be a catered interrogation about my career and lack of promising suitors. There's no reason for Carter to be here, but his wide grin and calculated eyes tell me he didn't fly in to hit the slopes.

He stops inches from my side of the booth and peers down at me. "There you are." With our height difference, I'm eye level with his tan designer belt—his crotch is in my face. *Dick.* "Aren't you going to say hello"—he tosses a glance at Miles—"and introduce me to your friend?"

Said friend keeps his attention fixed on me, unwilling to entertain the man who's demanding his. Laid-back and unserious is Miles's default. His body language reflects it, with his outstretched legs under the small wooden table and the finger casually tracing lazy circles over his half-full glass. He's unbothered on the outside, but the amusement faded from his gaze the minute Carter interrupted our date.

Date.

One thing at a time.

"Carter." I aim a glare up to reach its target and set my mouth in annoyance. "Why are you here?"

A dry chuckle rattles the camel sweater over hunter-green slacks. There could be six feet of snow on the ground, and Carter would still model those bony ankles in Italian leather shoes with no socks. I'm no better in my heels, but every man I've met with sockless ankles thought he was God's gift to women, and their ringleader is standing next to me.

Unlike Miles, Carter moves with a confidence sponsored by an Ivy League education, the opinions of low people in high places, and years of his fan club feeding his ego. The man is fine, but I never fell in line, which makes me both irritating and intriguing to him.

The corner of his mouth twists before it settles into a stiff smile, one formed after years of practice on Capitol Hill. "I told you I'd come for you." Bitterness spills into his voice as he cuts his blue-green eyes at Miles, who hasn't moved. "Who's your friend?"

I sigh. "Go back to wherever you came from, Carter. I'll see you tomorrow."

"I'll leave in good time. Does he not speak?" He flashes a grin. "That's a new one for you, Em. Maybe he—"

"Maybe he's trying to figure out who the fuck you think you are coming over here so reckless." Miles leans back and waits with a grin of his own, challenging Carter to keep up his antics.

Twice Carter's size in muscle, Miles would have no trouble knocking his ass out if he wanted. I'm sure he wants to, but grown men don't engage little boys in their childish games. Boys like the one still hovering over me. The entitlement and lack of basic manners for anyone he perceives to be beneath his social status is why I stay far away from Carter, and most of the people in our families' circles.

Maybe that's the reason I fix my lips to utter words I never imagined coming from my mouth. But they slip out with ease as I turn to face Carter and raise my chin. "Miles is my man, and I won't tolerate any more of your disrespect."

Chapter 11

Miles

If Emma wasn't sitting across from me stunned by her own words, I'd check her for head trauma. I damn near choked on my drink the second "my man" left the soft pink lips that have kept me in a chokehold since she let me taste them.

Women have tried their luck at cornering me into a commitment, but no one ever claimed me as a way to defend me.

She's still staring at Carter, who hasn't gotten the hint to bounce. It's unclear what they are to each other, but there's no mistaking Em's dare for him to say something else. She gets annoyed, but I've never seen her fury, the way it hardens the lines of her mouth into a scowl and coils her satin curves.

The Carters of the world roll off my back thanks to years of practice toughening my skin. The shit is laughable, but if he keeps pushing up on Em, his ass will roll out of here on a stretcher.

He blinks slowly and looks between us. "Your man?" His brows bunch; his eyes widening on the woman whose poker face is back in place.

"That's what I said."

"*Him?* He's not your type."

I know this prick with his ankles out in ten-degree weather isn't casting stones. I'm about to tell him to fuck off but stop at Emma's head shake. It's subtle, but I catch it.

Go off then.

She shifts half her body and stands to lean into Carter's personal space. He flinches. *Bitch.* "Who I see is none of your damn business. Now, if you don't get out of my face, I will call my father and have you explain why you're harassing me on taxpayer dollars."

His jaw ticks at the threat, and I rise to my full height when his eyes flicker at Emma for putting him in his place. Carter is tall, but I'm taller and big enough to cast a shadow over his lanky frame. He steals another glance but refuses to face me head-on. *Thought so.* "I'll see you tomorrow," he says in a sneer to Emma. "Be ready to leave by six."

"Make sure you note my plus-one. *We* will meet you in the lobby."

Carter swallows his pride and steps back so he doesn't run into my frame when he leaves.

Emma and I watch him stomp to the other side of the restaurant. Then she sinks back into the booth with a heavy sigh and rubs her temples.

I push over my bourbon, and she reaches for it with a nod. Our fingers graze before she takes a long sip. "Thank you."

We sit in silence as bookends to a paper "Reserved" sign on the table and unspoken words, which I cut through with an amused smirk.

"I'm your man now?"

"Don't start."

I laugh at her groan but ease up. If she needs to pretend we're together, whatever is going on must be serious.

"I don't know what the hell that was." She lets out a breath and swings her thick hair over her shoulder.

This close, I have a full view of her beauty. Emma is stunning. Her mouth and downward-turned lips in a seductive pout are my favorite, second to the fire in her eyes under thick, sweeping lashes. I push down the need to be close to her. She overwhelms my senses enough as it is.

There's a draw to Emma that's different from other women. I can't put my finger on it, but I want to fuck her out of my system. I'll lose interest, though. I always do.

I scratch my chin. "So, tomorrow."

Emma waves her hand. "Nope."

"Does it require fancy shoes, or can I wear Timbs?"

"You're insufferable."

"Thank you." My smile shows off all my pearly whites. "Where we going?"

"Nowhere together, Miles."

"I beg to differ if you're calling me your man. Now what did you sign me up for?"

Our staredown is a chess match. I won't push Emma to explain why she roped me into whatever she did. The feelings I have for her are foreign, but if she needs me to play along on some bullshit, I can do that.

Emma studies me. Her shoulders drop, and her claws retract. "One of my father's donors is hosting a fundraiser for his campaign."

I nod. "And that asshole in the ankle pants will be there?"

She snorts, her cheeks tipping into a smile. *There she is.* "Unfortunately, yes. Carter is my father's chief of staff. Has been for over a decade."

"Anything else I should know?" Like whether I need to bury his sockless ass in a ditch?

Here you go.

I shake off the desire scratching at my chest and reach for my glass to drain what's left.

Were those two ever together?

Why do you care?

"No," she finally says. "I've known Carter since he interned for my father. He's pretentious and doesn't mind his business, which should be on the East Coast.

I hear what Emma doesn't say, the attraction laced with annoyance. Carter means something to her, whether she chooses to admit it or not. It's clear she means something to him.

Again, why do you care?

"I'm around tomorrow, and I'm game to go." I keep nonchalance in my shrug. Terrence is balls-deep in his wife, and I don't have shit else to do besides work. It's not like I mind dressing up for some overpriced dinner to show off sexy in a suit.

Emma's brows sinks. "Are you sure? I would skip it myself, but I deal with being an ungrateful daughter enough." She drops her lashes but recovers. "I should go."

"You, uh, wanna crash at my spot?" It takes effort to rattle Em, and seeing her like this bothers me.

The way she cuts her eyes could split diamonds. *Shit*. "In the spare room, for you to clear your head and not listen to the sexathon in your suite. It's yours if you want it." I shrug. "Don't make it a big deal. I don't want you to lose a lash pouting."

Emma's laugh tumbles in a huff. "Ass." Her bottom lip slides between her teeth to consider the proposal. "Maybe I will. Keep your side locked." She pierces me with a look meant to intimidate. "I will punt your balls through your chest if need be."

"Damn, Em. Why can't I be nice? Here." I pull out my wallet and push over my extra key card. "Keep it for when you want your own space. Me and my dick will be on the other side of the door if you need us."

A slow smile builds. "Don't tempt me to run up your room service bill."

"Order me a lobster."

It's eleven thirty by the time I step into my room. I toe off my sneakers and pad across the carpeting, through the shadows filtering in from the window, to the bathroom for a shower. The gym was empty, so I hit the weights and released pent-up tension in a way that didn't involve my hand. It takes a steel grip on my washcloth not to fist myself tonight, but I cleaned my ass without incident.

I'm halfway to the kitchen area for a midnight snack when a sniffle from the adjoining door blends into a wheeze.

"Em?" I knock. She doesn't have asthma, and she better not have a dick in her mouth. Another wheeze. "Emma. Open up."

The lock clicks mid-knock, and Emma swings open the door in a huff. "Why are you banging like you're the FBI?"

My mouth goes dry at the fabric that's pieced together what she calls pajamas. It's a silky one-piece with strings around the waist that exposes the dips of her thighs. Her nipples press against the V-cut fabric above the curves of her breasts.

My eyes drag down her bare legs and red toes for a second time. She hasn't said a word because she's too busy staring at my dick print. "I'm up here, kitten."

In a rush to get to her, I almost kicked down the door with a towel wrapped around my waist. My erection is still pointing at Emma, wanting her to stop gawking at it and put it to use.

After a long delay, she finally catches herself and clears her throat. "I—what?" Another peek when I flex my hamstrings. "Stop distracting me, Miles!"

"Me? You're the one over here either choking or sucking dick, Weezy Jefferson. I knocked to see if you're okay."

Her wide eyes contort her face. *Someone's angry.* "You ask how I'm doing *after* you accuse me of having a penis in my mouth? Can't I laugh at the TV without you high jumping to conclusions?"

Sure enough, an episode of *Living Single* plays in the background. On the king-sized bed is a small spread of fruits and cured meat.

"Can I go back to minding my business, or do you want to check the closet for a man in hiding?"

My jaw clenches. She better not have a man in this fucking room. I need a release, but since my chivalrous ass gave up my spare room, that leaves my own, someone else's, or one of those play areas in Ravenous. The first is out of the question. The second would require me to get dressed and go out, and the third would have me hunching over a woman in public, which isn't my thing. Not usually, anyway.

Even if I did find someone to take the edge off, it won't make me forget the woman who's glaring at me for giving enough of a damn to do a wellness check.

I track the change in her breathing and the flush creeping up her neck. My interrupting one of Kyle and Max's fights doesn't have her this heated. Her nipples pebble under my gaze, and she conceals them with crossed arms.

If she hadn't gotten into it with Carter tonight, I'd drop my towel so we could get into each other. But I gave Emma the room so she could have her own space, and apparently eat through her feelings in pajamas that seem impossible to get into, which means...

"What are you doing? There's no one in the closet!"

"Hush." I storm into the middle of the hotel room, grab the fruit tray, and head back to mine with a pissed-off woman on my tail.

"Aht, aht!" I spin on her, careful to keep my towel in place. "I'm hungry, and you have a whole Sam's Club situation on that comforter. This is mine—and stop eyeing my dick!"

Her sharp inhale sends a shiver through her, one that parts her lips and triggers the pulse beating in her throat. Allowing her into my space was a bad idea.

She's everywhere but under me.

I shut the door in her face and lock the only barrier keeping me from fucking her senseless. "Go to bed!"

"Did you just—" Her fist hits the door. "That's my fruit tray!"

"Sharing is caring!"

"You're an ass hair!"

"Yeah, yeah." I settle on my bed, merely feet from the door that's become a microphone for her insults. "I'll see you tomorrow night. Ooh, blackberries."

"I rescind my invitation! I don't want you there!"

"Too late!" I wrap my lips around a strawberry. "Ankles expects to see you with your *man*." The last word comes out in a nasally attempt to mock her. I crack up at Emma's frustrated bang on the door and how quicky we've shifted from attraction to fury.

"You get on my damn nerves, Miles."

"You'll survive."

Chapter 12

Emma

That asshole stole my fruit tray. Miles's audacity and the whiplash he gave me kept me up half the night analyzing a man who's both an issue and an equation I can't solve. I'm not in the habit of dwelling on people or situations that lack significance in my life, but a woman has her limits, and fucking with my snacks is high on the list.

Miles surprised me with the compassion he showed last night after Carter's unexpected drop-in. I can take care of myself, but I didn't mind someone having my back for once, someone other than Justice. He was a quiet anchor opposite me in the booth, holding space for me to handle Carter while also having zero tolerance for his disrespect.

The "my man" declaration left us both confused. It was a slip that escaped my lips without effort, and I didn't register it until it stood proud for all to see. I don't claim men, but dare I say the words felt right in the moment? Miles wouldn't call me out for seeking a lifeline. He's a dick at times, but he's not an asshole like Carter, who'd relish in my downfall before dangling it over my head and pretending to care. Miles doesn't owe me anything, but he had my back. He's...a surprise I didn't expect.

The same sensation that kneaded between my ribs at Justice and Terrence's reconciliation squeezed and tugged last night at the seductive scent beyond the door that separated me and Miles's rooms. I swallowed back drool at the Adonis before me, in a white towel hugging his waist and the water droplets clinging to his chest.

Until he took one look at me and barked at me to go to bed.

"Em, did you hear me?"

"Sorry, what?"

Justice tilts her head, her worry lines on high alert. "I'm staying in."

"You'll do no such thing."

"I should. We haven't spent much time together on this trip since—"

"Since you and your man started coating the hotel sheets in bodily fluids?" I smirk at her blush. "No apologies necessary, Jay. Are you happy?"

Tears well at the smile pursing her mouth. My friend is in love and will never not cry about it. "Yeah."

"Then by all means, reclaim your time and that dick."

Our cackling bounces across the chandelier and down the four-poster bed in her room. I wouldn't resurface for most of the trip if someone laid good pipe for me to put up an "Under Construction" sign, either. Justice has never once judged me for my vacation escapades, and I refuse to give her shit for hers.

She deserves to live her fairy tale out loud.

"Are you sure, Em?" Trepid eyes search my reaction with a selflessness I've admired for years.

"Yes, but—"

"And were there times I did my own disappearing act without apology?"

Her answer is a small nod.

"I'm okay, Jay. I'll always be good."

"Okay," she says softly and reaches for a hug. Her and her Hallmark ways. "You know I—got it, sorry!" She pretends to lock her lips to hold in the apology she's itching to give. "Where are you off to tonight?"

I turn away to fiddle with the knot in my silk robe. "Dinner. Nothing fancy."

Minus the private jet.

A squeal too enthusiastic for this conversation rings in my ear. "That's right! How was last night's date? Did you match with the person you wanted?"

Did I.

"It was a surprise," I say with caution.

"Uh, what was that?"

"What was what?" The tips of my finger graze the side of my face, careful not to disturb the curly updo that took an hour to pin.

Justice's brow hikes. "That expression. You already said you like a man here."

"I said I was unsettled."

"Same difference."

Nope, not doing this. I hop up from the wingback chair with an eye roll. "Your little black dress is cutting off circulation to your common sense."

The breath I'm holding burns my throat. If Justice suspects something is off, we'll spend the next four hours dissecting feelings I don't have for a certain fruit-stealing penis wrinkle. What is there to talk about? Miles and I messed around. We might have sex. It's not breaking news, but if Jay is this giddy about the prospect of something more, I'll take this to my grave. Damn those Hallmark movies, for real.

"Don't you have a man to let down?"

Justice is meeting with Preston, and Terrence is meeting with Madison to tell each of them about their reconciliation.

Time drags on through silent looks until my cell vibrates in my pocket. Justice nods to it with a smirk. "You should get that."

I sigh and pull it out. "It's not a big deal."

The butterflies in my stomach still at the message from Carter, reminding me to meet him in the lobby in ten minutes. My hair and makeup are done. All that's missing is the floor-length gown hanging on my door, the one I brought in case of a special occasion or emergency.

I don't bother with a response. After his stunt last night, he can stay on read. I know when to be downstairs. The question is, will Miles? I haven't seen or heard from him since yesterday, and I don't have his number to ask if he plans on showing up. Justice does, but then I'd have to explain why I need it, and Detective Nosy is already eyeing me with a toothy grin.

"It's him, isn't it? The man."

"This conversation is over," I say in a huff over my shoulder on the way to my room.

We really did luck out with our suite.

The palette of linens and shades of gray against hardwood flooring and the backdrop of the valley next to the fireplace are reason enough for Justice and Terrence to hole up in here.

I swipe the dress off the French door and toss my phone on the bed. Justice plops next to it like she has nowhere to be. I figured she wouldn't let up, but damn. "My father requested I attend one of his fundraiser dinners." The robe pools at my feet, revealing my low-slung black thong bodysuit. Changing in front of each other has never been an issue since Justice and I started doing it in high school. "I'll be back later tonight."

"That could be fun. You love good champagne, and maybe you'll bag a congressperson," Justice says with a smile even she doesn't believe in. I'm in store for a night of highbrow cuisine and stuck-up politicians who feed off each other's bullshit. The perfect way to spend a Saturday night.

The straps of my black dress settle in place. The slit is high on my thigh but not high enough for my mother to lose a pearl over the "indecency." I step into the bathroom for a final look.

"Who's picking you up? I know it's not your daddy," Justice calls from the room. She's been around long enough to notice him missing in action. I spend more time with her family than my own.

My stomach grumbles. "Carter." I step back into the room to catch her teasing grin.

Justice's hands lift in surrender. "I'm not saying anything, except"—here we go—"you two have chemistry and years' worth of pent-up sexual tension. I get he's—"

"A self-absorbed asshole."

"But maybe he'll change his tune if he knows he has a real shot with you."

Peel away Carter's looks and conquerer mentality, and you have a man I can't stand pretty much every day of the week. On paper, we work. Beyond that, I'd speed up to the "until death do us part."

"Don't hold your breath, sweetie. Enjoy your night, and good luck."

She stands for another hug. "You too. Have fun."

The elevator opens to a casual flow of hotel guests shuffling between the front desk and the restaurant bar. Singles' retreat activities have wrapped for the week, leaving the option to pack up and head home or enjoy the grounds for one more day. I chose the latter for this trip, to get us home on Monday instead of Sunday. A four-day work week after vacation is simply nonnegotiable.

Carter stands next to one of the fireplaces near the entrance, earning every bit of the *Grey's Anatomy* nickname Justice gave him. His black dress coat hits his calves and matches his classic tuxedo and leather shoes.

Blue-green eyes lift from his phone in a slow drag up my champagne platform heels to the wrap coat belted around my frame. The collar hides the plunging neckline of my dress, but Carter stares like he sees through the fabric.

He takes a step toward me and reaches for my hand. "You look amazing." Soft lips ignite shivers when they press to my skin. My inhale isn't sharp, but he catches it in his gaze that has yet to leave mine. "Where is your *man*?" His voice carries a bitter edge.

"He'll be here."

He better.

A low rumble of laughter builds in his clean-shaven throat. "We'll see."

Time is many things, but it's not a liar. By six thirty, Carter is ushering me to the car to head to the airport, leaving Miles wherever he chose to be instead of here with me.

"Can I get you anything else, Mr. Davis?" The flight attendant all but purrs in his face with a stare that makes it clear she's more than okay getting bent over at cruising altitude. This is her third check-in. Our trip isn't long enough for this level of customer service.

Carter leans back and sips the bourbon she poured him two minutes ago. He flashes a grin in appraisal of her slender body in a navy dress as she leans and juts her breasts in his face.

If it were anyone else, I'd say, "Get yours!" and mind my business. But I don't need the visual of Carter pushing her onto her knees seared into my brain. I'm horny as it is and pissed I'm heading towards a good-dick dry spell, *and* I got stood up tonight.

Was ghosting Miles's only option? I still don't know what had him so angry last night, but it couldn't have been bad enough that he didn't slip a note under the door or leave one at the front desk. *Something.*

We're not friends, but I expected better.

"No updates?"

Two men might get smacked tonight, starting with the one in the seat across from me showing his ass and a full set of perfect white teeth. A considerate human being wouldn't gloat at another's pain—but that's not Carter. He enjoys watching me squirm, especially after I claimed a man I waited around to show but never did.

I shoot him a hostile glare and toss my phone into my clutch. Why am I looking for texts like Miles has my number? "I told you the last time you asked, something came up."

Now I'm lying for him. Great.

Carter drops his elbows to his thighs and leans forward with narrowed eyes. "Know what I think? I think you wanted to save face in front of your parents and picked the first bum—"

"Bum?" Miles is many things, but a bum isn't one of them.

"Bum, Emma." His scowl deepens. "You and I come from a different circle. Someone like that isn't fit to be on your arm and will disappoint you every time."

I fold my arms, annoyed that this flight is taking its sweet time. "Enlighten me, oh wise one. Who's fit to be on my arm?"

Carter's gestures to himself, and it takes everything in me not to laugh in his face. Impatience seeps into features I once fawned over. "Em," he sighs. "We could rule Washington if you knew what was good for you."

"Wow." I choke out a laugh and lean toward the aisle to find where the flight attendant went. "Let me get you someone who will entertain this nonsense."

"I'm serious, Emma."

"No, I'm serious, Carter," I snap. "You seem to be under the delusion that I need to be on a man's arm to unlock a new level I don't have a key for my damn self. Save your *I Have a Dream* speech for someone else."

The words I uttered last night slide into memory. I shake my head for calling Miles "my man" like I'm not strong enough to stand on my own. The disappointment cuts deep, at myself for pretending to have a man in the first place, and at Miles for ignoring me so effortlessly.

To hell with him and Carter.

The ten-minute ride to the hotel was silent after I stormed off the plane ready to battle whoever else wanted some. Carter rightfully chose to shut the hell up, opening the door to our limo and sneaking glances when he thought it was safe. Tonight isn't the first time we went at it, and it won't be the last.

I check my coat and proceed down the red carpet with the fakest smile for photographers. Carter guides me into the crowded ballroom with a hand on the small of my back. Steel blue and gray lights streak across campaign donors and career politicians swarming white linen tables and bars stationed around dark hardwood flooring under the gleam of chandeliers.

My father spares no expense with his fundraisers or the chance to plaster his face on every wall within a mile radius.

"Let's get this over with," I say over my shoulder. I march in with my head high and enough anger in my veins to hold a lifetime of grudges.

My parents are nowhere in sight, but a congressperson close to my father comes into view alongside a man molded to his tux.

"Emma! So nice to see you." Congressperson Daniels pats his companion's shoulders with a broad smile. "Allow me to introduce you to someone."

I clamp my jaw tight and stare.

Son of a bitch.

Chapter 13

Miles

I expected the heat of Em's anger when we saw each other tonight. She all but spat out my name after she attempted to eviscerate me with her glare. My standing her up wasn't intentional, and it comes with an explanation, one that stalls at the hurt pushing against the mask she's trying hard to keep in place.

Emma doesn't strike me as someone who allows her emotions to rise to the surface, and it wouldn't surprise me if part of her anger she reserved for me is frustration with herself for caring.

"You two know each other?"

My nod is for the congressperson, but my eyes are still on Em. "We're together," I say to narrowed brows and a glower that wishes me a lifetime of ass-whoopings. "Had to leave her for a meeting with Richard that couldn't wait." I lift her hand to my mouth and kiss it. "I'm sorry, baby."

If Emma wants to curse me to Hell and call me on my bullshit, she has the bullet to take the shot. I'll stuff my hands in my pockets and carry on with my night if she wants to dead the "my man" charade. I don't owe anyone here a damn thing, and I couldn't care less what these people think about me.

She's a different story.

Emma pretending my absence didn't affect her does something to me.

Congressperson Daniels opens his mouth to speak, but I brush him off to take the woman who I'm faking is mine on the dance floor. "Excuse us."

The string lights hanging from suspended garlands cast a glow from the nape of Emma's neck to the small of her back. My dick bricks at her black dress dipping to the top of her ass, and I nudge her forward into a spin to put distance between us. We settle in a casual sway to whatever the band is playing.

"You good?"

She trips over her own foot and cuts her eyes somewhere across the room. "Fine."

"You sure about that? The lip between your teeth and your two left feet say otherwise." I chuckle as she trips over my black loafers. "Damn, baby, can't you hold a two-step?"

My laugh folds into a groan at her heel digging into my big toe. "Funny now?" she taunts through red lipstick.

I shift us around another couple and subtly shake out my foot. "There better not be a scuff mark on these motherfuckers."

"If there is, you deserve it." The look Emma hits me with is too heavy for our usual banter.

"I'm sorry I didn't reach out," I tell her. "I thought I could get back to the resort in time, but I got caught up with something here."

Her eyes cut back to me with wry amusement. "What could you possibly have to do here?"

I don't typically account for my whereabouts but feel the need to with her. "A meeting with two congresspeople about cybersecurity. They were in town for this fundraiser. I consulted them on a couple of projects and had to fly out last minute. It didn't dawn on me that I didn't have your number until I touched down. We'll correct that later."

"Cybersecurity? Is that what you do?"

My head tips from side to side as I search for a simple explanation. "Mostly, yeah." There's much more it than that, but it usually flies over people's heads. Not that I talk about my company or the work I do.

Em's lip sinks between her teeth. She considers the info I hit her with, turning it over in her mind. Like I said, I don't talk about my work. But for her, I will.

"Makes sense." She chuckles at my frown. "You're loud and obnoxious sometimes, but you're also calculated." Her eyes linger on my face. "You don't let too many people close, but you protect the ones you do."

The air shifts to release some tension. My senses heighten, noting the rush of pink staining Emma's amber cheeks. Her throat works against the pulse points that flutter as she swallows. A quiver surges through her veins when I bring her closer and inhale the scent radiating from her body. She settles against my chest at first but catches herself and backs away from my grasp, taking the warmth of her curves with her.

I clear my throat and drop my hands into my tux pockets. "Want to tell me about your family I'm about to meet?"

Whatever moment we had blew off this dance floor like a wig in the wind. I tell myself not to sweat it. We're not like that, and we should keep it that way. The draw I'm feeling toward Emma is for fucking purposes only. Everything else is a side effect of not having had her.

You sure about that?

Em's gaze gets lost somewhere between my lips and chest. She rights herself and lifts her chin once she realizes she zoned out. "I—this was a mistake, Miles."

She moves to walk away, but I hold her wrist. "You're not someone who jumps to claim a man the way you did. I'm here, and I got this suit on." I lift her chin and stare down at her. "Let me help you."

"I'll handle it myself." She jerks away.

"Now it makes sense."

"What does?" An arched brow lifts.

"Why you and Justice are so tight. You're both stubborn as hell."

"Says the guy who won't take no for an answer."

"Aye, don't say that shit so loud." I scoff. "My mama and GG raised me right. I'd never push up on a woman like that; I was trying to help. Since you don't need it"—I step back—"do you. Lover Boy has been looking over here since we stepped onto the dance floor. Have fun explaining this to him and whoever else."

"Wait!" Emma's hand clamps around my bicep. "This is stupid." She sighs and looks away. "Just for tonight." She studies my face. "We'll keep this up until dinner is over, then we'll pretend I didn't say you were my man. This changes nothing."

"Don't spare my feelings. I ain't losing sleep over you." Her ass is still frolicking through my dreams, but she doesn't need to know that. Emma *and* her attitude can go if she keeps this up.

"Good."

"Good." I pull her back into my middle on instinct. My hands twitch to explore the soft lines of her back. Holding Emma brings me a strange satisfaction, one I push away. "So, what's the deal?"

"It's an election year, which means I get calls to show up to campaign events so my family looks like the united front we're not. I dodge most of them thanks to fashion weeks, but the ones I do attend are...rough."

"How so?"

Awkward laughter ripples through the air. "Don't worry, you'll have a front-row seat." Emma pats my chest at the sound of the dinner bell. "Time to meet the family."

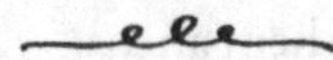

I never cared enough about a woman to meet her family, and I'll send a prayer of thanks up I dodged ever doing it for real. Who *wants* to sit through this shit?

Emma's parents only speak to her whenever cameras roll around. They're so caught up in shaking hands and small talk about who's here that they completely iced her out.

Carter has been in full peacock mode since we sat down, pointing out who he knows like we give a damn. For her sake, I hope Em never fucked with him. He's a clown and a bitch, stealing glances from the other side of the table like he'll say out loud what's playing out on his face.

Between us are Emma's cousin, Blair, and her mother, Lily. The former hasn't stopped humping me with her eyes, and the latter was already two sheets to the wind before she plopped into her chair.

I nod to the server when my dinner plate touches my charger but quickly regret it. There's not an ounce of seasoning on this shit.

"Here." Emma slips a container into my hands under the table.

I cough to hide a laugh once I peep the label. "I know you didn't just pull out some Lawry's from your bag."

"Never leave home without it," Emma says with a smile. "You'd think expensive dinners came with better food."

I brush off the urge to taste her smile by removing the Lawry's top and going to work on this bland-ass chicken. Her laughter is the first trace of happiness on her face all night.

"As white as this shit is, I might need to douse this chicken like them high school kids did them aliens."

Emma covers a snort and reaches for the seasoning. "*The Faculty* is a good movie. I saw it in theaters when it came out." She shakes her head. "I was alone while my father met with another senator. That movie had me signing up for chemistry class just in case."

We stare at each other before bursting into laughter.

"You watch horror movies?" I dig into my chicken breast, thankful for the spices from my childhood clinging to my tastebuds.

"Yeah. Not the new stuff, but I love the classics. I have a *Friday the 13th* movie marathon at home."

"No shit." Em at home with slasher flicks, of all things, seems counter to what I know of her, but it's dope. Also. "What you know about Lawry's?"

Her lip quirks. "Justice's parents use it. I picked up on a few things when I'd go over for dinner, which was more time than I spent at home."

"Because your parents went out all the time?"

She nods. "Something like that."

Tension slithers back to the table. Emma shifts in her seat, uncomfortable with the topic of her parents. But she refuses to falter or give any indication that their absence affects her the way it does.

"I watched *Gossip Girl*."

"*What*?" Shock riddles her face, bending it into a grin.

I shrug to downplay one of my guilty pleasures. If it keeps that smile on her face, I'll throw in *Buffy the Vampire Slayer* too. "It kept my attention, low-key. You got most of the cast at this table." I point to her horny-ass cousin. "Blair." The prick still eyeing us. "Carter." I nod at her aunt, who's a second away from falling asleep in her soup. "Lily."

My nose drifts back to Emma's perfume. "What's your mama's name again?"

She tilts her head a breath away from my face. "Juliette."

"There's one of those too," I say, my gaze dancing from the intrigue in her stare to the lust on her lips.

"Oh really?" She inches closer.

"Mm-hmm." I follow suit.

"Care to let us in on your conversation?"

We break apart at the terse voice and face lips thinned into a straight line. Emma's mother casts a commanding look between her daughter and me. They have the same moss-green eyes. Her ivory complexion reddens under the mound of diamonds on her neck.

"Nothing important, Mother. Just passing time." Emma straightens and smooths the cloth napkin over her lap. "Did you need something?"

"You haven't said a word about your companion for the evening."

The word *companion* twists with curt disapproval she doesn't hide. Juliette assumes Emma brought a fuck buddy to this fancy-ass dinner, and while that might be almost true, I won't give her the pleasure of disrespecting her daughter at this overdecorated table.

There are enough "Juliette" roses to make Martha Stewart sneeze.

I cross my ankle over my thigh and rest my arm on the back of Emma's chair. "What would you like to know, Mrs. Douglass?"

Emma leans over to brush my tux. "You're asking for it," she says through her teeth.

I reach down to pat her arm. "Did you forget this is your fault, kitten? You owe me," I say with a wink.

"Let's start with where you're from and how you met my daughter."

"Didn't you pick him up at the singles' retreat you're at this week?" Carter asks Emma in cold sarcasm.

"A one-night stand? That's digging low for a date, even for you." Blair purses her fillered lips and flips her copper hair over her shoulder. Nutmeg eyes turn to me. "Certain activities should be more...private."

To Em's credit, she remains indifferent, evidence of the years of experience she's had in dealing with her family's bullshit. My family and I take jabs at each other, but never like this. The only people not piling on are her pops, whose back is now to us as he chats with a man at another table, and Lily, who's snoring softly on a makeshift napkin pillow.

This fucking night.

"Our relationship is new, and Miles is far from a one-night stand," Emma says in a tone far too gracious for this interrogation. "I went to the retreat with Justice and—"

"Em and I ran into each other in Paris during the September fashion events. I was in the city on business, and our chance reunion turned into a private dinner cruise on the Seine and a stroll across the Louvre courtyard. We've known each other since Justice and Terrence got together fifteen years ago. I surprised her on this trip because I couldn't stay away."

Emma's cheeks color under the heat of my gaze as I take her hand and kiss her knuckles. Her breath catches, and our eyes lock before I look away. I might not date, but laying it on thick is a specialty, and I hit the spot every time.

Blair stares in awe while Juliette considers me with less contempt than before. I didn't mean to interrupt Emma, but I had to jump in at Carter's lips shifting to show his ass again tonight. He's one question away from me hemming him up at this fundraiser.

The only person I can't face is Emma—not because I don't want another glance. She's gorgeous, with layers I want to peel away to learn more about her. What excites a smile, and what brings her peace? T and Jay are family, which makes Emma someone I care about by extension.

Therein lies the problem. I want to help Em, but I can't allow myself to care beyond the facade we're creating for her family. I thought we could fuck a few times and be done with it, but it would be more than that, because *she's* more than that.

Emma is becoming an addiction, and it's getting harder to fight the cravings.

"To answer your question, Mrs. Douglass, I'm from Newark." I say it how we say it back home: *Nork*. I'm not about to play with these people.

"Newark." Carter washes the word down with merlot. Shit is as bitter as he is. "Kinda far from the block, aren't you?"

I rub my goatee and crack a smile. "You learn that word from JLo, Crispin?"

"Carter."

I shrug. "Brick City is my home. I still visit when I'm not traveling, but my block these days is the one in Jersey City with properties I own, and the house I have in Virginia." I have houses elsewhere, too, but that's none of his business.

Juliette's brow arches. "Impressive, Miles. Did you attend one of the Ivy Leagues?"

"I went to Bodie University, same as Emma. Got my undergrad in intelligence and cyber ops and mostly hop between New York City and DC when I'm not out of the country." I smirk at Carter and reach for my wineglass. "Not bad for a kid from the *block*." I take in his sour face with an amused chuckle. Bro is trying hard not to pout.

I came a long way from life in South Newark. My mama did her best to keep me out the street but had to focus on holding down the house after GG died when I was ten. That woman was my heart. She kept me glued to her hip after school, watching her stories. By eleven, my mama was working a part-time job on top of double shifts at the hospital to keep a roof over our heads once the rent went up. I stayed away from the dope block around the corner from us but ran errands for Shine, which turned into fast money boosting cars once I hit middle school.

I was always over at Terrence's abuela's house after his mom moved in with him and his sisters. Had it not been for them, and Professor Jelks snatching my ass up, who knows where I'd be. Not here in a $6,000 custom tux in a fishbowl for snobs who've had life handed to them and turn their noses up at someone who did what was necessary to save himself and his mother. They hear Newark, see me, and think I'm an exception and not one of many who'd run circles around them, especially if they had a leg up from generational wealth and not the constant need to operate on survival mode.

This shit—the fancy dinners, ego stroking, and women like Blair salivating over my dick because of my hood—ain't real, and it doesn't impress me.

The band starts up as servers move around white linen tables to drop off dessert. Senator Douglass already gave his speech in front of the podium. We've yet to meet, and I don't know if he prefers "John," "Senator," or what. Politicians get real uptight about their titles. At least introducing myself will end this round of LinkedIn questions bordering *Family Feud*.

Emma's dad and I share the same mocha complexion, only he has thick brows and full lips that now spread into a smile like he's campaigning for our vote. "Miles, is it? Carrillo told me a lot about you." He stretches out his hand and nods to the congressperson beside him. "I had no idea you two worked together."

All it took for this table to perk up was a fellow member of Congress to validate my existence. The only people unfazed are Emma, who's on her phone, and her aunt, who's still knocked out. Unlike Carter, I don't kiss anyone's ass. Unless it's in the bedroom. My work speaks for itself.

Lorenzo's smile is easy. I've seen it countless times on video calls these last nine months. It's a throwaway that comes with a flash of gray eyes that used to sear through my damn soul if I rolled up late to his class.

"This young man is the reason I introduced my last bill," he says, like he didn't school me in data analysis throughout college. "His knowledge of cybersecurity and technology are exceptional. I've tried to get Miles into our Los Angeles office, but he is a hard man to lock down."

"You've done alright without me." I'll save the *old man* for when we're not in mixed company. It might look like we just linked up, but Zo and I go way back.

Professor Jelks taught information systems at a college in Newark when I was coming up, and he introduced me to Lorenzo my freshman year at Bodie. Zo was an adjunct professor when he wasn't raising hell in City Council. He got his start in East LA and translated his hustle into serving his community through policy that reflects their needs and not the shit lawmakers pass off as effective change.

I don't fuck with many people, but Lorenzo Carrillo is a real one. How many elected officials do you know who handle their business and still get respect where they're from?

"Such high praise coming from you, Carrillo. Since my daughter and Miles appear to be an item, maybe she'll convince him to visit." Senator Douglass stands to shake hands with a couple passing by the table. Judging by the size of the dead carcass adorning the woman's shoulder, they're campaign donors. When he returns to his seat, he asks, "How long would you need him out there?" like I'm not here.

My traitor of a mentor lifts a shoulder, tempting the tattoo on his neck to peek out from his collar. He strokes his beard, which has more salt than pepper these days. "Only a few weeks—a month, ideally—to bring new members of my team up to speed."

"Nah, that ain't—"

"Emma has plenty of room in her home," the senator offers. "I was never comfortable with her living alone. Wish she'd settle down."

Her head finally snaps up from whatever had her attention on her phone. I suck my teeth at the poker game on Emma's screen and nudge her with my knee to focus. She really does zone out at these fundraisers, but now ain't the time for games. She better get us out of this shit before I turn off the lights.

Em looks between her father, who's trying to pawn me off as the boyfriend expected to live with her, and me. Said boyfriend. "Dad. Miles travels plenty for work, and so do I. Living together is a big step in any relationship." She shakes her head and looks to me for help. *You and this scheme are on your own.* "I—we're not ready for that yet."

"Consider it a test run," Carter says with a calculated stare. "If you're not a casual fling, this would be a great chance for John to support more data security initiatives." His mouth untwists from a scowl and shifts into a sly smile. "I don't mind representing our office. Plus"—he straightens in his seat and tips his head at Emma's dad—"increasing our bicoastal presence will help with the exploration."

"Exploration?" Emma frowns.

"Your father is considering a run for the presidency," Juliette reveals.

"Not this year," the senator clarifies. "Possibly next term. I've held my position for three decades and am grateful for the partnerships around the country." He nods to Zo. "If things continue the way they are, I'll start an exploration committee and throw my hat in the race."

"To the White House." A hunger for power flashes in Juliette's eyes.

The senator hits the table with an excited slap. "It's settled. I'll make arrangements for Carter to check in when I can spare him and will stay abreast of project developments. There are a couple of key senators on the West Coast I'll work with in the meantime." He leans over to Emma, who's morphed into an impressive shade of pale, and kisses her cheek. "Your support means the world to me, buttercup. Thank you for being part of this team."

He stands in a rush to walk after a small group, leaving me and his daughter speechless. How in the hell did dinner turn into cohabitation and me moving to California for a month? I'll be damned on both fronts.

Zo leaves with a smirk on his face, one I would knock off if he didn't spend hours a week in the boxing ring. He's inching up to fifty-two but keeps up with sparring partners half his age. I'll deal with his ass later, which leaves me to handle the woman who caused this shit.

"If you think I'll agree to this, you got me fucked up," I say through gritted teeth so as not to draw attention. Pretending we're together during dinner is doable. A month *and* living together? Fuck all that. Emma is fine, but even I have my limits.

Emma whips around in her chair to face me. *So much for discretion.* "Me? This is your fault."

"How the fuck does that math add up to you?"

"If you would've kept quiet about your job and degree, we wouldn't be in this mess. I don't have men over my house, and I don't need you stomping around my personal space."

That she doesn't have men over shouldn't feel good, but it does. I'm not sleeping with her, but I like knowing I don't need to toss shit into the ocean. Don't ask me why it matters, 'cause fuck if I know.

Back to her delusions.

"You need your head checked for real, letting your pops and his nut-sucker tell you what to do with your damn house. Zo and I got history. It was only a matter of time before he made his way to the table—one I wouldn't be at if I'd kept my ass back at the retreat." I should've pushed for today's meetings to be a video call.

Show up for Emma.

Have her back.

Look where that got me.

How she has me ready to bury myself deep inside of her one minute and toss her ass in my trunk the next is a hell of a superpower.

Emma stands, and I follow. "No one told you to come." She cranes her neck to hold my glare with a hand on her hip. "I can handle this myself."

"You got it," I say. "Now run off and tell Daddy that. Or are you still scared to speak your mind?"

Her eyes flash, and she steps closer, pressing her breasts in that deep-cut dress I've been trying not to eye all night to my chest. My dick hardens, but I stand my ground and follow her eyes to the swell pushing at my pants.

"You haven't earned the pleasure," I say with a twisted grin.

She scoffs. "The only place I'd fuck you now is in your dreams. You're such an ass, Miles."

"Honest. I'm honest. I'm not one of your fuck boys you can boss around. I'll always tell you what it is."

Emma presses into me. "This isn't happening."

"No problem."

"Good."

"Always am," I say.

Our showdown pulls all the air from the room. Fury and frustration tangle with a fire, threatening to combust. I should walk away, tell her to deal with this shit on her own. And for no reason other than all of the blood in my body rushing straight to my dick, I kiss her.

Chapter 14

Emma

I'm ready to tell Miles to go to hell, but his lips smother the words. His kiss starts slow and builds into an angry exploration of the recesses of my mouth. There was no warning, only action, sending the pit of my stomach spiraling through an unknown abyss. Here we are, arguing seconds before tonguing each other down in front of my family. Each kiss wraps itself in years of denial and yearning. We broke a seal we can't replace, and it's taking me further outside of myself.

Miles caught me off guard, and now I'm standing on my tiptoes to fuse myself with a man I've tried to hate for reasons now lost on me.

Hate isn't right. Dislike.

I *dislike* how obnoxious Miles is. How he seeps underneath my skin and settles like he has a right to exist there. Right now, I dislike his gentleness—the way he reads my thoughts and understands that my pushing him away is what I always do: handle shit on my own.

I break us apart, surrounded by the scent of his musk, and touch my swollen lips. I hazard a glance and find Miles searching my face with a determined expression. "Excuse me." I grab my black clutch off the table and head toward the entrance.

I need to leave. Leave this fundraiser. Leave Colorado.

I've loathed these events since my parents started collecting frequent flier miles to chase after flashing lights and people ready to kiss their ass because of their proximity to DC power. The private planes came once they amassed a certain status and realized they'd earn more political points standing next to a daughter they ignored most of her life. Not because they didn't love me; I just wasn't a top priority. I stopped caring a long time ago, which doesn't explain why I still showed up tonight. Or why he did.

Tonight, Miles made me his priority. He grounded me, supported me. Made me laugh. I haven't smiled at one of my father's fundraisers since I was too little to realize my own autonomy. Miles is pulling emotions out of me like he was meant to be part of my life.

Coat check comes into view at the other end of a marble hallway framed in crown molding and stuffy paintings of flowers. I'll go back to California, to the curated life waiting for me I formed without instructions on how to live it.

A hand circles around my waist and spins me. Miles's eyes narrow. "Dinner was shit, but why are you running out on dessert?"

My laugh catches us off guard. Only he can make the air lighter after my knees shook from that kiss in front of my family. Here I am freaking out, and he's asking about a piece of cake.

"I'm good."

"You sure about that?" The question rests in the space between us encased in silence.

Confused. It's the only word to describe my reaction to this back-and-forth we turned into a traveling act. Casual flirting. Sex without strings. That was our trajectory, and I royally fucked up by claiming him in a role no one will ever play.

"I'm fine, really. Thank you for checking on me, but you can stop now. Come to California if you want, but tonight is as far as this"—I motion between us—"goes."

"You done yet?"

"Excuse me?"

He leans his forearm on the counter while I hand my ticket stub to the attendant. "Being so damn difficult. Your family is on one, but I ain't about to pay for their mistakes." He passes his ticket but keeps his gaze on me. "Apologize."

"Are you serious?"

"Do you see a smile? I didn't have to come—and don't front like you weren't losing your shit when you thought I stood you up. You can go back to your mama with that lie."

Miles waits, and I roll my lips. No man talks to me this way. He's not trying to be rude; he wants respect.

"You're right," I admit to his smirk. "I shouldn't have snapped at you or got you into this mess."

"Stop saying that. We're..." He scratches the back of his perfect fade. "Shit, we're not friends like that, but we are friends adjacent. I show up for mine, and your affiliation with T and Jay covers you."

I snort. "Geez, thanks."

His shoulder lifts. "It's nothing."

"Do you kiss all your non-friends like that?" The memory of his lips on mine threatens to hold my breath ransom, but I keep it together.

Miles peers down at me with heavy eyelids. "Not all of them." A silken thread laces his voice.

"Good. For us." I brush a hair out of place and look away. "We'll see more of each other soon, and we shouldn't blur any lines."

"Is that what you want?"

"Yes," I lie.

— ee —

We stumble through the coat check door, lips locked and deep in moans. How we maneuvered back here after getting our coats remains a mystery.

"Hey, you can't be back here!"

Miles peels his mouth from mine and presses me into his side. He digs in his pocket and tosses two bills at the wide-eyed redhead. "Beat it, Archie. Go ride the elevators, and don't come back for thirty minutes."

The guy takes one look at the money in his hand, shuts the partition, and runs out the door he closes behind him. He can't be more than twenty and is clearly on a track team the way he sprints out.

"Thirty minutes?" I chuckle. "Think you'll last that long?"

"Shut up." Miles kisses up a hidden trail from my neck to my ear and licks my lobe to activate a shiver. "I told you that you haven't earned this dick. They probably cleared the tables by now, and I want my dessert."

I'm airborne before my gasp has a chance to escape. Miles moves us through racks of coats to the back of the room with my legs wrapped around him. Unlike the kiss earlier, this one is punishing, a demand for my tongue, which he sucks. The coat check room is small, like an oversized closet with a wooden side table and barstools next to the pass-through. At least these *Lion, the Witch, and the Wardrobe* coats give us some privacy.

Miles rips a fur coat from a hanger and tosses it to the floor. "I—" I squeal on the way to the ground. I'm now straddling him with my dress above my ass and my cleavage dangling in front of him. He buries his face in it with a satisfied groan.

"Miles!" I hiss. "This is somebody's coat."

He motorboats my titties and bites a nipple through the fabric. "They shouldn't be wearing that shit anyway. It's unethical. I'll leave money for dry cleaning. Now come ride my face."

My hands fly to the sides of his head when he pulls me to hover over lips he's licking in anticipation. The swell of his biceps locks me in place as he feasts with abandon.

I've had men eat my pussy, but not like this. Miles's mouth has the perfect suction, spearing me with his tongue and flicking my clit. His touch is ruthless, lashing me in circular motions up and down before changing speed.

My center pulsates as the first orgasm bursts through and careens into the room on its axis.

Holy shit.

I jump at the slap to my ass. "Did I not say ride my face?" Miles asks from between my thighs. "You better earn this one, passenger princess."

"I got your princess right here." A brow furrows before I slide my feet from behind me, grip the back of Miles's neck, and proceed to fuck his face. His hands move to my ass to deepen each thrust of his tongue.

He better ask for air in the afterlife.

Years of yoga and these platform shoes make holding up my body weight effortless. I could be here all night. The question is, can he?

The duet of our moans fills the room as I widen my thighs and drive as deep as Miles allows. My body curls at the rise of another orgasm, this one stronger than the first and taking its time to ease out. Miles sits up to catch me to his chest, his hardened length all but bursting at the seams for some attention.

Our stares thread through our labored breaths. I caress the side of Miles's face and grab his goatee. "Open." At my command, his mouth opens, and my tongue grazes his as I taste myself.

He holds me to his body for a kiss that lasts longer than it should. Eventually the sheen of our exertion cools, but not the desire we set ablaze.

There are lines I shouldn't cross with Miles, and I fear we passed the point of no return.

Chapter 15

Miles

"She left your ass, didn't she?" Zo chuckles into his tumbler and takes another sip. Had I known he'd be this annoying, I would've been on the first flight back to Jersey City.

I blow smoke into the night air and gaze up at the stars. "Remind me how much time I'd do for fucking up an elected official."

A grin stretches Zo's face as he leans into the patio lounger and closes his eyes. He kicks his feet up, folds his hands over his stomach, and tips his chin. "You'd never make it out the hospital."

Our laughter floats over the crackling fire pit. It's cold as shit outside, but between my blunt and our scotch glasses we never let get below two fingers, the Denver night isn't anything we can't handle. Zo does look wild bundled up in a coat and gloves with socks and slides. We both have on sweats, but I'll be damned if I let my feet out like that.

Monday came in a flash. One minute I was gripping Emma's ass for dear life while she rode my face like an Olympic equestrian. The next, we were back on the jet with Carter, who extended his stay at The Ravine. I haven't spoken to Em since her father's fundraiser and had to hear through the grapevine she went back to Cali this morning.

No "let's catch up" or "thank you for that tongue action." Nothing.

If I wasn't used to curving women, I'd take offense. Emma could've at least sent a text for being her plus-one to that bland-ass party. But that would require us to have exchanged numbers. I packed my shit and flew back here to cut up with Zo before I head to the East Coast.

"You're quiet."

Damn, can't a man be in his feelings?

The point is not to have feelings about anyone, especially her.

"Stop fucking up my peace." I puff on my weed scenting the wilderness.

A congressperson hooked Zo up with this house before he returns to a life of kissing babies and cutting ribbons. At this distance, he shouldn't get a contact high—like he doesn't light up on the low. There's no proof, but Zo's eagerness to legalize cannabis consumption for federal employees speaks for itself.

He scratches his chin and opens his eyes to meet mine over the flames. "It is peaceful out here. Not used to this much quiet, but it's nice."

I nod.

"Did all of your people leave?"

"T extended his and his wife's stay. He's gonna take her to another resort in Vail before they go home. They got months' worth of making up to do."

"It's good they worked it out."

I snort. "Who you telling? If I had to listen to any more of T's ass moping around, I'd make Justice a widow." Terrence tried to downplay the reality of Justice's leaving, but he wasn't fooling anybody—least of all me.

Just another reason to dodge attachments. If love had him ready to beg like that, I'll steer clear of that shit with my life. I love pussy, but I refuse to lose my mind over it. Though after I feasted on Emma's, I had to stop myself from following her back to Malibu to see what's up.

"And Emma?"

I take a pull and count the steps to ashing this blunt on Zo's forehead if he doesn't shut the fuck up.

He smirks like he's not out here reading minds. "Did she go home?"

"When do *you* go home?"

A laugh rattles his throat. "Touchy." He reaches for his glass. "In the years I've known you, I've never seen you kiss a woman in public."

"Em—"

"You got nicknames now?"

"Fuck you." I roll my eyes. "Anyway, Em told her people we're dating. I played along so she could save face."

The stare Zo casts damn near burns my face. "That's what you're going with?"

He stands and shakes out his legs. "Alright, *pues.*" *Here he goes.* "The fact you had your suit crisp and didn't blow up her spot tells me you care a little more than you're letting on. Nothing wrong with it. You should just be honest with yourself instead of acting industry, as the kids say."

I scrub a hand over my face and sink into my chair with a sigh. "Speak your piece, Professor."

Zo chuckles at his old nickname. He's aged since his Bodie days but wears it well. His salt-and-pepper game has women in his path stressed. They eat it up, along with the grin he's cracking now.

"I ain't got all night."

Zo's stride is casual when he walks up and pats my shoulder. "A man doesn't change his behavior for no reason. Might as well see where it goes. Bring your ass to California in a few weeks. Stay a month, and then go back to being a ghost."

I turn to face the house with brows higher than I am. "A few weeks?"

Zo looks over his shoulder with a crooked smile. "I've been with enough models in my day to know that the woman who's got you puffing up to Jesus will be hopping around fashion week for her job you told me about. Figure out whatever it is between you two before you have to be around each other. The answer is simple if you take your head out your ass." He turns back to the house and laughs. "It's a miracle your simple ass didn't fail my classes."

"Go to sleep, old man!"

"At least no one will be running marathons through my mind!"

I sit with the fire and Zo's words. I want more of Emma, but not if it makes it impossible to walk away. She's already a distraction, switching those hips across my thoughts like she owns the shit.

I can't afford for anyone or anything to throw me off my game.

Chapter 16

Emma

The lights dim, and a cotton candy glow rises from the all-black stage. Flashing lights go off as MHYSA's "power cuts" featuring Chino Amobi booms from hidden speakers. Models walk the runway in padded jackets, boiler suits, and low-crotch pants. Some strut in metallic heels, others in laced-up leather boots. Each look is different, but one thread unites them: Rêve, my new collection at Soie.

Working with in-house designers on high-end lingerie has been my longest commitment. Soie keeps me on the move and has ever since I was a wide-eyed intern out of college. I put in twelve years, running errands to work my way up to senior creative director. With no formal fashion training and an international business relations degree to appease my father, I worked hard to prove my eye for design wasn't a hobby, but an instinct.

And it's paid off.

My breath catches, and my chin lifts in pride when I see embroidered tulle and pearls roped together in intricate patterns and paired with Rustin designs. When I got the call asking to use our pieces for the fashion show, my yes was instant. I love the brand and its vision.

The theme, "Dystopian Uprise," centers models from historically excluded communities—often cast aside entirely or only sprinkled in by mainstream fashion houses—during the aftermath of the world's converging crises. There's darkness but also a resilience that Kojo, Rustin's founder and principal designer, will amplify in his upcoming spring/summer collection, "Utopian Promise."

A model steps on stage in a steampunk mad hatter corset and sky-high heels. She's wearing our sheer mesh thong adorned in crystal rhinestones, and it shines against her almond skin. Her hips sway in front of the photo pit before she spins on her stilettos to give photographers a view of her toned ass and pear shape.

Perfection.

Kojo takes his place and marches down the runway to a symphony of applause and whistles. We catch eyes, and I smile up at my friend as he winks and takes a bow. He's had his head between the pages of a comic or an Octavia Butler book since our sophomore year of college, and it shows in his work.

The lights come on to signal the end. An escort ushers me away from the growing crowd at the main door and into a small hallway beyond the backstage area. It's curtained off to conceal the chaotic shuffle of models and staff. It takes three minutes for a black car to pull up, and twenty minutes in traffic to reach my hotel in Gramercy.

My flight from California arrived late last night. I enjoy trips to big cities, but I'm thankful I requested a boutique accommodation tucked between quieter side streets. Well, as quiet as you'll get in New York. Everyone needs to recharge at some point, and my battery is hovering at low.

Kojo's after-party is at a cocktail parlor only a few blocks away. He swears it's a coincidence, and I won't argue with him. But I know he chose the location to keep me out past ten. He knows that when I'm not on vacation, I'm in for the night once I make the rounds and take photos.

I swap out my black balconette bra that crisscrosses at my ribs, the one I paired with heels and Rustin cargo pants. In its place, I slide on my dress.

Time to shine.

—ele—

The coat check attendant does a double take and runs into the door after accepting my jacket. I expected to turn a few heads tonight, but I don't want anyone in the hospital.

"Careful, sweetie," I say with a wink. "You're too cute to have a bandage around your head." He nods rapidly, shaking long stands of brown hair over his face. Then the young Josh Hartnett replica scurries away.

I've always appreciated shy men. They're quiet, eager to please, and do what they're told. Unlike some men. One in particular, who shall remain nameless.

Two weeks is the longest I've gone without sex of any kind.

Stressed? Get good dick.

Frustrated? Dick.

Happy? Angry? Lonely? The same answer applies.

I told myself the reason for my dry spell is because of the endless meetings I had once I got home. Not the man whose face I rode into the land of ecstasy, who's probably circling my waterfront property, hoping to slide inside. I don't have a welcome mat for a reason. My space is my space. Miles and his sexy ass need not bother me. *Tempt* me.

What we did can't happen again. Yes, he made me come so hard I damn near convulsed. If he wields power like that over my body without the D, I'm afraid to find out how he works that joystick between his legs.

It's a risk I can't take.

The fact he's still on my mind is both a problem and uncharted territory. It's not good etiquette to get eaten out and ghost, but there's only so much temptation I'll avoid before I let that man access my walls from the four corners of the earth. I'm living out of my suitcase for the next several weeks anyway. I need to get over him.

So here I am, in desperate need of a caffeine hit, ready to try out another distraction to pluck me from this damn coochie desert.

Aged chestnut flooring is my runway between sofas and chairs separated by crystals hanging from the black-lacquered ceiling. The intro to Missy Elliot's "She's a Bitch" kicks up. Heads pivot with every step my ankle-strap heels take. Minus the opaque cups covering my breasts, my corset midi dress is completely sheer, showcasing the curves of my hips in a high-waist thong. It's thick enough to cover most of my round cheeks but still gives more than a glimpse.

Kojo is in a Victorian room on one of a handful of velvet, button-tuft sofas. Gold sconces frame him and his company in a warm glimmer that bounces between ornate mirrors. Models, influencers, and press mingle with an occasional sip of their cocktails. The only person not drinking is my friend, who motions for me between his entourage of ass-kissers.

He stands and straightens his black and gold dashiki shirt matching his pants and vintage loafers. Kojo is a good-looking man—hazelnut skin, angular face, round lips, and dreads twisted into a bun—who pulls women and men.

But not me.

We learned early on we're better off as friends and left it at that. He's attractive, but there's no spark.

"Congratulations, Koko!" I extend my hands for him to take, and he holds them out to take me in.

"Damn, girl. Who are you trying to give a heart attack in here?" A low whistle exits his lips when I spin. "You always did have an amazing ass."

"Hush." I laugh. "What a show! I'm so proud of you, Koko. The designs, the set, the styling. You truly outdid yourself."

Kojo's bows in a cocky way that says he knows he's the shit. "Thank you, mama. I've been working with someone, and when I tell you she handles shit so I can focus on designing..." His hands form a chef's kiss. "The investment pays for itself."

"She did her thing tonight."

"I wish you two could've met. But she sprinkled her magic and hopped on a red-eye to London. Are you hitting any other shows?"

"I'm checking in with a few vendors in Milan. Have to get back to California soon." Kojo and I only see each other during fashion weeks, but we make it work.

He scoffs. "All work and no play." A brow arches as his eyes glide over my shoulder. "You are reeling them in tonight. Who will have the golden ticket?"

I sigh. "I need a drink first."

"Say less."

Kojo guides us out of the room to the bar down the hall. The setup reminds me of a speakeasy with ambient lighting, handcrafted wood, and brass fixtures. I order an espresso martini and almost down it in one go.

His frown twists his features. "Since when do you need liquid courage?" By now, I would've narrowed down my choices of who's coming back to my room. Unlike him, only one person will make the cut.

"I don't. It's been a long day, and my flight got in late last night."

"Go to sleep and try again tomorrow."

"Nope, I need dick tonight."

He releases a long breath. "Same. I'm ready for bed but need to get into something that makes me crack my toes and drool once I pass out."

The high five we share kicks off our quest for the evening. Kojo kisses me goodnight on the cheek once he finds a couple to share his bed. I have no such luck with any of the men filtering into what was once the VIP area for the Rustin after-party.

Most people affiliated with the show either left for another party or headed home, where my ass should be. I'm not just tired physically. I'm over using toys and want the real thing. I refuse to let jet lag be the only one fucking me tonight.

The bar is busy. Waves and a low fade catch my eye from my barstool. He's hard to see between a horde of people taking up space, but when the group parts, I get a better view.

I start with his Italian leather shoes, work up his legs and torso in an all-black suit, and smile at the prospect of a lover for the night.

That is, until it registers it's Miles.

And he's not alone.

Chapter 17
Miles

Real talk, shorty looks good tonight. I met Brandice last week after I stopped by to see my boy, Trey. He runs a security firm and has an office in Tribeca. The floor above is some type of rental space that fashion designers use. Brandice was there. She strutted into the elevator like she owned it, catching my attention with her long legs and smile.

We exchanged numbers but haven't been able to link up because of her schedule ahead of tonight's show. I appreciate a nice 'fit, but I don't follow fashion brands like that. Whoever did up Brandice deserves a raise. That thong she rocked had me about to choke on my drool. I don't know if the thing had crystals on it or what, but the shit was glistening, and it had me leaning against the back wall with my dick at full salute.

Brandice is the only reason we're here in Gramercy after her show and not back at her place getting to it. She had a stretch of interviews after her event but wanted to hit up whatever party the designer had. Judging by the crease between her brows, it's already over.

"Looks like you missed it." There's wall-to-wall people, none of which look like they pay attention to high-fashion magazines.

Brandice scans the crowd under the exaggerated lashes she still has on from the show and gets on her tippy-toes. She comes to my chest with heels on, so I don't know what she expects to see.

"Guess it did end. I wanted to catch the designer to thank him again." Her slick ponytail whips over her shoulder in the slinky gold dress she changed into before we got here. "My apartment isn't far." She reaches up and wraps her hands around my neck. "Ready for a nightcap?"

I stare into eyes that are a tawny shade of brown and not the moss-green from the dream I haven't been able to shake for weeks.

Emma gazing up at me.

Underneath me.

On her knees.

Her moans play on repeat, along with the memory of pleasure smeared across her face when it takes over. I haven't fucked anyone since before the singles' retreat, and I need a release to channel the tension coiling my muscles.

I'm ready to tell her let's go until mahogany hair flashes between people on the other side of the bar. I must need to fuck, because ain't no way I'm hallucinating over Emma, unless...

She's here.

"What?" Brandice frowns.

Shit, I am losing it.

I should get the hell out of here and take Brandice back to her place, but my mouth and feet clearly have their own agenda tonight.

"Nothing. Let's get a drink." I smile, but there's no energy behind it.

I'm already guiding her to the bar, focused on what I assumed was a figment of my imagination instead of Brandice's ass shifting the material of her backless dress.

Standing room opens up at the bar, but a Blue and Coke is the furthest thing from my mind.

I dodged the temptation to hack Emma's travel itinerary in order to prove to myself that no one has me sprung. Yet one peek over my shoulder has me ready to lean into whatever chokehold she has me in. Our eyes lock, and her brow raises, daring me to make the first move.

Giving up a night with Brandice to roll the dice with Emma is dumb as hell. She's ruthless enough to curve me, which would leave me alone with my dick in my hand. Ignoring her and staying with Brandice is less risky. But would it satisfy me?

Brandice looks at me to order, but I reach into my pocket for my phone with a sigh. "Gotta take a rain check."

Her voice rises. "Excuse me? What happened to getting a drink and going back to my apartment?"

"Something came up."

She stiffens, her sharp brows narrowed. It's a gamble to pass on one woman for another. Emma smirks like she didn't know what I was about to do. I should've ignored her on principle and stayed with Brandice, but the pull is undeniable.

I call a car to scoop Brandice, who's still staring at me like I lost my damn mind. Her irritation cools when she gets a text about some party in Brooklyn and asks me to reroute her ride so she can meet up with her friends.

No problem.

We're outside within six minutes, me pecking Brandice on the cheek to see her off and her reapplying makeup for a night out I never would've agreed to in the first place. I only go out to meet someone to fuck. My days of partying late are over.

I check my watch and pull up the lapels on my overcoat. If Emma expects me to go crawling in there to beg her, she's got another thing coming. I'm down for a good chase, but can't look too eager.

I put on my beanie, throw on gloves, and wait.

Chapter 18

Emma

What are the odds that Miles and I would bump into each other again? Pretty damn high, apparently.

The singles' retreat was pure coincidence, but this, weeks later at one of a hundred parties happening—in Gramercy, no less? Oddly specific and a little suspect, if you ask me.

I've been fighting for my life to get this man off my mind, only for him to show up in the flesh and with a model from Kojo's show. Miles loves to play games, and the fact I'm still here, at a loss for words while he left to carry on with his night, is a new low.

The stare he pinned me with caused a heatwave in New York City from between my legs. All I could do was smirk as I gripped my empty martini glass to steady myself without shattering it into thousands of pieces. The choice was clear. If I need one of those portable fans to cool off my pussy after *looking* at Miles, we should push aside any placeholders for the real thing: each other.

Does it make me a hypocrite after denying his advances? Of course it does.

Do I care at this moment? No, I do not.

Miles doused any rush of excitement I had when he bent down to whisper in his date's ear and told her, I assume, that they had to leave. Her back was to me, but her body language made it clear she had questions. He guided her to the exit by the small of her back.

Ten minutes ago.

I close out my sad tab of the extra martini I ordered once the after-party ended and head to coat check. Almost every eye is on me, but not the ones I want.

Miles did us a favor. With him, a situation of any kind has the potential to turn awkward, or worse. Rejection isn't something I navigate often, but I button my coat and walk into the winter night with my top knot high and zero thoughts he'd come back for me.

Liar.

It's ten o'clock. Early enough to hop to the nearest party and assess my options. But I don't want to. I want...him.

I jump at the figure who appears at my side until a familiar musk washes over me, calming my nerves while exciting my senses.

There's no mistaking Miles's intentions, which I hope starts with his mouth and ends with his dick. He's close enough to hear my heart thundering in my chest, but he waits. There's no move to touch me and no words to convey what needs no explanation. The lust in his eyes speaks volumes. Right now, it says sleep isn't on our itinerary.

I swallow to stop the blush inching up my cheeks. He left his date for me. A smile slips onto my lips, triggering one from Miles that widens into a grin.

Our walk to my hotel is silent. Miles shifts me to the inside of the sidewalk and keeps his focus ahead, allowing me to steal glances at his profile in a beanie and a long coat with the collar popped. All black everything, and, my, is it beautiful.

We reach the redbrick townhouse and climb the few limestone steps to the wooden door. Miles's face twists at the brownstone, but he follows me inside and up the creaky staircase to my suite on the third floor. He's so damn big, he has to duck into my room, and he looks out of place in the petite space with old-world charm.

I love modern luxury, but I also enjoy vintage sophistication from time to time. The room has a king bed with a button-tuft head-board, a cast stone fireplace, and a seating area. Miles is mugging like the furniture personally disrespected him. If this offends him, wait until he sees the bathroom.

His gaze snaps to my coat, which I place on the oversized chair in front of my bed. Judging by the tongue hanging out of his mouth, he didn't get a full view of my dress at the bar. My walk is slow to where he stands in the center of the room. I give him my back and look over my shoulder for him to unzip me. The low whistle of the zipper traveling from the top of my back to my ass is the only sound in the room. Until I gasp at the first kiss on my neck. My eyes close, and I tilt my head to give him better access.

Sex. That's all this is.

With his mouth still on me, Miles slides my dress down my shoulders and pushes it and my thong to the floor. A large hand reaches around to knead one of my breasts, while the other pulls me to his hardened frame. My lip sinks between my teeth to smother a moan as he gently rolls my nipple between his fingers. The other hand skates down my heated flesh to my clit.

Miles works me with a mastery of my body, switching peaks and changing speed, pumping his fingers into my pussy until my knees quiver. I come in choked curses, careful not to scare the older couple in the room at the other end of the hall.

Triumph shines in his eyes before they sweep over my breasts. The air around us electrifies, and he wraps a hand around my throat to pull me in for a hard kiss, one I'm more than eager to accept. My lips part at his demand, my mouth matching the long strokes of his tongue.

Our kiss is angry, balancing hunger and fire through pleasure. Miles can't keep his hands off me and holds my face in place. The intimacy sends me spiraling into a free fall without a parachute.

One of his hands slips into his coat pocket, the crinkle of a condom wrapper filtering through the haze of desire. I push down his coat, and he lets it fall to the floor as he unbuttons his shirt. His pants are next, and with the way I've been dreaming about this dick, it takes what little patience I have left not to rip his damn belt off.

I pull down his briefs to bring him to his knees with my mouth, but he stops me. "Not tonight, kitten," he whispers, his thumbs stroking my jaw. My mouth waters at the steel between his legs. Thick. Responsive. Perfect.

Miles sheaths himself, picks me up by my waist, and moves us to the wall next to the window. I wrap my legs around him and groan at the breach through my entrance.

Shit.

He pauses to search my face for discomfort and captures my mouth with his own. His moan at my fingers digging into his scalp jolts his hips forward. Miles spreads my cheeks, angles me towards him, and powers into my center in a staggered rhythm. The force knocks the breath from my lungs and rattles the pictures on the wall. I'm tossed into a wave I can't swim over or under.

My nails dig into his back to anchor myself as another orgasm builds. Miles buries his nose into my neck and pumps into me.

Sweat beads on his upper lip, and I swipe it with my tongue. Miles studies me, drinking in every expression with hooded eyes. He grinds into my pussy with slow circles and hits a spot that forces my head back in a scream for release. His pace quickens with deeper thrusts until I'm speaking in tongues. Then he releases a long moan and stills, his fingers digging into my ass to hold me in place.

That girth needs a warning label.

Miles walks us to the bed but takes his time putting me down. His lips return to mine before he leaves to handle the condom. I think he comes back with a warm washcloth, but I'm not sure. The man fucked me so good, I went straight to sleep.

Chapter 19

Emma

"**S**how me again!"

I sigh and pan my phone around the *Piazza del Duomo* from my window seat in the café to show Justice for the third time. It's in the low 50s in Milan, but it's a sunny afternoon, with tourists gathering in the square to check out the gothic cathedral.

"Happy now?" Her face is a dead giveaway that she is. Justice already squealed over my lunch, like a spring salad with fresh mozzarella requires applause.

"Very!" She cuts into her omelet with too much enthusiasm given our time zone difference. It's seven thirty in the morning in Austin, a minor detail for the woman who's ready for a virtual tour of Milan.

I wouldn't put it past her to try and squeeze herself through the phone to get here. Not that her forehead would fit.

Justice has been a morning person for as long as I've known her. She'd wake me up for high school when I stayed at her house while my parents were gone. The same bright-eyed smile and curls pulled up in a loose bun haven't changed in twenty years.

We text almost daily, but this video call is special. Galentine's Day has become a tradition since Justice discovered her inner Joan Clayton. No matter where we are on February 13th—me in Milan, and her at home this year—we check in for a date, assuming we're not already together on a trip. I'm happy to see my girl, but jet lag and a bouncy friend don't mix.

Justice forks another bite of her breakfast from the setup at her dining room table. Between the tiny bowl of mixed berries, the champagne bottle and orange juice for mimosas, and cheesy Galentine's Day decorations, my friend takes her holidays seriously.

"It's gorgeous over there, Em. Are you done for the day?"

I nod. Me and my crop sweater dress set are taking several seats. "Just met with the last vendor. Looking forward to a couple of days of rest before I head back to Cali."

Fashion week hasn't started here yet. Everyone is still in London before they hop over and then head to Paris. I've done the circuits, moved from one city to the next with the promise of couture, but I opted out this year. The allure is there, but after a while, it's tiresome.

Moving across time zones is no joke. I need my wits in order to bring to life a new campaign for Soie once I return. I also need to ready my mind to be in the same vicinity as *him*.

This trip to Milan is right on time.

No social calendar of events.

No distractions...like the one who ghosted me days ago.

"Emma!"

"Hmm? What did you say?"

Her frown softens. "You okay?"

Am I?

"Of course." It's where I want to be but miles from the truth.

Justice is in the throes of the honeymoon phase now that she and Terrence are back together. I won't disrupt that by telling her about Miles and I having sex. Before he left.

It's been four days since Miles followed me back to my room and laid it down so good I woke up facedown with drool on my pillow. I also woke up alone, which I usually prefer, given sleepovers aren't a habit. But Miles is different. He told me he doesn't share a bed with the women he sleeps with. It was wrong of me to assume he'd break his rule.

What we did, what we shared, deserved more than him running off in the middle of the night. I knew the sex would be off the charts, but damn can the man fuck. It wasn't just his ten-out-of-ten thrusts or his stamina that had me cracking every toe. It was his care—the way he devoured me with his mouth and cherished me with his eyes. Every touch was intentional, like he was in tune with what made me purr. And purr I did, over and over again.

We never exchanged numbers—another sign I shouldn't expect more. The problem is I want more. Sex, that is. The dick is too good to only try once.

If Jay found out Miles dipped his dick in me and went silent, she'd make Terrence pay him a visit. The drama is unnecessary, and I refuse to burst the bubble she's in with my mess.

Who knows if Miles is still coming to California to work with Lorenzo. Whether he does or not, I don't care. New York was a one-time situation. It's done, over.

If you say so.

"How was New York?"

"Great." I reach for my white wine to wash down acting thirsty over a man. "The Rustin show was gorgeous, Jay. My collection complemented Kojo's effortlessly."

Pride purses her mouth. "You don't give yourself enough credit. You've taken Soie to new heights. How's that new idea coming along?"

A smile blooms on my lips. "I'm playing around with a few concepts."

It's been a dream of mine to make our garments more accessible through a ready-to-wear collection. Justice doesn't know it, but she's my muse. I want to design a line for extraordinary women who don't recognize the authority they wield with their sexual empowerment.

Lingerie is more than an accessory for sex. There's a confidence that comes with knowing you're the shit, that your body is worthy of love and praise. That's what I want for femmes: to lean into their power, revel in the uniqueness of their form, and embrace their sexiness.

"Whatever it is will be incredible. Shit!" Justice hops up in a rush and barely avoids knocking over what's left of her mimosa. "It's almost eight. I gotta get ready for work. What time is it there?"

I check my watch. "Close to three."

Justice takes the phone to the kitchen and leans it on the paper towel holder on the island. "Oh, nice!" Her white oversized shirt rushes past the camera as she hurries to the sink with her dishes. If there's one thing Justice will do on autopilot, it's worry.

"Jay, slow down!" I dip my head to keep from cracking up in the café. "Don't act like you didn't lay out your outfit the night before."

She stops, and we bust out laughing. If only the people at her job could see their VP of marketing spinning in circles. Justice has her quirks, but she wears her heart on her sleeve, and she's the best friend anyone could ask for.

"Let me get out of here so you can enjoy your day." She catches her breath and chuckles. "Happy Galentine's Day, Em. There's a gift waiting for you at your hotel."

A twinge of guilt hits me in the chest. "I didn't get you anything."

"Not necessary." She waves a hand. "You're traveling, and you know I do the most. Besides," she smiles, "I have everything I need."

Terrence had movers ready to pack up Justice's studio the minute they touched down in Austin. He missed his wife and wasted no time rectifying the situation. She's back in the home they once shared, the corner house he bought her after she saw it on a walk.

I wasn't expecting her to call since they reconciled, but Justice will never miss the chance to show she cares. She's a walking Hallmark card when she's not freaking herself out.

"Thank you for the gift," I say and toss her a smile. I wish I was more sentimental, but it's not in my DNA.

"Cut the guilt. Gifts are *my* thing, remember? Go enjoy Italy—and send me photos!"

"Love you, girl."

"Love you too."

⎯⎯⎯⎯ ℓℓ ⎯⎯⎯⎯

"*Salute.*"

"*Salute.*" I take the negroni from the bartender. Gin isn't my liquor of choice, but when in Milan.

The bar is quiet, with only a handful of patrons sidling up to the polished mahogany bar that spans the length of the narrow room. Suspended chandeliers set on a low glow illuminate the floor-to-ceiling bookcases, which hold the finest liquor.

I smile down at Justice's gift on top of my hotel key card. It's a camera roll keychain with five tiny photos of us over the years.

Homecoming.

A random sleepover.

College graduation.

Our trip to Paris.

A selfie from last month's singles' retreat.

Over two decades' worth of memories captured in a trinket.

The verdict is still out on whether I'll grab dinner down here or in my room. Sleep is necessary, but so was pairing gold heels with this red satin dress.

A man in a gunmetal suit unbuttons his jacket and folds his long frame into the seat next to me. The sharp edges of his profile melt into a buttery smile, one he directs at me.

"*Ciao,*" he says.

"*Ciao.*"

"*Come si chiama?*"

"Emma."

His steady gaze rakes over my body. "Nicolo. *Piacere.*"

"Nice to meet you too."

The conversation switches to English, trading what little Italian I know for a discussion about our time in Milan. He's saying all the right things to keep my attention, and he's handsome. But he's not—

I stiffen at the dark stare cast over Nicolo's shoulder.

Miles.

Chapter 20

Miles

"*Ora puoi andare.*"

Italian isn't my strong suit, but Green Eyes can get the fuck on with his night. His brows cinch until he takes the hint and leaves without another word.

Emma is still in shock, which makes two of us. I don't chase women across the street, let alone out of the country. Yet here I am, straight from the airport after an eight-hour nonstop flight.

I lean on the bar, motion for the bartender, and order a negroni sbagliato without a glance at Emma or her wide eyes. She already has me acting out of pocket and using my frequent flier miles. I need a minute to get my shit together before whatever verbal jabs we're about to throw.

"What are you doing here?"

"Wanted a drink."

"A drink," she says to herself with a huff at my bullshit and shakes her head. She reaches for the key card on the counter and hops off the barstool. "I'll leave you to it."

"You left. Again."

The words hang in the inches between us, with me leaning against the bar and Emma on some ankle stilts. We're close enough for her breath to skate across my mouth.

I admire the curves of her pink lips as she licks them, and heat creeps up her neck. It's faint but matches the scarlet dress, the one that's kissing her body in all of the right places.

Emma's brows crease, twisting from confusion into full-on irritation. Her lips pucker, and she straightens to her full height, still inches below my eye level.

"As I recall, I woke up by myself." She grinds her teeth and throws up her hands. "Why are you *here*? How did you find me?"

"You left," I repeat, skipping over her question of how I'm standing next to her in a hotel thousands of miles from the one we shared in New York. With my line of work, the answer should be obvious, but I'm not about to explain it to her. "I told you I don't sleep in the same bed with the women I fuck. I came back Sunday, but you were gone."

"Did you expect me to wait by the phone for a call that would never come? I had to fly out here for work. You know what? It doesn't matter." Emma folds her arms and raises her chin.

"It does, and we're about to fix this." I step closer to inhale her perfume and smile at the hitch in her breath. "We're not finished, kitten." I put my credit card on the counter to close our tabs. "Did you eat?"

"Excuse me?"

"Did. You. Eat? Dinner." I nod at the bartender when he drops off the billfold and sign the slip. "Don't want you passing out on me once I take you upstairs."

Emma's scoff is mild at best. It lacks heat. "Don't flatter yourself."

I lean for my nose to graze hers and drop my voice. "Don't pretend I didn't put your ass to sleep the last time I gave you this dick."

She wants to be mad, to cuss me out and tell me to take my ass back home. The more I spend time with her, the more I discover her wants and desires.

Right now, my kitten wants to purr.

"Come on," I say.

Emma is more attractive than I remember. Her allure is an addiction, numbing all sense of logic. All I want is another hit. She's used to running shit, but tonight, that ain't gonna fly.

We barely make it inside the elevator before my mouth is on her, kissing, sucking, and licking every part of her skin. I capture her moan and pull down the thin spaghetti straps of her dress. Her breasts spill out, smooth and heavy in my hand.

"Fuck, you're perfect," I groan. Her legs quiver at the lash of my tongue against her nipple. I tease the sensitive peak between my teeth, then drag my tongue up her neck to slip into her mouth.

"Miles." Emma gasps at my thumbs rolling her buds between my fingers. She arches her back and presses her breasts into my face. Her mouth parts, her teeth grazing over her bottom lip. I cup her with both hands and grin as she watches me suck her nipples.

The elevator opens to the ninth floor. I pick Emma up and walk us to the end of the hall. My mouth never leaves hers as I pull out my wallet from my jeans, hover it over the sensor, and open the door.

I modified her hotel reservation and scooped up a key card before dropping off my bag in the other bedroom and heading out to find her. Hacking into systems is light work for me, which made Em easy to locate after she left New York. I always had access to her number, but I wanted to get it the old-fashioned way: with permission. A matter back home pulled me away before I could. A mistake I won't make again.

I stagger through the foyer with Emma rolling her hips over my dick, which is straining to get to her. I wanted to take my time and move her to the bed, but my fingers have other plans. I cup her bare ass and kiss her harder at her hand gripping my length.

Damn the bed.

"You were trying to get fucked tonight wearing no panties." She hisses at my fingers teasing her entrance. "Happy to oblige, kitten." I suck on each one coated in her juices.

Emma's eyes darken. "Fuck me now." She teases my lips apart and slides in her tongue.

I hold her tighter and set her on a nearby credenza. Her chest lifts at my hand traveling between the valley of her breasts to her navel. Her stomach contracts at the pressure to her clit, and a rush of heat floods her skin. Emma widens her legs as I take lazy swipes at her pussy, dragging my fingers further into her channel.

God, she's beautiful.

I drag a condom from my pocket and still at Emma's hands on my belt. Her eyes never leave mine as she unbuttons me, lowers the zipper, and pushes down my jeans. My dick bobs free as she takes it, lapping my head with her tongue.

"*Shit*, kitten." She has one more swipe before I bust in her mouth. "I won't last long if you keep that up and need to take care of you. Lie back."

I roll on the condom with the focus of someone diffusing a bomb. Emma's dress exposes her glistening pussy when I lift her leg. A raspy moan falls from her trembling lips as I push forward, stretching her walls.

My hands anchor her hips, and I drive into her. "Look at this pussy take my dick." I stare at our joined bodies. I'm mesmerized by the waterpark between her thighs, coating the condom. She whimpers when I roll my hips to hit her spot. "Fuck, baby. Cream for me."

I hover over her and pull a nipple into my mouth. Her cries muffle on a kiss, and I grind into her until we both go limp.

Chapter 21

Emma

I fell asleep again.

In my defense, my body gave out after the fourth round. Somewhere between dinner and the dessert we ate off our bodies after, Miles pushed one of my legs behind my head and let me have it. He was the one with jet lag this time, but he was still a damn lithium battery with no off button.

We showered and brushed our teeth before I went to sleep for good.

I lift my head from the silken pillow and crack an eye open at the clock on the nightstand.

11:42.

We closed the powder blue curtains that stretch from high ceilings adorned in crown molding to the walnut floors. It's pitch-black in here, minus the thin rays of light peeking through the ornate fabric and the door to the secondary room, which is now open.

"Good, you're up. Tired of hearing your ass snore."

Miles leans against the doorframe with a smirk, wearing ripped jeans and a white undershirt. It's a simple outfit, but he fills it out with a solid wall of a chest and the hard thighs he slammed into me for hours.

His body is a chocolate masterpiece. Natural in form and free of tattoos.

I wipe my mouth, checking for drool. "I do not snore."

His chuckle is deep. It's the same tone he used to demand orgasms from my body. "You sleep hard, kitten." He shakes his head and flashes a grin. "Sounding like a damn chainsaw."

"Shut up! You weren't even in here."

"Which says a lot."

This fool.

No man I've been with has ever possessed Miles's audacity. I'm used to flexing my dominance in the bedroom, used to men doing what I want and when I say. Miles is new territory. He's blunt, doesn't play by the rules, and doesn't back down. He calls me on my bullshit. I'd be lying if I said I'm not having fun.

I sit up and tuck the crisp white bedsheet into my armpits. Miles has seen every inch of me, but it's cold. "You're up early considering your flight to stalk me."

His tongue swipes over his teeth. "It's not stalking if we have unfinished business." He shrugs. "I only need a few hours of sleep, anyway."

Sleep. Alone.

Miles staying in the other room shouldn't annoy me, but it does. I don't sleep with every partner after sex, and I usually go home or back to my hotel room by default. The bartender at the singles' retreat was an exception, one I want with Miles. He's in a league of his own. Not because his best friend married mine, but because of the way he cupped my face to kiss me and pulled me close to stare into his eyes. I didn't know what to expect from having sex with him, but distance isn't it.

My phone buzzing on the bed next to me brings me back to the blue and white room. Carter's name flashes on the screen, and I answer with a sigh. "Yes?"

"Good morning to you too." His voice is alert for almost six in the morning in DC. Must be a swim day.

"What do you want, Carter?" I put the phone on speaker and place it back on the bed. Miles clenches his jaw but stays quiet in the doorway. I don't owe him anything—he's only here to fuck—but I don't need him assuming there's anything going on between me and Carter.

A husky whisper breaks the silence. "It's our day."

Valentine's Day is my least favorite holiday. Outside of Justice leaning into her Care Bear habits, I've learned to deal with it, regardless of whether or not it makes me itch. The cliché dinners, basic chocolates, and sappy cards. Who needs all that shit to profess love? I want to scream on principle every time I see a bouquet of red roses.

Miles flew in to see you on Valentine's Day. That has to mean something.

Bullshit.

He wanted another taste, nothing more. My pussy alone is worth a trip across the ocean.

"Happy Valentine's Day." My tone is flat and lackluster, like this damn holiday.

Carter pretends to declare his love every Valentine's Day because he knows I hate it. Nothing he says will grant him access to me the way he wants, so he'll line up whatever flavors of the week he can and be a commercial holiday fuck boy.

Drinks and head with one woman.

Dinner and sex with another.

He'll have roses and chocolates for each with neither the wiser.

Part of the reason I never subscribed to relationships is because I've seen men like Carter run game over the years. I learned to play said game and not let it swallow me whole. If the end goal is a loveless marriage for show, like my parents, I'll pass.

"Is that all I get?" Laughter rumbles in Carter's chest. "We'll have to fix that next week."

A knot twists in my stomach. "What's next week?" If Miles leads with audacity, Carter isn't far behind him.

"I'm coming to LA. Your father will be there toward the end of the week. I want to see you, Em. Maybe I could—"

"Nah, she's good." Miles steps into the room and heads straight for my phone. "Lay your head somewhere else, Crispin."

"*Carter*," he seethes but manages to even out his tone. "Miles. I didn't peg you as a fashion man."

Miles chuckles. "I'm not, but I support my lady. Find someone else to bother."

My lady.

"Since you're new here, allow me to help you out. Emma doesn't let anyone spend the night in her house. You should make other arrangements."

"My stuff is en route as we speak. We'll get at you once we get back." With that, Miles hangs up and walks out of the room.

His arrogance will have him six feet under.

"Um, rewind!" I jump up from the bed and storm after Miles, who's now pouring himself tea from a floral pot that looks like a dollhouse accessory in his paw of a hand. "What the hell was that?"

"What was what?" Miles stirs in sugar and sits on a baby blue chaise lounge. He stretches out, spreading his tree trunks for thighs, with one hand behind his head and the other balancing the tea cup on his leg. The corner of his mouth twitches at my unsubtle glances at his crotch.

Focus off the peen.

"You're not coming to California, and you sure as hell aren't moving into my house."

"Why not?"

"Because!" My hands slam onto my hips. Bare hips. I walk around naked in my house all the time, but I don't make arguing ass-out a habit.

Miles's grin dissolves as his gaze makes the steady voyage down my breasts to my navel. His eyes flicker when he reaches my pussy. "Who is Carter to you?"

"My father's chief of staff."

He considers my answer, licks his lips, and sips his tea. "You have until the time I finish this before I fuck you against that window."

My inhale is sharp, but I stand my ground and ignore the threatening flood between my thighs. "Look, I took this further than it needed to go. It was stupid to pretend we're dating. Go back to Jersey."

"Is that what you want?"

"Yes," I say too fast. The damn bulge in his jeans shifts, tempting me to stare.

He nods to himself, finishes his tea, and stands. "Okay."

"Miles, I'm serious."

Another nod. The empty tea cup is on the cart. Miles's steps are slow on his way to me.

"I'll tell my father we decided to stay friends. You're off the hook."

"I was never on one," he says with a halfhearted shrug and moves closer. "Tell your father or don't. I made a promise to Zo to be out there."

"Good." I suck in air but refuse to break eye contact when he leans down. Miles presses his hand against the wall and takes a slow drag up my neck with his wide nose. "This ends here," I say. "We go our separate ways once we leave Italy."

Carter's call was the dose of reality I needed to snap me the hell out of whatever is going on between me and Miles. We've spent more time together in the last month than we have in the last fifteen years. I don't do attachments, and I'm already questioning why he's unwilling to share a bed when we've spent so much time between each other's legs.

He lifts his head to pin me with a long stare. "You done yet?"

"We will be in a few days."

His mouth crashes to mine, and we spend the rest of the day on every surface in the suite. When it's time for dinner, we order room service. Away from foolish declarations of love and reminders of romance.

Chapter 22

Miles

I'm not a man who subscribes to the idea of happy accidents. Accidents rely too much on chance, and I'm too skeptical not to consider other forces at play. Chance is a vulnerability that will leave you defenseless if left unaddressed.

Every decision I make is based off of evidence. I scrutinize the details before I take action. It's a guiding principle of mine, one that's now being challenged by the woman who's sound asleep on the spare blankets in front of the fire.

Emma has me acting so far out of character, I question my own common sense. In one month, she breached the armor I put in place to keep myself from caring for a woman the way I'm starting to care for her.

The shit is irrational, like flying to Milan to see her after she dipped out of New York. Almost a month has passed since Colorado, and I've been struggling not to think about her, wondering how she's doing, and when the next time we'd see each other would be. The women I've been with in the past faded with time, but here I am, watching the glow of flames dance across her face while she snores into the night.

I don't believe in coincidence, but too many have occurred for me not to question if Em is supposed to play a bigger role in my life.

Aeris choosing us at Ravenous.

Matching after speed dating.

New York.

Random incidents forcing us to take notice.

I lift Emma from the ground, careful not to stir her awake or bust my ass over these blankets. Tonight was cold enough for a fire, but all of this cotton has to be some type of hazard.

We haven't left her suite since I arrived two days ago. I had to find an Italian alternative for Gatorade the way we've been losing electrolytes. We can't get enough of each other and fuck like there's no tomorrow—there won't be if Emma has her way. She doesn't want to see me in any romantic sense after this trip, and I'm not wasting time arguing with her if we only have a few more days.

I peel back the covers on her bed to tuck her in, careful not to press my lips to her forehead. That's another thing: kissing. Putting my mouth on a woman is an intimacy I don't give freely. But with Emma, it's effortless.

Tomorrow, we'll restart our routine. With the exception of lunch, when we walk to stretch our legs, every meal comes to the suite under a silver dome.

No romantic gestures.

No details about our lives.

No activities that veer into dating.

The setup is perfect for sex without strings, but the strings are here with us, whether we want to admit it or not.

Chapter 23

Emma

Coming to the store hungry was a stupid idea. I know it, my temper knows it, and my stomach, which is currently cussing me out in growls, knows it.

I pop another seedless grape into my mouth and glare at the wide-shouldered man in a tacky tropical shirt and khaki shorts, clothes not warm enough for February. His judgy eyes narrow at the next grape I pluck from the bag. He looks like he's contemplating a civilian's arrest.

"Can I help you?"

He shakes his semi-bald head, which is littered with dimples, presses his shopping basket to his side, and flaps off in worn brown flip-flops. When I'm not hangry, I'm not a confrontational person, but I contemplate bouncing a grape off the back of his head.

"It's not about dick," I mumble to myself, pushing my shopping cart with more force than necessary.

Beverly Hills Rent-a-Cop *is* a dick, but he's not the one on my mind.

Peen withdrawal a week before my period is deadly timing. Add in my need to eat, and I'll rip open every chip bag and hump the cashier for good measure.

The grocery store I'm at is a half-hour drive from my house. I don't come to Beverly Hills unless it's necessary, but this location is the only one in the vicinity with my favorite champagne.

My Milan trip ended yesterday. I shook off the jet lag by sleeping in, but not the frustration that's been following me around since Miles left Italy a day before me. I'd never spent more than two days with a lover but found myself losing track of time. Before I knew it, four nights has passed in a maze of clothes and blankets. We spent most days reciting the rhythms of our bodies, discovering new harmonies for symphonies of pleasure on the surfaces we christened. We avoided any signs of intimacy. We never slept in the same room or went on a date.

When it was time to let go, we did.

We ended on my terms, taking whatever pleasure we could during the days we spent together. It was perfect—*too* perfect—but ending it was the right call. Miles and I resealed the attraction we unboxed, and we'll never touch it again.

Miles attended to my every need without instruction. He took, but he also gave freely. The way he directed my body had me taking naps for the first time since I can remember, which I'm sure made the jet lag easier.

I can't shake him, his touch, or his scent. My name danced across his tongue in a rich baritone every time he moaned. Italy was incredible, but for my sanity, and to prevent pussy depression, I need to move on from Miles.

I'll call Zayn tonight. After I eat.

I lift onto the toes of my black heels to reach for a bottle of champagne and grab air. *What the?* I pat around for any hidden bottles but come up short.

"Not today, Satan," I mumble. I'm practically hanging off the shelf to do a pull-up I can't hold. Is it ridiculous? Yes, but I don't care.

A woman wants what a woman wants, and my champagne is nonnegotiable.

An employee confirms that the store is in fact sold out. One bottle remained, but someone grabbed it minutes before I came in. Just my damn luck.

I pay for my groceries, storm to my car, and take my ass back home. Champagne-less, hungry, and very horny.

My mind shifts away from my empty stomach, back to Italy and Miles eating me within an inch of my life.

You taste so fucking good, kitten.

Cream for me, kitten.

Let that shit drip, kitten.

The phantom touch of his words still tempts my thighs apart. Did he make it to California?

What would you do if he did?

I breathe a sigh of relief at the incoming call notification on my navigation screen. But then my eyes shift from the Pacific Coast Highway to the name in white letters. I'm too hungry for what will no doubt be an unnecessary debate about my life and the ways I've let it waste away. It's my business, not a topic for discussion. I push "accept" and straighten in my leather seat.

"Hello, Mother." A Sunday conversation is rare. *Any* conversation is, but Juliette Douglass will wear you down until she gets what she wants at whatever cost. What that cost is in this case remains to be seen.

"Emma." The two syllables lack a mother's warmth for her child, the namesake of the grandmother she claims to have loved. "Did you return from your trip?" Disinterest travels from the East Coast, where my mother is no doubt primping herself for a social activity.

"I got in from Milan last night," I confirm. She wouldn't care if I was in Italy or on *Sesame Street*. My mother never asks about my work or its related travels because she doesn't care.

"I hope you remembered about this Friday."

"What's this Friday?" I frown at the screen. She has a habit of committing me to events I never know about in advance, assuming I'll drop everything or that my father's staff managed to reach me. Friday night rings no bells. They can make arrangements with the Four Seasons. No one stays in my house, not that my family ever asked to.

Disappointment laces my mother's sigh, one she drags out for longer than necessary. "We're flying to Los Angeles to attend a fundraising event with a regional business council. It's a wonderful opportunity for your father. You will be there, yes?"

"It's the first time I've heard of it, but I can stop by," I say, pushing to the button for the garage door. My Mercedes pulls to the center of the two-car space, where I cut off the engine.

The garage door closes as I tap in the code and walk up the small set of stairs to access the main level of my waterfront property. My mother is still scolding me, but what else is new?

I step on wide plank floors and drop my keys into the small dish on an accent table in the mudroom area. It's small and leads to the kitchen I never use across from the living and dining space. The star of my home is the three-million-dollar view of the Pacific Ocean from the floor-to-ceiling pocket doors. My mother will never acknowledge my work, but blood, sweat, and heels afforded me what I have. I'm damn proud, even if it will never be good enough.

I'm across from my living room fireplace with a glass of wine by the time my mother finishes her speech on the importance of the Douglass family legacy and doing my part. I nod along and pepper in some "mm-hmms" while ordering sushi from one of my favorite spots nearby.

"Will Miles be your plus-one? You two are still together?"

My mother's question catches me off guard, pulling my focus away from the lobster roll on the takeout menu and toward the memory of Miles holding me under the spray of the showerhead. The silent glances we shared. Tender. Inquisitive. Reassuring.

I've contemplated every what-if scenario since the retreat, finding our way back to each other in New York, and him following me to Milan.

What if Miles comes to California?

What if we develop feelings that reach beyond sex?

What if I don't want him to leave?

My eyes drift to the waves outside the window that recede before crashing into hard rock. A steady pressure building until it demands release.

Miles and I could establish terms and conditions to keep our emotions at bay. Neither one of us would leave unscathed once it came to an end.

"This conversation is taking too long. Your father and I have a play to attend," my mother huffs. "No need to hide him, Emma. Your father confirmed Miles starts with Carrillo tomorrow. He's far from an ideal match but will have to do...for now."

My mother ends the call with annoyance as her only parting gift. It remains unclear what wedged us apart and put this much tension between us, but I stopped trying to solve that mystery decades ago.

I allow myself to float back to Italy, and an idea forms.

Chapter 24

Miles

"Took you long enough."

Lorenzo snatches the champagne out of my hand and scurries off to the kitchen. It's a row of white cabinets and a light granite countertop that he manages to keep clean between the mixing bowls and scattered groceries. He's serious about many things, and cooking is one of them. I'd clown him about the waist apron over his khaki pants, but not at the expense of dinner.

"You act like I was gone all day. Chill." I peek at the fish he's frying on the stove. "Why'd you need champagne so bad, anyway?"

He shrugs and puts a golden-brown piece on the wire rack. "Just goes with the shit. I like it with my *chilaquiles* in the morning, so you saved me a trip." He dips another piece of fish into the batter bowl, shakes off the excess to dip into a bowl with flour, and drops it into the oil. "Isabel loved that champagne. It stuck."

Lorenzo doesn't talk about his late wife often, but he doesn't have to. He keeps Isabel's memory alive by cooking the foods she loved in the house he bought after he lost her to breast cancer. What little money he had at the time went to her treatments, but he promised her the gated bungalow she saw on the bus route to her job.

They met at sixteen and got married at twenty. By the time he was thirty-three, he started teaching at college, and she was gone. We met at Bodie a year later and haven't stopped annoying the shit out of each other ever since.

"You should be thankful. There was only one left in that bougie-ass store. Guess you aren't the only one who likes that brand." I sit at the wooden dining room table.

I got to LA a couple hours ago and am already running errands. But Zo is letting me crash here, so I can't complain.

We rarely see each other living on different coasts. When Zo is in DC, he's knee-deep in public official duties. Not that I'm around. Work keeps my suitcase on the ready at all times.

Once the fish is done, we grab trays loaded with tacos, rice, and refried beans to take outside. Zo doubles back for a flannel and the drinks. The backyard is a small, covered deck next to an even smaller yard. Tall hedges border the perimeter for privacy, with pots of marguerite daisies, Isabel's favorite flower Zo gave to her. He has a condo he uses to entertain "company," and he'll stay there while I'm here.

"We good for tomorrow?" I grunt at the fish taco that's playing with my emotions. Zo dressed all of them in lime juice, chipotle sauce, shredded cabbage, and *pico de gallo*. Shit is good.

"You know where to pull up. I have a new intern who will work with you."

"Bet."

"*No seas pendejo.*"

I brush down my hoodie and blow out a breath. *Here comes the bullshit.* "What you on?"

Zo focuses on the champagne glass in his hand and chuckles. "You're in the same city as Emma since you hopped on a flight to follow her to Italy and have nothing to say."

"Technically, the same *county*. She's in Malibu," I say to be a smartass. A little over thirty-two miles separate us. Not that I'm counting.

He waves it off with a hand. "The point is, you're bound to run into her again."

"Not necessarily," I mumble around a bite.

"Please. You chase Emma to Italy after you ran into her at a bar in New York with a woman you ditched for her." Zo chuckles. "That shit is serendipitous."

"Nothing will happen while I'm here." My mouth tightens at his full-on laughter. "Shit ain't funny."

Emma made it clear our time together would end once we left Italy. She hasn't given an answer on keeping up a fake relationship for her parents, but what the fuck do I look like waiting around? I already followed her ass out of the country, and I'm not about to do that up and down LA. I don't chase pussy. Em's is top tier, but she needs to voice her wants.

"If you say so."

"I do," I counter.

"Alright," Zo says with his hands up and a goofy-ass grin.

We settle into our plates and go to work. A pot of daisies blowing in the breeze catches Zo's eye. He clears his throat. "I think I'm gonna rent this place out. It's time."

I pause. "Word?"

"Yeah."

The twentieth anniversary of Isabel's death is coming up. Part of my time out here is to make sure Zo is good. We don't talk about feelings, but he's been keeping my head on straight for the last two decades. We stumbled into each other's lives at a time when I needed guidance and he needed a distraction from losing his wife. He's more of a big bro than a father figure. Outside of Terrence, Zo is one of the few people I call friend and let close.

Zo dips after eight, and I let my thoughts drift back to Emma over my nightcap. What if we saw each other while I was out here? The sex is unmatched, and the chemistry is there. We also have a built-in expiration date. We can get each other out of our systems.

"Nah," I say to the empty backyard. It might be winter, but California and Jersey have different definitions of cold. A faint breeze picks up, catching the potted daisies under outdoor string lights.

Guys like me don't get the chance to be happy, even if they want it.

Zo did.

I take a long pull of scotch and let my thoughts wander into the night.

Chapter 25

Miles

I smell her before I see her.

Emma's scent has been recessed deep in my memory for longer than I care to admit. She hasn't changed her perfume in the fifteen years I've known her. Right now, her cedar fragrance with hints of floral is charging down the short hallway to the room that's been my office since I started at nine. I was in the middle of concocting a plan to see her when Rebecca, one of the interns, messaged me to say I had a visitor.

Emma beat me to our reunion, and I'm not mad about it.

The air shifts when she reaches the open door and knocks like I'm not already staring at her. Lorenzo's office isn't the smallest suite on the floor, but this shit has me looking like the dad from *The Incredibles*, squeezing my ass into this space they call a conference room.

"You coming in, or do you need an escort?" My voice lures Emma out of whatever trance she put herself in eyeing me in my suit. I don't always wear one, but a brother cleans up nicely.

I stand and button the dark gray blazer over a white dress shirt. Her eyes rake over my tailor-fit pants, moving down to my brown oxford shoes. My tongue darts out at her turquoise suit. It's a bold choice, one she pulls off without effort. Her high-waisted pants mold to her waist and toned legs, and the spaghetti-strap crop top in the same fabric shows a sliver of her amber skin above her belly. Once-curly hair cascades off one shoulder in thick waves.

"We need to talk." A brow arches in wait until I nod and shut the door behind her.

She takes the seat on the opposite end of the conference table, capturing my nostrils in the process with that damn perfume. I adjust myself and steeple my fingers on the table when I sit.

Her chin lifts. It's subtle. A gold chain dangles between her cleavage, flickering in the light. "I have a proposition." She mimics my hands on the table, showing off a pink manicure that matches her lips.

Flanked between the US and California flags, Emma looks ready to give a State of the Union address. I motion for her to continue.

"It's clear there's an attraction between us," she says, studying my reaction with narrowed brows. "I'm willing to explore it while you're here." *Aka, you want this dick.* "Provided we establish a few ground rules."

Interesting.

"What do you have in mind?"

She wets her lips and sits straighter. "You move in, and we make ourselves available to each other."

"*You* want to live together? The same woman who said no chance in hell?"

"I want unlimited access to sex," Emma says. "We had a test run in Milan after you moved yourself into my suite for the week. We're adding a few more nights in this case, and changing locations."

She's not wrong.

"Keep going," I encourage.

"No spending the night in the same bed." *No complaints here.* "Fridays are open for us to use as we see fit."

Say what now?

"You're cool with other sexual partners?" I ask for clarification.

"Are we exclusive, Miles?" The question is a challenge, one that reminds me this arrangement is purely to fuck and nothing else. Unlike other women, Emma isn't fishing for a commitment.

The stare I drill into her triggers a swallow. Emma shifts slightly in her seat, which is all I need to know. *Bullshit.* "Fridays open," I repeat and throw in, "in case we get bored."

I want to smirk at her glower but hold it in. I won't call her out. I haven't thought about another woman since we linked up in New York, and I bet Emma isn't itching to fuck on anyone else, either. This dick is enough to propel her to the next century just like her pussy has me humming ballads for no damn reason.

"Agreed." Emma's temper flashes in her tone, cool and demanding. *There's my kitten.* "I would also like to maintain the facade of a relationship during political outings with my father when he comes to California. They will be few and far between. By the time they're through, your time in Los Angeles will be up, and we'll go back to the way things were before."

Emma's proposal is a lot to take in. Sex without strings is how I operate, but living together? Shit, I have to think about that.

There hasn't been a woman to keep my interest or make me picture a life with her in it. Em already proved the first part to be a lie, but there's no way she goes two for two. Living together makes a hemorrhoid look like a good time. I don't commit—never have, and never will.

Back to unlimited sex.

"You're willing to open your home to me?"

"For fucking, not companionship, Miles. Sex, that's all it is. You'll have your own room and bathroom. We'll share common spaces. I'm sure it's better than the hotel you're in."

"I'm not in a hotel."

"Oh." Emma's shoulders tense. She nods and smooths her hands over her suit. "We can take—"

"Leave it, and I want one date night a week."

The words fly out my mouth before I have time to process what the fuck I said. Emma and I are similar. We want pleasure without the hassle of emotions. Yet here I am, requesting more time to get to know her beyond her body while living in her house.

Emma Douglass not only has my attention, she's got me questioning how I'll walk away when the time comes.

Her stare holds a million questions. "That's...doable." She clears her throat. "You can move in tonight if you want. My doors operate by keypad. I'll give you the code."

"I don't have much, but I can come through after work. What day are we having our date this week?"

Surprise registers on her face before she gives a nod. "I'm open."

"Good. We'll start tonight."

Moss-green eyes widen. "Excuse me?"

"Now who would've thought a date would spark that reaction and not you asking me to live with you?" I fold my hands over my lap and chuckle. "Isn't there some event on Friday? We should learn more about each other if we're pretending to be together." Zo told me about a fundraiser Emma's dad will attend. I planned to pull up on her then, but look who surprised me first. And offering her house, no less.

A warning that this is a dumb idea whispers in my head until Emma bites her lip and looks the other way. "How about Wednesday?" Hesitation trembles her voice. "I go back to work tomorrow but can meet you Wednesday around six."

It will be the first and last time she drives herself when I'm around.

We exchange numbers, so I no longer have to leave it up to chance or me breaking federal laws to see her.

Zo pops in as Emma leaves.

"Ms. Douglass, what a surprise." He extends his hand, his eyes shifting over her frame and then to me with a satisfied grin.

Asshole.

"I came to talk to Miles about a…business arrangement."

The motherfucker can't help but cheese. "Ah, yes. Let me not intrude." He motions to the now open door.

"Actually, I was on my way out." Emma tugs down her suit jacket. "Miles," she says to me.

"Emma," I toss back.

She struts out the office the same way she came in, leaving me with a giddy congressperson who has too much time on his hands.

"Don't start about that serendipitous shit." Zo mocks surrender at my pointed finger and rolls his lips to keep from laughing. "We're spending more time together, or we will. I, um, won't need your crib after all."

I get two seconds before Zo cracks up. He contorts his blue suit folding over in laughter, and the interns rush into the conference room to see why their boss lost his fucking mind. Zo barely smiles in public but is always laughing at my expense. The shit isn't funny. It just saves mileage and gas, when you think about it.

Your excuse for living with Emma is budgeting?

Fuck you too.

I shoo the entire office away and close the door. Zo wipes the tears out of his eyes and parks his foolish ass on the wooden conference room table. His laughter fades, but the tears in his eyes remain.

"Done yet?"

He puts a hand to his mouth and coughs. "Yeah. So how's that gonna work?"

"What?" I frown.

"You two under the same roof, spending time together and *not* catching feelings."

I shrug. "Simple. We come together when we need to come together and go about our business the rest of the time. I don't plan to be up under her, watching movies and shit. People do these arrangements all the time."

A situationship, friends with benefits, or whatever. I'm in town; we like to fuck. The end.

"Uh huh," is all Zo says, prompting me to kick his ass out the conference room once all that cackling starts again. I don't care if this is his office or not.

Emma and I will catch a cramp before we catch feelings. I like spending time with her when she doesn't annoy me and will keep my distance when she does. Problem solved.

"Thought I had to send a search party for your ass."

I grin at Terrence's dramatics and get on the 10. "What's good, bro?"

"Enjoying life and this woman finally back home."

We laugh.

The shit isn't a joke, but after seven months apart and Justice moving to the other side of Austin, I'm happy they're happy.

"Glad things are working out."

"Me too," he says, grinning like a cornball with that smile in his voice. "What's new with you? Haven't heard from your ass in like a week."

"And that was intentional. I'm not calling you the first Valentine's Day you're back with your wife. You probably just now let her up for air."

Terrence's laughter fills my rental car. *Thought so.* "Alright. How's Cali?"

"Nice. The weather is good. Just got off work."

"Look at you. Maybe this will keep your ass in one spot for more than two weeks," he chuckles, like he wasn't in and out of the country himself. "Did you head over from Jersey?"

"Nah." My grip tightens on the leather steering wheel. "Had some business to see about in a few spots."

If T knew Emma and I were fucking, he'd lose it. Any fallout would cause tension that would end with him in the doghouse or catching a stray. Jeopardizing mixed gatherings now that he and Jay are back together would be an issue. We have to be extra careful now that I'm staying at her spot.

"Always on the go," Terrence chuckles.

"I know you ain't talking."

Hair from his goatee bristles against the phone as he scratches his chin. "I'm straight. The right one will keep your ass at home. I won't lose her again."

We shoot the shit for the rest of my drive. I pull up to Emma's garage and park. "Let me let you go. I'll hit you up later."

"Enjoy the new spot. Talk soon."

"Tell Jay I said hi."

"Will do."

It's a short walk from my Audi to the door that separates the main sidewalk from the private entrance. Not one damn camera in sight. I make a note and punch in the code to the keypad. There's a waist-high gate the same weathered oak color as the wood near the front of Emma's house. The tiny thing separates the private beach from her front door in concept, but it isn't a practical security measure. Any serial killer could skip his sadistic ass up the steps from the level below without anyone noticing. The two lights on the side of her house aren't motion sensor and don't illuminate the full surface of her patio. The balcony in the back is a straight shot, just feet away, ready for someone to stalk her.

Said serial killer.

A greasy neighbor with a foot fetish.

Rich people don't put blinds on their windows, like they're cool with showing off their shit inside their fancy fishbowls. Fuck all that.

Emma is one of many waterfront homes off a road that feeds to the Pacific Coast Highway. Yeah, the view is nice, but how is she keeping herself safe with a Fisher-Price gate, questionable safety lights, and no window coverings? If there's no security alarm, I'll kidnap her myself.

A saltwater breeze sweeps over the back of my neck. I knock on the oversized wooden door and wait. I have the code but don't want to scare Em. Turquoise flashes by the thin window panel before the door opens.

"Why didn't you just come in?" Emma's face scrunches, twisting up her pouty lips and pulling her brows up toward her hair. She's still in her work clothes, minus the blazer concealing the crop top.

"I should've the way this setup has you ready for an intruder." I step past her, careful not to inhale her addictive scent. "Your security measures are shit," I tell her, toeing off my loafers. "I'll have everything set up tomorrow."

"The hell you will," Emma snaps. "You're here all of thirty seconds, and you think you'll turn my house into some *Criminal Minds* headquarters? Forget it."

"I was here for ten minutes looking at the bullshit you call security."

Her arms fold firm into her chest, pushing up the breasts I miss in my mouth. *Focus.* "I have security."

My lips twitch. "A nail file?"

"A security alarm, you ass," she seethes through a scowl. "I have a keypad down here and one in my bedroom. There haven't been any break-ins or concerns since I bought the place six years ago."

"It's getting an upgrade tomorrow." I already planned to work remote so I could settle in. I'll spend half the day playing Mr. Fix It.

Emma steps closer, her hands now on her wide hips. Anger sweeps across her face and anchors itself into her rose-tinted cheeks and tightened jaw. We stand toe-to-socks, neither of us bending to concede.

"This is my house, Miles. I won't have anyone telling me what to do here." Her voice is low.

I don't miss what she doesn't say. I had a front-row seat to witness it. Emma deals with enough of her family's meddling. It wouldn't surprise me if her decision to live on the edge of California was to keep maximum distance. Em is a boss. She takes no shit and commands respect. The same moss-green eyes impaling me for my audacity silently plead for me to understand. That her house is her sanctuary, impenetrable to control. I'm the first man she's allowing into her space, and with that comes trust. She wants me to fuck her, but not over.

"I want to keep you safe, kitten. Will you let me?" I keep my voice calm and my gaze steady. I'd set the world on fire if anyone harmed her.

Emma blinks away her fury and nods. "That's...fine." She studies me but shakes away a thought. "Come on, let me show you the house."

There's a chef's kitchen with a marble island parallel to a row of white cabinets. A small dining area converges with a living room next to a panoramic view of the ocean through glass pocket doors. I take in the wood beams on the ceilings and the steel loop that holds fresh logs next to the fireplace. Emma's living space is an ode to Pottery Barn with sand-colored seating and breathable linens. Blush and champagne accent pillows give a splash of color to complement the calacatta marble coffee table.

"It fits you," I say about her house, my attention on the black-and-white photos of Emma and Justice over the years on the mantel.

Three bedrooms are upstairs. Emma's, a spare room she uses for clothing storage, and the room she keeps for Justice whenever she visits.

"Is this okay?" Emma motions to the cream-and-taupe room. A large area rug covers most of the wooden floor, which matches the beams above. The bed is big enough for my size, but I need a desk large enough for the screens I had shipped, and a chair.

"This view is sick." I can't pull my eyes away from the open pocket doors leading to a private balcony. I'm starting to understand why there are no blinds on the windows.

"It is." Emma joins me at the threshold that separates the bedroom from outside. Barefoot, she reaches my shoulder without the pogo sticks she calls heels. It's different seeing her at home. Nice. Her shoulders aren't rigid, and she smiles more than I've seen—except for when she's around Jay.

Peace looks divine on Emma, which is why I look away from her profile and head downstairs. She can't be a distraction; only sex. We've fucked under the same roof in Milan for days. Her home is no different, if we keep sex the priority and out of my room. Having her so close tempts me to cross a threshold I've refused because of what's on the other side.

Chapter 26

Emma

Tuesday couldn't end sooner. Seriously, the bitch can hurry up and rename itself PMS. *Probably More Shit* is a good summary of my first day back after a month away. I always take the day off after I return from a trip, to settle in, but I spent most of yesterday preparing the room Miles will use. The last time Justice used it was over a year ago. I doubt he cared to lather up with the citrus body wash she keeps in the bathroom, which led to me shopping for toiletries and bigger towels. He's on his own with everything else and is likely making himself right at home, fucking mine up in the process.

I groan thinking about the text he sent two hours ago, about the flood lights and surveillance cameras he wants to install. They're probably already up, along with drones and missiles for the long list of burglars he thinks are waiting to break inside. I texted back that it was excessive, to which he replied about shipping his flamethrower from New Jersey. Thank God they're restricted in California. Also, why the hell does he have one?

My house is fine the way it is. No one is checking for me like he thinks, but I'd be lying if I said I didn't appreciate the gesture. No one has ever thought about my safety. Not even my father, a veteran

US senator who might have a long list of enemies, for all I know. He gets along with his colleagues from what I can tell, and he hasn't made national headlines for pissing off any particular group.

Still, it was nice of Miles. Unexpected.

I want to keep you safe, kitten. Will you let me?

Sex, this is just sex. It didn't happen last night, but maybe Miles was tired from his first day in Lorenzo's office. He only brought two bags with him when he came over, and he said he's been busy settling in today.

He was a little distant last night, a detour from our usual banter. I didn't push it and stayed on my side of the second floor, in my room, with a vagina in need of a tune-up.

Back to work and this mess of a schedule.

I lean into my executive chair and exhale a long, unsteady breath.

Every humanly possible meeting happened today, no thanks to my assistant cramming in a team brainstorming session, three check-ins with clients, and a budget meeting in a five-hour window. I had no time for lunch, which meant I was cranky and hungry and had to plaster on a smile without baring my teeth.

The prick who touched the stash of Twizzlers in my drawer will get a stapler to the forehead.

A tap on my office door has my fingers massaging my temples. If it's another meeting, *I'll* need a flamethrower.

"Knock, knock!"

"Ko—oh my goodness!" I run barefoot from behind my desk into Kojo's arms. Notes of basil and amber from his cologne tickle my nostrils as he pecks my cheek. "Why aren't you in Milan for the shows?"

He flicks a bracelet-clad wrist and walks into my office in patent-leather boots, black trousers, and a white tee under a black vest. "You didn't stay, and I have business here. When are you done? Quitting time was"—he checks his watch—"three minutes and twelve seconds ago."

Is it five already?

I reach for my phone to check my messages. Nothing new from Miles.

"Dinner?" I slip my cell into my pocket.

"Traditional," Kojo says.

"Drinks?"

"Expected."

I huff and roll my eyes. "Let me send out a few emails." I swat his ass perched on my clear glass desk on the way back to my chair and scoop up my YSL pumps. They're a standout against this red pant set. "Pick a place, but I'm not staying out late."

His face twists into a frown, tipping his dreads in a ponytail with his head tilt. "Why not? I'm only here until the end of the week."

What is my excuse?

Going out with Kojo is better than staying in the house with a tight lip and dramatic coochie if Miles is in another mood.

"You're right. Let's go."

"That's the third time you've ignored his call."

"Fourth." I hit decline again.

"Oop!"

My only response to Carter's calls and texts was a thumbs-up to confirm my father coming on Thursday, a tidbit the senator was too busy to share himself.

"Remind me why you two haven't fucked? The man is fine." Kojo tips his glass and takes a sip of Sazerac.

They never met, but a photo of me and Carter with my father was enough for him to question why I won't let the *Grey's Anatomy* lookalike play doctor.

I sigh and twist the stem of my martini glass in my hand. "Carter and I have what you call a volatile relationship."

At nineteen, Carter had his swagger down. The custom suits weren't in rotation then, but the cocky smile was, along with the red flags spelling out "trouble" in Broadway lights. He was my first crush, and he's still an anomaly.

Charming yet exhaustive.

Addictive yet enraging.

Like Miles.

I used to think my immediate attraction to Carter and our par-for-the-course back-and-forth were signs we'd fall into place. The senator's daughter with his chief of staff would be a match made in Washington if it didn't make my skin crawl. I have a connection to Carter by default, but something is off.

"Were you ever attracted to someone but knew if you got together, you'd lose more than you'd gain?"

Kojo nods.

"That's Carter."

I always follow my gut, and it says not to trust myself with him. *Carter or Miles?*

A dry martini coats my throat on a long sip. There are parallels to both men. Miles is exhaustive and enraging, but he's also nice—caring, even. He never tries to hurt me but possesses Carter's same ability to get under my skin.

"Sounds like a damn mess. So no Jesse Williams then. Who *is* in your rotation?"

"I, um. There's no rotation right now."

Kojo pulls another sip and tips his head from side to side. "Dry spells happen. I was in one myself until this morning." He crosses himself.

"It's not a dry spell. It's kinda been the same person for a minute."

"Define a minute."

"I don't know. A month, give or take a week or two." I scan the bar menu but freeze at the heat of his gaze on the side of my neck.

Kojo is a damn fool, staring at me with wide eyes, an open mouth, and the spring roll the bartender dropped off seconds ago now inches from his lips. "What?" I laugh.

He discards the roll and scans the room. "We need a table for this."

The spot Kojo picked is a cocktail bar in the Art District. The dark wood bar with matching molding and floors now has a crowd gathering for drinks as throwbacks from the '90s and 2000s play.

A booth opens for us in the corner, where I spend twenty minutes catching Kojo up on Miles and our volatile relationship, the singles' retreat, New York, and Milan. It's a relief to get everything off my chest. I haven't told Justice yet, because she'll make a big deal out of nothing. Weddings and soulmates will come up, and I don't need that drama in my life. Sex is the arrangement.

You keep telling yourself that.

By the time I finish, Kojo snaps his mouth shut and flops back into the leather cushion. My snort morphs into laughter. "Say something."

He wiggles his jaw before picking up a slice of the salmon flatbread between us. "I'm trying to figure out why you're here with me and not at home with more of that good dick."

We crack up.

"It's better to have space, you know? We're not trying to develop feelings."

Kojo's *Tuh!* draws the eyes of three tables. "You have a man in your house for the first time ever, and you want to play make-believe about not catching feelings."

"Did you forget who I am? I catch many things, but feelings aren't one of them. This is a temporary situation with the benefit of in-house penis."

Part of my allowing Miles to stay with me is to prove to myself that he doesn't have a hold over me. We'll have sex and see other people. When he leaves California, we're done. "I can handle it," I declare to Kojo, who's ready to tell me I'm full of shit.

Why is it so hard to believe I can get close without feelings?

Can you?

The intro to Keri Hilson's "Pretty Girl Rock" pumps through the speakers. Kojo grabs my hand to pull me to the makeshift dance floor, which is now full of people.

"Koko, I do not dance!" I lean back into the booth but get pulled out anyway.

"You don't do relationships either, but you're about to have a whole man!" He spins and sways me into a two-step. "Send me your measurements when the time comes. I call dibs on your wedding dress!"

It's past ten by the time I make it home. I reset the alarm, remove my heels, and head upstairs to my bedroom. Light peeks from under Miles's door. Did he hear me come up? There's no television in either bedroom that might mask the creaks in the wooden staircase.

"Whatever," I mumble to myself. So much for in-house dick.

I strip off my clothes, toss them into the laundry basket, and head to my bathroom, where I spend more time soaking under the rain shower and thinking about Miles than I should. Maybe this was a bad idea. I don't need a roommate, least of all him.

Another ten minutes of serums and lotions, and I'm back downstairs for a snack. Stress-eating is a habit I need to break, but I'm in peen withdrawal, and the source of my problem is feet away. I pop three more grapes into my mouth and close the refrigerator door.

The "Jesus!" I yell is a jumble around the fruit in my mouth at Miles standing behind the stainless-steel door. I chew on overtime and clutch my heart, which is doing sprints under my silk robe. "Announce yourself next time."

Miles pulls his black headphones off and frowns. "My bad. Got caught up in a simulation." He waves the phone in his hand as evidence. He scans me from my toes up to my thighs before his eyes land on my lips. "When did you get in?"

"Close to an hour ago. Guess you didn't hear me come in with those things." I point to the headphones curled around his neck.

"We still on for tomorrow?" I step back so Miles can open the refrigerator. He pulls out a refillable water bottle, unsnaps the top, and takes a generous sip.

"Yes," I say, too breathless at his stare. I swallow hard as I watch him drink. The suction from his mouth works the muscles in his neck, which is adorned with a single gold chain. His chest is bare, with pecs the size of my head on full display, glimmering in the moonlight.

Miles is blemish-free and every desire in gray sweatpants.

The intensity of his appraisal under thick lashes and hooded eyes has us reaching for each other at the same time. Miles anchors me to him with his tongue and picks me up. Our kiss is slow, a whirl of emotions through deep strokes. His thumbs rub circles into my back, and I sink into his embrace.

Cold marble sends a shiver up my spine as he lays me on the counter, licking and savoring my neck. His soft lips move to my collarbone, and he slips a hand through my satin robe to knead my breast. I hiss at the pinch to my nipple that he laps at with his mouth.

My fingers breach the band of his sweatpants and stroke his length. Miles bucks in my grasp and palms my pussy with his hand. I rock against the friction and moan into his mouth at the fingers he pumps in and out of me.

"Squeeze my shit," he says, curling to reach my G-spot. My heels dig into the counter to ride out the orgasm charging up my body.

"Oh my—"

"Let it drip." Miles sucks his fingers before diving between legs. He traps me in his arms and curls me to his mouth.

I don't know what school of eating pussy Miles graduated from, but I will create a scholarship in his name. He sucks on my vagina like it holds the meaning of life and never once comes up for air. The massage to my clit with slow drags of his tongue is my undoing. I try to wiggle free, but he doubles down, burying his face with a satisfied groan.

I need his dick. Now.

"Top drawer on your right," I push out between breaths. Miles frowns until he opens the drawer to find the stash of condoms I keep inside. Most are upstairs, but I have a few down here in case I'm in a rush.

He pulls out a gold wrapper he rips open with his teeth, his eyes trained on me. My body hums in anticipation. The muscles in his abs contract when he pulls down his sweats. His dick bobs, his head thick and angry. He sheaths himself, and I lick my lips.

Our gazes tangle when he reaches for me and steals my breath with a single thrust. We kiss at a lazy pace to match the rhythm of his hips grinding against my thighs. Miles pulls back to take in our bodies and rubs his thumb over my clit. He slides in and out with deep strokes before leaning over me. The tempo changes, and his ab muscles contract as he comes with my name on his lips.

"*Fuck*, kitten." Darkened eyes reconnect with mine as Miles stands. I move to get up but remain fixed on the marble by his hand. "I want to see you." His tone is soft, barely above a whisper.

I unravel my robe and pull the lapels open to bare myself to him. Miles's gaze is a gentle caress over my face before it travels the curves of my breasts, over my nipples, down my navel, and to my parted thighs. He's seen all of me countless times but relishes in every dip and arch of my body like it's the first time he's bearing witness.

Miles bends to inhale my nectar scenting the air and groans before taking a long swipe with his tongue. My body is vibrating, still high off the ecstasy we created on my kitchen counter, but I'm ready for another round. He tongues down my other lips while he replaces the old condom with a fresh one and sends us soaring until we both need water and a shower.

We clean up and say goodnight on our way to our rooms.

I remind myself sex is all this can be.

Chapter 27

Emma

Why did I agree to a date with Miles?

The request caught me off guard on Monday, and it still does now that Wednesday has arrived. I held back my curiosity tinged with excitement, because dates shouldn't excite me. They're not supposed to. They're a means to an end for a purpose that starts and ends with penis.

Any physical arrangement I've had is temporary and without any fillers to incite confusion. I don't need fine dining with candles or flowers to have sex. That's a good way to have a man following you home and crying all night on your doorstep. It happened before, with Mark, a transplant from Silicon Valley who was all too eager to tour the inside of my bedroom like he had a right to. I may not have a flamethrower, but I keep a Taser in my pocketbook, and Mark met it after following me home. It was the one time my father flew out to see me. I filed a restraining order as a precaution.

Miles isn't the type to lose his shit like that, but the fact we're living together and he still wants my time gives me pause. I haven't stopped thinking about last night when he held me in his arms after sex. We never spoke about it and carried on like kinda friends with benefits—more like friends adjacent—who are still figuring out what the hell they're doing. Miles left for work this morning before I made it downstairs. I was grateful for the distance, not that it helped clear my mind.

He's changing my rules like they were meant for him to break.

Miles texts at four to meet him at the Santa Monica Pier in an hour. Strolling around carnival games outside in February wouldn't be my first choice for a date. He's lucky it's not raining.

I shake my head and gather my things, still in disbelief that these heels will touch a boardwalk. On a *date*.

The drive takes less than ten minutes. I find parking and head to the ticket kiosk, where Miles stands. His back is to me, giving me time to take in the full muscular frame that sends a jolt to my clit. Miles is fine—there's no debate—but the way he wears a suit should be illegal. His hands in his pocket stretch the fitted fabric hugging every hard-earned muscle. And that ass. I love to dig my nails into his smooth flesh every time he rolls his hips into—

"There you are."

Miles turns with a smirk, like he caught me reliving last night on the kitchen counter. I was, but I won't admit it. His eyes glide up my figure, and he bites his lip. "You good in those?" He nods to my platform heels.

"They're comfortable."

"Alright, but if they start to hurt, I'm buying you sandals. Can't have you fucking up those pretty feet." He extends his hand. "Come on."

The wind chooses that moment to pick up the scent of his musk cologne. Against my better judgment, I smile and put my hand in his for our adventure.

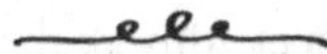

"Wait 'til I get your ass! Shit!" Miles's bumper car spins in a circle. It resets, and I push my handle forward to ram him again.

"Aye!" is all he yells before his car spins out again.

If I laugh any harder, I'll pee on myself.

Miles wanted to try out these inner-tube bumper cars and went easy on me, assuming I'd be too bougie to let loose. He quickly learned the hard way not to underestimate me the first time I pushed the pedal to the floor and rammed his car. The man never stood a chance to retaliate, which has me laughing through tears at his frustration.

At the end of our time, our cars stop. I unbuckle myself in a fit of giggles and take off as fast as my designer heels will go. I barely make it ten feet before Miles lifts me off the ground.

"I see you got jokes behind the wheel, Driving Miss Daisy!" He curls me over his shoulder with a smack to the ass.

"Put me down!" I squeal.

"For you to ram me again? Nah."

Only a few people are here to witness Miles carry me across the pier. At five eight, I'm not small, but he dwarfs me in size.

We reach a burger spot with outdoor seating. Light winds from the water deliver a chill, but it's nothing an LA hot dog won't fix.

"Are you sure you're not cold?" Miles shrugs out of his suit jacket.

"I'm good," I say through a bite of a crinkle fry. "Thanks again for the hoodie."

The pink tourist sweatshirt clashes with my outfit but keeps me warm. Miles bought it from a shop right before he won me the cutest stuffed red panda. Football was his sport of choice at Bodie, but his talent also translates to basketball.

Tonight was a pleasant surprise. We spent the last hour and a half hopping on rides and playing games. I didn't know what to expect coming here, but I don't mind the change in scenery.

It feels nice to laugh again.

"Thank you for tonight."

My hair has to be a mess, but Miles looks at me like I just walked off the runway. The corner of his mouth lifts. "You're welcome."

"Did you go to lots of carnivals growing up?"

He finishes a bite of his burger and shakes his head. "They didn't come through my neighborhood, but T and I tried to hit them up with his younger sister if we could."

From what little I know about Miles's childhood, he had a rough start and spent a lot of time with Terrence. Their mothers worked multiple shifts as nurses and single moms providing for their families. Terrence's Dominican grandmother watched him and his sisters—and Miles, from what Justice told me. He doesn't talk about his past much, and I never had a reason for him to disclose it to me.

"I never went, either," I say with a shrug. "They were always around Alexandria, but it wasn't an activity worth an appearance from my parents."

"They traveled because of your pops?"

"Yes, but they were also particular about what deserved their attention. Spending hours on amusement rides and eating junk wasn't their idea of a good time." I wiggle the hot dog in my hand. "These were a staple in Jay's house. We had them at least once a week."

What I don't mention are the excuses I made whenever Justice and her parents would invite me on their family outings, carnivals included. It didn't feel right to tag along when they'd already opened their home and heart to their daughter's best friend.

Miles considers me. "You stayed with her a lot?"

I nod and wipe my hands with a napkin. "At least twice a week, whenever my parents were away or stayed out too late. I was safe at home—"

"But you didn't want to be alone."

"Something like that." I force a smile, one he sees right through. "I had a key to her house by the time we hit our sophomore year of high school." I laugh at the thought. "Pretty wild given my background. I didn't stay all the time. Didn't want to impose."

"I get it. The staying away to not be a burden." The look on Miles's face is one I've seen in the mirror, and it's taken years of practice to cover. Wanting to belong.

Something flickers in his brown eyes, but he blinks it away. Miles and I might be from opposites ends of the socioeconomic spectrum, but we're two kids who clung to their chosen families for different reasons. His mother had no choice but to work multiple jobs that cost her time away from her son. My parents had all the privileges in the world at their fingertips, yet couldn't afford to stay at home.

We turn away, searching the lights illuminating the pier, far from any plausible explanation for the pull to each other and why the shared truths flow effortlessly.

"So, Friday."

"Yes," I say with too much eagerness. "My family and Carter will be there. I don't plan on staying beyond a quick appearance."

Miles nods. "We have a team meeting that might run late. I'll meet you there. Anything else to know?"

"You've seen them in action. My father is always in campaign mode, too busy to notice anything else. My mother will purse her lips at anything deemed unworthy of her time. Blair is"—I laugh—"Blair, and you met Carter." That sums it up: one wealthy, dysfunctional family.

"Why do you put up with it?"

I shrug. "Sometimes we want what we can't have. I love my family but wish things were different. What about you?" I flavor my tone with more enthusiasm. "Are you close with your mother?"

He nods. "We talk a few times a week when I'm not in Jersey or in a location with decent service."

"That's very sweet," I say against a sourness forming in the pit of my stomach. I'm happy for Miles—and Justice and Terrence. Growing up without a loving parent didn't hinder me from my dreams. I had access and privilege because of my father. What I miss are the moments, the lost opportunities to create memories without strings or stipulations.

I still feel the void at thirty-four. With all my success and confidence, I can't shake wishing I had family who called just because and told me how proud they are. So I tell myself as I continue pouring into my found family while holding onto remnants of hope with loose hands that, one day, my own will come around.

Miles takes our trays once we finish and guides us to the end of the pier. We stand in silence, taking in the breeze and the ocean's rising waves. The sun sets, trading its sherbet glow for moonlight over endless water. I love the white noise of the ocean. It's one of the reasons I chose Malibu as my home.

Thick arms wrap around me as a chill creeps into the air. Miles nuzzles his nose into my neck before replacing it with his lips. His mouth moves to mine for a lingering kiss, coaxing me into his warmth. The lines are blurring between us, and I can't find it in me at the moment to care. Maybe I will tomorrow, but tonight, I allow myself to feel.

Miles follows me back to the house and spends the rest of the night tending to my body. I wake up the next morning with a hum between my legs and a stuffed red panda on the pillow.

Chapter 28

Emma

"All those carbs will go straight to your waistline."

I roll my eyes and cut into my waffles and berries before taking an obnoxious bite. "Another reminder that you did not have to come given no one invited you." At Blair's huff, my smile spreads like the syrup on my plate.

She showed up at my office hours ago, expecting a red carpet rollout out in honor of her presence. The best Blair got was a swatch of linen fabric thrown at her feet. One of the designers in my office laughed at my gesture before Blair ran out in a rush. She's always suffered from rich bitch syndrome. My aunt pushed a silver spoon into her mouth and treated her ungrateful daughter like the world revolved around her. We never got along. Blair's envy of my father's political celebrity is why she weasels her way into events and always stands in front of cameras. She wants her own recognition.

What my father considers loving loyalty would crumble at his feet the second a spot on *The Real Housewives of Beverly Hills* opened up. Blair would shoot up Botox while whining over a salad if she had the storyline to be relevant. For now, I have to deal with her smacking on a tuna tartar tostada and crashing my lunch with Kojo.

We're meeting up with his new stylist who worked on his show in New York while she's in town.

Waves of chatter and servers flowing past tables drown out whatever Blair is ranting about. Something about the sparkling water not having enough bubbles.

I rush to Kojo when he walks through the door looking every bit of business casual in a color-block striped polo and black slacks. "Save me," I plead in his ear.

He frowns. "The copper blouse works with your shoes. Undo another button if you feel stuffy."

I smack his hand and snort. Three open buttons are enough. One more, and this restaurant will see more than my cleavage.

"My cousin is with me."

"Ooh, the one from Austin? Let me meet her!"

"Justice is my sister-friend. Blair is my aunt's daughter from Virginia."

Kojo's face drops with his tone. "They say charity starts at home. Take the tax deduction. Is she Ms. Pollyanna with the oversized ruffles on her sleeves?" At my nod, he peers down over his designer frames, clearly questioning why she came in here wearing flotation devices. "Let me introduce you to my plus-one. You two have a lot in common."

My brows tug. "We do?"

"She went to Bodie with us."

He extends his arm toward the woman on her way over to us. Here, in front of me, is the second person I never wanted to see today. Instead of a puffy-sleeved shirt with jeans, she's in a classic wrap dress accessorized to perfection.

"Madison." It's all I manage through gritted teeth.

"You two know each other?" Kojo's eyes dart between us.

I'm not the type of person to air out someone's funky laundry, let alone in a professional setting. But the longer I stand in front of Madison, the more my hands itch to reenact a *Love & Hip Hop* episode.

"This was a bad idea. I should go," Madison says, already one step closer to the front door. She chances a glance at me but quickly diverts her eyes to Kojo, who's still trying to piece everything together. "We'll work something else out. I—I have to go," she shouts over her shoulder.

"Explain to me why you have my stylist running in heels." Kojo leans back to watch Madison rushing across the street. At least she looked both ways before crossing—not that I wouldn't mind a bus taking her out. "Did she fuck your man?"

I surprise myself with a laugh. "She could never."

"Then why do you look possessed with the spirit of Tami Roman and ready to snatch her wig?" He sighs. "Madison will be my eyes and ears on shoots while I scout a new studio space. I don't expect you two to braid hair, but it would be nice if no one sprinted away if you're in the same room." He holds my hands and pouts. "Please."

"This is asking a lot, Koko." My lips curl at his *Puss in Boots* act. Widening his big brown eyes is the only way he begs.

"Fine," I grumble. "But she stays away. Far, far away, and only reaches out in an emergency and via email." Justice is my best friend, and Madison's crimes will not go unanswered.

"I hear you, Emmy!" Kojo all but screams in my face when he squishes me to his chest in a deep hug. "Madison is sweet once you get to know her."

"I'll be the judge of that," I push out, short of breath and nearly squeezed to death.

With my collection soaring, Kojo styling with the enemy is stress I don't want on my plate. I would already be on a video call with Justice if it wouldn't soil the honeymoon phase she's in with Terrence. I'll tell her about Madison later, once things are solid between Jay and T again.

> Madison popped up at my lunch.

Three dots form seconds after I hit send.

Miles

> Which precinct are you at?

A rush of laughter erupts. Kojo pins me with a look. "What?" He peeks over my shoulder, but I turn to send another message.

> I kept my claws away. Had her running as soon as she saw me.

"Let me see," Kojo pouts.

Miles

> Scared of you, kitten.

> You should be.

"Emma!" Kojo stomps through a whisper-yell. "Is that your man? Lemme see!"

Miles

Your breath is scary in the morning.

I snort and keep my nosy friend at bay with one hand.

You weren't saying that earlier with a mouthful of my pussy.

Miles

I got no problems with your other lips.

"Gimme!" Kojo snatches the phone at my cackle. He scans the text exchange with puckered lips. When his eyes meet mine, they scream for details. "Oh, I see your new housemate is working out just fine. The way you got this man eating your box like Cap'n Crunch. Don't get shy now!"

I swallow a laugh and ignore his taunt. "Give me back my phone."

"Can I get details?" He pinches his thumb and index finger together. "A few?"

"No." I snatch back my phone and smirk. "You lost that right with Madison, traitor."

"She's a brilliant stylist," Kojo all but whines. He pinches the bridge of his nose and lifts a hand to recenter himself. If there's one thing Kojo won't do, it's invite early wrinkles. "I will figure out how to make that situation work, but I need more context first. In the meantime, you need to keep that"—he points to my phone—"going. There's good dick, and then there's love. You have stars in your eyes, Em."

"I do not," I say with an eye roll. "We—"

"Are cute together, sending texts like teenagers. You don't do giddy, ever. You're smiling and laughing. It looks good on you."

Sex with Miles is incredible, but spending time with him isn't bad, either. Underneath his antics is substance. The real him. "You're reading too much into it," I protest, to prove friendliness does not equal love. "We text on occasion, but that's all it is."

"If you say so."

"I do."

Kojo clicks his tongue and lifts his hand as a way to say, *I guess*. He doesn't believe me, but that's okay. Miles and I are nothing more than friends of friends getting to know each other while sharing bodies. Our jokes and texts come with the territory.

We head to the table, where Blair is pouting about feeling left out. She suffocates us with a monologue on why she's the perfect face for future campaigns until Kojo dives into the nearest server for a check.

I put Blair, her to-go bag, and her delusions into a car and go back to work alone.

My phone buzzes with a text from Carter about tomorrow's event. I roll my eyes and don't respond. I've successfully dodged his attempts to see me all week, either with meetings I lied about or working too late for dinner or a nightcap. He knows better than to swing by my house. It's not like I'd get up from my sectional to answer the door at ten o'clock at night anyway.

A crisp breeze flows through the open glass pocket doors of my beachfront balcony. It's completely dark outside of the glow from my neighbors' homes. There are no curtains on any of the windows on the main level, though most face out to the water. The only way anyone would see me curled up under a throw blanket with a messy bun and a bowl of ice cream right now is if they walked along the private beach below.

I grab my glass, finish the last of the vintage merlot, and reach for my phone to text Miles. He hasn't messaged since our earlier exchange. Not that I expect him to.

"No. Keep some distance." I force myself to focus on the rerun of *A Different World* and not the man who's still out wherever he is. I only care because the tip of his dick has magic powers.

I refocus my Thursday night around the students of Hillman. Whitley is my favorite character, which is on brand, I know. She comes from wealth and appreciates the arts but handles her business. I'm not whiny, but I do love nice things, Denzel, and a good pantsuit. I always pictured Whitley with someone like Julian—aka Papa Pope from *Scandal*—but Dwayne worked. He was a nerd with a calculator who grew into his own.

Smart.

Former flirt.

You just described Miles.

A scoop of cookie dough ice cream goes down the wrong pipe, stirring up a coughing fit. Miles is from Newark and has more edge in his baritone voice than Dwayne ever could. He has to be good with a computer to do data security. As for being a flirt, there's nothing former about it.

Unlike his best friend, who took one look at Justice and vowed forever, Miles has more flavors of the week than Baskin-Robbins. If it has a pulse, a pussy, and consents, he's on it.

That's one thing we share in common: not circling back to the same partner. We keep sexual encounters about sex. Anything extra—going on dates and sharing about our past—guarantees getting caught up.

Who the hell has time for that?

Apparently you two, since you did all three last night.

"Kinda friends with benefits!" I shout into my empty home. I pull another mouthful of ice cream and sigh. "I'm turning into Justice."

Miles is probably out enjoying the LA nightlife, and good for him. If I weren't so comfortable in the creases of my couch, I'd be on the prowl too. Thinking about who he's with and what he's doing reaches beyond the boundaries of our agreement.

Does he know not to bring anyone to your house?

That's it.

I shake Miles from my mind and turn off the TV. If I'm thinking about him to the point of comparing us to Whitley and Dwyane, it's time to take my ass to bed.

Chapter 29
Miles

My fingers hover over the button to text Emma and ask if she's okay. I grabbed a drink at Bella's, a wine bar Zo opened on the east side, a short walk from his house. He's had the spot for years now, but I never made it over to Los Angeles to check it out. We got caught up talking about meetings he's lining up next week when he's back in DC. He's trying to get this bill right so it has a chance of becoming law. I didn't glance at my watch until after ten, when we both dipped to call it a night, tired from long hours.

I've been burning the candle at both ends, splitting my time between work with Zo and my own business in the evening. A handful of contracts are still active, and they require my attention—which I have less and less of since I moved to Malibu to stay with a woman who's now radio silent.

Em wasn't up when I got in last night. I thought about texting her to let her know where I was but brushed it off. We don't check on each other like that, though our random messages throughout the day make it move faster. The more I learn about her, the more I like her. Emma is cool people, with a fire personality to match the physical. She keeps me on my toes and stocking up on Icy Hot the way we go at it. I like giving her my time, which is more than I can say about any woman I've been with. I'm becoming more in tune with Emma, and I know when something is off.

She had an attitude this morning, giving me only short responses before she left for work. I assumed she slept on the wrong side of the bed the way she was wrangling animals with her snoring last night. I stayed up late working on research for a client and had to put my noise-canceling headphones on to drown her ass out. Not sure how that translates to a funky morning, but I'm not a mind reader.

It's now two o'clock with no signs of life, which isn't her—at least, not anymore.

"Mr. Walker, you have a visitor," Michelle, the receptionist, says through the intercom.

"Send her back," I say.

"It's a Carter Davis," she clarifies. Her voice is cautious, like he's breathing down her neck just to be an ass.

I hit the button to speak. "Send Crispin in." I chuckle at the echo of him stomping his ass up the hallway. Is this why Emma is so quiet? Can't be. The only man she backs down from is her father. Her mother, too, but I'm not touching that.

Emma owes me nothing, even if I wanted more or thought about what more would look like. So, I stick to our arrangement. It doesn't remove the urge to check in on her, but it is what it is.

Carter powers through the last stretch of hallway and heads for the chair at the head of the conference table. He unbuttons his tan suit jacket and sits with his eyes trained on me.

I lean back in my chair, smirking at the steam wafting from his ears. I haven't fucked with him yet, and he's already on one.

"When's your birthday?" I fold my arms over my polo.

It takes a minute for Carter to unlock his jaw. "Why does it matter?"

I shrug. "I got a gift for your ankles." My grin widens at his glare, showing all of my pearly whites. "What can I do for you, Crispin?"

He sighs. "How the hell did you get a job here?"

"Contract," I correct. "I work for myself, but the answer to your question is, I know my shit. Now, what can I help you with so you can get back to your job?"

Carter's nostrils flare, turning his light complexion a shade of pink. He unclenches his hands and folds them on the table. "I wanted to touch base for a bill status update. Do you have something to present to me?" He eyes my end of the table, looking for a presentation he's not getting.

I cross my ankle over my knee. "I don't have any appointments on my calendar with Carrillo's team for a legislative briefing, and I have a meeting in"—I check my Rolex—"eighteen minutes. I doubt you storm into other senators' offices unannounced, demanding people drop what they're doing to appease you. I can assure you, Crispin—"

"Carter," he fumes.

"—that shit don't fly in this office. Even so, are you versed enough in scripting, network security control, or intrusion detection to follow the conversation?"

His flush deepens to crimson. "I'm Senator Douglass's chief of staff. He's owed an update."

"And he will get one once it's ready and the primary sponsors of this bill approve any changes. He might tell you how far to bend over, but this little attempt at a pissing contest will get you escorted out the door." I stand. "Don't come back here on bullshit. Respect the staff in this office by making an appointment, or read the bill draft Carrillo sent you three weeks ago. Either way, your time is up."

Had it been another staff member in another office, I might've had a bit more patience. Maybe. But Carter can kiss the entire length of my ass. Zo doesn't like him and would laugh him out of his office for trying what he just did. I never respect people who abuse their power, and I won't entertain boys masking themselves as men and slithering around to get it.

Carter is the type to stab you in the back while holding a mirror. His pretentiousness makes my ass itch, but there's something calculated about him that's dishonest.

He stands and takes a slow stroll to meet me at the conference room door. We're close in height, but he could be a giant and I'd still knock his ass down to size. Our builds are different. He ain't floating with the heavyweights. He should punch in his own weight class, where it's safe.

"Need something else?" I hold his stare and wait for him to look away.

"Actually." He glances at his watch. "No. I'm on my way to Emma."

Carter visiting Em shouldn't bother me, but it does. So does the smirk he tosses back. She and I aren't together, but if she ever wanted to get serious about someone, she could do a lot better than Carter fucking Davis. He would never treat her the way she deserves. To be worshiped. Cherished.

My tongue drags over my teeth so I can reset and not give him a visit to the nearest hospital. Boys like Carter expect people like me, from around the way, to act out of pocket. It took a while for me to learn my lesson, and, luckily for this ankles-out motherfucker, I did.

"Hope you made an appointment with her. She's a busy woman." I know for a fact he didn't the way his eyes shift to the left. "Tell her I said hi, and I'll see her at home."

I almost pull out my phone to snap a photo as Carter's eyes widen once the words settle. He stares, speechless, searching for signs I'm lying. When he can't find any, the shock settles into irritation. In his mind, he's entitled to Emma, like she's some birthright and not a woman to earn.

"See you tonight, Crispin."

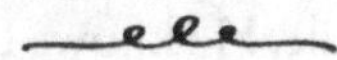

Emma is playing with fire. She never called or texted about this business-council fundraiser, giving me zero details about what I'm walking into. Luckily, Zo did, when he arrived an hour ago. I changed into a suit I had at the office in case a polo and slacks weren't the move. Turns out I was right. At least a hundred people are here, all dressed like they're going to the opera.

Emma's father glides through a crowd of suits and cocktail dresses, wearing a classic tux and the practiced smile of a career politician.

I don't know much about him, but I don't like the way Emma begs for his attention. She doesn't realize it, and I won't point it out.

He and I share a smile on the way to meet Lorenzo. "Miles." Senator Douglass pats my shoulders.

"Senator Douglass." I shake his hand.

"Please, call me John," he says with another politician smile. I know better than to call him by his first name in mixed company, and I'll dodge the bullet his wife will send into my chest without hesitation if I do. She's off in the corner with Blair, and they're turning up their noses at a woman. Is this not a fundraiser?

I scan the room for Emma while John and Zo start a conversation around me. I'm not trying to be rude, but work ended an hour ago for me, and they're not my priority.

"Carrillo tells me you've made wonderful additions to his bill," John says.

"We've passed benchmarks months in advance because of him."

I roll my eyes at Zo's smile. He knows I hate this shit.

"How's Emma?"

"Excuse me?" I glance at John for clarity and frown at his smile.

His eyes crinkle at the edges. "Emma. How is she? You're staying with her, yes?"

"I am, but I'm wondering why you're asking me about your daughter. Haven't you spoken to her?" His smile slips, teasing glimpses of sadness pass over his features before a corner of his mouth lifts.

"Unfortunately, not as much as I'd like," John confesses through a humorless laugh, one I don't find funny. "I've been here since Wednesday but haven't had the time."

"Wednesday?" My head snaps to John, who's looking at the wrong one for understanding. Zo's subtle headshake warns me not to cause a scene.

I spot Emma in a yellow off-the-shoulder dress and lick my lips at the fabric touching her curves. Her exposed thigh lengthens her toned legs strapped to black stilettos. By fashion standards, she's perfect—the most breathtaking woman in the room. But light is missing from her eyes. I search for the source of her hurt—outside of her father ignoring his only daughter for two fucking days—and take in Carter next to her. His penguin suit blends in with the others, making him easy to miss. She squirms at something he whispers, and I'm off.

To my surprise, she meets me halfway.

"Phone?"

Emma's frown is abrupt. Her glittery eyes narrow at my question. "Yes, I have it."

I pull mine out, scroll to her number, and put it to my ear. Hers rings seconds later. I smile once she answers. "It works," I say with a straight face, on my bullshit.

She rolls her red lips. "The line goes both ways," Emma says in defense. It's good to see her smile. I'll make it my mission to see another. Don't ask me why.

"Why you ignoring me all day?" If we have to have this conversation over the phone while standing next to each other, so be it.

Emma opens her mouth but closes it again. Her guard goes up to the moon right before she pulls back her energy. I hate this but can't say shit about it. We're not together. We fuck, text, and went on one date, but a relationship isn't part of the deal.

Still, one thing I won't do is pretend I don't care.

I tell myself Em's place as Justice's best friend is why I'm entertaining shit I wouldn't normally, but that's a lie. Maybe it's the fact she's been off-limits to me for so long that keeps my focus on her. I thought it would wear off after Italy, but I can't shake not wanting more with her.

She still won't play with me.

"You didn't think to reach out about tonight?" I shake my head and end the call but keep my eyes on her. "I'm not some random, Em. I came here as a courtesy, but never forget my presence is a choice."

Zo calls me back over to him and John. I meant what I said: I'm here by choice. Sex doesn't require pretending to be together, but I want to be here.

I chuckle at Carter, who's huffing and puffing in the corner. For someone who had so much to say in Zo's office, he's very quiet.

My phone chimes with a message from Emma.

Emma

> I appreciate you coming and I'm sorry I was distant.

Our eyes meet. I type out a response.

> No apology necessary for taking time if that's what you needed. I'm here for you,

Em. No one else. Let me in next time so I know what I'm walking into.

Emma

I'll work on it.

I smirk. Stubborn ass.

You better. Now bring your fine ass over here for a kiss. Gotta keep up appearances.

Chapter 30

Emma

Turns out the regional business council was only the first stop on tonight's tour. Everyone is so far up each other's ass, it's a miracle they're still breathing. At eight, we leave the ballroom for a private spot on the patio of an Italian restaurant. It's the kind you'd go to on a date, not to cozy up to donors. Each table seats six, and Miles and I are with my parents, Carter, and Blair. Lorenzo had the sense to leave before we got here, and more power to him.

At least forty of us are squeezed together at round tables. We're under outdoor lights hanging from the pergola. Servers keep grazing Miles's head with their ass every time they twist to move between tables. I was cracking up until he threatened to switch seats, which shut me right up.

My breath caught when I saw Miles tonight. Men in suits are nothing new, but my thighs threatened a fire rubbing together at his BDE in a black suit and matching dress shirt.

I tried to put distance between us today, but he charged through it and called me out. It was the right thing to do at the time, or so I thought. In our week together, Miles grew from an acquaintance to a true friend. Not reaching out today wasted what little time we have together. I like texting him just because, and I find myself wanting to reach out more throughout the day to ask about his. It's weird to think we were at each other's throats for so many years. I've enjoyed our time together thus far, but I'm not rushing to shout it from a rooftop.

Miles's groan mimics a growl when another server bumps his chair. "Don't start," he says with a stony expression. But there's no heat behind it, and, sure enough, it morphs into a grin at the laughter I'm fighting to keep behind the napkin over my mouth.

His gaze turns serious, cascading from my eyes to my lips. "You're beautiful," he says, just for me to hear.

"Thank you," I whisper back.

We don't break our stare until my mother clears her throat.

"Colette's daughter is expecting," she announces across the table before cutting into an olive she could have popped into her mouth whole. "She invited us to Diana's shower."

"Diana and I haven't spoken in years, Mother." A fact she already knows. "With the new collection, work is too busy for me to leave right now." Could I squeeze in the trip? If I wanted to. Will I? Of course not.

"Maybe if you focused more on meaningful relationships and not your job, you'd have a husband and a child," my mother retorts. "She's on her third, building a legacy, while you're"—her face scrunches—"playing with fabrics."

A muscle in Miles's jaw ticks. His eyes soften to assess me, then darken at my okay. He glances at my father, whose attention is elsewhere, as usual. The fact that he arrived late Wednesday and this is the first time we've seen each other should sting more than it does. Maybe I'm finally numb to it after all of these years.

"Those *fabrics* are part of a multimillion-dollar brand I helped build. I don't need a husband, and I don't want kids. *My* legacy will live on just fine."

I never wanted children. I always saw myself as the fun aunt who'd drop in, inject my friends' children with sugar, and leave. I enjoy my freedom and won't let anyone guilt me into feeling unfulfilled or incomplete for choosing not to procreate or raise a child. Parenting comes in many forms, and it isn't a milestone or a box to check off by a certain age. It's a calling I never felt in my life.

If my mother paid attention to the needs I expressed and not the demands she wants to impose, she'd know that. Instead, she shifts her attention to Miles, whom she already insulted with her dig about "meaningful relationships."

Her violet evening gown sparkles under the canopy of twinkling lights. My mother is a beautiful woman with an ugly heart. "You'll have to forgive us, Miles. We're not used to Emma keeping a companion for longer than a month. She rarely commits to anything."

"I think she made it clear where her priorities are." Miles straightens and reaches for my hand. His thumb rolls over my knuckles. "My mother loves me unconditionally, so you'll have to forgive *me*. I'm not used to this."

Our corner of the room stills. Every other table carries on as the antipasto hits the white linen, unaware of the gauntlet Miles dropped. No one, not even my father, who found yet another reason to scurry away, has put my mother in her place. Carter, of all people, lifts his head from his phone to check if Miles still had his head on his shoulders. Blair is a fawn caught in headlights, unsure if it's safe to blink without permission.

I want to laugh my ass off. For once, Juliette Douglass is speechless, and it took Miles two sentences to do it.

"In the time we've shared, your daughter had her collection featured in fashion week, flew to Milan to meet with vendors, and is working hard to sustain her success." Miles directs his words to my mother. "I'm not a parent, nor do I want to be, but Emma's happiness should be your focus, not trying to contort her into a box or control her."

My heart cracks open, flooding warmth into pieces of me that were frozen over but are now regaining circulation. I'm not an emotional person, but in this moment, I want to feel every single feeling. Mainly gratitude for my friend.

"You're so unappreciative," Blair stammers from next to my mother, whose gaze is lost in the distance. "Your parents give you everything, and you throw it in their faces to chase after lust and gold."

Laughter tips my head back. This dinner might get me committed. "Says the person who followed me around work, begging to be part of one of my campaigns. Do us all a favor, Blair: stop *chasing* after other people's lives and live your own." I push my water glass to the middle of the table. "I'm not that thirsty, and you clearly need this more than me."

Miles's lips twitch over his drink.

"Where did I go wrong with you?" My mother laces her voice with every ounce of disdain she can muster. Her ice-cold stare is as pale as her ivory skin. I've always questioned if part of her regrets me. Now I know. "First your embarrassment of a profession, and now bringing this hoodlum—"

Her rant ends prematurely to a wave of gasps. Conversations stop as our private area goes pitch-black. Servers scramble to figure out the source of the power outage and why it only affects our section and not the entire restaurant.

"Let's go." Miles pulls me up and guides us through the landmine of tables. We reach the front of the building, and he signals for the valet to get our cars.

"You deal with that shit on the regular?" He glowers and turns away.

"What?"

"Them speaking to you wild as fuck!" Maple eyes darken into thunderclouds. Miles steps back to check his temper and scrubs a hand over his face. "Shit isn't cool, Em."

You think I don't know that?

My brows furrow. "I've dealt with that my whole life. It's nothing new or anything I can't handle—"

"Yourself." He nods. "You always got it and don't need anyone else."

I hesitate, baffled, trying understand Miles's reaction. The desire to protect me reflects in his eyes like a possession. "Why do you care so much?" My gaze flicks up to find him staring down at me.

The air shifts through a series of exploding currents prickling my skin. Miles is so close, I feel the heat of his body. Drops of moisture cling to his smooth mocha skin over brows once drawn downward and easing into the handsome face I've admired. My fingers yearn to touch him in a way I haven't before.

"I should go." The words release on their own, pulling me away from Miles, trying to understand the wedge I'm resecuring between us.

He searches my face in a fury of glances that land against my skin like forehead kisses. "Are you okay?" The rich timbre floats above a husky whisper.

My weak smile clings to the edges of my control. "I will be." I can give him that. "I've had enough excitement for one night and want to clear my head."

He unfastens his stare and releases a breath. "I understand. Just"—his gaze rakes over my face, pulling his brows back together—"text me at some point to let me know you're okay. Please."

"I can do that."

The valet arrives with my car. I slip in and speed off.

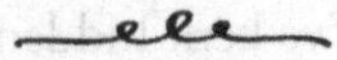

Aged wood groans as my five-inch, patent leather pumps amble over its weathered surface. Neon lights shine over quiet ripples succumbing to the ebbs and flows of the ocean.

I drove around lost in city lights and thoughts that sped too fast to catch until I found parking near the last place my head was clear enough to revel in the moment. I never intended to come back to the Santa Monica Pier, but this stretch of boardwalk is helping me process. It's close to ten, which means it's almost midnight in Austin. Too late to call Justice with the time difference.

She doesn't know about my arrangement with Miles that has him sleeping down the hall from me every night. I'm assuming he hasn't told Terrence given Justice hasn't flown over here to rip me a new one for keeping such a secret. I never meant to withhold it, but I also didn't imagine the sequence of events from the singles' retreat until now.

My feelings for Miles are changing. Every sense leaps to life in his presence—the way he cares for me as much as he brings my body pleasure. Miles stepped up for me tonight in a way no one ever has. I take care of myself, I always do, but a weight released when I wasn't the only one defending myself at the table. Miles became my knight, protecting my peace not out of obligation, but because he cares for me.

Sex anchored us, but we've transcended that now. Roots grew, stretching below the safety of the surface, and that scares me. The more time I spend around Miles, the more I lose my touch. I'm revealing parts of myself I've kept hidden for so long I forgot they existed, and it's all because of him.

My pointed-toe red bottoms stall at the figure down at the end of the pier double-fisting two hot dogs. Miles stops mid-bite when his eyes drift to me. That's another thing about us we can't seem to escape: chance run-ins.

"Are you stalking me?" Humor nestles itself in my voice.

Miles hikes a brow. "Who was here first? One of the interns in Zo's office mentioned a stand here with Japanese-inspired hot dogs. I was too busy to make it for lunch and figured now was good since we didn't have dinner." He chuckles to himself and looks away. "Can't stop running into you."

My smile spreads at his. "Guess not."

When I reach him, Miles hands me a hot dog with fried onions, teriyaki sauce, and Japanese mayo, and I devour it. We exchange nods between chews and settle in at the end of the pier to watch the moon dance over the ocean.

"You good, Em?" Miles's eyes drift to my profile from his perch against the railing. His forearms rest over the metal, placing his body at my eye level. Miles looks good in a suit, but his overcoat and beanie tipped to the side send me back to New York. Him waiting in the shadows, walking back to my suite, and thrusting us into an unforgettable affair.

Pleasure tightens my breath, and I release it with a sigh. "Yeah. Just embarrassed at this point."

He frowns. "Why?"

"I feel too old to let them affect me the way they do. When do I allow anyone else to act like that? I'm over it."

"So be done," Miles says matter-of-factly. "Stop holding on to things that no longer serve you. If that includes your family, you have other people who care about you. Justice. Her parents. T. Me."

I'm caught off guard by the vibrancy in his voice. "Me" is a velvet murmur that takes flight, set free from a place of longing.

Miles stands to his full height, the magnetic pull and lure of his musk moving me to him. His gaze travels over my face, searching for the mirror we hold for each other. When he finds it, he swallows, his gaze compelling me to hear his heart.

"You asked me earlier why I care," he says. "You're too incredible to deal with unnecessary bullshit from the people who should love you the most." His words are a stroke to my cheek, with adoration lighting his eyes.

I'm clueless as to what this means for our arrangement, but we'll worry about it tomorrow. I take Miles by the face and press my lips to his. "Thank you. Not because I need saving, but for showing up when it means the most."

"I got you, kitten. Them lights aren't coming back on until tomorrow." He pulls me to the corded muscles of his chest and kisses the top of my hair.

I stare for a beat before it sets in. "*You* did that?" My eyes damn near bulge from their sockets.

"Damn straight," he says with a grin. "Call me the hoodlum hacker. I'll turn off every light in the city before they disrespect you again in my presence."

We bust out laughing. I stumble back in my heels, grip my sides, and keel over with delayed snorts. It all makes sense why he was on his phone.

Pink stains my cheeks from my cackling. I blot the tears form the corners of my eyes and swallow. "Let's go home."

We hop in our cars and race off to Malibu.

Chapter 31

Miles

"This legislation tracker is legit. It paints a clear picture of all the states that need to step it up. Great job."

Paco, one of Zo's newest interns, shrugs off the compliments to dig his shoe into the carpet. "It was nothing."

"Nah, don't downplay what you did. Own that with your whole chest."

The kid is a buck thirty wet in a department store suit two sizes too big. His confidence hasn't hit its growth spurt yet, but we're working on it.

"Sorry, Mr. Walker."

And that.

"Do I look like Morgan Freeman? I told you to call me Miles." I'm all for respect, but I don't need to feel like a church elder whenever I step into the office. I'm old as fuck compared to the rest of Zo's LA office staff. They're all in their early twenties or thirties, except Paco, who's eighteen.

"My bad, Miles," he says under a crown of shaggy brown hair that needs a trim.

"I won't hold you. We'll go over regulations and areas to strengthen later. Take an early lunch if you want." Or scratch your nuts—I don't care.

"Okay, thanks." Paco waves and exits the conference room.

Zo has a job lined up for him once he graduates high school. The kid needs some guidance with his gear, but he's smart as hell. His full ride to a nearby college takes the pressure off his household to pay tuition and will have him on Capitol Hill in no time.

I call Zo for our first check-in of the week. He picks up on the second ring.

"*Bueno, bueno.*"

"Aye, what's good?" I adjust the tie I've been itching to take off since I came into the office.

"Same shit, different Monday," he chuckles. "Thanks for sending over Paco's database so quickly."

"The shit is good, right?" As my GG used to say, Paco is smart beyond his years.

"He reminds me of you."

I smack my lips. "Never once did you see me dressed for a tent revival at Bodie." The scholarships I got eased my pockets so I could keep my closet tight. Paco should wear what makes him comfortable, but we'll help him find a size that fits.

Zo laughs out loud but catches himself. "Leave the kid alone. We all have our starting point. Keep it up with the data and research. We might get a public hearing on the bill in the next few months."

The US lacks a comprehensive data protection law for consumers. Zo wants to fix that with his federal bill, and he has a real shot if things keep up he way they are. My consulting role isn't a requirement for its success, but it pushes his efforts to the next level. I'm not an in-office person, but being here isn't a pain in the ass yet. Zo has a good team.

"How was dinner on Friday?"

A pain in my ass. "I cut off the lights," I say, and Zo starts cackling. "You're a better man than me dealing with that bullshit. Em's family is on one."

My mama and GG never played about family, taking the chicken out of the freezer before they got home, or mac 'n cheese. They loved me and got me right when I needed it, always keeping my best interest at heart. It's wild that Emma grew up in such a toxic-ass environment. There's no question why she keeps her guard up, though it's a motherfucker to take down.

"John talks about his daughter all the time," Zo says. "It surprised me to see their family dynamic."

"He needs to come correct with her. Emma doesn't deserve that."

"Look at you, taking up for your lady." The grin in his tone is loud as hell.

"Don't start," I huff.

"Whatever you say, *carnal*. You've been quiet about leaving."

Trying not to think about it.

"Don't you have taxpayer money to waste?"

"There's something between you and Emma whether you take your head out your ass to see it or not. Life is too short to not go for it."

Zo ends the call, leaving me in an empty conference room with a lot on my mind. It's instinct at this point to defend Emma when it should be just about sex. I wanted to comfort her Friday after witnessing the uncensored version of her mama's mouth. Fucking with the electricity by hacking into the city grid was the only response outside of knocking Carter's ass out for not standing up for a woman he claims to care about. I went to the pier to calm my ass down with a hot dog and figure out why I cared to intervene.

I'm not a praying man but tossed up a request for a sign—and then came Emma on the other end of the pier. She wore the same look of confusion I did, but we met each other in the middle of the boardwalk and let the night take us.

Em saying *Let's go home* felt natural. Right. We fucked on every surface and corner of the house we share. The sex was phenomenal but tethered us to the connection that's veering us away from friends with benefits. We're sinking into a foundation neither of us wanted in the beginning, and we're putting up less of a fight as the days stretch across the calendar.

I only have a few weeks left in LA and never had any intention of leaving in a relationship. Yet, when the time comes, I'm not sure how I'll say goodbye.

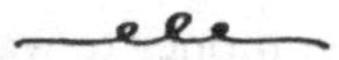

"Why do they eat yogurt in front of the Met?" Emma screws up her face through a bite of popcorn.

I shrug. "It's what Blair and The Minions do."

"The who?" She passes me the popcorn bowl.

"Minions." I point to Blair's homegirls.

"Oh." Em nods like she won't ask me fifty more questions.

We started watching *Gossip Girl* over the weekend and are trying to get through at least two episodes a night. Every now and then, she cracks a joke about me liking the show. The shit is entertaining. They'd have me under the jail if people so much as farted some of that bullshit my way. Emma pretends she doesn't like it, but I can tell she does.

Her mahogany hair whips over her shoulder when she spins toward me on the opposite side of the couch. "You thought I would be like Blair?" she asks around a mouthful of popcorn. "*Blair*?"

I chuckle at the daggers forming in her eyes and raise my hands. "All I know is, you were a senator's daughter who came from money. You kinda dress like an Upper East Si—" I dodge a pillow and laugh. "Now that I know you better, I would never."

She sips from her wineglass. "Well, if I'm Blair, you're Chuck."

"The fuck I am!" I almost catch a cramp rolling my neck her way. "His ass should've caught a few charges the first episode." I shake my head and shovel popcorn into my mouth. "Chuck Bass," I mumble to myself. "You saw the shit he wore to play ball on the court. Ain't no way."

A grin forms and tips Emma's head back with laughter. Her eyes are closed, her lips parted to release a full-hearted melody that squeezes my chest. Emma is beautiful in whatever she wears, but now—hair down and makeup-free in a fuzzy crop top and shorts set, cackling her ass off—she's the most gorgeous she's ever been. Completely free and relaxed.

Coming home to this is foreign, but it's the best Monday night I've had in a long time.

Home.

Emma wipes a tear and catches her breath. "You know I'm kidding. You're more like Malik Wright from *The Game*."

"That tracks," I nod. "Terrence is a ding-dong like Derwin, and Justice is Girl Melanie in the flesh." Shit, my dynamic with her is similar too. "You remind me of—"

"Do not say Tasha Mack."

"Nah, that's my mama—and that's nasty, since we fuck. I was going to say Dionne, Derwin's publicist. She made her own bread, was about her business, and took no shit off anybody."

"Good choice." Emma shifts back to watch *Gossip Girl*, but my eyes never leave her profile.

My mind wanders to an episode we starred in two years ago in the hallway of our best friends' house. What would life look like if we were different people, people who believed in relationships and opening up enough to try?

My phone chimes on the coffee table with a text. Emma catches the message when she hands it to me, flaring her nostrils as she looks away.

Brandice

> Hey, stranger. Interested in a nightcap this week?

"Big plans?" Her eyes flit to the phone in my hand.

I haven't seen Brandice since I left her to be with Emma. But we've texted once or twice, which is how she knows I'm in the area.

"This is the first time Brandice is reaching out to link up," I say. "She was the one I was with at the bar that night—"

Everything changed.

"Looks like you'll have a redo once you get home." Dare I say Emma looks pissed?

"Actually"—I peek at the incoming message—"Thursday. She'll be in LA for a shoot." My gaze swings from my phone to Emma and her tight jaw. "You'll crack a tooth mugging me that hard."

She squirms into her sectional and flicks her hair over her shoulder. "I'm not mugging anyone," she huffs.

"You look jealous, kitten."

"I'm not."

"Sure about that?" I don't know why I'm goading her to admit what we both haven't. The lines between us have blurred.

"One night open for other people," she says, reintroducing me to her guard, which is now back in place. "We agreed to it, and it's not a problem. I might meet up with someone myself." She returns to *Gossip Girl* and grabs the popcorn bowl.

Lying ass.

Em might think she's running things and keeping me at arm's length, but I see her—*all* of her. You have to earn her trust for her to feel comfortable enough to stay. That takes time, a gift I'm not used to giving.

Brandice is cool, a knockout with a tall, athletic build dipped in subtle curves. It's not a bad idea to get something going since she lives in New York and I'm out of here in less than a month. My usual reflex would be to get up with whoever holds my interest, but I'm not moving like I did in the past.

Brandice

> My shoot wraps at six. There's a dinner spot next to my hotel we can try.

I've been following Emma's lead since she made the rules. Going out with other people never came into play last week, but maybe she wants the flexibility to get down like we used to.

Emma shuts down the conversation when I ask again and reminds me we're not together. I don't know why the shit pisses me off, nor why I'm going back and forth like we *are* a couple. If she says she's cool, I'll take her at her word.

> I'm game.

Chapter 32

Emma

This week can munch on my ass. Monday was wall-to-wall meetings that made coming home to dinner and *Gossip Girl* a breath I was eager to exhale. Everything was perfect until the text that shifted the air, thickening it until it was no longer breathable.

I made a mess of my arrangement with Miles. I was in my feelings, not because he said yes to Brandice, but because of how hard I pushed him. I've tried hard to dodge how effortless it is to fall into each other. There's no safety net, which makes intimacy an act I'm avoiding at all costs, because the price is too high. I've had men hurt my feelings before, but no one I let close enough to break my heart.

Until him.

Two days blurred together. We barely texted Tuesday, when he was out with Zo's staff all day, or Wednesday, when I took an unexpected day trip to San Francisco for work. Now it's Thursday. The night Miles goes out with another woman.

He had no business glistening this morning in a sheen of sweat after his run. We caught each other in the kitchen. Him shirtless in compression leggings under basketball shorts with a beanie tipped to the side for no damn reason. Me cramping with a mess of curls plopped on my head and cotton pajamas that are comfortable but no match for the well-muscled body moving around my appliances with ease.

We sat at the marble island with a reusable water bottle and two coffee mugs between us. "I won't be back until later," he told me, his focus on the waves crashing in the distance. He wanted me to ask him not to go. To stay for me.

So I ripped the Band-Aid off by reverting back to my old self, where feelings lose their daggers because there are none.

Now, I have no dick, no contact, and am in the fight of my life with my period. Here I am, tucked underneath a heating pad with a bowl of ice cream and a horror movie while Miles is on his date with Brandice.

"Shit." My hand flies to cradle my head thanks to the brain freeze I caused chewing through a bite.

Miles's date started hours ago, at six. It's past eight—not that I'm paying attention. Day is already turning to night in a streak of sherbet pastels across the sky.

Him out with Brandice is a good thing. He's leaving in a few weeks, back to a reality that doesn't include me. We'll see each other in passing should our schedules overlap visiting Justice or Terrence. We'll hold the memories of us as a blip in time when we surrendered to unspoken passion we gave language. Then we'll move on, because that's who we are.

"Time to go upstairs." Lying on a sofa, pondering why opening myself up to Miles terrifies me more than *The Conjuring* is not how I'll spend the rest of the night. It's no secret how dates end, and I don't need to replay all the possibilities in my mind of a model taking my man out for a spin.

My man.

"He is not," I say to the home furnishings around me who are bearing witness to the demise of my common sense. Claiming Miles and talking to myself are grounds to call the therapist.

I lift my battered body from the couch, grab the remote, and scream at the figure on my balcony.

The glow from the television teases a wide torso and thick legs. The beach is private. No one should be on my deck. I have nothing to defend myself with outside of a spoon with remnants of rocky road ice cream on it and a heating pad.

Knuckles tap against the glass door. "It's me, Em," the baritone voice says.

I blow out a breath, grateful that I didn't manifest a killer from the movies I've been flipping through all night. "Why are you on the balcony?"

"Having a conversation through a door for the hell of it." He snickers. "I told you to let me install the one-way window film." His grin deflates when I step closer. "You sick?"

I scoff. *Typical.* "If you must know, it's my time of the month." I smooth out the fluffy gray robe Justice got me for my birthday. My mother would have a heart attack if she saw me looking like a JCPenney catalog, but comfort beats expensive sleepwear tonight. I feel and look like shit.

Miles takes in my bare feet and face. My hair is a thick, curly pineapple on top of my head. Unsexy to the max. He should get in his car and go back to wherever Brandice is. She's likely runway-ready and not engaged in hand-to-hand combat with a menstrual cycle.

"Will you open the door?" The rich timbre of his voice washes over me.

I step back to let him in and fail miserably at blinking away the confusion on my face at his presence. He's staying here but isn't supposed to be *here*.

Prying myself away from the attraction holding me in place is damn near impossible. It's overpowering, daring me to look Miles in his probing eyes. There's desire in them, but also affection.

He steps closer. "You in pain?"

"I'm uncomfortable," I admit, not that it isn't obvious.

He nods and toes off his shoes to place near the back door. He rinses out my empty ice cream pint, tosses it in the recycling, throws the spoon in the sink, and grabs the heating pad. I'm airborne before I process him moving us upstairs.

My eyes balloon as Miles carries me bridal style. "What are you doing?"

"What does it look like?"

I open my mouth to scold him until he walks through my bedroom and heads straight to the bathroom. I skimped on a large walk-in shower for space to have a freestanding tub.

Miles sits me on top of my double vanity. "Salts and bubbles?" I hold in a chuckle at his question and point below my feet. He drops to his haunches and pulls out a wire basket with my bath accessories, but not before his thumb skims up my calf. I shudder at his touch and watch in silence as he tests the water temperature, sprinkles salt, and squirts aromatherapy bath liquid.

Once it's ready, Miles scoops me off the counter and carries me to the bath like the distance is a trek and not a few feet. I unknot my robe and let it pool at my feet. His eyes smolder at the curves of my naked frame. I don't feel my best, but I look good. He steps out for me to discard my tampon and pulls the pouf next to the tub once I'm in.

The lights dim on command from the remote in his hand. I sink into the tub and moan at the first strokes of a sponge on my shoulders.

"This okay?"

My eyes flutter closed. I lift my chin to expose my collarbone, which he cleans. "Yes."

Miles bathes me and massages my aching muscles, sending me to heaven. He erased every pain and discomfort with hands that have yet to leave my body. His touch isn't sexual. It's soft, a steady pressure devoted to my well-being.

"Did you have a good time tonight with Brandice?"

He studies me. "It was alright." His fingers trail down my neck. "She's someone I can kick it with who's down for whatever."

I pull in a breath and nod. Of course they hit it off. It's neither surprising nor unexpected. Miles is fine to the fifth power. I don't know Brandice personally, but she's attractive. They're both single and free to do what they want, and a tryst is no different than our setup. Hell, she's in his backyard. Why not sample each other now?

My mind understands the logic, but my heart twists. As casual as I've been with partners, I don't want to share Miles. Not his time, and certainly not his body.

You need to tell him.

Feelings are territory I don't wander into intentionally. I've had them before, but never this strong or this quick. I thrive on being in charge, and a relationship has too many variables that leave you vulnerable. Does Miles feel the same, or is this kind of attention for whatever woman holds his interest?

"Do you take a lot of baths when you aren't feeling well?"

"That's the question you want to ask me?" A shadow of annoyance crosses Miles's face at my change in subject. His forearms flex over the lip of the tub as his gaze sharpens. He breaks his stare to reach for my foot. "I'm not into them, but my mama was. She had all types of lotions and shit from catalogs. She worked too much to use them, but I added to her collection with the money I made. Now I pay for her fancy spa visits."

My smile switches to a groan as his firm hands rub the arches in my foot with perfect pressure. "You're a good son."

"I try to be." He chuckles. "Deborah Walker will always have the best. I take care of mine."

He tugs on my other foot, exciting a fresh wave of pleasure. I sit back, my nipples peeking through the now bubble-free water and catching his eye. My breasts tingle under the stroke of his unwavering eye contact. "Feel better, kitten?"

I suck my lip between my teeth and damn near purr. This man is good with his hands. My body settles, every ache long gone. "Yes," I say through a moan that arches my back.

"You asked about Brandice," Miles says, his eyes still on me. "I could fuck her, but I don't want her. We both know she and anyone else are a distraction." My breath hitches at the deep circles he rubs into my thighs. "Aren't you tired?"

"Of?" My clit pulses.

"Fighting this. We are inevitable."

His mouth collides with mine. Miles kisses me like it's the first time his lips are discovering mine. He slips his tongue in my mouth and presses me against the hard shell of his chest. Water sloshes in the tub and sends a wave into his dress shirt he removes without pulling his lips from mine.

Miles strips off his clothes, and we head to the shower. He covers my body under the spray and backs me up against the white tile wall. I writhe beneath him as his hands brush my nipples, exploring the soft lines of my breasts. He bites my lower lip, and I whimper, digging my nails into the muscular flesh of his ass.

Miles makes me melt.

Under him.

On him.

For him.

He breaks us apart in a groan when I yank him to me by the dick. "Emma." His voice is hoarse, hanging on to the last thread of self-control. "You don't feel well, kitten."

I kiss his chest and tug again. "Put me to bed. Please." I suck his lip into my mouth and rub his tip up my slit. Any cramp I had put itself in time-out the minute his length came out to play.

Miles turns serious, his warm brown eyes fixed on me. "I missed you."

My fingertips sweep across his cheeks. "I missed you too."

He leans into my touch and grazes his lips over my hand. We share a smile before Miles steps out of the shower to put on one of the condoms we keep around the house. My legs wrap around him, and I quiver when he slowly enters me. Heat ripples under my skin as his hands cup my thighs to deliver cautious strokes.

"You okay, kitten?" Miles rolls his hips and thrusts me against the wall.

"*Yes.* Right there!" I tighten my arms around his neck to brace for the first orgasm charging through my body.

"Shit, Em," Miles says through gritted teeth, knocking at a spot that has my next orgasm on standby. He sucks on my neck and pistons into me. The slap of our skin carries over the steady hum of the shower. He lowers into a squat and pumps his hips to grind our pelvises together.

"Take every inch." He kisses my slack jaw and curls me to suck on a nipple.

Passion pinches through my veins. I don't remember how many times I cry out before I jerk in his arms. Miles's thrusts turn erratic. His legs widen, and I grip his ass as he drives home.

"*Fuck,*" he groans, swirling his hips to draw out the last of his release.

Miles drops a kiss onto my nose. I'm not ashamed when he picks me up and puts me on the countertop to take care of the condom. He returns with a washcloth and cleans us up.

I vaguely remember him towel-drying me. I put in a tampon, brush my teeth, and run through my nightly skincare routine on autopilot.

Then I pass out once my face hits the pillow.

He really did put me to bed.

Chapter 33

Miles

Emma has me by the dick—figuratively and literally. I'm trying to slip out of her bed to pee, but every time I do, her hand darts straight to my shit with a baseball-bat grip. I will myself not to brick up, but my man is ready to go again, as am I.

"I'll be back," I whisper to the side of her face, like she can hear me through all that snoring. Em wasn't kidding when she asked me to put her to bed. She's out, mouth open, sounding like a construction site. It's cute and oddly doesn't grate on my nerves.

I don't sleep with anyone, but tonight I'm breaking my rule, one of many I've already broken. Emma is different. She makes me want more time with her—even to listen to her engine-starting, snoring ass.

Brandice was never an option. I met her for one drink to make up for ditching her, told her goodnight, and watched a car take her wherever she went. We left it on a good note. Every woman I've dealt with was clear on what it was. I told myself until I get Emma out of my system, there won't be anyone else. But after last night, I don't want her out of my system. The truth is I never did.

Emma is my match. I felt it years ago but never understood the pull to her every time we were in the same vicinity. I avoided it as long as I could, not because I couldn't develop feelings for her, but because I wasn't sure if I could love her the way she needs to be loved.

Commitment doesn't come natural to me, but I want to try for her. I haven't got a fucking clue what I'm doing, but not having Emma close is no longer an option.

I tuck a loose curl behind her ear and smile at the thin line of drool falling from her plump lips. Emma would have a fit seeing herself so disheveled, but she's never looked more beautiful.

She keeps herself together, always in some high-end outfit with heels and her hair, nails, and toes done. Tonight was the most casual I'd seen her, in that fluffy-ass robe with Justice's name all over it. Now we're both naked underneath the covers, and it's a struggle to not imagine her in one of my shirts that would reach the tops of her thighs.

I've stared at her long enough to catch misdemeanors, so I remove her hand from my dick.

Does she feel the same way? Is she capable of opening her heart to let me in?

Emma cuddles against my chest, smearing drool. "Stay. Please." The request is so faint that I doubt she realizes what she mumbled in her sleep. When she nuzzles into my side, I wrap an arm around her, kiss her hair, and close my eyes.

We have a lot to figure out, about us and our self-imposed deadline. I care for Emma, and I don't want to hurt her. I'm also in over my head, swimming against a current of water I've never tread before.

Tonight, I hold her in my arms and get the best sleep of my life...after I slip away to pee.

Chapter 34

Emma

Miles cured my cramps and my weeklong dry spell coming home last night. I knew he would come back eventually—he's staying here—but our relationship took a turn with his confessions.

We are inevitable.

We broke a lot of my rules between him spending the night in my house—a first for anyone—and period sex. He said he never sleeps over, but he could have fooled me with the way he held me against his frame like he didn't want to lose me. I don't do cuddling and will always gravitate to the farthest end of someone else's bed.

That didn't happen last night. I wanted Miles, every part of him, and couldn't keep the surprise off my face when I woke up to find him watching me sleep. He stayed, with me and in my bed.

My pussy feels like it took a fastball in one of those batting cages. I fell asleep after our shower and the deep strokes that put me straight to bed. This morning was a different story. I checked Miles's back for batteries the way he harpooned me. He's not a one-minute man, but what I'd give to have time to recover from the horsepower between his legs. The towel we put down kept my bed from looking like a crime scene.

Muscles I didn't know existed ache. I pride myself on setting the pace in the bedroom, but I'm a sore loser with the biggest grin this morning.

Miles would helicopter his dick in my face if I admitted he bested me. My confession is unnecessary given the way I go right to sleep after one of our triathlon fucks, but it's the principle of the thing.

His phone buzzes for the third time in two minutes with the strength of my strongest vibrator. It's facedown to conceal whoever keeps calling at six a.m. on a Friday. The phone goes silent before it dances across the nightstand again.

Miles feels around for the device, slapping everything but the phone until he picks it up. "What?" The pillow smothering his face filters the bass in his tone but not the irritation.

"Miles Devonte' Walker! I know you didn't answer the phone like that!" comes from the other end of the line before it goes silent.

He sits straight up with wide eyes he rubs. "Shit," is all Miles says before his phone buzzes again. He hits a button on the screen and gives a tired smile on the video call. "Hey—"

"Don't *hey* me! I have half a mind to hop on a plane and see who you think you're talking to with that *what*."

Miles chuckles and scrubs a hand over his face. "Ma, chill. I'm almost forty."

"Boy, you ain't too old for me to go upside your head. Keep playing with me, and I'll stand on a chair to pop you good, with your tall ass. You still in bed?"

Miles scratches his goatee. "It's six a.m. over here. How are you?"

They update each other about their week. Miles and Terrence's mothers are gearing up for an eight-day cruise that leaves in a couple of days. It's cute how they make a tradition out of traveling now that their sons retired them.

I manage to pull on a silk cami from my nightstand drawer and am halfway out the bed before Miles's mother clears her throat.

"What is that?" she asks.

"Just Emma," Miles says casually, like us in the same bed is old news.

There's no way—

"Oh, can I speak to her?"

My eyes mushroom, and I dive under the covers. I flatten myself as much as humanly possible to blend in with the bedding, which is now shaking from Miles's laughter.

"How does she know?" I whisper to Miles through a crack between the duvet and pillowcase. Miles is in my bed, bare-chested. It doesn't take a detective to put two and two together. She's too far away to smell the sex in the air, but my post-coital glow would be a dead giveaway.

His hand reaches under the covers to squeeze me for reassurance, but he ends up stroking my breast. *Pervert.* "Ma, you can't put people on blast like that. Ease up."

I pop my head out from the duvet to glare at him. "How does she know?" I ask again, moving far away from the camera. To his credit, Miles keeps only himself in the frame.

"I'm sorry, baby. You talk about her on almost every call, and I haven't seen her since Terrence and Justice got married," she confesses.

"*Ma*, chill please," Miles groans.

"You talk about me?" I stare up at Miles waiting for him to reveal the punchline of his joke, but it never comes. Is he turning red?

"Sure does!" his mother chimes. "Swore me to secrecy and everything!" She backtracks at Miles's eye twitching. "Of course, I don't know the details, baby. That's between you two. My boy was excited to see you at the retreat and said he'd see you again in California. And that he was staying with you, but that's it. He's never spoken to me about a woman, and I've heard great things from Robin," she says about Terrence's mother. "You two get back to your business. Miles, don't be a stranger, hear?"

"Yes, ma'am," he grumbles.

"I'll call you later. Bye, Emma!"

"Goodbye!" I say.

After he hangs up, Miles stares off into the distance in a trance. He shakes his head, leans over, and kisses my forehead. "Morning, kitten." He can't look me in the eye, and I don't blame him. If my mother told my business like that, you'd never see my face again. He finally peeks at me and rolls his eyes at my grin. "Don't start."

"You like me, *Miles Devonte' Walker*?" I mimic the bass in his mother's voice and shriek when he dives for me.

"You got jokes now?" Miles's sinister smile deepens as he pulls down the duvet to tickle me. "Don't talk shit and run!"

My head flails from side to side to avoid bites to my neck. There's no use fighting Miles or the feelings we have for each other. "You told your mother about me?"

Miles winces, a flush deepening his mocha complexion. "Not like that. We don't have a weird relationship. I just"—he blows out a breath and steals a glance—"I don't know, Em. Fuck. I'm not good at this. You're in my life, and I didn't want to hide that shit. I mention you in passing, but the moments are adding up."

I pull him down and seal his lips to mine. He jerks at first but softens, curling me into his chest. Every doubt and fear drains to give way to the passion radiating from my core. An uncontrollable sensation bursts from within, freeing me. Fulfilling me.

His lips touch me like a whisper. "What am I going to do with you?"

"Don't let go."

I groan at the sting of my nipple between his fingers and gasp at a flick to the other.

Miles's dick hardens in my hands, which are wrapped around his length. "Damn, woman. *Shiiiiit*." He rises to straddle me and presses my breasts together to slide himself through. I curl my chin and let my tongue swipe his tip. He shudders, but not before he makes the *hoo-hoo* sound like the animated Pillsbury mascot. He hates it, but I love it.

I sit up, grab his firm ass, and swallow his dick to the back of my throat. It took some deep-breathing exercises, but I got it down—literally. My tongue twirls his crown before it makes long, ice-cream licks up his shaft.

"*Shit*, baby." Miles jerks. "Fuck." His hips move at a lazy pace until another giggle freezes his movement.

Miles becomes a statue when he's getting good head, and it doesn't stop me from bobbing and slobbing for him. I cup his balls, and he damn near sings.

That's another thing about giving him head: he doesn't last long—at least, not with me.

I slurp down his release and hollow my cheeks for a hard suck to pull out one last giggle.

"Want eggs?" Miles points to the skillet with the spatula, then swivels back to the stove at my head shake. The muscles in his back flex as he moves between two burners. He's shirtless in basketball shorts and slides after working out at the gym an hour after we finally got out of bed. The pheromones wafting from his body will attract every animal in heat within a ten-mile radius to scratch and sniff the Michael Jai White body on display.

Having a man cook breakfast isn't normal for me, but it's a sight I can get used to. He loads up his plate with eggs, tomatoes, sliced avocado, and turkey bacon and balances it and two coffee mugs as he joins me at my shiplap top dining table. Miles absorbs half of the upholstered banquette Justice and I found at a flea market in Pasadena and places his plate next to my parfait of mangoes and mixed berries.

He bows his head to say grace. Then he says, "What you got going on today?" His forearms dwarf the circular table as he forks his first bite.

"Meetings about a photo shoot in Big Sur next week for our collection," I say. "Going over mood boards with hair and makeup, pulling looks together to make sure they'll work on shoot day. Re-assessing the budget and finalizing the shot list."

Miles nods into a sip of coffee. "Okay, boss lady. Work your magic. When do you go up?"

"Wednesday. We'll do an extra style-out the day before the actual shoot on Friday."

He nods again and says, "I'll move some stuff around to make it," between chews.

I choke on my coffee. "You—what?"

"I go where my lady goes."

My lady.

It takes a long sip, but I swallow the compulsion to squeal and flip my hair. *Get it all the way together.* "I don't want to take you away from work," I say.

"It's nothing. Plus, I need more time with my lady. She missed me."

"Miles—" My breath skips as his thumbs rub circles into my thigh under the table.

He drags me over to him so our knees touch and flips up one of the edges of my silk robe. I'm bare underneath, giving him full access, and he takes advantage with an evil grin.

"I'll leave her alone for the rest of the week. Next week, though? It's on." I bite my lip at his thumb inching up higher. "Sucking on this pussy." He moves higher. "Stretching out this pussy." I moan. "I want my baby to sing for me."

I damn near convulse at the graze against my lips and fight gravity to keep my head from falling back. I'm a mess of nerves, from my period and him teasing the bundle below that's screaming for more of his attention.

Miles pins me with a teasing smile. "I'll show you some love too. Until then, it's me and Bernadette."

"Bernadette?" My question comes through a snort.

He lifts a shoulder like he's not about to say something reckless. "Me and my lady are about our *Good Times*."

We bust out laughing.

"You are a fool!" I throw a napkin, and he dodges it.

His charm is on full display, along with all of his teeth. Miles licks his thick lips. "I meant what I said, Em. We're inevitable. I want more time with you in the open, whenever you're comfortable. I want to try."

An odd twinge knots my stomach. It tells me to settle back into the facade I've perfected over the years. To not let anyone or anything penetrate my armor and wound me.

"I've never had a serious relationship, and I don't want to mess this up," I confess. "What we have could implode if this goes wrong."

There it is. All of my cards on the table.

Vulnerability has always been a weakness in my eyes. You expose yourself to unnecessary pain if your guard is down, but the loss of *not* taking a chance could cost a world of regret.

Miles's voice breaks through my thoughts. "This is a first for me too, baby. We're more than the arrangement we have. I know you feel it. It's okay to be scared. You're not alone in that. If you want this, we'll figure out the rest together. Distance. Justice. Terrence. We'll deal with it as it comes. You and me."

"You and me," I repeat.

I take his hand and make the leap.

Chapter 35
Miles

"Is there a reason you picked to meet at this bougie-ass place on a Saturday? They got breakfast in the hood, and I know they use seasoning."

I stand to dap up Rico and settle back into my seat. Here two seconds and already complaining. "How many street cameras do you see outside?" The fool strains to count in his head, furrowing his brows. "Exactly. We'd blend in, but there's too much surveillance."

The hood is already overpoliced, and with LAPD pushing to tap into private cameras to expand its network, linking up over there was a nonstarter.

"And what the hell is this?" Rico motions around the people who are funneling in and out of the restaurant. "We're two Black ass thumbs sticking out for no reason."

"Speak for yourself. The only one here who looks like a thumb is your ass." I snicker at the lack of effort it took to get him in his feelings. Face all scrunched up like he smells his upper lip. "Professional athletes live over here. If anyone stares, they're probably trying to figure out what team you're on."

Thousand Oaks is an affluent city outside of LA with mansions and expensive rides. Aside from a few lust-filled glances from women who are curious about our endurance for reasons other than fitness, no one is paying us any mind. Rico and I are both tall with athletic builds. His tracksuit and my joggers and long-sleeve tee make it look like we just came from practice, which feeds into an image I don't mind portraying for this meeting.

I don't conduct the type of discussion we're about to have over the phone or on the computer. A Thousand Oaks is a twenty-five-minute trek from the house, but the sunshine and promise of more money in the bank make up for it.

Right on cue, Kristie, our server, rushes to the table with an extra water and intrigue in her eyes at the curly-haired light-skinned guy sitting across from me. Rico favors the actor from *Good Girls* who is always talking crazy to Elizabeth. I had to tell her twice I wasn't Trevante, but she doesn't seem to give a damn the way she keeps licking her lips.

She takes our drink orders and damn near faints when Rio cracks a smile and winks, sending her scurrying off. We're in a corner booth, our backs to a faux moss wall and our eyes on the front door.

"You finish the traffic analysis?" Rico sips his water.

"I did. There were no red lights, so I gave it to Unc," I say.

"Good, good. Thanks for helping with the dry cleaning." Rico lowers his chin. "No spots. Still clean."

I'm helping Rico and his team assess if they were under surveillance. It's part of the services I provide on a case-by-case basis, fighting corruption and some of the most unimaginable shit. I'm what you call a floater, someone who pops in for clandestine operations, to gather intel and provide system support. Some rare missions require me in close proximity, to hack a database or monitor an area.

The company I run assists businesses with ethical hacking to evaluate security measures and provide data protection. But below the surface, I help expose shit by hacking the impenetrable without leaving a trace. I've scaled back on the projects I take on, but I always stay sharp.

Rico reached out about a job involving US officials dabbling in some scandalous activity. Oligarchs funneling millions into businesses and campaigns for their own personal gain are nothing new. The shit has real-life consequences that always end with a power grab and everyday people caught in the crossfire.

My client pushes his phone to the middle of the table and talks about some crazy ass goat video while I position an electronic device underneath to inject a signal to access data on his burner phone. Screen hacking requires no physical contact with the device so long as you keep the phone facedown. I'll get what I need without issue or anyone around us suspecting a thing.

I nod when the transfer is complete, ask Kristie to box up my orders, and tell Rico I'll swing by the dead drop on my way back to the East Coast in a few weeks.

I make it back to Emma an hour later. By one o'clock, I'm showered after a run up the beach and bored out of my fucking mind with the movie she's forcing me to watch. It's the second one since she scarfed down my steak and eggs I brought back. Imagine my surprise when the parfait I ordered her sat on the kitchen counter. I like fruit but ended up making turkey sausage, which I had to share, and more eggs.

Emma is living her best life, gnawing on a chocolate bar I picked up for her on the way home. She's in one of my hoodies she found rifling through my drawers. It's my favorite—go figure—a worn, light gray Bodie sweatshirt that hovers at the top of her thighs. She giggles at a scene, her laughter floating up and into my chest.

"How much longer until this is over?" I push down the big ass bun smacking me in the nose.

She peers up at me and rolls her eyes. "Not a Ryan Gosling fan?"

"I'm not a hater, but this movie is corny as shit."

"That would be hating, Miles," she laughs. "No need for jealousy."

I brush Emma's hair out of my face to stare down at her delusional ass. "I know you slipped on one of them rocks outside if you think that's true. I've been your mattress for the last two and a half hours and have a chest twice his size." I wiggle the pecs she's been using as pillows for a reminder.

If Terrence or Zo saw me on the couch debating Ryan Gosling movies, I wouldn't hear the end of it. This isn't normal behavior for me. Yet I didn't think twice about pulling a blanket out of the closet for a movie marathon at her request. I picked the last movie, *Inception*, which she fell asleep on. That little nap has her bouncy as hell now for a dude who deserves a drink to the face for these whack-ass pickup lines.

"Ain't nobody jealous of that man," I reiterate, making Emma laugh. "You've seen me in a suit. Shit, I sparkle."

She cracks up like it's the funniest shit she's ever heard. "And you wear it well." She pats my thigh and nestles into me when I pull her closer. I find myself cheesing more and more in her presence.

I'm learning more about her.

The way her nose crinkles when she's pissed off at a scene in a movie or one of her books.

The twitch in her lower lip when she pulls it between her teeth at a happy thought.

The unrestricted grin she gives me when I take her into my arms.

Em isn't big on showing emotion, which makes the glimpses she gives of herself a gift I'll keep fighting to earn.

Sex with Emma is on another level, but time with her without it is just as good. There's an ease about us that fits. I kept my word and haven't touched her while she's still on her period. We fill the time with food, sitcoms, and cheesy-ass romance movies when she isn't on her horror kick. We sit outside and watch the sunset too.

Yeah, I'm definitely not telling Zo or T about this.

I nibble on her ear and whisper, "You've seen better game."

Her snort morphs into laughter at my expense. "Please. You could never pull me when you opened your mouth. You're fine, but that game you speak of? Questionable."

"I know you're not talking shit in my clothes"—I tug on the sleeve—"after eating my breakfast. Now I know you have head trauma." I shake my head and huff. "Questionable game. Bernadette knows better."

Bernie better come on. I miss her, and Emma needs reminding that I'll have her facedown snoring into a pillow.

"Since you're so fly, give me my shit back."

Em's hands snap to my wrists like she could stop me from taking back my hoodie. She dives to the other end of the couch, or at least tries but doesn't make it. I snatch her up, grinning from ear to ear at her irresistible smile and damn audacity. She doesn't have an ounce of makeup on, and she's perfection.

Her moss-green eyes widen when I flick her off and tug a sleeve. "Wait! What about a bet?"

I fold my arms over my chest and smirk. I'm shirtless, and she's making it clear she needs dick with that gaze. "Let me hear it."

"You and me, tonight," she says, licking her lips. *My kitten needs attention.* "Meet me at Gio's at seven. We'll pretend not to know each other, and whoever buckles first has no game and has to do whatever the other says."

This is what happens when you watch corny-ass romance movies. But if I get a W with some role-playing sprinkled in, game fucking on.

I lean forward and drag my tongue over my teeth. "Don't come crying when I hurt your feelings."

Emma gets in my face so we're inches apart. "Tonight will be another reminder that you've met your match, Miles."

I might love this woman.

Chapter 36

Emma

I lost. Bad.

I didn't doubt that Miles's charm, and his arrogance would be at a hundred. Toying with him about his game was fun, but victory was in his maple gaze when he looked me over and accepted.

I was confident, but I'm also no fool. I spent a good two hours pleasuring myself to build up the endurance to resist him, to fortify my pussy at all costs. My victory dance was ready. I can't two-step to save my life, but I had everything in place.

The insulated structure for a private dining experience on the balcony.

Candles and champagne.

The spicy fried oysters he says are "good as shit."

My game was solid, guaranteed to force Miles to kneel before my five-inch heels. That was until he walked through the restaurant doors in an all-black suit that bent to the hard planes of his body and excited my senses.

Our eyes met in the mirror over the bar, where I waited for him as he crossed the dining room and stood next to me without uttering a word. The fragrance of our arousal coated the air between us. I faced him head-on and held back a grin as his gaze traveled over my face to the vegan leather dress painting my curves. I was at the home stretch until flashbacks of him between my legs broke my concentration.

It was a mistake to allow my eyes to slide down the outline of Miles's back muscles. The slow burn crawling up my throat was a warning I ignored as I got lost in his profile, which came with a fresh fade and a trimmed goatee.

My disloyal knees buckled when I stepped off the stool, earning a side-eye and a twisted smirk. "That was fast," was all Miles said before we went upstairs, fogged up the plastic panels, and ate like we didn't test the table's weight limits.

Today's walk of shame has a new meaning, and it comes with a side of salami.

I swallow what's left of my pride and smile at Michelle. "Hello. I'm here to see Mr. Walker," I tell the receptionist.

The phone on her desk rings. "One moment, please," she says, turning her attention to the call. Her brown eyes widen, and she bites her lips to keep from laughing. *Miles*. "Here." She passes me the phone.

"You'll kiss my ass twice before I say it," I blurt. Michelle is no stranger to our banter.

Miles's laughter tickles my cheeks, but I remain strong. "So testy on a Monday. What's wrong with saying you're here to see a winner?" His arrogant smile shines through the silence.

Michelle pretends she's not eavesdropping and mindlessly clicks her computer mouse. You only need a day around Miles to get caught up in his foolery. Said fool has me on the phone when he's feet away.

I hang up, tell Michelle goodbye, and set off down the hall. Miles is in the conference room, leaning back in a chair next to the door. His arms are behind his head too big for his body with that stupid smirk.

"Put those claws away, kitten, and let me look at you."

He chuckles at my sigh. I adjust my jeans and the picnic basket hanging off my arm. As the loser, I have to do what he wants. I expected some type of sexual favor, but he surprised me with his in-office lunch request. Why I'm in jeans when he's in a white button-down shirt and olive slacks remains a mystery. I paired my denim with an ivory blouse and a turquoise blazer that matches my heels. Other than naked, this is as dressed down as I'll get.

I walk into the conference room and drop the basket in front of him. Miles pulls me to his lap when I try to sit next to him. I protest but still at the squeeze to my waist.

"Chill," he says against my pendant earring. His voice is low, deeper than the playful tone that goaded me on the phone at the reception desk.

Miles reaches around me and opens the basket, adjusting me off his now erect penis. I roll my hips and smile at his groan. "Don't think I won't fuck you in this conference room. Emma!" He nips at my neck.

His playfulness is a breath of fresh air. It's been fun to let loose and relax, something I rarely do without a vacation. I enjoy pleasure, but until him it was all work and no play unless I needed a sexual fix.

A grape presses to my lips. I suck it into my mouth, along with the fingers holding it. Miles hisses but continues to feed me. He never misses a moment to touch me or take care of me. I've done the latter myself for so long, but I enjoy the attention.

"What's going on in that head of yours?" Miles switches to a cube of mozzarella cheese, and I swallow.

"Thinking I could get used to this." I accept another piece.

Miles pulls me closer. "Funny. I was thinking the same thing," he says. He studies me before he shakes away the thought. "You should make more bets you know you'll lose." A grin spreads across his face at my slap to his chest.

I could get lost staring at his face. The way his eyes soften in appraisal and his lips seek mine. I'm not into intimate displays of affection, but I give in to the overwhelming sensation of kissing him.

Miles's lips are gentle. He anchors me to him, submitting to my tongue exploring his mouth. He's a tornado force who savors when I take the lead. I lean into the hardness of his chest and drag my nails against the textured hairs of his goatee.

He sucks on my top lip before rolling his tongue over my bottom one. "Feel better?"

I kiss his smile with my own. My "yes" comes with a sigh—not from the blocks of meetings that will take up today and tomorrow until my team heads to Big Sur on Wednesday. My stress level is at an all-time high, but it's manageable because of the man who demanded a picnic lunch to pull me out of the chaos awaiting me back at the office.

"Good." His thumb rubs circles into the small of my back, taking away tension with every swipe. I need an appointment with my masseuse but have no time. Miles pecks my cheek and holds me when I burrow against the side of his neck. "I gotta handle a few things, but I'll meet you up there Wednesday night. Don't forget to pack more than heels."

How I let him talk me into camping while we're up there is a testament to the magic between his legs. He's charming, but charisma alone isn't enough for me to rough it in the wilderness or wherever he'll have us staying.

Laughter rumbles up his throat at my groan. "Relax, bougie," he says in a tone to taunt my disinterest in bug spray and peeing outside. "It's part of the resort. I'mma take care of your ass and have you skipping home the same way you're about to skip back to your office."

Miles stands with me in his arms, bridal style. My hands wrap around his neck. "Where are we going?"

The answer is the private bathroom in the conference room. He closes the door and places me on top of the granite countertop. His hands are firm on either side of me as he presses his nose into my neck.

"I can feed you this meat or eat my dessert. Which one do you want? You're not going back to work stressed either way."

My lips find his. Miles leans into my center and rocks his hips, teasing me through my jeans. I reach for his belt, grab his length straining against his pants, and pull out a groan at my squeeze. "Take care of me, please."

Miles's expression softens at my request. Yes, I want dick delivery, but I also want...more.

His inhale is sharp, his voice now a murmur. "I always will, kitten."

I lose track of how many times I come. We leave the bathroom, him with a satisfied smirk and me with frizzy hair, a cramp in my leg, and shaky knees. He and I finish lunch in the conference room before I head back to my office, grinning and with a pep in my step.

My eyes cross in front of my computer screen. It's a fight to stay awake and not pack up and leave the office early.

"You have a call on line two."

"Thank you, Mal," I say to the intercom and hit the button to take it. "This is Emma."

"Is that happiness I detect?"

Any hint of a smile drains from my face at Carter's voice. It's smooth with hints of a pretentious asshole waiting to piss me off.

"Unless you want to place a sizable order for lace panties, why are you on my phone?"

"Testy." A deep rumble of laughter vibrates down the line. "How are you, Emma?"

"Busy."

"That you are. We haven't seen you at any of John's campaign events."

We.

Carter is so far up my family's ass it's a wonder they don't claim him as a dependent. I was over the Illuminati known as DC politics when I was little, and now I'm a grown-ass woman.

I wasted so much time trying to be worthy of my family when they never deserved my time. I have people in my life who love me and support me without conditions. I don't have to chase their affection in order to feel it.

I am enough. It's a full sentence and requires no explanation.

"I didn't feel like it," I say honestly. "My life is here, in California. I am not a prop to use for political polls. My father signed up to sing and dance for campaign donors. I didn't."

"Would your act of defiance have something to do with Miles?"

That gets my attention and hikes a brow. "Are you spying on me?"

"Looking out for you. One of us has to since you're not thinking clearly." Carter sighs. "There's something not right about him, and I'm not talking about Newark. I asked around, and it appears your friend has been cozy around Washington."

My face twists. "And? Is that a crime?" Miles has clients all over the place. That he has some in DC isn't surprising, given he has a home in the area.

A home you haven't seen.

"He's dangerous, Em. His résumé appears clean, but he's hiding something."

I don't know the people Miles associates with. I always thought military or mafia, which might be true. But he never served and doesn't have any ties to organized crime as far as I know. The secrecy around his job has been a running joke—like Tommy from *Martin*. I never asked questions because I never needed to know.

Does that mean he's dangerous?

"You'll find anything to make an issue out of, Carter. Miles is working with a congressperson; he can't be that much of a threat. Just admit you're jealous. I never brought anyone around my family, and it pisses you off he's still here."

Carter takes a long pause before he speaks. "What better way to bring down a politician than to date a senator's daughter? I'm not saying he's a spy or anything ridiculous like that, but he's too cozy with people around us and clearly does more than assist with malware. You say you've known him for years. Why did he choose to pursue something with you now? It doesn't add up, and I want to keep this family safe.

"You're important to me, Emma. You were always mine. Had I known you were ready to entertain something more, I would've made my move. We're perfect. You know it, and so do I."

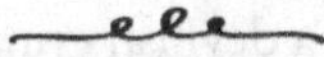

Salt air from the ocean tangles with the strands of my loose bun blowing in the wind on the silent ride home.

Carter's call was short. Just long enough for him to toss a grenade and clear the area. Miles and I open ourselves up the more time we spend together, but there are still missing pieces to his life, answers to lots of questions I haven't asked.

I pull into my garage, next to the Audi Miles is renting while he's here. We haven't discussed when he'll return to the East Coast. Having someone in my space required an adjustment—to his stomping, loud conversations, and morning shits too foul for words—but I haven't felt the urge to dismember him...yet.

He's actually a good housemate. He's clean, keeps the fridge stocked, and weaves into my life without wanting to overpower it. His thumbprint around my home becomes more visible each day.

Like the stainless-steel grill and hammock on my balcony that weren't there this morning.

"Hey, baby!"

Miles waves with tongs in his hand. He's barefoot in a pair of low-hung sweats, a black apron I don't own covering his shirtless chest. The muscles in his biceps flex as he flips whatever is on the grill.

"Hope you're hungry," he says, his full attention on the dinner he's making. His gaze flicks to me and my open mouth with a chuckle. "I can feed you this dick the way you got that jaw ready."

I kick off my heels with a devilish grin. "And have the neighbors hear your giggle?" Miles groans at my hand over his sweats to grip his length. "I'm down if you are." I lick his ear and bite.

He shudders but bumps me away with his ass. I fall into an outdoor chair with a cackle and my hands up. "We don't speak about that outside of the house," he grits through his teeth, the tongs pointed at me. "It only happens with you and that voodoo mouth."

"*Voodoo mouth*?" I bust out laughing.

Miles adjusts himself and looks around for signs of nosy neighbors. "Exactly what I said. Got me sounding like a cartoon character."

"You know you like this mouth."

He grunts, waves me off, and turns back to the grill. "Take your ignorant ass back inside so I can feed you. Dinner is almost done."

I set the table, and we eat the steak and lobster Miles grilled to perfection along with some vegetables. Two hours later, we're in the hammock to watch the sunset. This thing takes up most of the deck space, but it's cozy.

I'm nestled against his warm chest, now free of the apron he tossed in the laundry basket.

"Thank you for cooking," I say up to the stars. He really outdid himself.

"You're welcome, kitten." His long fingers knead the achy muscles in my shoulders. "I'll rub you down after we get upstairs."

That's another thing about living together: free massages. Yes, they come with his penis at the end, but who's complaining about that? Since we confessed how we feel about each other, Miles sleeps with me. He converted his old bedroom into a home office with more screens than Best Buy and has the flexibility to do it because of his job.

His job.

My phone call Carter pops into my head. His conspiracy theories are out there, but that doesn't mean questions are off the table.

"Carter called today," I say haphazardly, running my fingers through his.

"Oh really? What did Crispin want?"

I snicker at his nickname. "To warn me about you. He says you're dangerous and wonders why you're in my life now when we've known each other so long."

Miles tenses under me, the hardness of his muscles protruding into my skin. "And what do you think?" His tone is low and even.

"I told him he was full of it."

"No, Em. I don't give a damn what you said to him. I want to know what you think."

My brows knit. "Are you mad?"

"I'm waiting for you to answer my question."

It's impossible to face him without risking us flipping over. I can't see the disappointment on Miles's face, but I hear it in his voice. We sit in silence, him wondering what more he needs to do to earn my trust and me searching for the right words.

"You're not with me to uncover any government secrets." Miles is sleeping with the wrong person if he wants to take down Washington. "But it would be nice to know more about what you do."

I want to hold every piece of himself he stores away.

Miles adjusts me on his chest. He's quiet, but the tension in his muscles eases. "I can't get into details, but I take contracts to help gather information. I don't assist extremists or entities that want to harm everyday people in pursuit of power. My data security company is my main focus. I won't lie to you and say I don't like to hack, but I'm not out here breaking into the Pentagon or some shit."

The hammock picks up a steady sway. "And politicians?"

Miles snorts. "I work with people trying to tip the scales toward equity, not those who want a power grab. Zo is the main politician I've worked with, and he'll be the last. I have no interest in them otherwise."

"Yet you're with a senator's daughter." Amusement shines in my tone.

Miles drops a kiss on my knuckles. "I'm with a woman who takes no shit and changes everything she touches for the better. You're my quiet place, Em. Every day I spend with you feels like home."

I let my tears fall freely. Miles isn't the only one changing. He exposes me in ways that should frighten me but don't. "You are my safe space."

We try to make love in the hammock but bust our ass in the process. I knew jeans were trouble.

Chapter 37

Miles

Emma Douglass has me in my feelings. Witnessing her in her element fills me with pride.

I got to Big Sur last night and have been with her since the 7:00 a.m. call time. There are all types of Pinterest-looking boards with fabrics and pictures of models in lingerie. I don't know what half of this shit is—computers and codes are my thing—but with all the moving parts at play, Olivia Pope has this shoot handled.

Em moves between her team of photographers, makeup artists, hairstylists, and assistants, working with the models she handpicked for the photo shoot. The weather held up, the threat of storm clouds clearing for sunshine. Models pose under an outdoor shower in front of a backdrop of mountains and redwoods.

Everything is running according to her shoot plan, and when it doesn't, she pulls an ace out of one of the jumpsuit pockets clinging to her hips.

I almost had to wrestle Emma to get food in her stomach with all the back-and-forth she's doing.

In the resort spa for interior shots.

Outside on the balcony to capture the Pacific Ocean.

We compromised: she'd take the plate of vegetables and hummus I made for her if I kept my ass quiet in the corner. Fine with me. All the food she ordered for the shoot is over here anyway.

Did I try to trip her at some point to fall into these shoes I brought? Damn right, I did. Only a person itching for corns and blisters stays in heels all day, but, as Emma told me with her full chest, "This isn't my first rodeo, Miles. I'll be damned if I pair sneakers with this outfit."

Like Chucks don't go with high fashion.

"She'll learn today," I mumble to myself, shaking my head at Emma's stubbornness.

Usually my mama is the only woman whose well-being registers as a priority. Justice gets an honorable mention, but she's not on the same level as Emma. The instinct to check on her is second nature at this point. I never cared about a woman I fucked until I pressed Emma into the wall of her New York City hotel room and released fifteen years' worth of pent-up desire.

The truth is, I've cared about Emma before we became intimate. I always have, even when I denied it.

Eleven hours pass until the photo shoot wraps. The sun, once searing the shit out the back of my neck through the window, now illuminates the crew who's packing up the ballroom. Three empty trays I had zero shame eating are next to my laptops on the table. I stretch out my arms and legs and ignore the models stealing glances. I look good in a Henley and denim, but I only have eyes for the woman currently lost in laughter next to a photographer.

Em covers her exhaustion with a smile. *I'm* tired from watching her, but you'd never know she walked a marathon the way her eyes crinkle. Her thick curls are in a knotted bun, and her navy jumpsuit has no wrinkle in sight. My tagging along has to do with soaking up as much time together as possible, but also ensuring she takes care of herself.

She air-kisses the last photographer and walks over. Gravity pulls at her smile, and her ass drops into a lounge chair. She kicks her feet up onto a metal seat across from me. "Done," she says with a heavy sigh.

"You handled your business today. Great job, kitten." I close my laptops and reach for my bag under the table.

Emma sinks further into the upholstered seat, minutes from falling asleep, and smiles. "Thanks for coming."

"Told you I wouldn't miss it."

Her voice softens. "I appreciate it, Miles."

Our eyes lock with the same sensation that heats my chest whenever I'm near her. Images of a wide smile playing across her lips and her cheeks flushed from orgasms hurtle through my mind. We've only scratched the surface together. There's more, and I'm looking forward to the journey.

"Let's go, kitten." I sling my bag over my shoulder and move around the table to pull her up. Her ass really might fall asleep here. She squeals when I toss her over my shoulder. "There's a hot bath with your name on it."

My dick surges to life at her groan and takes three reminders to calm the hell down. She had a full day and needs to rest.

Dick will also put her to sleep.

True.

Her body relaxes into mine. "A bed sounds amazing."

"And it will be, just not the one you booked. I had your bags moved. Did you pack your camping boots like I asked?"

"You know damn well I don't own any."

I shrug. "Shame."

Emma tenses when I walk us away from the main elevators in the lobby to the back door. It's a trek on a trail to our campsite, but this isn't the first time I had her ass this close to my face.

"Miles?"

"Emma?"

"Why are we leaving the hotel?"

"I told you I pitched a tent," I say, sidestepping large stones beside the wooden staircase. "You thought it was a game? Hey! Keep them claws out my ass." The slap to her butt shocks her enough to stop digging those talons into my skin. She knows I like that shit and will fuck around and have us falling down these stairs.

Her frustration would be adorable if I weren't dodging dick shots from her legs, which are kicking in protest. "I'm not roughing it!"

"Chill. I'mma get you relaxed. You'll be howling at the moon in no time."

"Kitten?"

"Hmm?"

"You're purring again."

"Shut up!" I chuckle at the elbow to my ribs that's nothing more than a love tap and pour more hot water into the tub. Steam rises, a warm contrast to the chill in the night air.

I wasn't kidding when I told Emma we were staying outside.

The resort she chose has a campground for glamping, or whatever you call the bells and whistles to make tents and washing your ass in the wilderness a memorable experience. I wasted no time reserving the area near the small lake so we could claim it as our own. We have the restrooms to ourselves and can hit up the restaurants if we want.

It's a peaceful spot. Where else can you fuck in the woods in a king-size bed without interruption? We tried sex on the balcony back in Malibu, but between her nosy-ass neighbors and the Whitney Houston high notes Emma hits every time I knock her spot, we'd catch a charge before either of us came.

She has full range to scream down our outdoor suite, and she has the last two nights. With all of her hollering and snoring, she scared off Yogi Bear and his squad.

I rolled the dice that Emma wouldn't give me the finger and march her fine ass back to the hotel for an en-suite bathroom and four walls. She surprised me by agreeing to stay in the tent and has been up under me and on top ever since.

My arms snake around her, stroking her soft skin now glowing in the moonlight. Her back is to my chest, and our eyes are cast up to the stars dotting the sky above the trees.

Emma's sigh is deep and peaceful without her work schedule weighing her down. She threads our fingers together and kisses my forearm. "Do you camp often?"

"No, but I like traveling to places where it's quiet." I kiss the top of her shoulder and rest back against the tub. "Nothing beats unplugging."

"Because of work," she says, grasping my need to step away. Emma knows about my data security work but not the specifics of the private contracts I take. Those details are need-to-know.

"I don't stay in the same place for long. Once I'm done, I'm done," I say. The homes I do have are simply to collect mail. "Do you travel outside of work?"

"My annual girls' trip with Jay. Other than that, it's Milan and Paris every year for my job, and I'm not complaining."

"Are you living or keeping busy? I know it well," I say. "Jumping from one project to the next. My mama got sick years back, which had me reevaluating how I was moving. Life is too damn short to not enjoy it."

Emma tips her head back to look at me. "What did you do?"

"I moved like I had a battery pack in my back that I never recharged. My mama kept up the same hustle since I was a kid and found herself in the hospital. I took care of all that once I got established and promised her the world after I retired her. Deborah Walker has enough stamps on her passport to put me to shame." I chuckle. "She forced me to slow my ass down, so that's what I did."

Being with Emma is opening me up to truths I never expected to reveal. I like sharing with her and want to create more memories with her.

"It's sweet how much your mother cares." Emma swallows to school her expression and shifts the conversation away from the topic of family. "Where do you like to go?"

"Iceland. Namibia. Ecuador. Minnesota."

"Minnesota?" Her eyes snap to mine, the promise of a teasing smile now spreading across her mouth.

I nuzzle into her neck and nip at her silky skin. "The forests are dope. There's good stargazing."

"Aren't you full of surprises?" The edges of her lips curl.

I'm an enigma to her, not because she judges how I grew up or carry myself. Emma calls me on my bullshit but sees beyond my layers, straight to my core. I want to expose more of myself so that she feels safe enough to do the same.

I reach for the pail to add more hot water. "Japan is nice. I take two weeks in the Kyushu region at least once a year. There's a beautiful coastline, hot springs, and historic sites."

"Sounds amazing."

"You could come with me...if you want."

Damn if this woman doesn't have me nervous as fuck. I never felt the need for a travel partner but struggle not to make space for Emma in my life. I want new adventures with her, for her stubborn ass to give me lip before we christen a room. I want more of Emma's smiles and the chance to see where life takes us. I want to earn more pieces to the puzzle that creates her masterpiece.

I'm about to tell her never mind to save face, but then she turns around and kisses the outline of my mouth. "I'd love to," she whispers.

Our lips collide on a moan as she rolls into my erection. The tent I rented is spacious enough to fit a tub for the two of us, and Emma proves it when she pushes me into her warmth. Sex without condoms was a mutual decision on this trip, and it's new territory for us. We never shared such intimacy with other partners—one of our many firsts together.

Emma slips her tongue into my mouth and grinds her hips. "You're not tired of me yet?" Her body shudders as my fingers knead her nipples.

"I'd follow you to the ends of the earth, kitten."

With a kiss to her collarbone, I cage her to me and sink further into her. Emma matches me thrust for thrust. We cry out under the moon, scaring the shit out of every forest animal from here to the Pacific Ocean.

Chapter 38

Emma

"Did I not tell you he'd be a disappointment?"

I tear my eyes away from the fabric swatches quilting my desk and look up at Carter, who's fixing a cuff link in the doorway. He grins at my glare. "A phone call would've saved you the time it took to fly out here and be ignored."

"Maybe if I treated you like an afterthought, I'd get more of your time."

Carter's barb reaches its target and detonates. He pushes off the doorframe to waltz into my office in a wheat suit tailored to his frame. He flew thousands of miles to rub salt in my wound; he doesn't care if it stings.

Miles left. Vanished without a trace or a forwarding address.

It's a reality I'm still wrapping my head around.

The extended stay in Big Sur was everything I never knew I wanted. Miles and I tethered ourselves to hidden parts of us we rarely uncover. I saw him. I bared myself to him.

Miles was a man at peace, comfortable in nature's white noise, the sound he uses as an escape. Behind his unapologetic mouth and wild antics is a person with a gentleness reserved for a few.

It was perfect until it wasn't.

We returned to Malibu Sunday and made love on the beach underneath the stars the entire night. By Monday, it was back to our routines. He left for work, or so I thought, and never came back. His computers, clothes, rental car. All gone. One day of silence stretched into four.

Now every moment of last weekend is on repeat as I look for a clue to explain how Miles could walk out of my life so easily after everything we shared. Something distracted him when he checked his computer before bed on Sunday, but nothing set off alarms or explained his abrupt departure.

Clearly, I was wrong.

I don't stay in the same place for long. Once I'm done, I'm done.

The confession doesn't match the parts of himself he showed me.

I want to try, Em.

It's okay to be scared. You're not alone...

Nothing makes sense.

"Did he have the courtesy to tell you he was leaving?" Carter steps closer, his head tilted, his ego ready to press another button. "Imagine my surprise when I stopped by Carrillo's office and heard Miles ended his contract early. Gone without a trace." His brows narrow, hardening his eyes into stone. "Did you get bored of him, or was it the other way around?"

Miles never attempted to reach out. My calls went straight to voicemail, an automated reminder of my place in his life.

Proof he was okay came as a slap to the face when I called Lorenzo's office and he informed me Miles left the state. Lorenzo and I don't speak, but he's close with Miles and knows we're together.

The twist of the dagger was sharp and steady when I heard the question he didn't ask: why didn't I know?

Miles plays games, but I never thought my heart would be one.

Carter isn't fooling anybody with his pop-in. He never came to see me alone and waited until Miles left California to play in my face. My father gets updates on Lorenzo's data security bill in Washington. The only time he wasn't too busy to make the trip to California was when it involved donors. He's yet to ask for updates about my relationship, let alone my well-being. My father didn't send Carter here, which doesn't answer why he's in my office. On a day when Congress is in session, no less.

He's here with his condescending tone. For what? To get the upper hand, see me worn down in despair?

I sit back in my chair, wrinkle-free and without a hair out of place.

My blouse and slacks: designer.

My stilettos: imported.

My smirk at Carter's inability to read me: priceless.

"What's your play, Carter?" I'm confused about why Miles left, but I'm not broken. I will pick myself up. I always do.

"You're a smart girl, Emma, or so I thought?" His tongue drags over his lips. "You've wasted enough time impersonating a relationship. He cleans up well, but he isn't your type—nor does he belong in the same vicinity as this family, as he's proved."

My gaze roams over the lean muscles spread out in my office chair. Carter has aged well over the years. He's still handsome and keeps himself tailored to perfection. But he's a coward at his core.

"You wait until Miles leaves California to express your affection while gloating at my expense? I'm surprised my father took you off the leash and let you fly over. Do us both a favor and get out."

Carter stands and buttons his suit jacket with a glower. "You'll regret this, Em. I'll give you time to lick your wounds and come to your senses. We're tied together, whether you like it or not."

I'm not my mother nor my cousin. Power and the pursuit of fortune don't move me, least of all into a relationship. If I ever choose to tie myself to one person for the rest of my life, it will be for love. I've felt its absence for so long, but I know a crumb is not a meal.

"Remember your responsibilities, Emma. John expects his only daughter by his side before the primaries. You've blown off this family long enough." He steps closer and brushes his thumb over my jaw. His voice lowers. "Don't shut me out. I have everything you need."

My skin prickles at Carter's hand on my neck. The grip isn't tight but forces a sharp inhale at his lips hovering over my mouth. "Stop fighting us," he whispers.

"I've had enough of people telling me what to do." I peel his hand off, step back, and nod to the door. "Goodbye, Carter. Go find the real reason you flew here."

Something is at play. I'm not sure what, but Carter's charm can't mask it. I trust my gut.

The same gut that told you to trust Miles?

Carter is right about one thing: Miles is a disappointment I never saw coming. I don't want to believe it, but I won't make the same mistake twice.

Chapter 39

Miles

"The surveillance network is compromised," I confirm with a final keystroke. "You have twenty minutes."

"Copy," Shane says through his earpiece, ready to lead his team of three through the compound layout we studied down to the bolts.

"You've got eyes in the air, and I'm monitoring all CCTV." I scan the three computers in front of me for potential threats. "Stay on this frequency."

Days of gathering intelligence and a mock search gave us the window we needed to attempt this rescue mission. The compound has many safeguards in place that pulled me into the field to gain access from a closer distance. It was a risk that took days, but I spoofed the network undetected.

I'm pissed that I had to drop everything without notice, but I owed a favor, and I always pay up. I didn't know how bad the situation was until we were in the air, halfway out of the country.

I need my head clear for this one. Lives depend on my focus, and I can't afford any errors or distractions. The outside world fades beyond my screens. It has to until it's safe.

"Miles, clear to go?" Shane asks.

"Clear."

Chapter 40

Emma

Two more weeks pass in a haze of work projects and deadlines. Each day without Miles is one in which I curse myself for caring about him. The silence and disregard cut deep, but I'm numb to the bullshit.

"Are you sure the dates work?"

"Yes, for the fourth time." I force out a laugh.

Terrence exhales a strangled sigh. "Good—okay. I know you're busy, but I won't say no to help with the flowers and decorations. I don't want to mess this up."

I swirl soy sauce over my lunch platter. "It will be perfect." It's hard not to smile at the lengths he'll go to for my friend.

The man about to hyperventilate on the other end of the phone is planning a vow renewal for him and Justice. Terrence has been stressed for a good month about getting everyone together at a secluded Mexican resort, and he's fighting for his life to keep from freaking out at the hint of something going left. His and Justice's mothers are already praying hard, which should tell you how determined Terrence is to put a smile on his wife's face.

Justice ugly cries at pet commercials and will fall out like she's at a funeral once this comes together. She deserves someone who loves her this hard.

So do you.

I force away the thought. What's a fairy tale for some is a nightmare for others. "I'll call the resort to square away the ceremony decorations," I say, to his relief. "You approved the reception menu, so we're good for now."

"Thank you, Em. I don't know what I'd do without you."

"Just keep loving my friend."

"Always." The smile in Terrence's voice is loud and clear. "Hey, we might be heading over your way before June. There's a contract I need to wrap up with a client in LA. Jay is gonna take off a couple of weeks for you two to cut up and do whatever it is you do."

"Our business," I say around a bite of sashimi. Bottomless mimosa brunches and getting Justice to shop someplace other than Target are the most of our good trouble. God knows I need my friend here.

Terrence laughs. "Just don't do anything that requires me to put up bail money. Miles and I—"

"Miles?" At the sound of the name I refused to utter the last twenty-three days, a thin strip of tuna falls from my chopsticks, splashing sauce over the documents on my glass desk. "Shit."

"You okay over there?"

"Yeah," I mutter in a fury, scrubbing my desk to death. "What's going on?"

"There's a potential investor for the training facility out there. It's been a bitch getting on his radar, but we'll make it work."

Terrence is hard at work creating a space for athletes and production companies to use in Austin. He'll work close to home and expand his services without traveling around the clock. Time away from Justice was an issue in their marriage, so he took steps to show her she's a priority.

I guess that's what people do when they're in love. Something I clearly know nothing about.

"You'll get it. Let me know if I can help." Terrence is a good guy who deserves everything that's coming his way.

Miles and I will have to face each other at the vow renewal, if not sooner, but that doesn't mean I can't ignore his existence until then. One disappearance was enough to show me where I stand. The armor I always keep firmly in place will be ready.

"Did it come?"

"Yeah." I lift the to-go bag up to the phone. "Yours?"

Justice smiles and holds hers up.

Everyone deserves a best friend who forces a girls' night and doesn't take no for an answer. Justice called after work and told me to clear my evening of nonexistent plans the second I said, hello. We ordered each other's favorite food for the video call that, hopefully, does not include a hot seat with my name on it.

"You want to tell me what's wrong now or after we eat?" *Spoke too soon.* Justice pulls out her Greek chicken platter from the bag and positions the phone across from her on the dining room table. "I know, Em."

Know what?

I follow her lead with my shrimp dish, careful to sidestep any hints about my love life or lack thereof. "What makes you think something is wrong?" I uncork a bottle of merlot to wash down the lie and shrug. "Carter came by the office," I offer.

Justice frowns, and it's a fight to not laugh at how much she looks like a Mowry twin without trying. "Isn't Congress in session?"

"It is."

"Weird, but that's not it. You've been distant. We haven't spoken much in the last couple weeks, and I want to make sure you're okay."

Am I okay?

Relief eases through my chest on an exhale. She doesn't know about Terrence's vow renewal.

"Em."

"Yes?" I snap my attention back to Justice, whose brow furrows. She eyes me with a questioning gaze, pleading for me to open up. I bite my lip and look away. I miss him, and I hate that I do.

"Don't hide yourself, Em." I drop my lashes to conceal any hurt that might be visible from fourteen hundred miles away. "You're my best friend, my sister. I know when something bothers you, and it's okay to name it. I won't push you, but I'm here if you need me. Okay?"

A stab of guilt buries itself in my chest. I hate keeping this secret from her. Justice and I tell each other everything. The good, the bad, the messy. I wanted to talk to her about Miles, but the potential of what could go wrong kept me from shouting it from the rooftops. Everything is different now that the very thing I fought to keep from exploding in face shattered my heart in the process.

"I fell for someone." My voice cuts through the silence. "He opened my eyes and heart to a world around me I ignored for a long time."

"Sounds beautiful, Em."

I brush away a tear and push out the words before my voice breaks. "Everything I thought I'd lose letting him in, I gained. Until he proved me wrong." *Damn you, Miles.* The torment I've tried to ignore the last few weeks overwhelms me. "I don't want to feel this anymore, Jay."

He left me when I told him not to let go.

Tears spill down my cheeks. I don't sob. I don't scream. The pain weighs me down, and I don't know how to carry it.

Justice weathers the storm with me. She doesn't speak or tell me it's okay. She doesn't make promises about it working out or finding someone better. She sits with me, the same way I sat with her.

I wipe my face, embarrassed I allowed myself to feel for him.

"There's a red-eye I can take to reach you by morning," Justice says.

"Not necessary, but thank you. Can you do me a favor?"

"Anything."

"I need to forget and don't want to bring this up again." The only way to do that is to revert to how I was before Miles and close the door to my heart for good. Love and forevers are for people like Justice, not me. "Promise me we'll never talk about this again, and pretend I never brought it up. I need that, Jay."

She considers my request, her internal conflict about prying for more to heal the wound evident in her stare. "Okay. I promise," she says through a watery smile she holds up for me. "Movie time. *Jason Takes Manhattan*?"

My favorite.

"I love you, Jay."

"Love you more."

Chapter 41

Emma

I sank to a new low that happens to be at the bottom of a martini glass. I chase down the burn with a gulp of vodka.

Heads are on a swivel around the hotel bar, homing in on the red strapless dress that's hugging me in all the right places. My lips, which are the same color, twitch over the rim of the glass before I take another sip and swivel toward my unexpected companion tonight, a move I'll regret in the morning.

"You're still a bitch."

Madison chokes into her champagne and coughs around the French 75 that no doubt went down the wrong pipe. She waves off the dig with her gel manicure. "I'm a good person once you get to know me!"

"You mean once you get past your thirsty ways of running after married men? You're lucky you didn't catch a beatdown."

Her mouth falls open, but she quickly closes it. "You're right." She nods, her hazel eyes slow to reach mine. "You don't fight, do you?"

"Do I look like I'd chance ruining this dress over you?" My face screws into a scowl. The floral appliqué and corset bodice curving around my body is for the red carpet, not jail.

Tonight's field trip off my couch did not include this on the itinerary. A photographer I know is in town for a shoot at this hotel. Harmless, right? Take one guess who the stylist was.

Is no other stylist available in Los Angeles?

Madison and I stayed on opposite sides of the bar during the post-shoot get-together. Over time, people filtered out, sliding us closer until eventually we were three chairs apart. I had no issue ignoring her, but she wore me down. There is only so much "Emma, can we please talk?" and "I'm sorry, I made a mistake" I can take. Madison was on the verge of tears, like that would move me to empathy. Who the hell cries at a bar on a Friday night, anyway?

I should leave, but the only thing waiting for me at home is a half-pint of ice cream and reminders that I'm alone. The goalpost moves whenever I try to turn off feelings I never wanted in the first place. I hate the way they claw at my chest with surgical precision. I'm not supposed to care, but I can't find my way back to the time in my life when I didn't. It wasn't that long ago, but now it feels like a lifetime away.

"I appreciate your willingness to sit with me."

"Like I had a choice."

Kojo already doubled down on Madison as his go-to stylist, which is a Rambo-sized knife to the back if you ask me. I barely stomach people on a good day, and any serving size of Madison Monroe will fuck up my gut. Kojo swears there's more to her than deception and showing her ass, but I don't believe it. I'll only reconsider if Justice decides to extend Madison an olive branch one day. Her heart is too big for her own good. Until then, left on read.

Eric Dane behind the bar keeps giving me dirty looks for not reacting to her endless loop of apologies. If only he knew the full story of her fuckery. The only thing keeping my ass planted on this barstool are his handcrafted cocktails, but he should direct that silver fox stare at the person on her apology tour.

Yet you're still here.

Like I said, I unlocked a new low. Peeling myself away from *Gossip Girl* is a shame I carry. Leaving my house was essential tonight, for my sanity and to reduce the snack bits falling into the cracks of my sofa.

Go to the hotel, have a few drinks, get a room, and get over Miles. That was the plan. Not sit next to Madison, who's still pouting.

"Are you done cursing me out in your head?" She twists her barstool my way, her black bodycon dress touching her knees.

"Give me a few more minutes."

Madison's heart-shaped lips twist into a frown. At least she looks remorseful when she lets out a breath. "I really was a bitch."

"Was?"

Her eyes drop to her glass. "I can't apologize enough for my behavior at the singles' retreat. Before." She shakes her head. "I was in a bad place and wanted...there's no excuse for how I treated Justice. I never expected Terrence to leave her while they were together."

"You're not that delusional." I toss a glance her way. "Maybe you are."

Denying Madison's beauty is a waste of time. Her thick lips, thighs, and wavy, cinnamon-brown hair would knock a celibate person unconscious. The couple of months Madison and Terrence had in college were never a match for the fifteen years he spent adoring Justice.

I level her with a look I hope sears into her forehead so she remembers it the next time she gets the urge to be awful. "Consider yourself lucky the day you have a friend who becomes your sister. Justice is everything good in this world. She didn't deserve the games you played. I've made my fair share of mess, but there are lows too low for even me. You can't fix past mistakes, but you can glow up, grow up, and move forward."

Madison's eyes fill with tears. "Trust me when I say I feel awful. I've done a lot of soul-searching since the retreat. Work I should've done years ago. I'm not a person who plots and schemes to take people down. You're right"—she sniffles—"Justice didn't deserve that. I clung to the wrong things for jaded reasons, misinterpreted someone's kindness. Seeing Terrence at a retreat I booked on a whim felt like a sign we'd get another chance at love. My right hand was itching—"

"An itch is the reason you acted a mess?" I fix my would-be nemesis with a stare.

"It's something we believe back home," Madison says. "If your right hand is itchy, an old acquaintance will cross your path."

"What about the left?" I must be buzzed if I'm entertaining tales about unlotioned hands.

A high-arched brow lifts. "Money is on the way."

We clink glasses.

Do I like Madison? No.

Am I all femmes of the world securing the bag? Absolutely.

But that doesn't absolve Madison of her behavior.

My smile fades. "No more games. Our paths might cross, but you have to make up for the harm you caused."

"Yes, I do." She swipes at a tear. "Can I ask you something?"

"You haven't been quiet yet." I put my glass on the bar and motion for her to get it over with, all while avoiding another look from the bartender.

"Are you okay?" She hesitates. "You don't owe me anything—least of all an explanation—but I recognize it. The mask to make everything look like it's fine when it's not." Her grip tightens around her champagne flute. "I wore it for many years. Still do."

Melodies from the instrumental music piping through hidden speakers fill the silence. A large mirror spanning the length of the honey-wood bar reflects low-hung chandeliers, top-shelf bottles, and two women who might have more than their pasts in common.

"When is feeling ignored enough?" The question slips out before I can catch it and tuck it away.

"Let me know once you find out," she says in a ragged whisper laced with tension.

"You know what? Fuck this." I throw both hands up and earn the bartender's attention once again. His eyebrows sharpen at my outburst. "I don't want to feel this anymore." My hands motion around my heart, which has caused more pain than pleasure.

Not true, and you know it.

"No more!" Madison jumps at the bass in my voice but nods with doe eyes and zero understanding.

The more I replay Miles's leaving, the more pissed I am for caring. His dick is exceptional, but I lived without it before and I'll do it again.

The TED Talk for my spirit, sponsored by the good people at vodka, is a masterclass on empowerment and not letting a penis of any kind fuck you over.

"No more tears."

"No more!" Confidence trickles into Madison's voice. "He left me for another work emergency, like I'm luggage he can put down and pick up whenever he wants. I'm sick of it."

"That's right!" Also, what? "Who—"

She lifts her chin and guzzles the rest of her champagne cocktail. "If he wanted me, he would come and get me, but I'm not waiting around to find out."

Now I'm lost. All of that groveling tonight did not come with CliffsNotes about a man and work emergencies.

"Rewind," I say. "What man are you talking about?" A lover, obviously, but I want details with no crumbs spared.

I'm so caught up trying to piece it together that I miss Madison's parted lips and her brows reaching for her hairline.

"Miles," Madison whispers.

My stomach drops and takes my jaw with it. Please God, no. "*Miles*?"

"Miles," she repeats, her wide eyes locked over my shoulder.

A figure from behind casts a shadow over me. Musk invades my senses. I fight the attraction, but weeks apart will have you acting out of character.

I shut my eyes, unable to contend with the reality that the man I let insert himself into my life only to leave me in shambles is here. The hairs on the back of my neck prickle as he leans over, his mouth an inch from my ear.

"Kitten."

Chapter 42

Miles

Emma has ten seconds before I peel her off the barstool and toss her over my shoulder. We wouldn't make it far with the way my restraint is about to snap after seeing her for the first time in weeks. I fucking missed her. She hasn't faced me yet, but Madison's shock is enough for the both of them based on her jaw on the floor. I'll ask Emma why they're together later. After I get her home.

She finally spins around on her barstool. I step back at her snarl, not because she frightens me, but to keep my nuts a safe distance from her knees. They're oiled and ready to go.

"Save it." Emma dismisses me with a hand and stands, pulling the see-through dress squeezing her hips for dear life back into place. "Are you good?" The question is to Madison, who's still trying to piece together why I'm here.

She blinks twice before answering. "Yes." Then she clears her throat, her gaze bouncing between me and Emma. "I have a room here. Did you two—"

"Not your business," Emma says matter-of-factly. "You and I aren't there yet, but this was nice." Her half smile hints at the possibility of mending...I don't know what.

"It was. See you around. Miles." Madison's light eyes sweep over me until she groans at her phone, which is ringing on the bar counter. She sighs and picks it up. "What excuse is there today, Preston? You'll always make it up to me."

The billionaire dude from the retreat?

Madison scurries off in a huff, leaving me to rush after Emma, who's already walking out the door.

Emma speed walks through the tiled hotel foyer, determined to get to the valet and dip like I don't know where she lives. It's a home we've shared for weeks, one I want to make permanent. If she'll let me.

I slow my pace to take in the ass she'll tell me to kiss once her silent treatment eases. If only she knew I dreamt of holding her in my arms for the last twenty-five days.

A pimple-faced valet attendant rushes out of the booth and trips over himself to get to her. I rub my fingers over my lower lip and chuckle at how quickly he folds in her orbit. Emma's lure is without a doubt addictive. You'd think she was royalty with all the bowing this guy does. He's yet to get her car, doing everything he can to hold her attention.

I post up inside the glass doors, never once taking my eyes off the woman pacing up and down the sidewalk, ignoring me.

Her Mercedes pulls up, and Em hops in and speeds off. I give my ticket to the kid still watching her taillights and am in my rental car minutes later.

——◆——

Sizing up the wide door I'll have to scale to get to Emma's townhouse is a matter of physics once I arrive at her spot. I usually go through the garage but decide the front gate is better. To my surprise, the private entry is unlocked. The floodlights I installed months ago announce my presence. I test my luck with the front door. I still know the code but won't enter if it's locked. Sure enough, the long handle opens, and I take a cautious step into the foyer.

It never crossed my mind that Emma might shoot my ass, but the unlocked doors and dimmed recessed lights are some don type shit. Would she snipe me and tell the police I broke in, or bury me alive on the beach? The latter requires manual labor, but I wouldn't put it past her.

I inhale deep, toe off my sneakers, and head past the illuminated path from the kitchen to the living area. Emma stands before floor-to-ceiling glass doors that reflect the dark ocean under the moon.

A month and a twelve-hour flight to Los Angeles gave me time to think about the mess I got myself in. I'm good with numbers and codes but come up short with Emma. I never stayed in one place or spent so much time with one person, but I couldn't reach her fast enough and never thought twice about going to her. I fucked up, but I want to fix it.

I left on autopilot. I packed up all my shit and bounced, the same way I've done countless times. I never had someone at home and had to get my head in a zone. I just hope it didn't cost me everything.

Emma refuses to look at me through the glass. She deserves more than a bullshit excuse about why I left so abruptly. I had to wait until it was safe.

One step turns into several until I'm inches from her. She stiffens at my touch but remains stoic. "I'm sorry I broke your trust." I murmur the apology into the air, which is scented with the perfume I've missed for too long.

Emma's lack of reaction is a double-edged sword. She's not one for affection or displaying it. But her indifference toward me now hints at detachment beyond repair.

"I'm sorry, baby." I look for signs I didn't lose her for good. I may not know what this is, but now that she's in my life, I can't imagine another day without her.

Emma's resolve doesn't falter when I hold her. The front of my jeans grazes the back of her dress. Goosebumps form as my hands glide down her bare arms, and I pull her into my center. My apology is still a chant that's yet to crack her armor.

A mix of fire and ice whirls in Emma's glare when she faces me. She's silent but shoves at my chest over and over, building force with every push.

I let her move us, never taking my eyes off her or repeating the same apology. Emma can push me into next morning if she wants. Shit, my ass deserves worse. Her fire means there's still a chance.

"I didn't want to leave, kitten. Please let me explain."

My brows knit when her hand finds my belt. I step back. "Em, wh—"

"Shh." Her fingers press to my lips as her other hand makes work of the leather. She yanks the buckle free and palms my dick, pounding at the zipper. *Fuck*. She's on her tiptoes to reach my ear. "We'll fuck until it's time for you to leave. Once Monday comes, we'll go back to not speaking to each other."

Ice hardens around the words she hurls at me. They're the same ones I told her at the singles' retreat a lifetime ago. I shake my head at her determination to reduce what we have to a weekend-long fuck.

The shit hurts.

"No." I shake my head again and push away her hand. If she keeps staring at me like that, I'll bust in my jeans, but I want her to hear me out.

"*No?*" Emma hikes a brow. "If you're not here to share your dick, leave the way you came."

"I'm trying to apologize, Emma. I'm sorry. What we have—"

"Is over," she snaps. "Your time in California is up. You made that clear when you packed up and left without telling me." She huffs out a laugh. "You had the decency to tell Lorezno but not me. Everything you said to me was a lie, because if you *truly* cared, you wouldn't have done that." Her chin lifts. "Sex without strings is what we do best, and that's all I'm willing to offer."

"Em."

"Take it or leave it, Miles." Hurt dances in eyes once full of light, now embers.

I walk Emma across the room until her back hits the glass. Her breath hitches at my palms slamming onto either side of her. I don't want to scare her, but I will be damned if she doesn't think there's more between us. "Zo got a one-line text in the middle of the night before I left," I whisper to her profile. She refuses to look at me. "I wanted to call you to explain, but everything went to shit, and I had to focus so I could get back to you."

"One month, Miles." Emma's reply is low, tormented. "No phone call or email. Only silence. I let you in, into my home and my he—" She swallows hard to bite back tears I'll kiss away. "I have enough people in my life who walk in and out of it whenever they need something from me. I wanted you to be different. I wanted you not to let go."

Shards twist and tug through my heart at having caused Emma pain. "You're my home, Em." I kiss her eyelids as they flutter shut. "What we have is real. I care, baby. I fucked up, but I can explain if you let me. Don't shut me out."

"Why? You did."

My lungs give way to the anguish tightening my chest. I'm a problem solver, but I don't know how to fix this. *I* am the problem, a risk Emma took that proved to be a threat. My throat works to pull in air at the thought of losing her. I *can't* lose her.

"Please." Her voice retreats to a hushed whisper, trembling her lips apart when I press into her and claim her mouth.

I pull her closer, devouring her with my tongue and every word I've yet to tell her. Emma moans into my mouth as my fingers slip under her dress, coaxing her to dig her nails into waves that are now a tiny fro after my weeks away. Her hands drift to my beard and tug. I lift her to wrap her legs around me and revel in the touch of her thighs.

I'm lightheaded from all the blood in my body rushing from one head to the other. I want to fuck her until she can't walk straight, but I want her trust and heart more. "I'm not them, baby," I say against her mouth about every person who disappointed her. I'm not a perfect man by any stretch of the imagination, but I want to fix this.

We make it upstairs to her bedroom and stumble onto her mattress in a tangle of clothes and moans. I kiss every part of her as she straddles me.

"You have no fucking idea how much I missed you, kitten." I grab the back of her neck and pull until our heartbeats touch.

"Condom," she says and breaks us apart. I frown at her reaching into her nightstand for a foil wrapper but say nothing. She shreds the last sign of her trust with her teeth, sheaths me, and rises to her knees. I widen my legs and shiver as her pussy sucks me into her heat. "Fuck, baby."

My grip on Emma's ass tightens, and I spread to encourage the hips she rolls in a circular motion. I'm seconds from busting a nut but squeeze her tight and pump into her anyway.

"Miles!" Emma's eyes roll to the back of her head, exposing the soft column of her neck, which I suck.

It's a fight to steady our pace. The thought of being away so long and ruining what we had has me on my feet. I angle Emma's body, scoop my hands over her shoulders, and drive home.

She is my home.

Sounds of our skin slapping and her cries fill the room. My quads will be on fire tomorrow but fuck if I care. Emma unravels, her hard, pink caramel tips bounding inches from my face. Her stomach tenses as she squirms in my arms.

"Look at me." I kiss her chin and quicken my pace, grinding my hips to hit her spot.

Pleasure floods Emma's moss-green eyes. Her lips part on a pant, her legs quivering and her chest heaving.

It's on the tip of my tongue.

Three words.

Eight letters.

I've never told a woman I loved her. It took a minute to figure out that's what this is, but I love Emma, and I don't want to go back to a time when that wasn't my reality.

My balls rise as I slow to lazy strokes, dragging them out to rub her clit over my pelvis. Emma shudders, a sign that her next orgasm will put her to bed as I release inside the condom. I come so long my toes strangle the area rug. She slides a hand down my cheek dotted with sweat but says nothing.

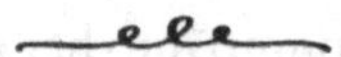

"A distress message came in from an old colleague. He had to rescue someone he loves. I packed fast and was out before dawn to catch a chartered flight. Zo got a three-word text that said I wasn't coming back to the office. But I was coming back for you, kitten."

I brush a strand of mahogany hair from Emma's face, careful not to wake her. She passed out before she could give me the silent treatment or another excuse as to why we can't make this work. I didn't get a chance to explain where I was, but I need to get it off my chest.

"Shit went down when I got there. I had to switch gears and focus, which was hard because I kept thinking about you. Every time I tried to call, something popped off that needed my attention. Time escaped me, Em, but you never did. I should've tried harder, and for that I'm sorry.

"I caught a tail and spent the last week and a half moving between countries to shake it. There's protection in place for my mama if shit goes south, but not for you. Not yet. But I'll never let anything touch you and will keep you safe. That's why I had to stay away."

Light from the window scatters over the ceiling and onto Emma's back. "I never meant to hurt you or leave the way I did. I moved out of habit, and it won't happen again." My fingers trace the curves of her shoulders. "You were never just a fuck, kitten. I care too much for you."

In the weeks we've spent together, I fought every reason I had to walk away. But the more we filled our days with each other, the more those reasons faded into the background. Distance has kept us miles apart, but Emma is an enigma I want to explore.

"I told you I want more, Em," I whisper next to her. "That wasn't a lie. I want your time. I want to earn your heart. Will you let me love you? I can't promise I won't fuck up, but I want to try. I am trying."

I kiss Emma and pull the covers up to her neck. She'll tell me to leave tomorrow, but I won't have her thinking I left her again by sneaking out.

She mumbles something and reaches for me.

"I'm here, kitten."

Chapter 43

Emma

"That's all for today. Great work, everyone." I shuffle papers into a folder to the chorus of conference room chairs sliding over marble.

My team's chatter fills our workspace as people cluster to discuss lunch options while filtering out of the glass-framed room bathed in natural sunlight. I'm never one to work through lunch and always wrap all weekly meetings before eleven thirty.

Rêve is taking off, earning features in coveted fashion magazines. Sales have tripled since our fashion week Rustin collaboration. Everyone, from editors to social media influencers, has the name on their lips, a testament to the people who were just gathered in this room. This is my seventh campaign at Soie, and I'm damn proud.

Gianna charges down the hall. A bouquet of long-stem red roses covers her face and the top half of her pinstripe jumpsuit. Her single-strap nude heels stop inches from my pointed-toe pumps.

"Glad I caught you," she says in a muffled huff behind at least forty roses. "These came for you." She passes me the oversized bouquet.

"Thanks. Is there a card?" Trying to squint to find one in the wilderness of petals is pointless.

She peeks around the mega bush and tosses the golden ponytail stretching down her back. Gianna's features settle into a light scowl. She's not upset, but the sharp lines of her cheekbones make a resting bitch face that's perfect for the camera.

"Didn't see one," she says. "Mal said you have a visitor in your office. Maybe they came from him."

Him?

My lips wiggle into a smile Gianna spots. "Ah."

"Ah, what?" I move the bouquet to my hip.

"That." She points a blush-colored nail at my neck, which is turning the same hue. "You serve many looks in this office, but shy isn't one of them. Who is he?"

Persistent as hell.

"I don't know what you're talking about." Miles never visited me at my office. I always came to Lorenzo's for appearances in case word got back to my father. The people at Soie are vultures and will latch on to any bit of gossip. I like my tea, but I don't need to be on the menu.

Gianna's grin widens. "Uh-huh. Mal said he's fine," she says, looking over the roses I'm squeezing like a lifeline. "You've had a glow about you recently. Now I know why." She winks and struts off.

Miles and I talked about why he left—when I was awake to process everything—but I'm still cautious. What's to stop him from leaving like that again? He promises he won't, but I already took a gamble on opening up once, and I'm not sure I'll survive the heartache again.

Miles has made his presence known since the day he barged back into my life weeks ago.

My eyes dart around the hallway like I'm holding company secrets in my arms and not the fragrant bouquet of flowers. The verdict is still the same: red roses are too cliché for my taste, but these are beautiful. Thick, too, like the man waiting in my office.

Miles and I could hit any daily exercise goal with the amount of sex we have. It's a good thing I live next to the ocean. Without the loud waves crashing into rocks, my neighbors would think my house was a murder home with all the screaming. He stays with me in my bed until I fall asleep before he goes back to his old room to give me the space I asked for.

But no matter how hard I fight him, he refuses to leave.

"Miles." I casually walk past him leaning on the front of my desk with folded arms and legs crossed at the ankles. He's in fitted black slacks and a cream-colored polo, looking like Jake from State Farm if he powerlifted.

He glances over his shoulder before standing to his full height, which is overbearing for my office. "Hello to you too, kitten." The pet name skates up the pulse point in my neck, beating an SOS message to my vagina. *Calm the hell down*. There is no good reason to be breathing this hard.

I keep my back to Miles and my focus on these big-ass flowers. Did he send them?

"I wanted to see about lunch."

"Not necessary, but thank you." I sit in my office chair and crane my neck to reach his eyes. "Anything else?"

This dance we do always ends the same way. He asks me out, and I say no in an attempt to keep our relationship strictly about sex. It's safer at the surface, but the pull to the deep is hard to fight.

"Nice flowers." He nods to the bouquet I stuffed between framed campaign shots. "Secret admirer?"

My brows dip. "You didn't send them?"

The corner of his mouth tips into a cocky grin that's too fine for any man to wield. Miles is back to his fresh fade and lined goatee. His beard and mini fro were giving Zyair Malloy from *Mea Culpa*, which had me singing Kelly Rowland melodies to the ceiling.

My nipples harden at the memory.

Focus.

"You might not think I pay attention, but I do, kitten." Miles rounds the desk, pinning me between his thick frame. I steady my breathing at the musk permeating off of him with confidence and a leveled gaze to match.

"Red roses aren't you, baby. They're mass-produced and easily accessible. You're one of a kind. There are some thorns, but I'll prick my finger every time to hold you." His lip sinks between his teeth at the drool no doubt pooling from my mouth. "You also hate red roses like you do Valentine's Day."

He remembered.

Staying away from Miles is next to impossible. He's determined to get us back to where we were before he left. His apology was on repeat until I told him I'm willing to take it slow. While I understand the unusual circumstance he was in, I'm not equipped to be with someone who can leave for weeks at the drop of a hat.

Once was enough. I already have too many people in my life who think they can pick me up and discard me whenever they like.

"I'll see you tonight?" I ignore his frown and lift my chin. He knows what I'm willing to give.

Miles stares but nods. "I'll be there." He stuffs his hands into his pockets and leaves.

I order lunch and check emails. My cell rings—Carter.

It's been weeks since he showed up at my office. I have no energy for a sparring match today.

"Carter," I sigh.

"Do you like them?"

"Like what?"

"The flowers," he says in an oddly calm tone.

I lean back in my seat and swivel toward the grand floral display. "You sent them?"

Humor laces his tone. "Don't act surprised, Em. I wanted to do something nice to apologize. I'd like to start over."

"Start over."

"Back to the way things were, when we weren't arguing. We work, Emma. I'd wish you'd see it."

What in the entire hell is happening?

"Is someone sick, Carter? Did you find out you have three days to live?"

Carter's bark of laughter has me looking at my cell sideways. I can count on two fingers the number of times I've heard him laugh when it wasn't at someone else's expense. "Give us a chance, Emma. A real one. With Miles gone—"

"He's not gone."

Our conversation fades from Carter professing his love to hushed stillness. "Emma." My name is bitter on his lips. *There you are.* "You're smarter than this. He left you once, and he'll do it again. It was always us. We've wasted enough time. I'll treat you better. I'm better for your family."

"I was waiting for your ego to show. We tolerate each other, Carter. You're in love with yourself and my family." I chuckle. "Miles is a bigger threat to you than I thought."

"He's nothing!" Carter's hand slamming onto a hard surface echoes through the phone. "I've been here, and I'm not going any-where. You'll see."

By four, I'm running on fumes between meetings when Mal comes in with a vase of flowers in a mason jar and a brown paper bag.

"Aren't you popular today?" She winks before walking out.

These are more subtle than the roses eclipsing half of my space, but they're beautiful nonetheless. Blush and sherbet-orange garden roses bloom in an arrangement of ranunculus, anemone, solomio, and eucalyptus. The colors are soft touches of off-white hues.

I pull the small card from the envelope and smile.

Got you something to match your free spirit instead of that "off with her head" shit on your desk.

I snort at his *Alice in Wonderland* reference. My favorite Disney movie.

These reminded me of you.

See you soon,

Miles

PS: Open the bag. I know your ass is grouchy this time of day.

"You don't know shit," I mutter to no one through a smirk. But I am getting grouchy, and I am low on snacks.

I pull out Greek vanilla yogurt, oat clusters, a small container of mixed berries, and a Heath bar. All of the necessary ingredients for a mini parfait.

"Damn you, Miles."

My vision blurs at his random act of kindness, pushing against the last of my resolve to keep him far away from my heart, which he already took up residence in long ago.

Chapter 44

Miles

Is it too much to ask to eat pussy in peace?

I ignore my phone for the third time. Whoever it is will have to pray about it. I'm busy.

Emma's body quivers under me, tightening the vise grip of her thighs, which are about to pop my head off. "What you running for?" I nip her clit. My hands curl around her outer thighs to pull her further into my mouth.

"I'm. Coming. Again." Emma surrenders to the orgasm, bucking her hips. She plants her feet on the bed and rolls her body into the hard strokes of my tongue. Em's scream floods her bedroom in a mix of pants and cries.

I slurp her nectar and French kiss her lips. Emma's pussy has me swinging my feet in the air. I could suck on it all day, and I plan to stay between her legs like I pay rent there. I'm tired as hell from the red-eye I took from Jersey, but I have my priorities, and Em is number one.

Leaving Emma for weeks again took effort. Business on the East Coast required my presence, but I called and texted. Yeah, that's not normal behavior for me, but I'm trying. I even used a few of those love emojis.

To my surprise, Emma responded, a sign that the journey back into her heart won't take a lifetime. I'd wait one if necessary, but at this point, I'm doing everything but begging. Shit, I'm ready to move in if she says the word. I already snuck clothes into a drawer, and she hasn't tossed them, so that's progress.

My phone rings again, then Emma's.

"Ignore it." I lick my way up her body and into her mouth.

Em missed me, whether her stubborn ass wants to admit it or not. We're meant to be together, and now that I have her, I refuse to let her go.

I suck her tongue and pump three fingers into her pussy, which is ready for me to consume. My crown pushes through her entrance, stretching walls I haven't felt in weeks.

"Miles." My name is a knot in Emma's throat, low and sultry in tone. A desire to trust glitters in her eyes.

"I'm here, kitten." I kiss her and push in another inch.

Our phones go off again. Emma's *Sister, Sister* ringtone for Justice is loud and annoying.

"I know you're not."

"It's an emergency," Emma mumbles into my mouth.

"So is this dick."

She chuckles and slaps at my chest. "We only call each other this early if it's serious."

"Fine, but make it quick," I grit out and slide back down her body, slapping her pussy when she scoots away. "Stay still."

Emma picked Jay up from the airport yesterday. They spent half the day together before Em dipped for a night shoot. This better be an emergency. Jay's my sister, but she is fucking up my time with Bernadette.

"Terrence is cheating on me with Elena from *The Vampire Diaries*. Do you want to go on a coffee run? I can't work the machine here. Tony Stark left no instructions."

Say that one more time.

I pop my head up from between Emma's legs to verify that I heard what the fuck she just said.

Justice blows out a frustrated breath. "I went out with SiSi last night, over in West Hollywood."

"Uh-huh," Em says, trying to follow along.

"Terrence was out after a business meeting. When I went to my car, he was across the street with some guy and a woman." It's hard to follow Justice with her sobbing every three words while licking Emma into my mouth.

Cheating and Terrence don't belong in the same sentence. He came out to Cali a week ago to wrap up a contract with a client and take a business meeting that will change his career. Nowhere on that itinerary was stepping out on his wife. He loves Justice too much. But if what she's saying is true, he can get this ass whooping right now.

I lose it when Justice sobs again, something about a hotel and some Pop-Tarts.

Fuck all this.

The room goes silent at my growl. "I'll fucking kill him myself," I mutter.

"Miles, please calm down. I don't want anyone to get hurt," Emma pleads away from the phone's camera.

"I'm not about to argue in whispers," I bark, damn near on mute. "Take care of your friend, and I'll handle mine." Emma knows what's up, that she might as well meet me at the nearest police precinct with my bail. T knows better. He can catch this heat for fucking up my breakfast.

Em reaches for me when I move off the bed but drops the phone. She scrambles for it and accidentally puts me face-to-face with Justice, whose eyes and mouth are the size of saucers.

"*Miles?*" Her face is pale and her eyes are puffy.

"Are you still at the house? Justice!" She jumps at the bass in my voice. "Are. You. There?" Now is not the time for a commercial break in her head.

"Y-yes."

Say less.

I toss the phone back to Emma, who's still arguing for me to stay. Terrence is my brother. I love him to death, but I'm not above knocking his wig off if he was disrespectful to his wife. Ain't no way stepping out is in his DNA, not after his father walked out on his family. But if Jay saw the shit, she saw the shit. For all her cockblocking and whining, she doesn't deserve any of this.

So off to a celebrity's house I go. Like I give a fuck about the superhero who lives there. T is staying at a former client's house in Malibu, and I'm about to assemble some shit on his lawn.

Emma and Jay's conversation is a blur I'm not trying to hear. I throw on sweats and slides and drive the short distance to the address T gave me weeks ago. It's a private compound with Flintstone futurist properties that look like they've seen its share of orgies and lava lamps. There are at least six acres of land for alpacas, chickens, and whatever else to roam outside.

I know somebody got some good weed over here with these flower child vibes.

I barely get my rental car in park before I hop out and walk around every damn bush in Malibu to the egg-shaped door with a long handle and no other security measure. I bypassed the initial system at the front gate with my phone, so I guess Tony Stark and his people are living free with nature.

When I open the door, Justice is on the steps in an oversized tee and leggings with a Rudolph nose and a pout. Terrence is in the foyer wearing a wrinkled navy suit that looks slept in, and that's all it takes for me to pick him up and slam his big ass to the ground.

It costs nothing to mind your business and stay in the house. The energy I had rolling up is the same energy I got in return when Terrence all but tossed my ass back outside. I'm protective of Justice, but he's just as protective of Emma.

"Are you fucking kidding me?" he barks in a 'fit of dark blue wrinkles, his hands on his hips. "*Emma?* Out of everyone, you go after *her?*" Thick brows crease into a frown. Add a curly black wig, remove about eighty-five pounds of muscle, and you have Robin Davis. T has his mama's scowl down to the foot tap.

I need a blunt after this. Possibly some Bengay too.

T's integrity remains intact, but so does the hostile glare he stabbed me with after squaring things away with Justice. He adores her, and he isn't in Cali to fuck around, but shit hit the fan real quick when it looked like he was out with another woman. They sorted through all of that, with Justice revealing she had more than one surprise with her on the flight from Austin. She's pregnant. I'm ready to pop bottles, but T still has a fade with my name on it.

The problem with choke-slamming someone you assumed was cheating is if you're wrong—and if you bench close to the same weight—you might get hemmed up after they catch their second wind. Based on the baseball grip around my neck when T marched me outside to "talk," I knew he'd try to fling me off the porch like Uncle Phil did Jazzy Jeff after Emma and I got caught on our video call with Jay. I didn't tell him because I wanted to avoid this reaction—not because I'm scared. I'm still bigger. I know my reputation—I lived the shit. But I wanted space for Emma and I to figure out what we are to each other. T and Jay would never know if it was only a few taps and nothing else. We planned to keep it casual with an expiration date, but life happened, and we grew into something I never imagined but will fight for with all I got.

Fighting Terrence is another story. I expected a little heat from him, but I'm not about to be outside scrapping next to no zoo animals.

"I'm not paying for your mistakes when you screw this up," he scolds. "I love you, man, but this one is too close to home. End it now." The fury emanating off him will have me in an ice bath if this goes left.

I should've stretched first.

"Can't do that, bro," I admit.

"When you break Emma's heart, you'll hurt Justice. I won't have it."

Already did, and I'm working like hell to heal it.

GG told me at a young age that when you find love, you might not have the right words or know what to do, but your soul will whisper to theirs. Emma speaks to me in ways no one else has or ever will.

"This is different. *She's* different."

Terrence folds his arms across his chest. He really needs an iron, and a shower. "Is your community dick worthy of her?"

I take a deep breath and scrub my goatee. It's a struggle to put into words everything I feel for Emma. She's changing me for the better.

"I can't explain it, but I'm drawn to her, man," I say. "It's like I've been blind for so many years and can finally see."

What's been in front of me the whole time.

Terrence's smile widens into a grin. "You're in love with her." He winces at his ribs, sore from when I tackled him to the ground.

I want this—Emma's pleasure and joy—every day. The love and affection she fights out of fear I'll hurt her is there. I just need her to trust me.

I love her. I want her, however she'll have me.

"I never thought what you and Jay have was in the cards for me," I confess. "But I want that with Emma." A group of alpacas walk by in a slow stroll of kazoo-like hums.

Every man in Emma's life let her down, and I'll prove to her I'll keep fighting for us. The ball is in her court. When she's ready, I'll be there.

Chapter 45

Emma

"Are you mad?" I peek over the rim of my sunglasses at Justice in the lounger next to me. She's still staring, arms and ankles crossed in a cutout cover-up dress. It would make me nervous if her face wasn't bunched up like she's about to tell Roger to go home.

"If you're asking if I'm upset that you've kept your relationship with Miles a secret for months, and the fact he's been staying with you—"

Here it comes.

She reaches for my hand. "No. Disappointed that you felt the need to tiptoe around me? Sure, but I'm not upset. Now, surprised is a different story. Are you sure you want to be with him?"

"Don't talk shit on my name!" Miles shouts from across the pool where he and Terrence sit, legs grazing through the surface of the illuminated water, wearing matching coconut tree swim trunks. I'm not even going to ask how they coordinated that.

"Don't make me pop you again, Miles Devonté!"

"Aye!" Miles points a finger at Justice with a tight lower lip. He rubs the back of his neck at the memory of her smacking him and mumbles something to Terrence, who snickers and leans back on his towel.

Justice's smirk says it all.

Once she put together that Miles was the man at the singles' retreat and the one I cried about on our video call, she let him have it. After Terrence had his talk with Miles, Justice found a step stool and went upside his head for leaving the way he did. She chased him around with a spatula until Miles pleaded with Terrence to get his wife. Justice might be a hopeless romantic, but she gets her licks too.

"As I was saying"—Miles looks away when Justice hits him with a playful stare—"it took a minute to get over the reality of you two actually together. That said, I'm surprised it didn't happen sooner." She studies me. "Have you told him how you really feel?"

"No."

She frowns. "Em."

"I love him," I release into the night air, freeing me from the fear of uttering my confession.

I love his gentleness.

The pauses he takes before kissing me.

His intelligence. His protectiveness. His wildly uncensored mouth.

"I know," she says quietly. Justice motions to Miles. "Now tell him."

"We—I—it's complicated, Jay."

Miles and my gaze meet under a starry night. We spent the rest of the day with Justice and Terrence. We went out to lunch and swung by my house for our bathing suits while Jay and T stopped by the store to get food to grill for dinner.

Most of the evening has been by the pool. Miles and Terrence are still getting in a few laps. Justice and I got out an hour ago to unprune and catch up.

My best friend is pregnant. Justice let the news slip during her argument with Terrence. Her confession stopped time. I couldn't reach her fast enough, and we shared hugs and tears.

This is the first time the four of us are together since Miles and I became more than friends. Our dynamic shifted, but not in the way I imagined. Being with Miles and our friends feels like the last pieces of a puzzle coming together. We always fit, but we shuffled to squeeze in the wrong spot when the best place was by each other's side.

I can admit that now, but it doesn't remove the fear that something will go wrong.

"I hate to break it to you, but from what you've told me, you two have been in a relationship whether you want to admit it or not. You're making time for each other, and that's beautiful." Light from the pool glimmers over her pecan skin with gold undertones. The warmth of her smile echoes in her voice. "Tell him, Em."

My gaze reaches for the stars. Night extends beyond the domed concrete home, past the echo of waves from the Pacific Ocean in the distance. Lights inside the house glow over the backyard and pool, where Miles sits studying me.

It's hard to let people in. To trust. I don't make room for many changes in my life, but I don't have to with Miles. Even from a distance, he's been a part of it, our connection rooted in our love for our best friends. We found each other when we weren't looking, where we least expected.

"It's okay."

I tear my eyes away from him. "What?"

"To let him love the parts you don't think are lovable."

Justice kisses the top of my head and gets up. Tears cloud her vision. "Take it from me, Em: don't run from what you want. Even if it scares you."

She and Terrence head inside hand in hand, fooling no one. They're about to ride Tony Stark's headboard into the next cinematic universe, and good for them. The backyard wakes with shimmering lights as Sade's "By Your Side" croons through outdoor speakers.

Subtle.

I guess they finally found the controls.

Miles moves to the edge of the outdoor daybed, the long planes of his muscles at rest after a night swim. Moonlight filters through the canopy and dips over his freshly cut waves and broad chest. He's watching me with a fixed gaze that stokes a fire inside my belly.

He sees all of me.

My strengths.

My weaknesses.

The soft parts of me I push away to be resilient.

The two of us in the same space are magnetic. I've tried to fight the pull, but I come alive when I'm with Miles. He unlocked a part of my heart I never wanted to uncover, and now I want it to be free.

So I stop fighting and allow my heart to lead—straight to him.

Miles lifts his head when I stand between the power of his legs. All the features I love are on display, but it's the love reflected in his eyes that shines the brightest.

I caress his cheek and bend down for a kiss. He yields to my lips, which move slowly against his. Warm hands slide down my arms to my waist and anchor me in place. I don't rush the stokes of our tongues but can't get enough.

My mouth raises, inches from his. "I love you," I say above my thundering heart, which is whirling at the declaration I've never given any man other than my father.

Miles clasps his arms around my body and buries his face against my belly. He holds me there, his lashes fluttering against the eyelet pattern of my cover-up. Every one of my curves molds to the contours of his muscular frame. In a single motion, I'm in his arms, bearing witness to the deep longing in his gaze.

"I love you beyond this lifetime, Emma." Miles presses his lips to mine and eases me onto the outdoor daybed.

I suppress a sigh and let go.

Between each "I love you," he plants kisses on my neck and collarbone. Our kiss deepens once his mouth is back on my lips. His tongue massages mine through long, surrendering moans. Desire flares in Miles's eyes. He frees me from my dress, unable to control his need to touch me.

He lifts to release his board shorts. His dick bobs free and taps my stomach as he nudges my legs farther apart with his knees and pushes through my entrance. Pleasure tightens and explodes with every inch he takes.

Miles swallows my gasps and thrusts harder, angling his position to trigger a fire that burns my skin. My lips tremble at the vow he repeats with every glide into my soft flesh.

To love me.

To protect me.

To be my safe place.

Skin to skin, under the arena of stars, we step over the threshold and into the unknown.

Together.

Chapter 46

Emma

Miles and I spent the night at the superhero compound, as he now calls it. We christened the guest bedroom and made breakfast with Justice and Terrence, the latter of whom stepped away shortly after to train his client. It was the perfect start to the perfect weekend, doing nothing and everything. We stayed in with movies, went out for dinner, and watched the sunset over the Pacific. On Sunday night, Miles and I took them to the Santa Monica Pier for our first double date, which ended with him and Terrence chasing me and Justice after we lit them up with our bumper cars.

Having my best friend here unlocked another part of me. I miss Jay and wish we lived closer. We see each other at least twice a year, but I want more memories. I've spent so much time creating distance in my life. I've missed out on a lot in an effort to dodge the hurt. But I get her for the rest of the month—Miles too with Terrence, who thanked me for finally keeping him in one place long enough.

True to his word, Miles hasn't left for more than a week. He hopped back to Jersey a few days ago to check in on his business interests on the East Coast but calls and texts every day. He thinks he's slick coming back with extra clothes to pop into my closet, but

I roll my eyes and look the other way. Miles has been filling up space in my life, and I love it.

I love him.

I've been on my phone all morning, responding to his texts about him missing me.

Miles

Might go to the ER.

Why? Are you hurt?

Miles

Dick won't go down after that performance.

My snort morphs into a cackle. *Idiot.*

Last night's video call included me taking a dildo while a jeweled anal trainer was inside me. Miles lasted thirty seconds before coming in his pants. He loves Bernadette, but there's a new star in town.

Miles

How is she?

My eyes roll.

Deloris is fine.

Miles

Excuse you. That's Deloris Van Cartier.

It's too early to be cracking up over nonsense. Only Miles would name my ass after Whoopi's *Sister Act* character. It's so random, and it borders on blasphemy, but that's him.

"I'm not going to dignify that with a response," I say to the potted plant next to me on the couch. It's a "love fern," one Miles swears will grow if it hears good vibrations. I waited for him to play the Marky Mark song when he brought it home, but he scoffed and walked off.

Smiles have taken up residence with Miles. Life is funnier, lighter.

I settle back on the couch with my coffee and the ocean's soundtrack. Sunlight stretches across the living room, electrifying the gold accents in the room. Justice is coming over soon to work remotely while Terrence trains his client. I've been scaling back in the office where I can, so she and I can spend time together while she's in California.

My phone rings on the kitchen counter. Probably Jay saying she's on her way.

I stall when I see the incoming call from my mother. My hand slips over my hair in a high ponytail as I set down my mug to answer. "Hello?" The letters run into each other in a scramble to understand why she's calling.

"Could you please come out?"

"You're outside? My house?"

"Emma, I did not fly all this way to answer questions from a public sidewalk." My mother restrains herself from scolding me but can't mask her frustration. She sighs. "Please, sweetheart."

Someone died. It's the only explanation why she's here.

Juliette Douglass does not waste outfits on unnecessary travel, and she never says please or calls me sweetheart. Ever. Death or an apocalypse are more likely, and I'm not sure she'd visit me before the world ended.

I slip on Miles's slides by the front door and clomp out to the main gate. I'd have an easier time walking in shoeboxes. The man has boats for feet.

My mother adjusts her vintage Chanel purse, which is hanging over a black sheath dress that screams funeral.

"Who died?"

"Don't be ridiculous." She waves me off but stops herself from walking into my house. Her fingers flex before they reach for me and brush the tops of my shoulders. I frown as her face moves toward me before she reroutes for a pat on my back and heads inside.

At least she tried to hug me.

My mother stands in front of the open pocket doors, focused on the glittering light scattered across ocean waves coming to life. Wisps of her auburn hair stretch from her controlled bun to touch the breeze. Her posture eases as she softens the delicate muscles in her back to release the perfection she upholds. She's out of place here in my home, which she's criticized on more than one occasion for being too casual. Her stilettos have only crossed my threshold twice in a decade, but she never misses an opportunity to remind me of my shortcomings.

As if she catches herself, the rod in her back reanimates. She turns her eyes to me. "My approach with you has not been helpful. I'd like to make it up."

"Okay." If she's expecting another response, I've got nothing.

A smile sets in place, one that doesn't reach her eyes. Smiling isn't normal behavior for my mother. This one looks forced, like she's straining the muscles in her cheekbones and thin lips to accommodate the effort. Her eyes flicker to the T-shirt I'm wearing—one of Miles's. It touches above my thighs and clashes with the version of a daughter I no longer strive to reach. I still love my outfits and will never trade heels for flats, but I'm discovering that I have layers, and wearing my man's shirt while he's away is one of them.

"Let's have dinner tonight," she says in a voice too soft to be her own. "We'll make up for the years lost."

"I'd like that." The breath I take solidifies in my throat as years of emotion swim to the surface. I've wanted a better relationship with my mother—practically prayed for it. I don't know what sparked her change in heart, but coming all this way to see me during my father's campaign means more than she'll ever know.

A chill shifts through me at my mother's half smile. "Very well. Hera at seven. I'll send a car."

Her smile remains etched in her ivory features as she lets herself out and leaves me wondering what I signed up for.

The black town car pulls up to an industrial building that looks like an all-glass skeleton. A man in a black suit and matching hat opens my door and extends his hand. "Good evening, Ms. Douglass."

He leads me through a lobby of fountains and marble to a glass elevator, where he presses the button for the eighteenth floor. The car slides up to a quiet melody of classical music and opens its doors to an empty restaurant.

"Your party awaits," he says at my struggle to hide my confusion. "Enjoy" is all I get before he's back in the elevator.

My black heels take cautious steps over dark marble. Every table and chair is empty. So is the bar. I turn toward the ceiling-high windows that reveal the LA skyline and gasp. There, in front of four tables pushed together, is my mother...and Carter.

Her lips curl into the same smile she had in my house. She makes her way to me, her eyes never leaving mine. Her target. "So happy you could make it." She kisses me on my cheeks.

"What is all of this?" I lift my eyes to the candles scattered amid rose petals on the table and freeze at Carter's lean form filling out a tux. His mouth is set firm, his bronzed skin magnifying blue-green eyes that pierce the distance between us. He scans my patchwork lace bandage dress with an approving grin.

"I told you we'd make up for the years lost." Something flickers in my mother's eyes when she repeats the words she said hours ago in my home. Words I thought conveyed a willingness to repair our damaged relationship. Not an ambush. She motions to Carter, who approaches on command. "I've failed you, Emma. I should've intervened earlier."

"What are you talking about?"

"You've had more than enough time to waste on men who aren't a good fit for you or this family. Carter is worthy of us. He'll take care of you, and he won't run off like that thug. How could you think so little of yourself to not want more—not *be* more?"

A wave of nausea hits me as Carter's hand closes over mine. The touch is far from loving, and it tightens under his grip. "I told you I'd show you, Emma," he says through clenched teeth. "I want to marry you."

"You want permanent admission into this family," I spit back and snatch my hand away.

Clarity chooses that moment to touch the shoulder of my younger self, the one who desperately waited all these years for her family to love her without conditions. I've shielded her so much, I never set her free.

Stop holding onto things that no longer serve you. If that includes your family, you have people who care about you.

Miles's words coax me to loosen my grip on a hope that's hurt too much to carry. It's time to let go.

My "No" echoes through the empty restaurant. "And I really fucking hate red roses."

"Emma!" My mother's curt voice steadies for a lash. "This is your last chance to be happy. To have a family."

"I have one, Mother! I have people in my life who love me no matter what. In case it wasn't clear to you, I've always been enough, with or without a man. I'm the happiest I've been in years because I'm finally letting go of things that never meant me any good. If you want Carter so bad, you marry him."

"Isn't it customary to ask permission from the father before proposing? John, did he hit you up first?" The warmth of Miles's chuckle sends a shiver down my spine.

He's here.

I leave my mother and her jaw on the floor to rush to him. Miles gathers me into his arms, buries his face in my neck, and exhales. "Kitten," he whispers.

"I missed you." I pull him tighter. He kisses his way into my mouth, demanding a moan I freely give. Miles breaks us apart and plants a kiss on my forehead before stepping back so I can greet my father. I'm shocked to see him here.

"Hi, sweetheart," he says, pulling me to his middle. My father gives good hugs. If only he made time for them. "What is the meaning of this?" He looks over my shoulder at my mother and Carter, who's eyeing the exits.

"I'm helping Emma secure her future," my mother says matter-of-factly.

My father frowns. "You said you came out here to spend time with her. This isn't right, Juliette."

"What isn't right is you allowing her to waste every opportunity we've given her. You were too soft, and now she's fallen for"—her hand waves at Miles in a T-shirt and jeans in disgust—"that. He's a threat with a juvenile record! Carter looked into it. Vandalism. Theft. Assault. *This* is who you want your daughter to date? He's below us!"

"He has shown *our* daughter nothing but love and respect since we met him," my father roars, silencing my mother and catching me off guard. He never raises his voice. "His past does not define him, nor is it a mark of who he is today." His gaze drifts to me, with years of sadness forming tears in the corners of his brown eyes. "I owe you a lifetime of apologies, sweetheart. I've let my career and other influences"—his eyes shift to my mother and harden—"get the best of my judgment for too long. I own that, and I'm sorry I hurt you."

A sob racks my insides and releases years' worth of heartache. I look at Miles with blurred vision whose smile tells me everything will be okay. He brought my dad here from the East Coast after I texted him this morning and told him what my mother said when she came over. No matter what, he'll always come back to me.

"You have a good man, Emma," my father says so only I can hear. "One who protects you and those you love more than you know."

"I rarely hate being right, but my suspicions were correct," Miles says to the other end of the room. "I knew you were a calculated little shit, but"—he whistles—"this is some Grade A madness."

"You will not speak to me that way!" My mother meets his accusing eyes without flinching, like she didn't just insult him seconds ago.

Miles chuckles. "Respectfully, ain't no one talking to you, Juliette. You *think* you have power, siphoning it from other people. But you've never been a factor. I'm talking to Crispin."

Every head turns to Carter, who lets the faintest smile slip. My eyes swing to Miles, whose gaze is still locked on Carter. If he so much as thinks about running, it's his ass.

"What's going on?" I look at my father, who nods to Miles.

"Big donors spending money to influence political outcomes is nothing new," Miles says to Carter. "The *Citizens United v. Federal Election Commission* ruling at the Supreme Court made it easier to funnel millions—billions, even—to buy what we call democracy with money from undisclosed sources. A network of wealthy elite could push forth judicial nominees with the same money they use to buy legal groups that bring cases to courts with their people in place to rule in their favor." He scratches his goatee and chuckles. "It's hard to track the source of dark money—damn near impossible. But there's always a thread."

Carter shifts on his feet and lifts his chin.

"One of my clients is fighting the concerted effort against voter suppression. Lawmakers and judges across the country are enshrining disenfranchisement laws, all backed by dark money from a network hell-bent on our demise."

Miles steps closer, shaving the distance between him and Carter to mere inches. "While you were watching me, I was watching you attend special fundraisers and private events with these same judges and lawmakers you thought were flying under the radar. That took me to a deeper dive. You couldn't pass the LSAT, but your buddy from your Ivy League did, and he's conveniently running for attorney general and is backed by the same network. Now he's courting Blair."

My mother's gasp fills the room. Her nervous gaze turns to Carter like she's seeing him for the first time. "What are you saying, Miles?"

"Crispin is a pawn for a network of wealthy elite who are buying this country through the courts, Congress, and the White House. As chief of staff, he oversees John's policy development and has one of the greatest influences in the office. I'd bet the network assigned him early on to see how far he could push their agenda. Why else do you think an exploration committee into a presidential bid is popping up now? John's desire to be likable and appease donors makes him a great puppet."

"You know nothing," Carter glowers.

"Em, do you know why Carter started pressing up on you in your twenties? Around the time you turned twenty-six?" Miles asks over his shoulder. "That was when the Supreme Court ruled on *Citizens United*, making it easier for wealthy special-interest groups to shape campaigns through unlimited spending. Carter likely took the opportunity to safeguard his influence on your father by being a love interest for you, if not his right hand on Capitol Hill."

Shock and rage hold my breath hostage. I can't believe any of this, but I trust Miles without a shadow of a doubt.

"You have no proof, and who do you think people would believe anyway, hmm?" Carter's head tilts in a sinister smile. "A man with a pedigree, or a thug with a record?"

My feet take off on their own to slap the smirk off Carter's evil face. I wind up for a punch, but Miles pulls me back. "Easy, kitten," he whispers against the shell of my ear. My body softens at his breath on my skin. "I love you, and I won't let you go to jail for me."

"You won't be far if we kill him together," I whisper back.

"I'm marrying your ass." Miles presses a kiss to my cheek and moves me behind him. We'll need to discuss that later. Offing Carter is one thing, but marriage is a jump I'm not ready to take just yet. "Crispin, your car is waiting for you. Say goodbye to John's ass, because you won't be kissing it for a while. My guess is fifteen years to life."

All the color drains from Carter's face. "John, what is he talking about?" His eyes flit between my father and Miles under hiked brows.

My father shakes his head and sighs. "I loved you like a son," he says, his voice low and tormented. "How could you do this and steal from me, no less?"

"What is he talking about?" I ask Miles, whose arm is now around me.

"Money laundering through bullshit contracts. Bribery. Crispin has a shell company to conceal his assets. He got too greedy, which made it easier for me to trace." Miles shrugs. "Not bad for a thug with a record."

"Hey." I grip his chin and turn him to look at me. "None of that."

Miles is playful and prideful at times, but I see the vulnerability he's hiding behind the mask I want removed permanently. "You're brilliant, amazing, and one of the best men I know. I love every part of you, in this lifetime and the next."

His lips crash to mine, trembling with every kiss he takes. "I fucking love you." He clasps my body to his.

"I fucking love you back."

Authorities flood out of the elevator to apprehend Carter, who kicks and screams. He mumbles about it not being the last we hear from him before he's carted off in handcuffs.

"We can fix this. I—I didn't know, John. I swear! We're still a family. We'll make it work," my mother pleads in a rush.

"Enough!" My father expels a deep breath. "Enough," he repeats softly. The light in his eyes is dim when he faces me. "I have a few meetings with trusted colleagues about this network and the extent of its power. Miles, you owe us nothing and gave us everything. I'll never be able to repay you, but if the time comes for you to marry my daughter, you have my yes right now."

My father cuts my mother off when she tries to speak. "Our daughter is happy and in love, Juliette. I will not hear another vile word about Miles or his past. Let them be. Some of us should marry for love." His confession is so quiet, I have to strain to hear it. My parents met in college, but they never discuss their love story. They just are, which explains why so much was hiding in plain sight, even for me.

"If you find it in your heart, I'd love to spend time with you before I go back to Washington." My father takes my hands and looks to Miles. "I'll make this right, but I know it will take time."

"She's deserves better, John," Miles says with no hint of humor in his tone.

"I know." My father nods. "I know." His gaze shifts back to me. "I should go. The authorities will likely have questions about all of this." He huffs out a laugh. "*I* have questions about all of this. I love you, Emma. Always have, and always will."

We hug before my father leaves. My mother is hot on his trail, begging for him to forgive her. She said nothing to me—or Miles—and I'm okay with it.

I'm more than okay. I'm at peace.

Miles looks down at me. "You alright, baby?"

"You just unmasked an episode of *Scandal*." I laugh and wipe away a stray tear. "But yes, I am."

His lips press to my forehead as he pulls me into his warmth and holds me. "I'm not sorry what I found, but I am sorry this shit touches people you love. I'll always protect you, kitten."

"I know. Do you have to go back to Jersey now?"

"Nah." Miles shakes his head and smiles. "I'm finally home."

"I love you."

"I love you." He kisses me with a grin. "And Bernadette. And Deloris."

My head tips back with laughter. *Only him*. "Let's go."

We leave the restaurant hand in hand with Miles singing "I Will Follow Him" from *Sister Act*.

Epilogue
Miles

*E*ight months later

"How is she?"

"Pissed but playing it off," Justice says with a giggle. "She almost threw out your flowers."

"Damn, that's cold." It's not like I had red roses delivered.

"This is Emma's first Valentine's Day with someone she loves. The holiday isn't her favorite, but she's in her feelings that you're not there. Your trip took too long."

"Well, excuse the fuck out of me for flying to the other side of the world and back." I chuckle. "I wasn't exactly jerking off in the Outback." My kitten deserves the best. If that means digging out a diamond by hand from an ethical mine in Australia, so be it.

Low and gentle, Justice says, "I know. Did you get it?"

"I wouldn't be going to face her wrath otherwise." I signal to get off the turnpike and groan at the glow of brake lights stretching beyond the ramp. I landed in DC instead of Newark to handle some business and drove back. The weather is threatening to dump a shit ton of snow, and I didn't want to chance the airline canceling my flight.

"Don't screw this one up."

"Aye." My eyes narrow at the navigation screen like Justice can see me. "That was a fluke," I say at her laughter.

Emma and I went back to the singles' retreat last month. It was supposed to be a getaway for us to reminisce and dabble in some bondage at Ravenous. The resort screwed up the reservation that had us in the honeymoon suite. I never intended to propose, but I figured, what the hell? We had the flowers and champagne to celebrate.

Why not bypass an over-the-top ceremony and elope? It made sense to me, but Emma pulled my ass together. She gave a speech about the people most important in our lives not being there. She also chewed me out for my audacity to entertain what she calls microwave nuptials. The discussion turned into an argument that ended with us naked on top of the dining table. Had I known asking about a quick marriage would activate a new level of freak, I would've mentioned using Burger King to cater.

We don't need a marriage to validate our relationship, but I want her in every way possible and would say "I do" tomorrow—hamburgers or not.

Em has revealed more parts of herself to me since we got together close to a year ago. I didn't think marriage would be in the cards for us. Not yet, given the shit with her parents. But I hopped on a plane two weeks ago to cut a diamond from the earth, based on her reaction at the retreat. My lady wants me to come correct, and I'll show her better than I can tell her.

Making a diamond into an engagement ring took longer than expected. I couldn't get home before Valentine's Day. Em still thinks

I'm blowing it off for work, but I still have three hours before the day ends.

The East Coast has been our home since the holidays. We spent Christmas with my mama, who iced me out for her new friend like I wasn't shit. She and Emma are as thick as thieves, and I couldn't be happier. Even if I'm an afterthought in their presence.

Emma and I also saw her dad. Things are still tense, but they're working on their relationship with a therapist. John is still sorting through the aftermath of Carter's deception but faces everything head-on.

He refused to sweep the betrayal under the rug. He's been working with a communications team that specializes in crisis management. They're on loan from family friends who own a DC law firm and are handling it. Chanda is a real-life Olivia Pope. Through political scandal and a divorce, John came out on top. Voters looked at him as an honest man who won't tolerate betrayal.

Emma's mom put up a fight but found her bags packed after the stunt she pulled with Carter. We'll never know if they worked together or with the network I unearthed, but Juliette is on her own. John had an ironclad prenup and cut her off. She got a condo outside the DMV but lost access to the circle she prioritized above her family. Through therapy, Emma is learning that love is a choice. She's choosing to sow it into people who have her joy and best interests at heart.

As for Carter, his ass is behind bars. He hasn't said a peep about the people he works for, likely because he wants to stay alive. They're ghosts in the wind who erase any breadcrumbs that lead to their identities. I gave the information I uncovered to my homegirl in Baltimore. She's an investigative journalist dedicated to bringing darkness to light.

I turn onto Marin Boulevard, grateful to leave the traffic to the Holland Tunnel in my rearview mirror.

A baby wails over the phone. "My godbaby is up. Time to put on the cape, Mama," I say to Justice. "Kiss them both for me and tell T I said what's up."

As if on cue, Terrence grumbles. "I got it," he says, half asleep. I imagine him hurrying off to the nursery, and I smile.

We were all surprised to learn that Justice and Terrence had two babies on the way: Edith and Graciela Reyes. Emma and I flew to Austin last month to meet our godchildren. We're still set on no kids but are buying a house nearby to be closer. Cali is nice, but family is where the heart is. Time with T and Jay during their trip out west cemented the decision. Em and I will still travel and float between our properties but want to remain connected.

Austin has emerged as the fashion capital of Texas. With a growing demand for luxury and designer events, Emma got the green light to open a Soie office in the city. It will take time to get up and running, but we'll be closer to our friends, and Em will also have Kojo nearby. He relocated to the area months ago after opening a design studio.

"Have a wonderful time away, and take care of my friend," Justice says.

I plan to knock the Mario coins out of her pussy.

"Will do," I say.

I pull up to the curb of my condo and dap up Marquis before handing him my keys. I drove up my Audi R8 after swinging by my Virginia house and visiting Justice's mama. She wanted to see the ring for Emma and sobbed before hopping on a video call with my mama, who damn near fell out like it was the first time she saw it. My mama called me every two days while I was in Australia asking for updates but gave the BET performance of her life with all that hollering on the phone. Between the gorilla grip that Jay's mama had me in and the trio of squeals once they called Terrence's mama, I never thought I'd make it out on time—much less with my hearing intact.

The mothers showered Emma with love during Jay and T's vow renewal ceremony in Mexico last year. Their affection was right on time, given Em's fallout with Juliette. That woman has yet to reach out to her daughter, but Emma has three mamas now who pour into her—their bonus daughter. We now have a blended family with those who love us the most.

I hit up Em's pops out of respect before driving up to Jersey. John had given me his blessing last year, but he didnt't know I'm dead serious about loving his daughter for the rest of my life. I'm also serious about him treating her right.

Emma is endgame; there are no two ways about it.

The wind picks up on my walk inside the building. I tighten my peacoat and step through the parting glass doors. This place has everything you need—and then some. It's a stone's throw from the city, a major plus whenever Emma has a fashion event. The security is also legit. We have a private elevator. Our condo has panoramic views of the skyline and a split-level terrace with an outdoor jacuzzi.

The elevator door opens to concrete flooring and high ceilings. I drop my bag, pull off my Timbs, and walk through the foyer. Sade's "By Your Side" is crooning through the speakers. It has become the song we play almost every night while we watch the sunset.

Emma is on the large sectional that overlooks Manhattan. She's in one of my hoodies, her hair tossed up in a messy bun. Snowflakes coat the night sky as city lights streak through the living room. Emma sighs and sips her wine before reaching for her phone.

Emma

Hi.

Hi. Like your gifts?

Emma

They're nice, thanks.

I roll my lips to suppress a chuckle. She's pissed.

I had presents delivered for each day I wasn't here. A stuffed animal from the Santa Monica Pier arrived last night, and flowers today. I planned to wrap my dick in a red ribbon, but we'll see how the night goes.

You mad, kitten?

Emma

I'm fine.

Liar.

I haven't had to travel for work in almost half a year. With Em splitting time between New York and LA for fashion events, I follow her around these days. My sudden departure sparked suspicion.

Emma

Just checking in to see how work is going.

I got what I needed.

The five-carat diamond ring weighs heavily in the box in my pocket. I had the jeweler add two small stones from GG's wedding ring. Emma has my heart, and now she'll carry a piece of the woman who helped shape me into the man I am today.

Emma

Good. I'll see you home soon.

"Happy Valentine's Day," she mumbles under her breath.

"Happy Valentine's Day, kitten." Emma startles at my voice. She whips her head around to face me, her brows knitted and eyes wide.

"Wh—what are you doing here?" She clutches her chest. Shock dissolves into a smile that dents her cheeks.

"I need a reason to come home?" I chuckle. Emma rises to her knees when I reach her, still in disbelief that I'm here. I tip her chin and peck her mouth. "I wouldn't miss our first Valentine's Day." I kiss her again to savor her taste and lift her from the couch. "Fuck, I missed you."

Our lips crash. My dick swells at the weight of her in my arms. Emma slips her tongue into my mouth and grinds her hips against my pelvis.

"I missed you, baby," she pants. "So much."

Her breath catches at my fingers grazing her entrance. I pump a thumb in and out. "Look at this greedy pussy sucking me in," I say and bite her bottom lip. She whimpers. "Em?"

"Yeah?" She groans when I remove my hand to cup her face.

"I want this for the rest of my life."

Emma's eyes search mine. "You have me in every way." She presses her lips to mine and wiggles her booty. "Now fuck me like you've missed me."

"I'mma stretch your walls and contort those legs." I nip at her neck and walk us back to our bedroom.

"You talk too much, Miles."

"And you're about to choke on this dick. Get those vocal cords ready to scream and suck." I kiss the laughter rumbling up her throat and sprint the rest of the way.

"Miles!" Emma squeals.

I toss her on the bed, spread her legs, and eat.

An hour later, we finally come up for air to catch our breath and eat dinner. Emma had two sushi platters in the refrigerator, which we placed between us. We're in front of the fireplace next to our bed with a picnic spread, butt-ass naked, surrounded by blankets.

I kiss Emma's shoulder and hold up a tuna roll she sucks into her mouth. I hiss at the flick of her tongue over my fingers. "I'll pin you down and fuck you right here if you keep it up."

Desire dances in the flames reflected in her eyes. "Promise?"

"I love you. For real." My smile spreads at her laughter. "I've never experienced the happiness I have with you. You're it for me, baby."

She sucks in a breath and stares, her eyes brimming with tears. "I love you too."

"Don't cry, kitten. I didn't mean to get sentimental with my dick out." We snicker. "The shit just hits me."

Emma nods and takes my hand to place over her heart. "You unlocked a love inside me I didn't know was possible. Thank you for seeing me and loving me without conditions."

Well, shit. I might let some tears fall too.

"Alrigh"—Emma wipes her eyes and laughs—"We don't do Hallmark. Do you want to watch a movie?"

"We're getting snowed in and have nothing but time." Outside is a curtain of white with low visibility. "Another horror movie?"

She leans back and squints. "How did you know I watched them?"

"Lucky guess."

Her finger trails down my pec. "What about a rom-com?"

"Oh, hell no. I thought you said no Hallmark!"

She laughs. "Nothing cheesy. Just something for the occasion."

"If it has Ken in it, I'm out." I have already sat through four Ryan Gosling movies. One more, and I will personally ask for his autograph if I ever see him on the street. *La La Land* pissed me the fuck off. Emma was crying all hard, and I was shouting at the TV. Right person, wrong time, my ass.

"What's the matter? Can't handle romance on Valentine's Day?" Her lips curl in defiance.

I scoff. "I'm smooth as a baby's ass."

"Care to bet? You and me, this weekend," she says, wrapping her arms around my neck. "No fancy restaurant this time."

A brow hikes. "Do you remember what happened the last time you bet me?"

"Whoever proves to be the least romantic has to do whatever the other person says."

I lean forward and press my lips to hers. "Don't come crying when I hurt your feelings again."

"This is payback, Miles. I may have lost the first time, but I won't lose again."

My grin widens. "You sure this is what you want? I'mma pull out all the stops," I warn.

Like déjà vu, Emma gets in my face so we're inches apart. "Do I need to remind you that you've met your match?"

My gaze steadies on her. I could spend a lifetime telling Emma how much I love her, and it wouldn't be enough. "No," I say, my voice thick and unsteady. I lace our fingers together and kiss her forehead. "I'm game."

Make no mistake, I'm handing Emma her ass again. I planned to wait until we left the country to propose, but it feels right here, snowed in at our home. I would never force her to uphold the bet, but you best believe I'll add extra razzle-dazzle.

"You've got a deal, kitten."

"Alright. What are we playing for?"

A slow smile eases over my face. "Forever."

THE END

Acknowledgments

I'm not gonna lie; this one was hard. Once *The Seven Month Itch* came out, many folks hit up my DM and asked about Emma and Miles's story. I was happy with the enthusiasm, but your guess was as good as mine as to what would happen. The good news is that I had a title. (That counts for something, right?) The bad news is that the story didn't come to me... at all. When I tell you I was nervous I would miss my deadline because the story was as stubborn as an ingrown hair, believe me.

I knew Miles and Em would need to account for their whereabouts at the singles' retreat. Ravenous was a total surprise, as was the rest of this novel. I also knew Em and Miles lived on opposite coasts and had to somehow come together in a way that challenged them to stay. Politics is a wildcard, but it's a part of my identity. I'm too unserious to ever run for office, but my day job centers around policy advocacy. You saw tiny glimpses in *Ella Gets the D*, and I wanted to kick it up a notch since I had the runway, given that Emma is a senator's daughter. Eventually, I'd love to do something that veers down the political path (maybe a romantic suspense). I also love Zo (again, completely random) and have a story idea about him finding love again.

What developed between Em and Miles was completely unexpected. Over time, I heard them more clearly and allowed them to dance how they needed to. They are my favorite couple to date, and I hope you enjoyed their story as much as I did getting them to the finish line.

Miles has a special place in my heart and is my favorite cinnamon roll hero to date. (Sorry, Julian!) The mouth on him! But he also has layers I wanted to show. It's easy for society to constrict you to a box. As he said, he's not an outlier. When I wrote him, I saw the people I grew up with and those I know—Black men, especially—often painted in broad strokes. They are more than their stereotypes, and I wanted to hold space to unpack the idea that there is always more than meets the eye.

My sweet Emma. I loved her as Justice's best friend in *The Seven Month Itch* and wanted her to take up residence in her soft era. She's always been fierce, but vulnerability is one of the best superpowers she unlocks. I enjoyed peeling back her layers and her dynamic with Miles. They set the world on fire physically, but their love extends beyond this lifetime. (Sidenote: Baths and picnics will forever be a vibe!)

Found or chosen family is big for me and will always be present in my books. Love is a choice, not an obligation. We see Emma choose to love Miles and also herself as she learns when to hold on and when to let go of relationships.

Now, for the Academy Award speech (kidding).

I want to thank my developmental editor and beta readers, who were patient while I cursed the manuscript and threatened to bury it outside. Time is rarely on my side, but that's what it took to listen for the story. Thank you to my sisters-in-law and other folks in the bookish space for the words of encouragement. The finish line for this project was at the top of a very steep mountain. Your support helped me climb when my arms felt too heavy.

What can I say about my real-life cinnamon roll husband? You picked me up and brushed me off when I wanted to give up. I love you in this lifetime and the next.

To everyone who's stuck by me since my debut and loved these characters—and to those discovering my shenanigans—I hope you enjoy the journey. Miles will likely appear in another book or two, and Emma will make a couple of appearances in Madison and Preston's book, which is up next.

Until the next one.

Madison and Preston's story is next in the Chance at Love Series.

KEEP READING for the first chapter of Justice and Ter-*rence's story, *The Seven Month Itch*!

The Seven
Month Itch
Chapter 1

Justice

The *thwap* my head makes startles me awake. I wince at the sting and peel myself off the cold, hard glass that offers zero protection from a throbbing jaw or the stream of light aimed at my eyes, ready to burn my retinas. So this is the life of a crash test dummy on the verge of blindness.

Christmas on a cracker, that *hurt*. At least there's no drool.

Snow-covered pines race past the shuttle in a blur. My breath paints a fog across the window when I lean in for a closer look. I'd smile if it didn't hurt.

On any other day, a winter wonderland would excite me. I'm a sucker for Hallmark, and this view has all the ingredients for a movie set in a scenic small town with nosy townspeople and a feel-good ending.

But today is a nightmare. I'm not in a holiday movie, escaping the big city to save my family's tree farm—nor in my childhood home, in front of the fireplace with a book, hot cocoa, and a frosty view of our yard, which is covered in a fresh blanket of snow. Heck, I'm not in the comfortable bed I left in Texas this morning.

I'm...where are we?

Emma, my captor, shakes me like an exorcist from my attempt to go back to sleep. This is the bowels of Hell. Everything hurts. My face. My eyes. The shoulder her manicured talons grip to keep me in place.

She's one glossy fingernail away from getting tossed out of this fancy Sprinter to become one with nature. Unless she has a hot shower and a warm bed in that bottomless designer bag she calls a purse, we have nothing to discuss. I've never been to Kansas, but the urge to click my heels together three times to wake up from this bad dream masked as a getaway wrapped in "good intentions" is tempting.

Very tempting.

Regret isn't a third wheel on our annual girls' trip, but after our plane touched down in Denver three hours ago, she is present and accounted for today. And do you know what she thinks? This singles' retreat is a big mistake. The kind that requires holy water and a tetanus shot.

A *singles' retreat*.

My enthusiasm is right up there with a rectal exam. What does one do at a singles' retreat anyway, besides act single and retreat when necessary?

How Emma convinced me to come remains an unsolved mystery. Oh, that's right—I had no choice.

The artist formerly known as my best friend forced me to step away from work and go on vacation. Not by gunpoint, thank God, but to reclaim my time from the mess that's become my life.

Sounds good, right? It was, until I read the fine print that included random men with unlimited access to this awkward Black girl in the middle of the woods for a week. Em thinks we'll have an unforgettable time. I think black-and-white photos of our younger selves will pan across a screen as a narrator describes the events that led to our deaths.

Two best friends dared to have the adventure of a lifetime. But little did they know their snow-filled escapade would end in a bloodbath and their heads mounted on snowmen.

Can't wait!

My chest tightens at the driver's alert. We're ten minutes away from our destination, which might as well be a murder cabin with no cell reception. I stare out the window and scowl at the grin in the reflection. Spoiler: it's not me.

Heifer.

It's all fun and games until we find ourselves in some sex dungeon with leather head harnesses, greasy granddaddies, and a steel door to mask our screams. A singles' retreat is *not* what I had in mind when I told Em I would *think* about life as a single woman.

A blind date? Doable, if there's a swipe left function that teleports me back home and drops me in a pair of sweats.

One of those Christian dating apps so I can try out the username @PsalmLikeItHot? Sure, why not?

What happened to meeting someone in the grocery store bread aisle or at the post office? We share a "hello" and a laugh over jams and stamps. That's more my speed. Baby steps that lead to coffee weeks later, *not* a singles' retreat. But, you give an inch, and your overbearing friend signs you up to run a marathon in heels that rub your baby toes raw.

Emma threatened to stage an intervention if I didn't get on the plane. I questioned her sanity and asked if an air marshal was on board. This was *after* she posted an ad online for a Good Samaritan to escort me to the airport. An ad. As if human trafficking and serial killers aren't a real thing. Thank Baby Jesus someone—me—had the sense to remove "Operation Save Her Coochie" before I landed in the back of an unmarked van, or she ended up in a federal prison.

But did that stop her? Not a chance.

She booked flights to our snowy retreat behind my back and flew to Austin from Malibu to make sure my butt was on the plane. She even worked with my assistant to guarantee I had this week off so I could make the trip. In the forest, in the middle of winter, God knows where.

Was there no place available on the beach? Bikinis and mai tais got Stella her groove back. Why not me?

I pull myself up from the cocoon of my reclined leather seat. These windows do nothing to block out the sun. "You should be thankful this little stunt didn't pan out like a *Law & Order: SVU* episode, Madam Kidnapper."

Her chin dips to lower the designer shades now on the bridge of her nose. Moss green eyes dare me to look away. "Let Detective Stabler try," she says with a smirk.

Emma Douglass is as unapologetic as the day I met her two decades ago. We enjoyed detention on our first day of high school after our homeroom teacher overheard Em say he looked like a predator on *America's Most Wanted* who kept young girls chained up in the closet. In her defense, Mr. Shaw did give off magic potion vibes. His wild beard and unkempt gray hair favored Dr. Vink—with a va-va-va—from *Are You Afraid of the Dark?* But mad scientist living in his mother's basement was more his speed, not kidnapping. At least, I hope not.

She told me we'd be friends that day, the same way she told me to get on the plane with no sudden moves today. Em gets under my skin, and she'd have zero issue committing a felony offense, but I can't live without her.

Emma grew up the daughter of a US senator and a mom who gives the Beverly Hills Housewives and their Botox dealers a run for their money. Her parents are Blair Underwood and Milla Jovovich look-alikes—the ultimate DC power couple, fit for a Shonda Rhimes drama.

With her mom and dad lusting after private jets and crustless sandwiches, our bond strengthened over the years. She spent many nights at my house, which translated to home-cooked meals my mom would whip up on days her middle school class didn't suck her soul. My dad, God bless him, has a brilliant mind as an engineer, but he couldn't boil water in Hell. He did his best to step in and make dinner for "his girls," but we kept the fire department and local pizza shop on standby.

Our home was humble compared to Emma's, but it was comfortable, full of laughter, and the occasional burnt meal. It was a far cry from the fancy political galas she endured, but a place she called home. Em will lose a limb before she parts from her designer labels, but with us, she felt seen. Not like some heirloom her parents showed off for the cameras and later ignored.

We took the same classes in high school and attended Bodie University together, much to her father's disappointment. Senator Douglass wanted Emma to go to his alma mater back in DC, but he lost that debate to his iron-willed daughter. She stayed in California after we graduated, left the San Diego area for Malibu, and never looked back. I packed up what little I owned and headed to Texas as a newlywed.

Our annual girls' trips became a tradition during spring break. We plan them together, so it should've been a red flag when she asked for my credit card but never revealed the itinerary. February is the month of our trip—or so I thought. My soul almost fell out of my butthole this morning after her attempt to break down my door with stilettos like we needed to leave for witness protection.

Emma was wise to wait until we were midair and I was two drinks in to tell me we were off to a singles' retreat. First, who has a weeklong singles' retreat? Second, what inspired her to spend our girls' trip looking for love? I'm fresh from the Land of the Broken Heart, and she...well, she hates romance but seems determined to get me back on the dating scene. No matter how many times I tell her I'm okay.

That's because she knows you're not.

Whatever.

It's not that I *haven't* thought about it. I've been...busy.

Is a swan dive into work after your marriage hits a brick wall an unhealthy coping mechanism? Sure, I'll admit it. But at least I scored a promotion and a fancy new title. That has to count for something, right?

Seven months of grief and resentment passed in a suffocating haze that never relaxed its grip. The wounds are still fresh, and I'm not ready to face the music. Divorce is a foreign tune I don't want to learn, at least not yet.

The urge to hit the reset button after a relationship that started when I was a freshman in college isn't there. Who in their right mind gets their heart stomped into the ground and jumps at the first chance to give it to someone else—at a retreat, of all places? Not me.

My pulse trumpets as we turn down a private entrance. Gravel and ice crunch in a symphony under the weight of the tires. I grip my armrest and steady my breaths. Everything clenches, including my vagina for good measure.

"Stop preparing for a crash landing and open your eyes," Emma says next to me.

Post lights and white fencing lead to a hotel the size of the place in *The Shining*. I don't need to look at a map to know I'll freeze to death in the hedge maze if there is one. With my luck, terror twins with pigtails in matching outfits will follow me around the halls. Perverts might be more survivable.

My eyes lift to a view that takes my breath away.

The resort sits at the bottom of a valley. It's a mountain scene straight out of a Christmas movie—the kind where you kiss in slow motion as snow floats from the sky. Maybe if I rent a car and drive it into a ditch, I'll meet some hot local who's good with his hands and builds rocking chairs for elders in his spare time. I'll bake cookies for the rest of my life if it erases all reminders of my failed marriage.

Okay, this place is gorgeous. I bet Mariah Carey has a chalet off the property and yodels her Christmas songs to wake up the town during winter. It's that over the top.

Maybe I *will* recharge and clear my head here. Christmas was painful back home with my parents, who flooded me with questions about my ex, if I'm okay, and my daily fiber intake. They meant well, but they treated me like a wounded animal in one of those commercials with the Sarah McLachlan song, the kind you can save with the change in your purse. It was my first Christmas as a woman on the road to divorce, and I didn't have a chance to sulk with a bottle of wine and watch *The Holiday* like I wanted.

A change in scenery in a place that doesn't remind me of my ex will do me good. If that means I entertain the company of strangers like a twisted *Bachelorette* episode with true crime potential, so be it.

The shuttle door swings open, pulling the heat and the last of my patience with it. A man in a gold-and-black uniform with a fancy row of buttons dips his head inside. He's missing the white gloves and tiny hat, but the pompous look is present in his glare.

"Welcome to The Ravine. Please watch your step on your way out. We hope you enjoy your stay," he says to me. Or the sky. It's hard to tell who he's talking to with his nose in the air. What a charmer this one is.

"She"—I nod back at Emma—"took me against my will. But I promise not to press charges if you turn the heat on outside." I take his hand to get out and smile. His scowl etches deeper into his features, and I shrug.

Guess sarcasm isn't a language they speak in these parts.

Em and I join the small group that files out the Sprinter and trudges over a path of snow toward the entrance.

Ropes of garland curl up the entrance's four columns like holiday ribbon. The first-floor windows still have wreaths in the center that I know cost more than a month's salary. It's not hard to picture this resort in its full glory during Christmastime.

How Emma found a seven-day retreat in the middle of nowhere still baffles me. Come to think of it, maybe this trip has nothing to do with me. She watches videos of men chopping thick slabs of wood in suspenders and pants that squeeze their cheeks. She would die a happy woman if she found herself a mountain man who's the perfect blend between the Brawny paper towel guy and Chris Evans.

She'd *still* haunt me in the afterlife for not getting under a new man fast enough, but there'd be a postcoital smirk. "Tie yourself up in pleasure, not a relationship" is her mantra. She enjoys all flavors of men the world offers without the need to settle on one.

A gust of wind scrapes up my spine. Our friendship can freeze outside by itself. Where are those *Shining* twins to take their first sacrifice?

"Did you have to pick a place below freezing for us to visit? The feeling in my toes is still back in Austin." I pull my jacket against my chest for warmth, but it's pointless. There's no escape. Mr. Uptight walks along the plowed path with a gold-plated luggage cart and gestures for us to follow.

"Enough with the complaints, Jay. Is it too hard for you to say thank you?" Em breezes into the foyer on the stilts she calls heels and checks her Cartier watch like she has somewhere to be. "By the way." She turns to me. "You only have thongs to wear while you're here. Thank me later."

I'm sorry, *what?* A tundra *and* booty floss. The thing will grow icicles by the time I peel it from my crack. "Emma!" I say in a stage whisper.

Her leather heels screech to a halt on the wide plank floor. She raises a hand and levels me a stare. *Here it comes.* "Save it, your majesty. You had months to move on. You don't want your man back—or so you say—fine. Jay, you're cranky. You need dick—*good dick*—to knock those cobwebs off that coochie before it closes up for good."

Good dick reverberates through the immaculate lobby. Heads turn to stare at the woman who hasn't had sex in months.

Me.

Pay no attention to the lady in Prada with the mouth of a trucker, folks. What you see is what you get. My face is numb, but my cheeks aren't red from the cold.

Kill me now.

So it's been a minute since I had sex. Seven months, one week, and four days to be exact, but who's counting? Do I miss it? Of course. Is it necessary for everyone to know my neglected vagina is about to go on life support? Nope, it's not.

Seven months isn't *that* long. Is it?

She cuts me off again. "I make no apologies for who I am. Now pick your jaw up from the floor so we can check in." It's pointless to argue. I grab her arm in a rush and follow the bellperson with a knotted stomach in tow.

I stumble when we turn a corner and enter the great room. *Holy shiplap!* I died and went to HGTV heaven. This resort is all about luxury and doesn't pull any punches.

Windows stretch to the angled ceiling, which has too many exposed beams to count. There are three stone fireplaces with mantels draped in garland. Clusters of tufted sectionals and oversize chairs in a palette of creams and taupes invite guests to the warming stations. I don't know whether to grab a novel from one of the bookcases or prep for high tea.

"Give it to me." The corners of Emma's mouth curl in triumph.

I roll my eyes and bite back a smile. "You were right. Thank you."

Check-in is a breeze, with no signs of hedonism, and I thank God for small favors. A nap, a good meal, and a thick pair of wool socks are at the top of my scavenger hunt list.

The front desk attendant hands us our key cards. "You're in one of our grand suites on the seventh floor, which should accommodate your every need."

"Does that include a mountain man with a giant—"

"Tool belt!" I cover Emma's mouth and flash a smile. "She has a love for flannel and appreciates skilled tradespeople." Wrong answer.

She rips my hand from her face. "Yes, this one needs someone to snake her drain. *Deep.* Send him up with the thickest *tool belt.*"

God, it's me again. Where is my friend's off switch?

We stumble to the elevators next to the desk, out of view of the attendant, who has turned an impressive shade of white. "Can we *please* put the peen talk on hold until we get upstairs?" I push the button in a huff.

Emma meets my eyes and sighs. "Okay. No more dick talk for today." She motions to me. "Just do me a favor and do *something* with that hair and that outfit when we get upstairs."

I frown and look down. Black jeans, a khaki-colored knit sweater, and black motorcycle boots. Did she expect New York Fashion Week after she gave me two minutes to change out of my PJs? If she wanted a "moment," as she calls it, she should've picked out my clothes while she packed my suitcase.

She ignores my glare. "There's a kickoff mixer tonight. I need more from you than that 'don't touch me, I'm on my period' outfit. It's fine for riding a plane—but not a man."

I don't pretend to take offense. Emma is the senior creative director of a luxury lingerie company. They sell crotchless panties that cost more than the GDP of a small country. The Kardashians look like nuns compared to the people she's around on an average day. My friend stands tall in six-inch stilettos, ready for the runway and not the snow. Her crimson blouse plunges to her cleavage, which gold chains hover over in a sultry trail to black leather pants that grip her hips.

"You never know who you'll meet here." Her voice trails off to a place far away, one I'd like to be instead of at this singles' retreat. Back home, in my queen-size bed, safe from stranger danger and mounds of ice.

A side glance at Emma's hand to her throat draws my brows together. Does she need the Heimlich? I follow her line of sight and freeze.

Terrence, my soon-to-be-ex-husband, is here.

© Frenchy Press LLC

Tanvier Peart is a future bestselling romance author with a healthy obsession for snacks and happily ever afters. She is a good girl with kinks who spends her days working on policy and enjoys the wild life of being a wife and soccer mom. By night, she writes and reads romance books with steamy scenes. When she's not lost in the land of smut, Tanvier enjoys long walks down snack aisles and the chorus of grunts at the gym.

Want to stay up to date on all of Tanvier's bookish news? Sign up for her newsletter:

https://tanvierwrites.substack.com/

Connect with Tanvier online:

@tanvierwrites

(Instagram, TikTok, Threads, Facebook)